# UGLIES
## Shay's Story

ALSO BY SCOTT WESTERFELD

**Uglies**
**Pretties**
**Specials**
**Extras**
**Bogus to Bubbly: An Insider's Guide to the World of Uglies**

# UGLIES
## Shay's Story

Created by
**SCOTT WESTERFELD**

Written by
**SCOTT WESTERFELD** and **DEVIN GRAYSON**

Illustrations by
**STEVEN CUMMINGS**

Ballantine Books  New York

*Uglies: Shay's Story* is a work of fiction. Names, characters, places, and incidents are the products of the author's imagination or are used fictitiously. Any resemblance to actual events, locales, or persons, living or dead, is entirely coincidental.

A Del Rey Trade Paperback Original



Published in the United States by Del Rey,
an imprint of The Random House Publishing Group,
a division of Random House, Inc., New York.

Del Rey is a registered trademark and the Del Rey colophon is a trademark of Random House, Inc.

ISBN 978-0-345-52722-6
eBook ISBN 978-0-345-53510-8

Printed in the United States of America

www.delreybooks.com

2 4 6 8 9 7 5 3 1

Toning and lettering: Yishan Li
Coloring assistant, front-cover artwork: Espen Grundetjern

# CHAPTER 1

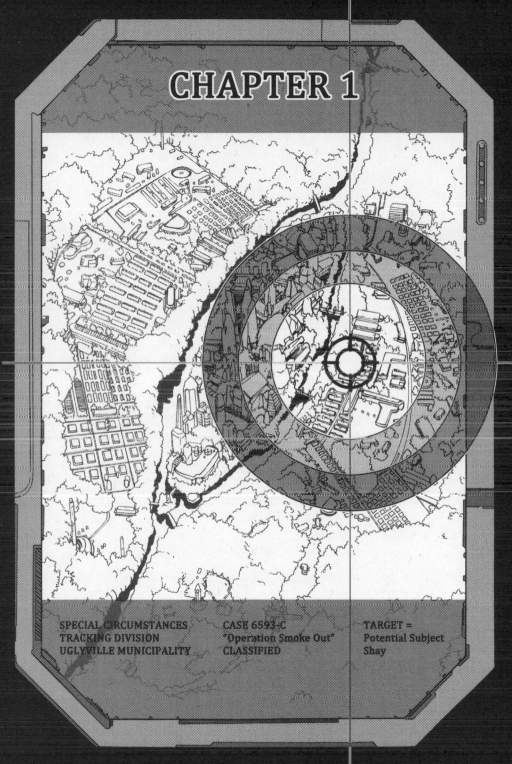

SPECIAL CIRCUMSTANCES
TRACKING DIVISION
UGLYVILLE MUNICIPALITY

CASE 6593-C
"Operation Smoke Out"
CLASSIFIED

TARGET =
Potential Subject
Shay

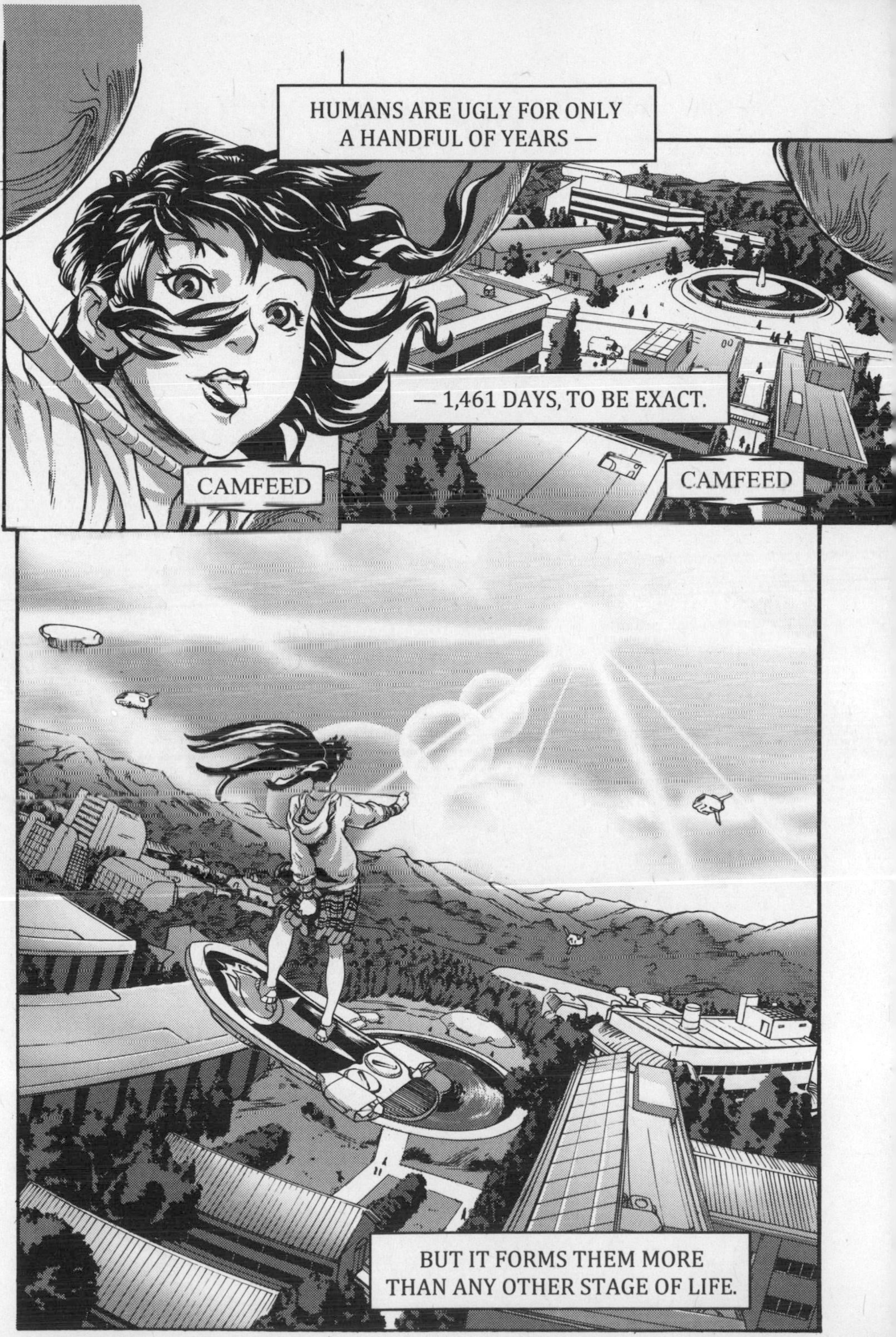
HUMANS ARE UGLY FOR ONLY A HANDFUL OF YEARS —
CAMFEED
— 1,461 DAYS, TO BE EXACT.
CAMFEED
BUT IT FORMS THEM MORE THAN ANY OTHER STAGE OF LIFE.

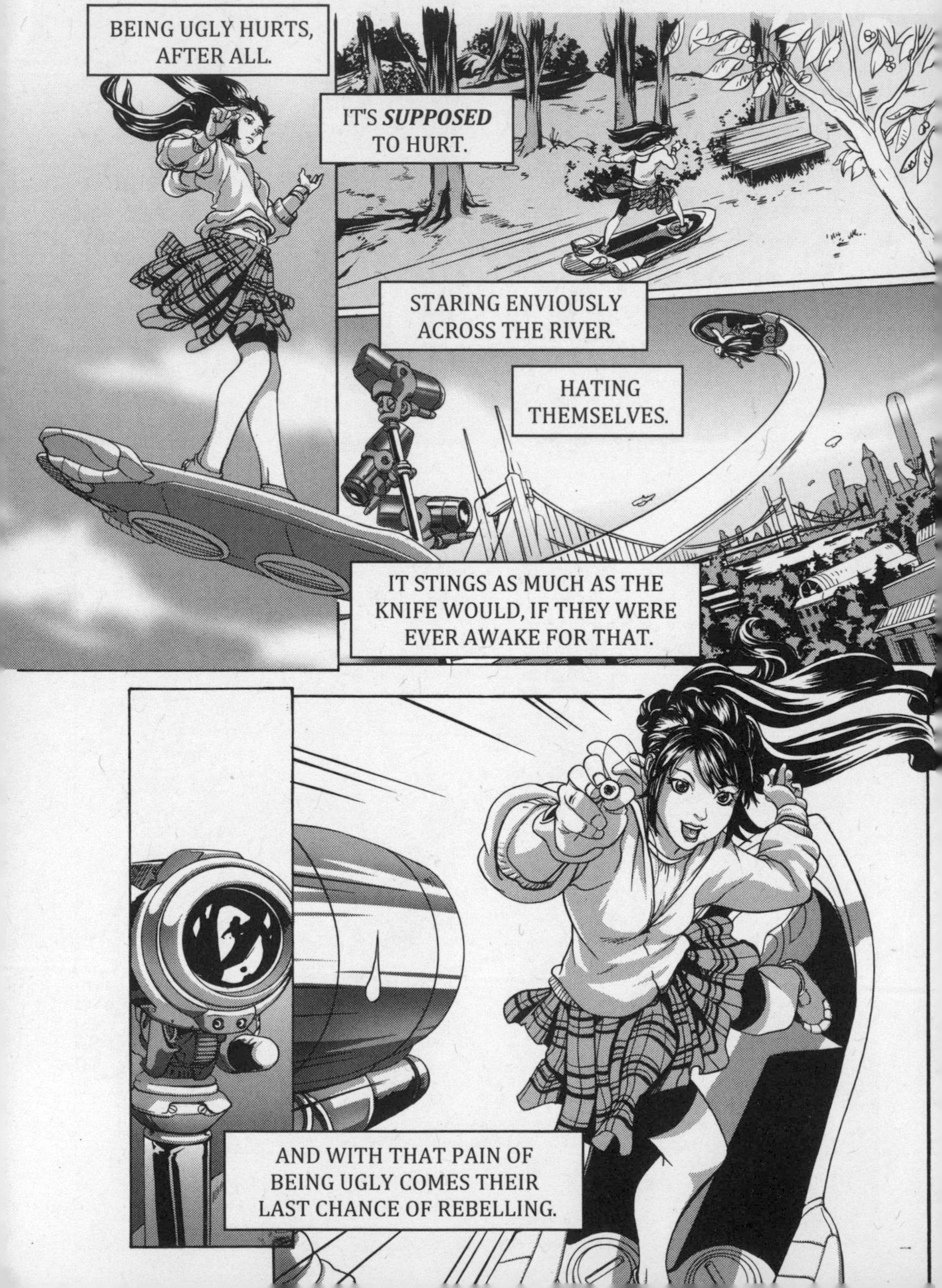
BEING UGLY HURTS, AFTER ALL.
IT'S ***SUPPOSED*** TO HURT.
STARING ENVIOUSLY ACROSS THE RIVER.
HATING THEMSELVES.
IT STINGS AS MUCH AS THE KNIFE WOULD, IF THEY WERE EVER AWAKE FOR THAT.
AND WITH THAT PAIN OF BEING UGLY COMES THEIR LAST CHANCE OF REBELLING.

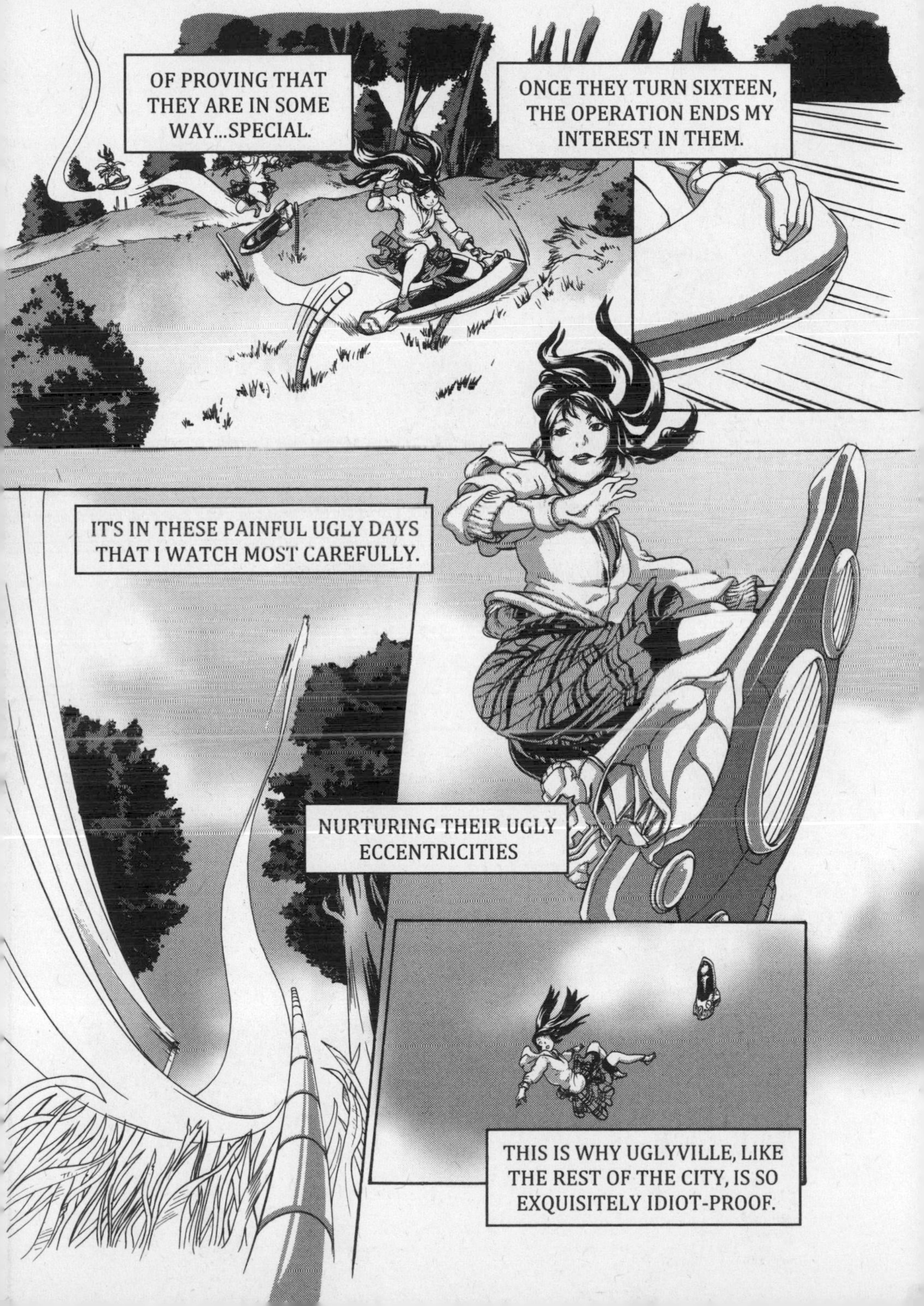
OF PROVING THAT THEY ARE IN SOME WAY...SPECIAL.
ONCE THEY TURN SIXTEEN, THE OPERATION ENDS MY INTEREST IN THEM.
IT'S IN THESE PAINFUL UGLY DAYS THAT I WATCH MOST CAREFULLY.
NURTURING THEIR UGLY ECCENTRICITIES
THIS IS WHY UGLYVILLE, LIKE THE REST OF THE CITY, IS SO EXQUISITELY IDIOT-PROOF.

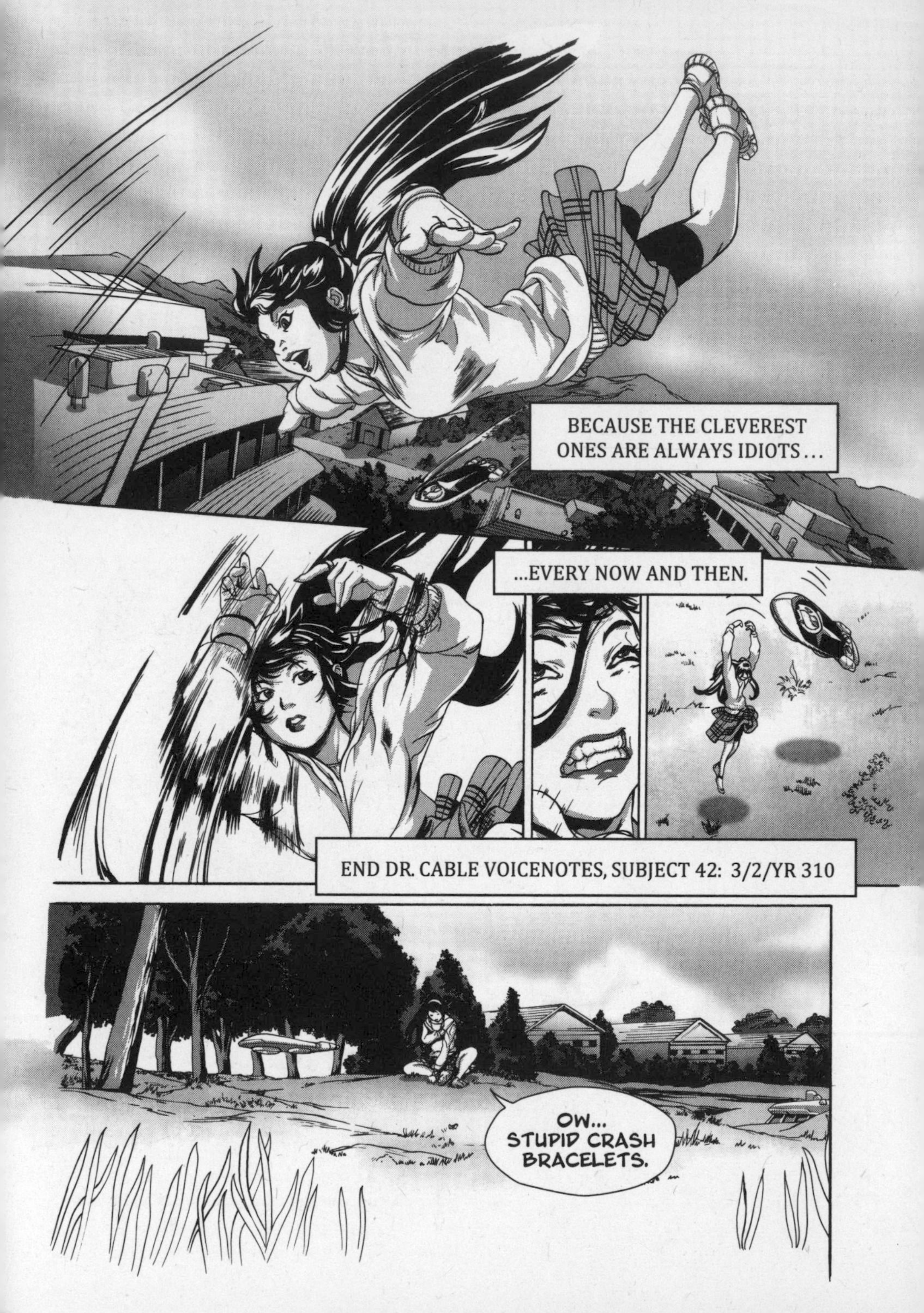

BECAUSE THE CLEVEREST ONES ARE ALWAYS IDIOTS . . .
...EVERY NOW AND THEN.
END DR. CABLE VOICENOTES, SUBJECT 42: 3/2/YR 310
OW... STUPID CRASH BRACELETS.

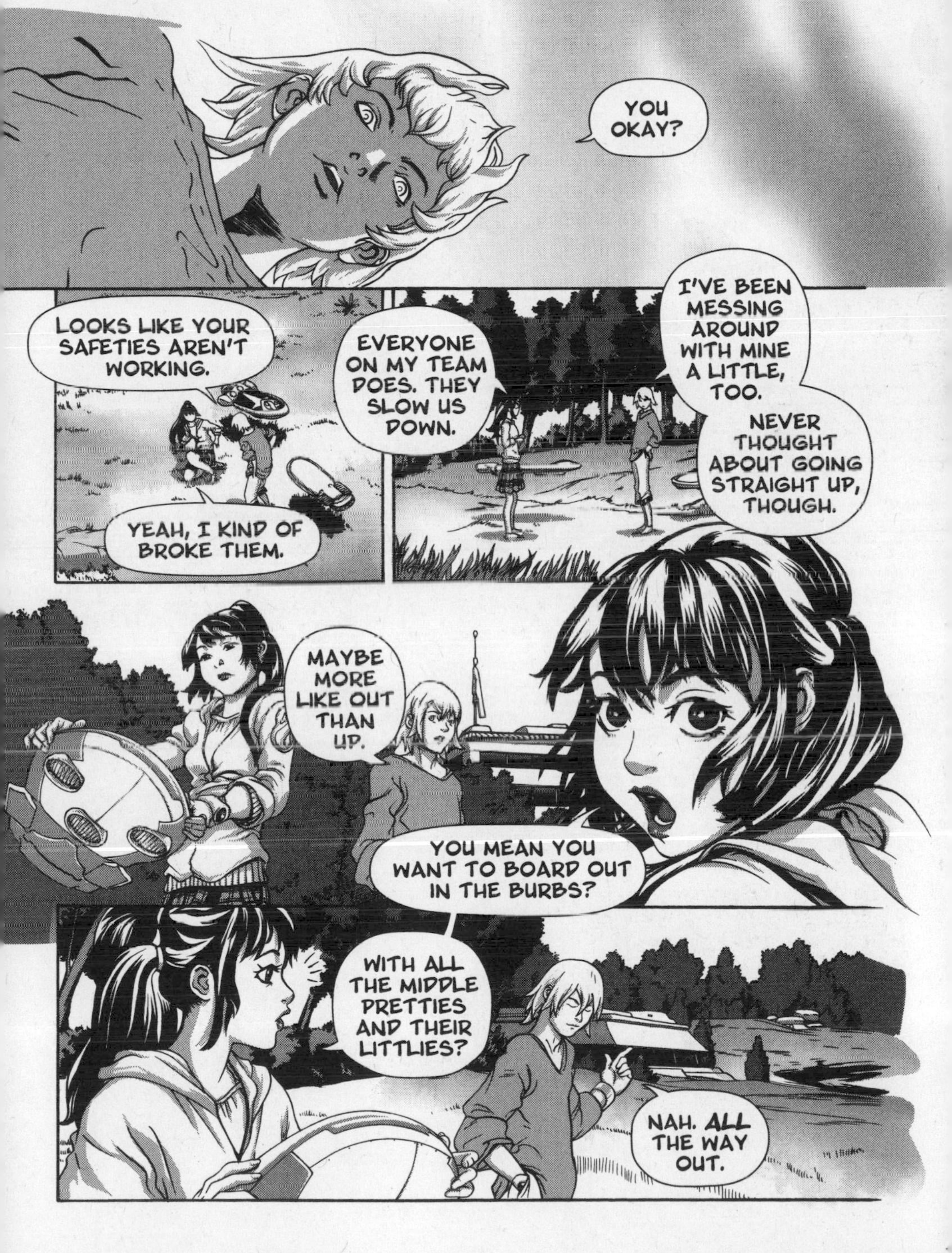
YOU OKAY?
LOOKS LIKE YOUR SAFETIES AREN'T WORKING.
YEAH, I KIND OF BROKE THEM.
EVERYONE ON MY TEAM DOES. THEY SLOW US DOWN.
I'VE BEEN MESSING AROUND WITH MINE A LITTLE, TOO.
NEVER THOUGHT ABOUT GOING STRAIGHT UP, THOUGH.
MAYBE MORE LIKE OUT THAN UP.
YOU MEAN YOU WANT TO BOARD OUT IN THE BURBS?
WITH ALL THE MIDDLE PRETTIES AND THEIR LITTLIES?
NAH. **ALL** THE WAY OUT.

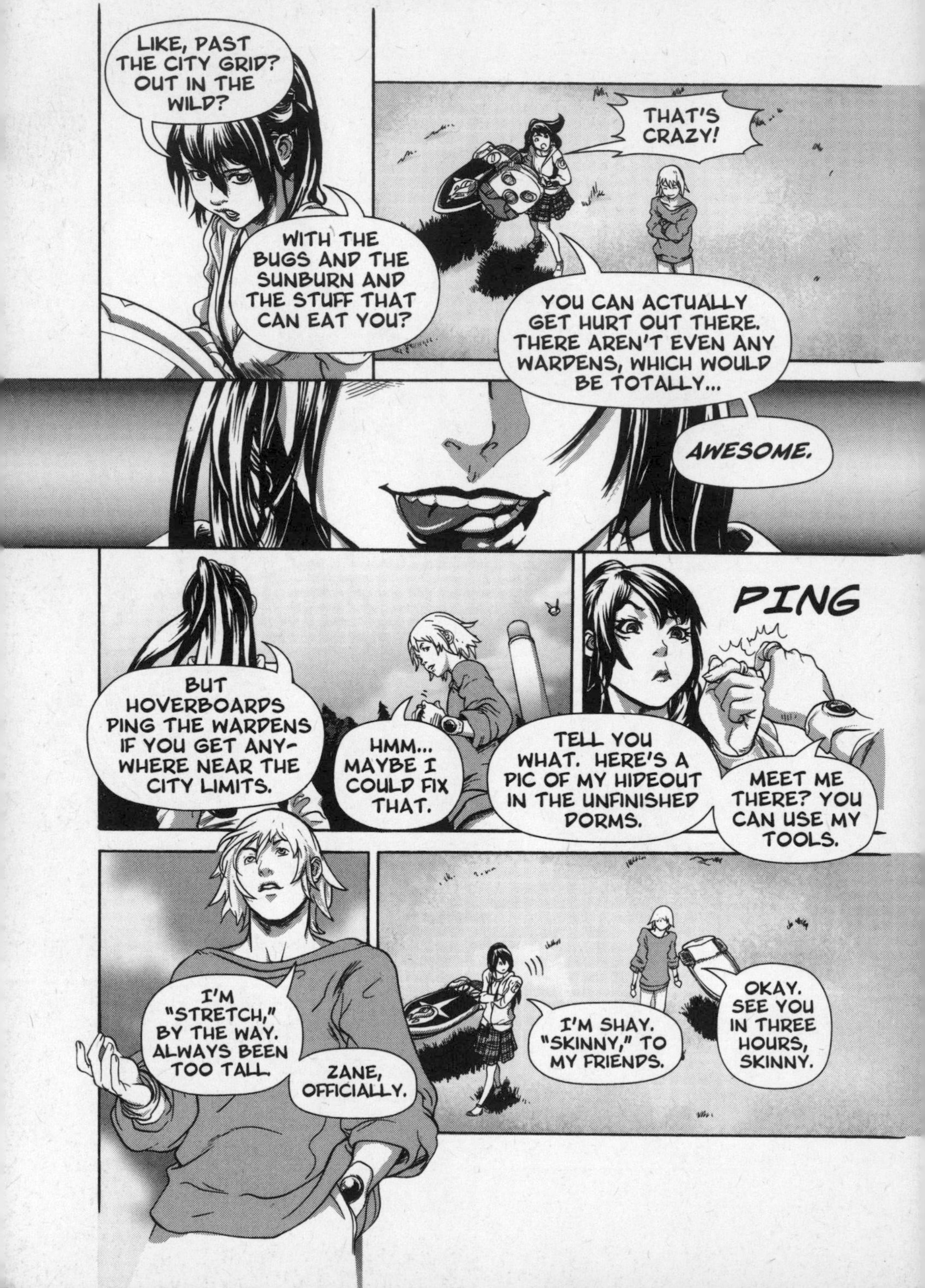
LIKE, PAST THE CITY GRID? OUT IN THE WILD?
WITH THE BUGS AND THE SUNBURN AND THE STUFF THAT CAN EAT YOU?
THAT'S CRAZY!
YOU CAN ACTUALLY GET HURT OUT THERE. THERE AREN'T EVEN ANY WARDENS, WHICH WOULD BE TOTALLY...
AWESOME.
BUT HOVERBOARDS PING THE WARDENS IF YOU GET ANY-WHERE NEAR THE CITY LIMITS.
HMM... MAYBE I COULD FIX THAT.
PING
TELL YOU WHAT. HERE'S A PIC OF MY HIDEOUT IN THE UNFINISHED DORMS.
MEET ME THERE? YOU CAN USE MY TOOLS.
I'M "STRETCH," BY THE WAY. ALWAYS BEEN TOO TALL.
ZANE, OFFICIALLY.
I'M SHAY. "SKINNY," TO MY FRIENDS.
OKAY. SEE YOU IN THREE HOURS, SKINNY.

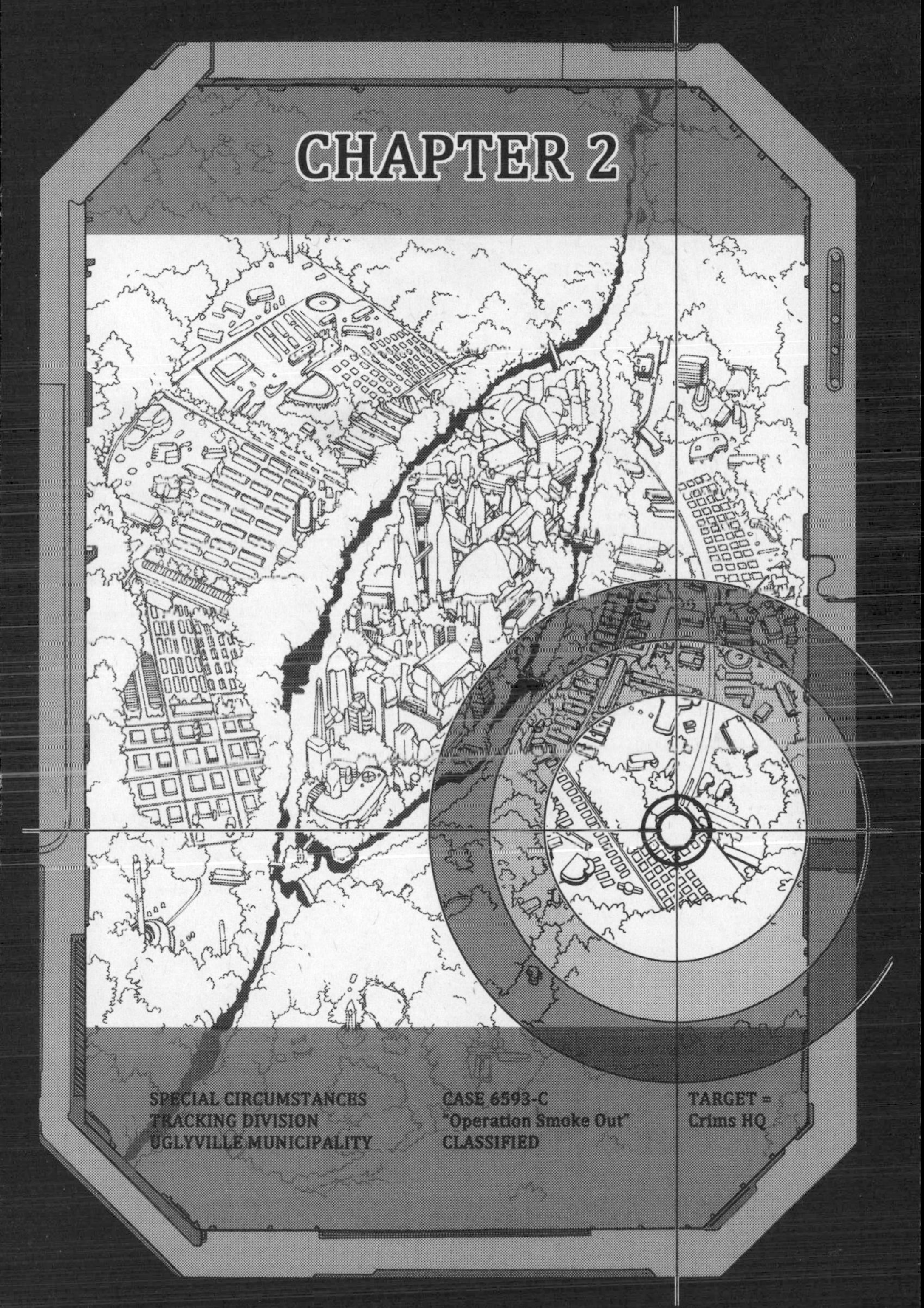
CHAPTER 2
SPECIAL CIRCUMSTANCES
TRACKING DIVISION
UGLYVILLE MUNICIPALITY
CASE 6593-C
"Operation Smoke Out"
CLASSIFIED
TARGET =
Crims HQ

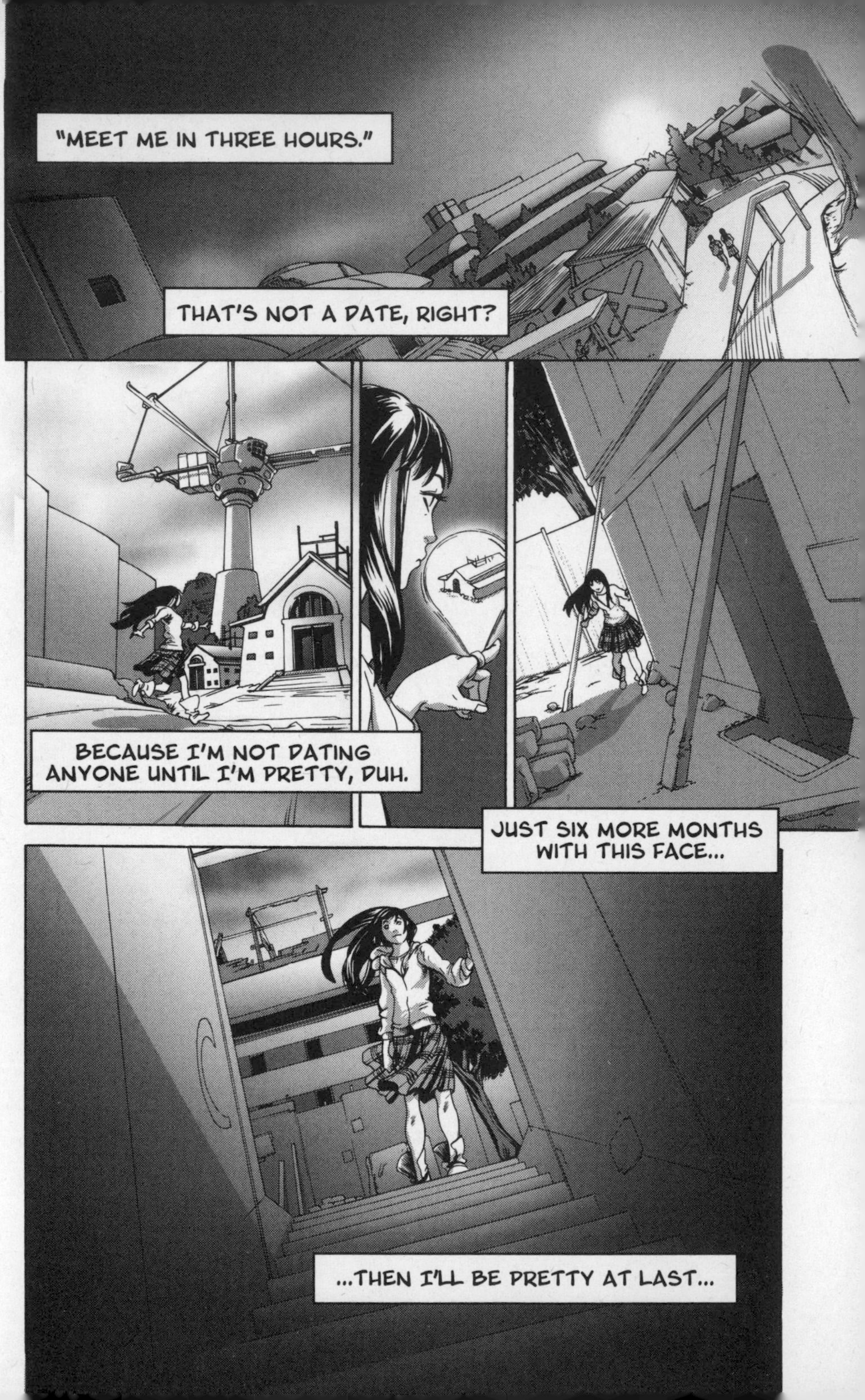
"MEET ME IN THREE HOURS."
THAT'S NOT A DATE, RIGHT?
BECAUSE I'M NOT DATING ANYONE UNTIL I'M PRETTY, DUH.
JUST SIX MORE MONTHS WITH THIS FACE...
...THEN I'LL BE PRETTY AT LAST...

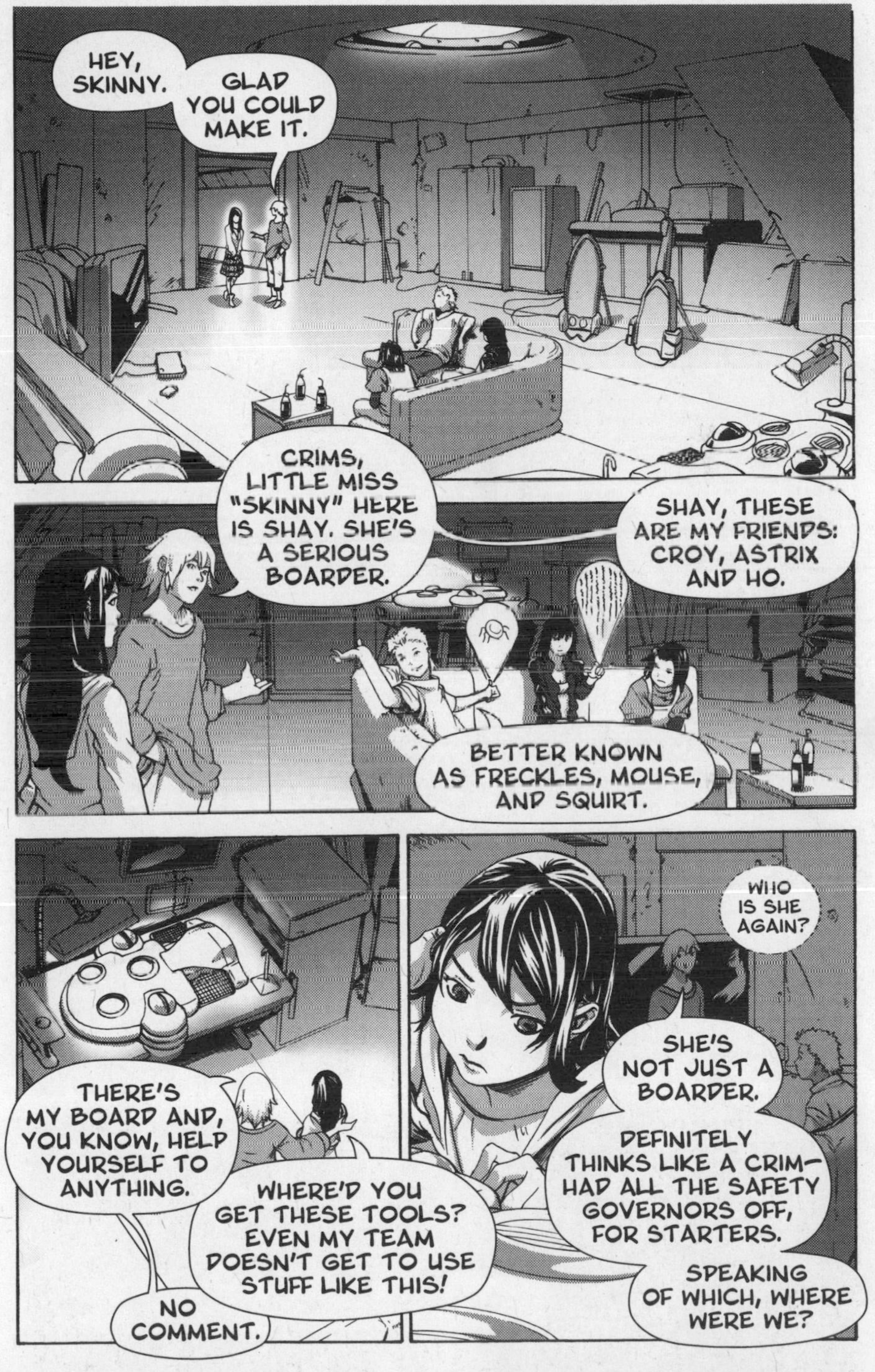
HEY, SKINNY.
GLAD YOU COULD MAKE IT.
CRIMS, LITTLE MISS "SKINNY" HERE IS SHAY. SHE'S A SERIOUS BOARDER.
SHAY, THESE ARE MY FRIENDS: CROY, ASTRIX AND HO.
BETTER KNOWN AS FRECKLES, MOUSE, AND SQUIRT.
THERE'S MY BOARD AND, YOU KNOW, HELP YOURSELF TO ANYTHING.
WHERE'D YOU GET THESE TOOLS? EVEN MY TEAM DOESN'T GET TO USE STUFF LIKE THIS!
NO COMMENT.
WHO IS SHE AGAIN?
SHE'S NOT JUST A BOARDER.
DEFINITELY THINKS LIKE A CRIM—HAD ALL THE SAFETY GOVERNORS OFF, FOR STARTERS.
SPEAKING OF WHICH, WHERE WERE WE?

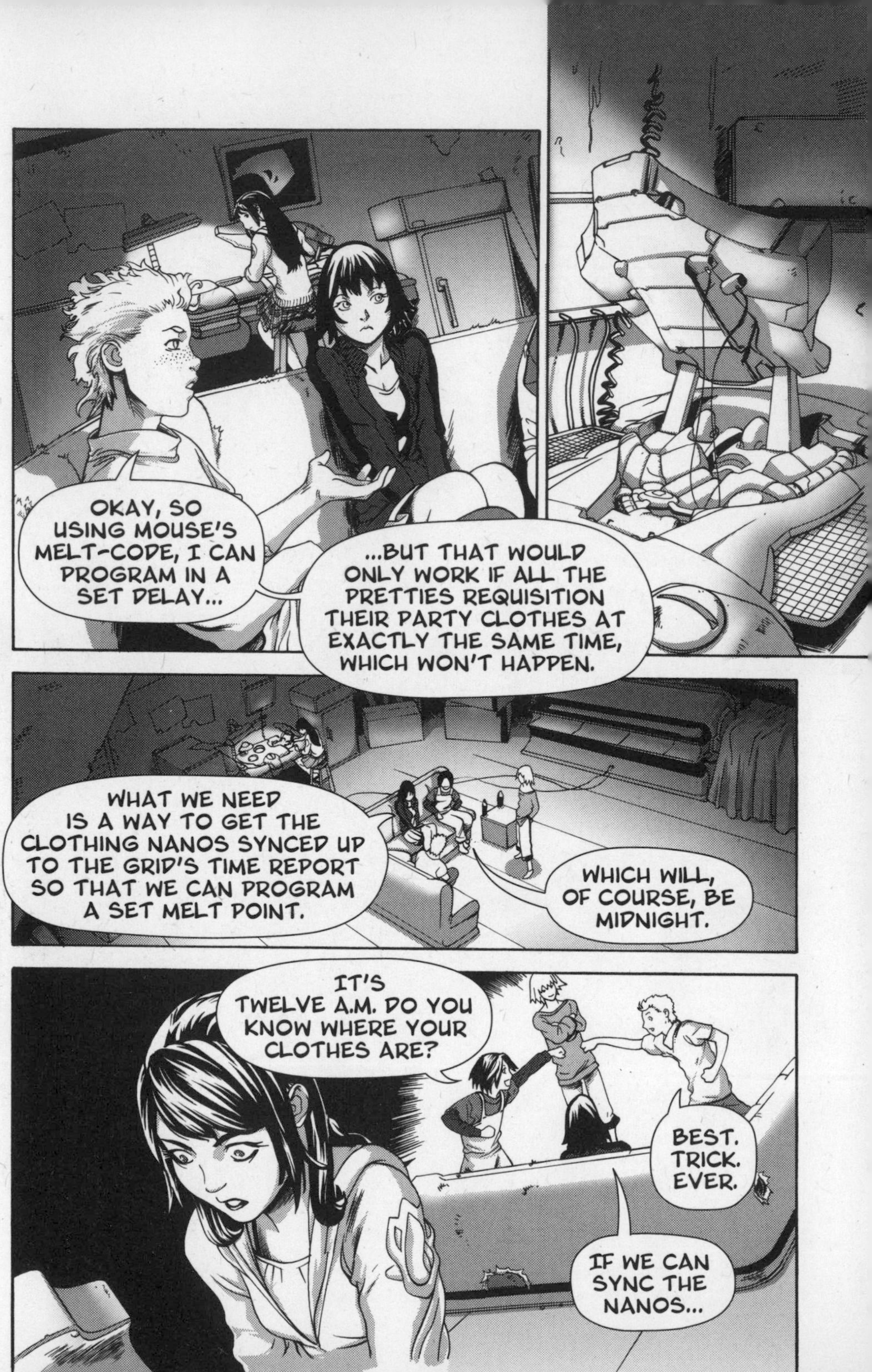
OKAY, SO USING MOUSE'S MELT-CODE, I CAN PROGRAM IN A SET DELAY...
...BUT THAT WOULD ONLY WORK IF ALL THE PRETTIES REQUISITION THEIR PARTY CLOTHES AT EXACTLY THE SAME TIME, WHICH WON'T HAPPEN.
WHAT WE NEED IS A WAY TO GET THE CLOTHING NANOS SYNCED UP TO THE GRID'S TIME REPORT SO THAT WE CAN PROGRAM A SET MELT POINT.
WHICH WILL, OF COURSE, BE MIDNIGHT.
IT'S TWELVE A.M. DO YOU KNOW WHERE YOUR CLOTHES ARE?
BEST. TRICK. EVER.
IF WE CAN SYNC THE NANOS...

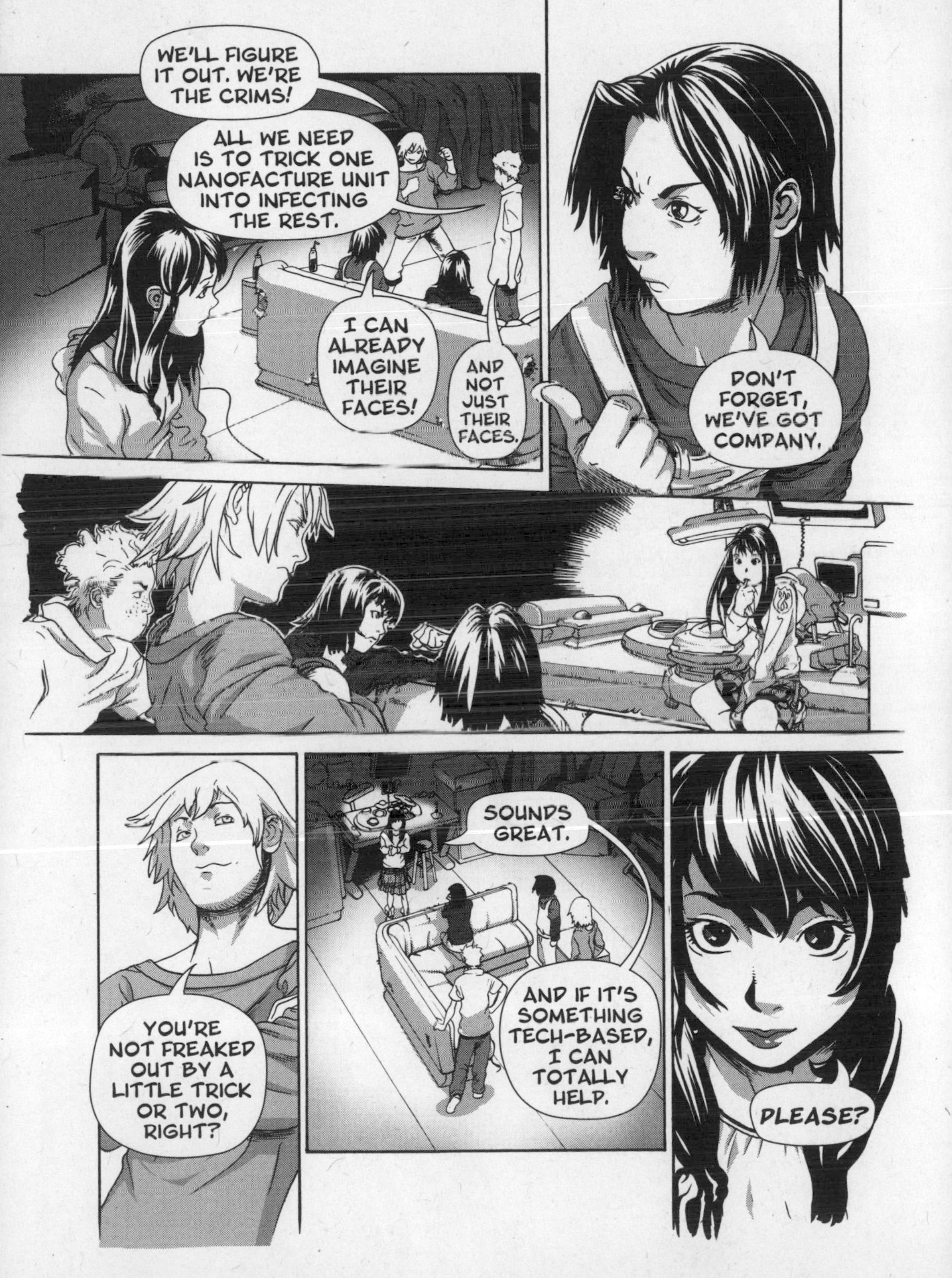
WE'LL FIGURE IT OUT. WE'RE THE CRIMS!
ALL WE NEED IS TO TRICK ONE NANOFACTURE UNIT INTO INFECTING THE REST.
I CAN ALREADY IMAGINE THEIR FACES!
AND NOT JUST THEIR FACES.
DON'T FORGET, WE'VE GOT COMPANY.
YOU'RE NOT FREAKED OUT BY A LITTLE TRICK OR TWO, RIGHT?
SOUNDS GREAT.
AND IF IT'S SOMETHING TECH-BASED, I CAN TOTALLY HELP.
PLEASE?

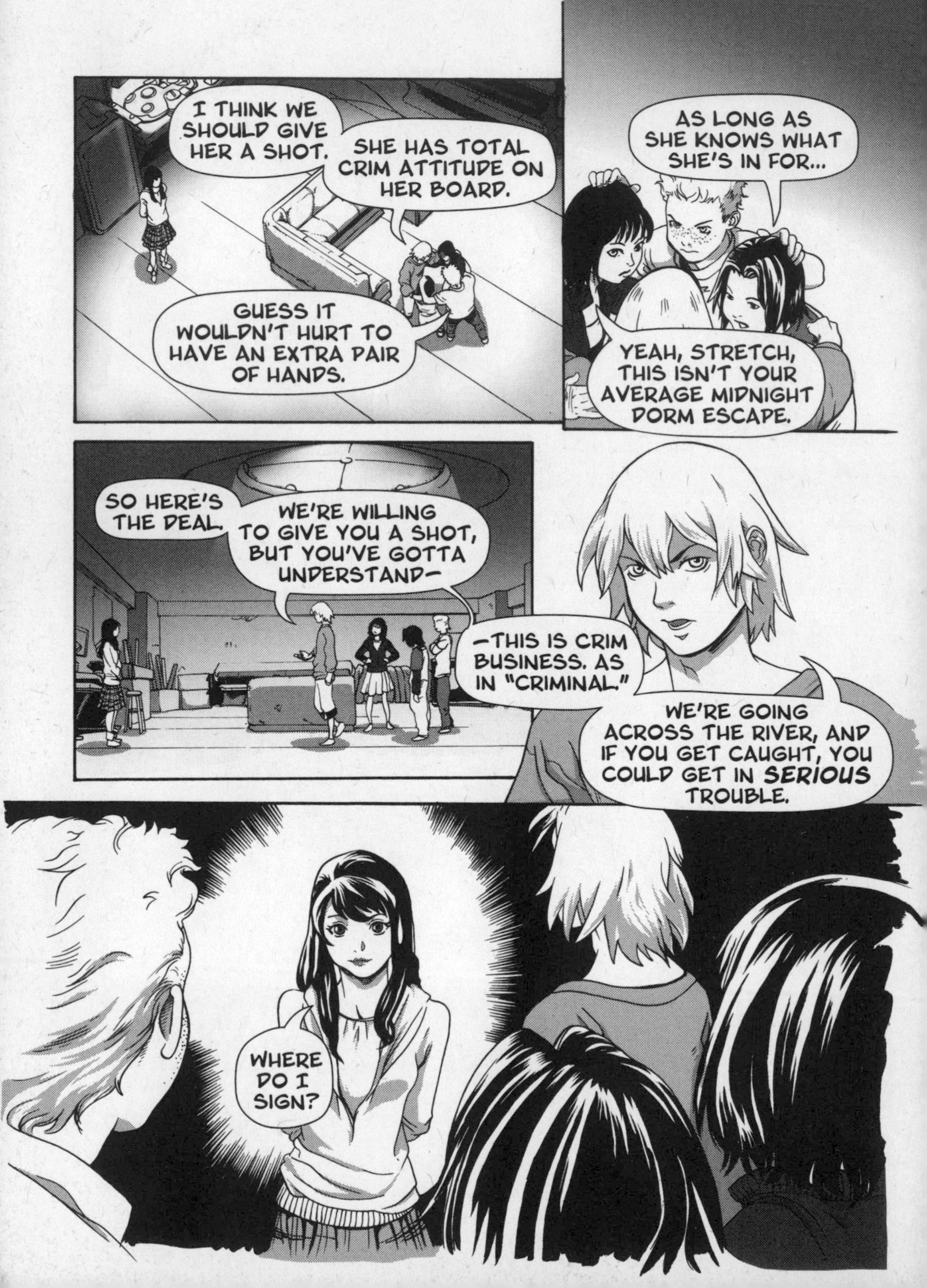

I THINK WE SHOULD GIVE HER A SHOT.
SHE HAS TOTAL CRIM ATTITUDE ON HER BOARD.
GUESS IT WOULDN'T HURT TO HAVE AN EXTRA PAIR OF HANDS.
AS LONG AS SHE KNOWS WHAT SHE'S IN FOR...
YEAH, STRETCH, THIS ISN'T YOUR AVERAGE MIDNIGHT DORM ESCAPE.
SO HERE'S THE DEAL.
WE'RE WILLING TO GIVE YOU A SHOT, BUT YOU'VE GOTTA UNDERSTAND—
—THIS IS CRIM BUSINESS. AS IN "CRIMINAL."
WE'RE GOING ACROSS THE RIVER, AND IF YOU GET CAUGHT, YOU COULD GET IN SERIOUS TROUBLE.
WHERE DO I SIGN?

# CHAPTER 3

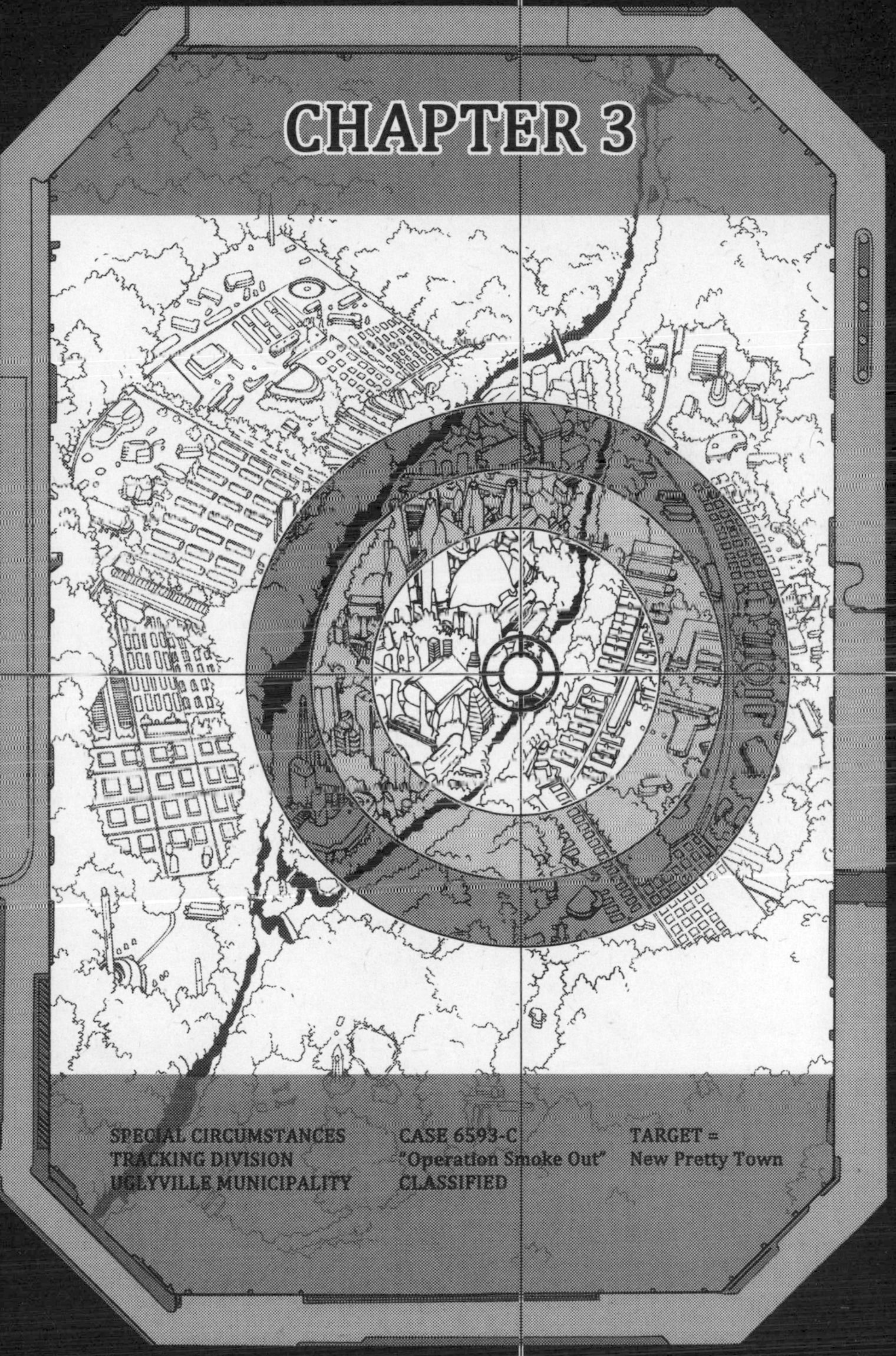
SPECIAL CIRCUMSTANCES
TRACKING DIVISION
UGLYVILLE MUNICIPALITY
CASE 6593-C
"Operation Smoke Out"
CLASSIFIED
TARGET =
New Pretty Town

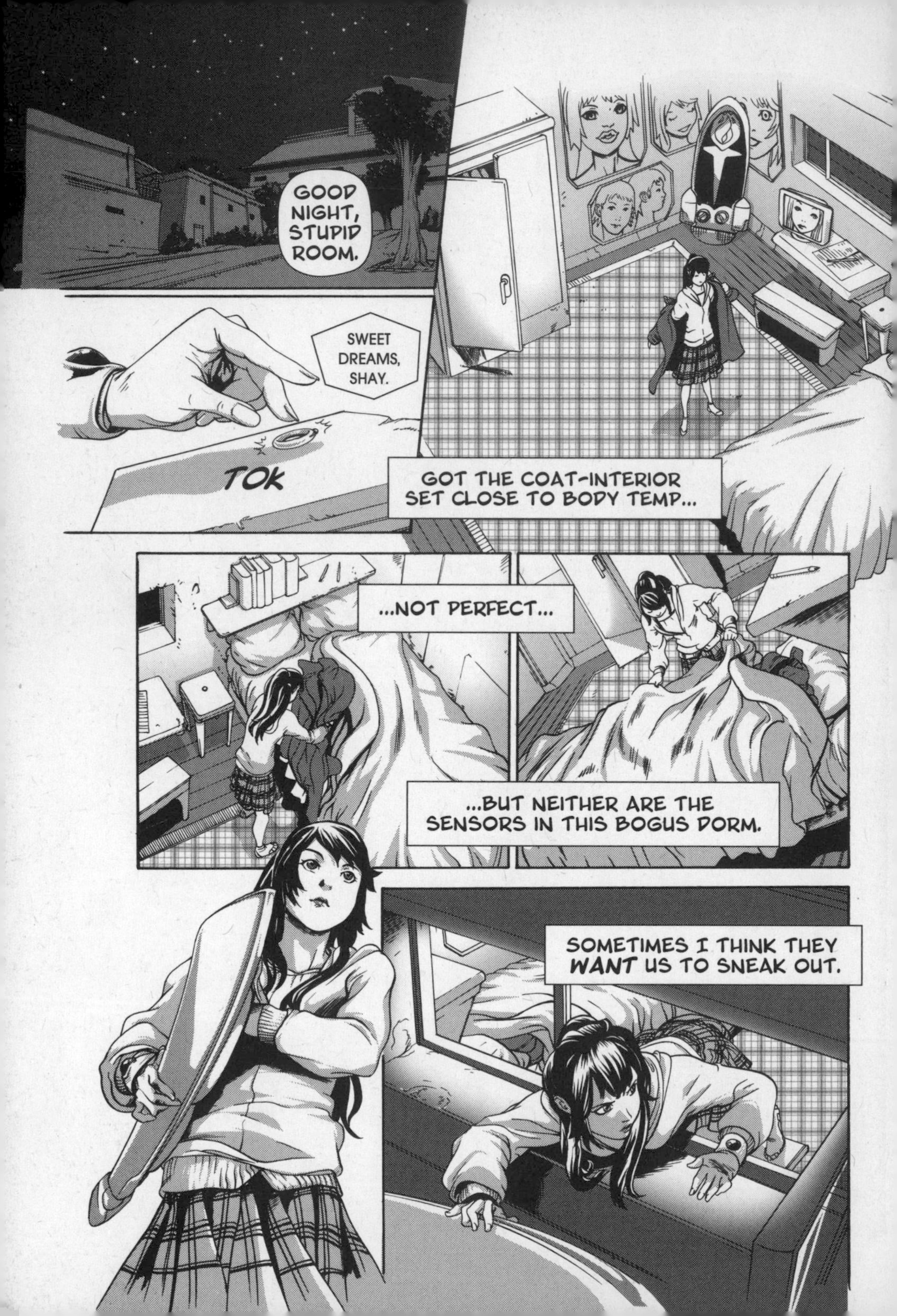
GOOD NIGHT, STUPID ROOM.
SWEET DREAMS, SHAY.
TOK
GOT THE COAT-INTERIOR SET CLOSE TO BODY TEMP...
...NOT PERFECT...
...BUT NEITHER ARE THE SENSORS IN THIS BOGUS DORM.
SOMETIMES I THINK THEY WANT US TO SNEAK OUT.

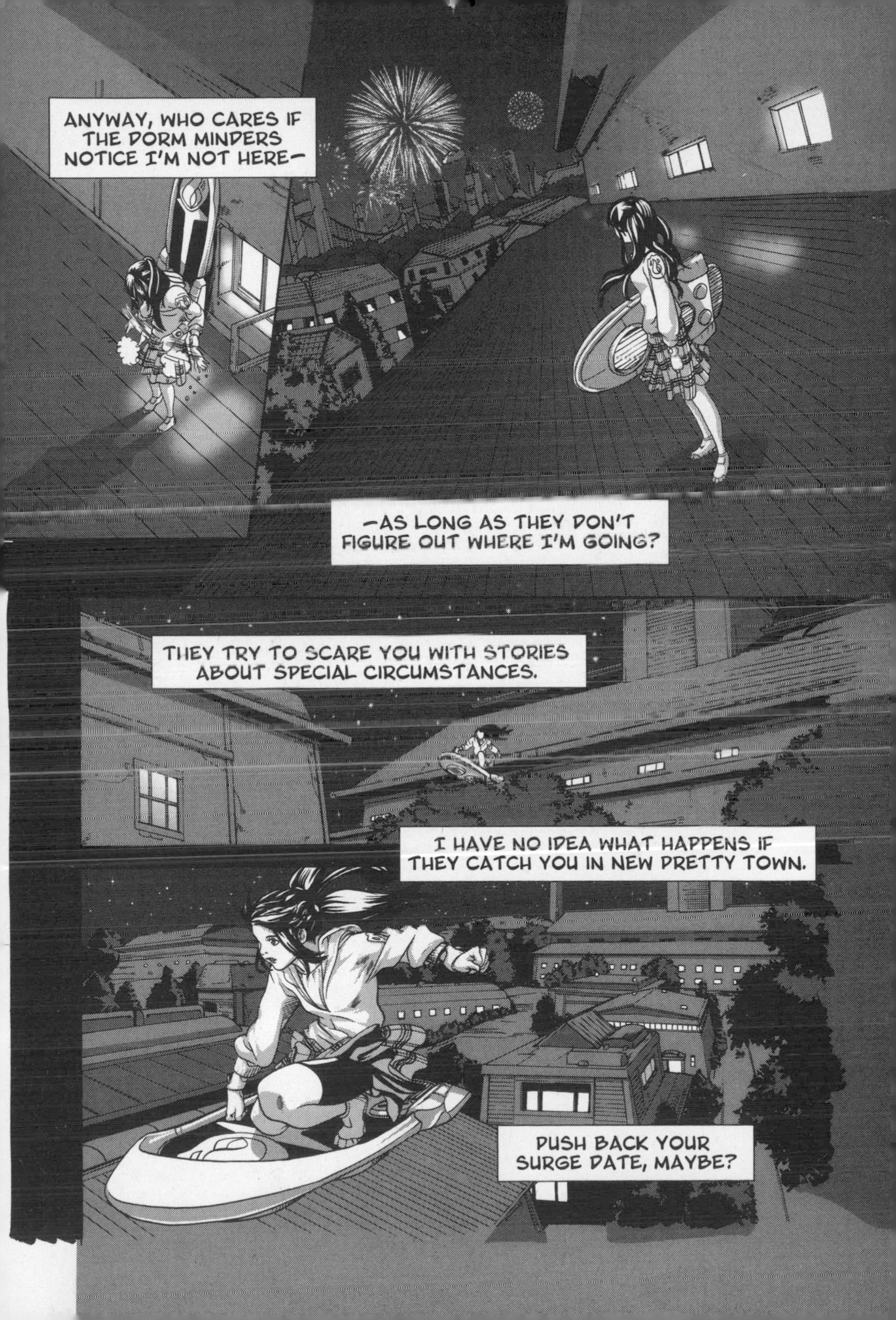
ANYWAY, WHO CARES IF THE DORM MINDERS NOTICE I'M NOT HERE—
—AS LONG AS THEY DON'T FIGURE OUT WHERE I'M GOING?
THEY TRY TO SCARE YOU WITH STORIES ABOUT SPECIAL CIRCUMSTANCES.
I HAVE NO IDEA WHAT HAPPENS IF THEY CATCH YOU IN NEW PRETTY TOWN.
PUSH BACK YOUR SURGE DATE, MAYBE?

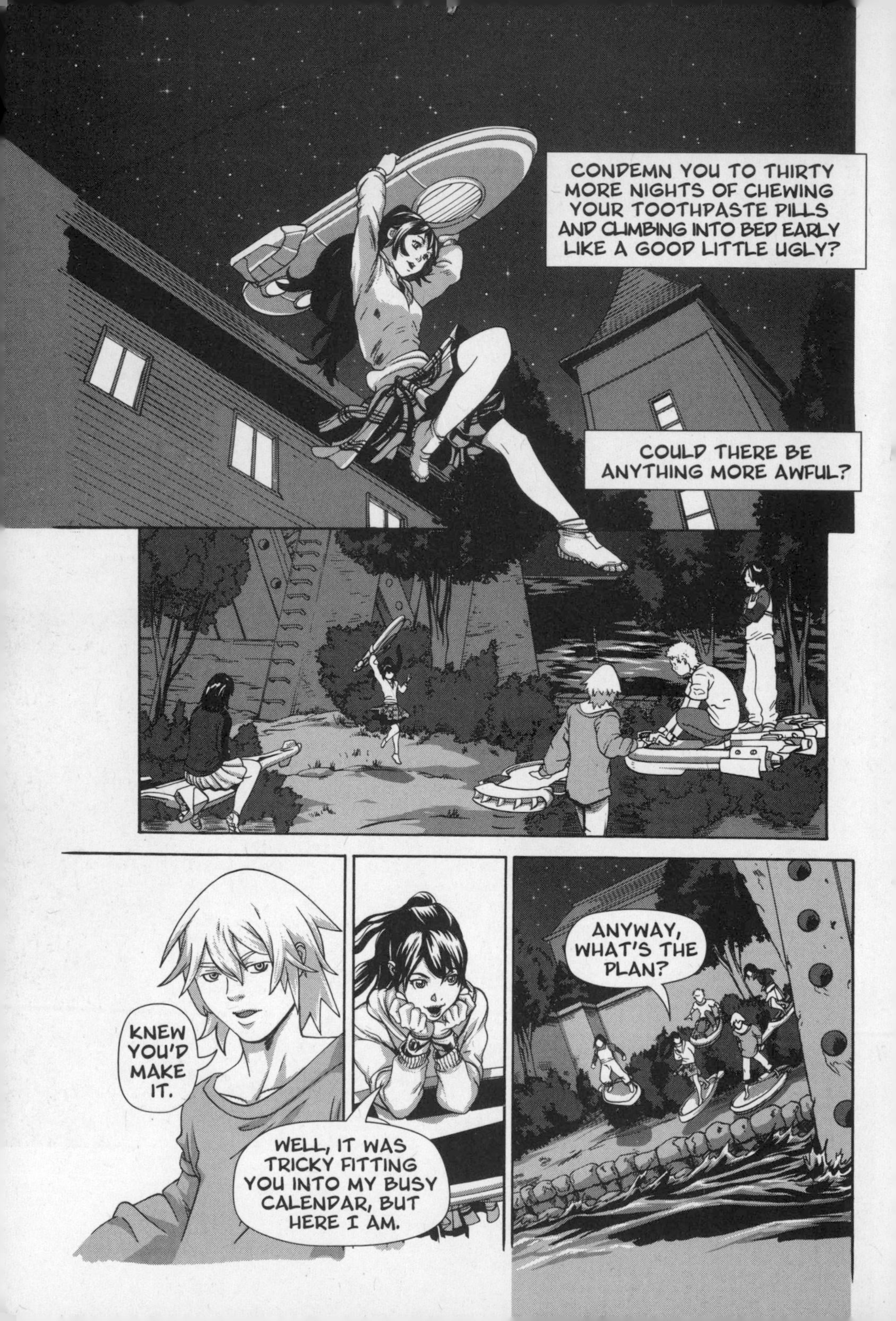
CONDEMN YOU TO THIRTY MORE NIGHTS OF CHEWING YOUR TOOTHPASTE PILLS AND CLIMBING INTO BED EARLY LIKE A GOOD LITTLE UGLY?
COULD THERE BE ANYTHING MORE AWFUL?
KNEW YOU'D MAKE IT.
WELL, IT WAS TRICKY FITTING YOU INTO MY BUSY CALENDAR, BUT HERE I AM.
ANYWAY, WHAT'S THE PLAN?

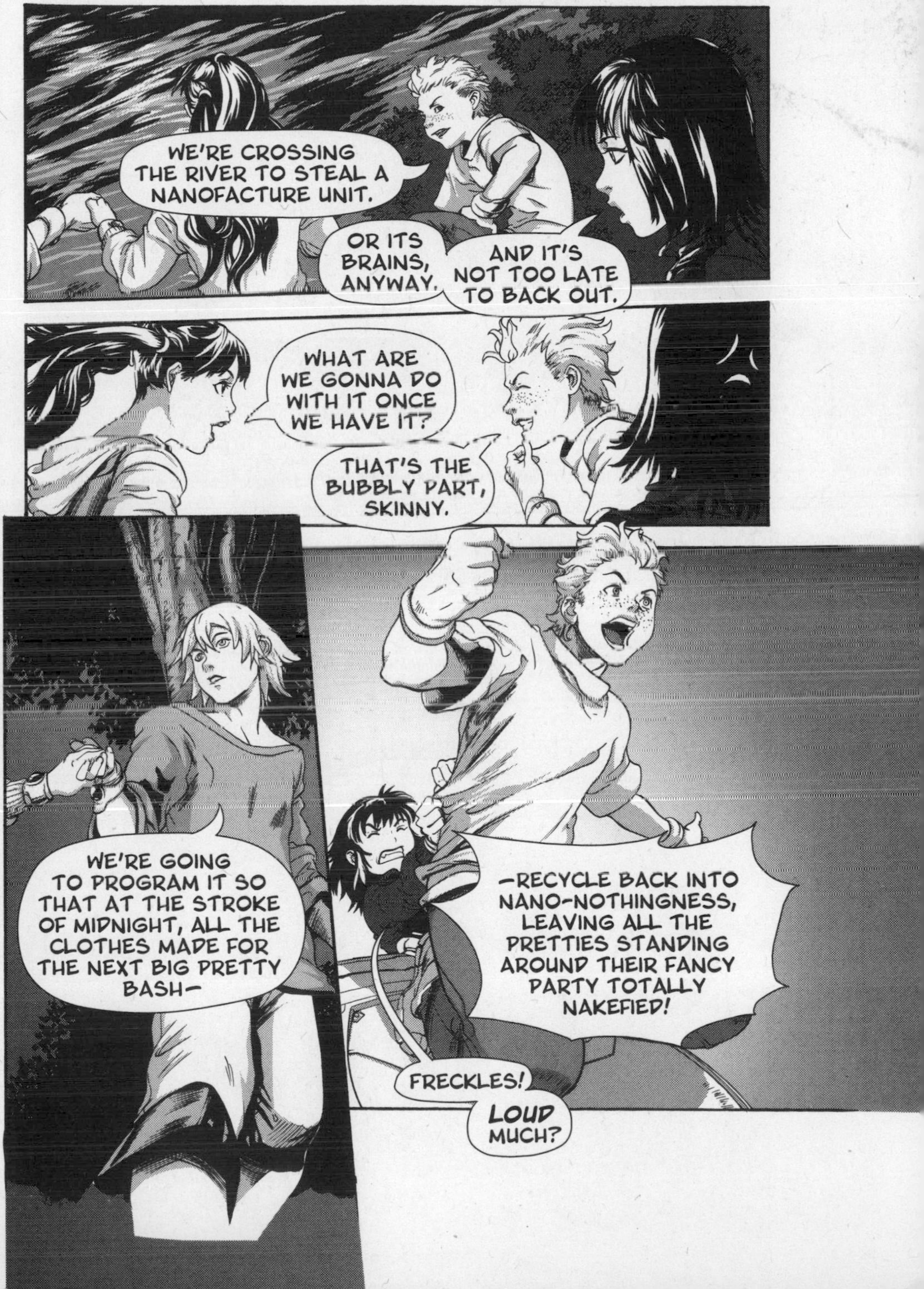
WE'RE CROSSING THE RIVER TO STEAL A NANOFACTURE UNIT.
OR ITS BRAINS, ANYWAY.
AND IT'S NOT TOO LATE TO BACK OUT.
WHAT ARE WE GONNA DO WITH IT ONCE WE HAVE IT?
THAT'S THE BUBBLY PART, SKINNY.
WE'RE GOING TO PROGRAM IT SO THAT AT THE STROKE OF MIDNIGHT, ALL THE CLOTHES MADE FOR THE NEXT BIG PRETTY BASH—
—RECYCLE BACK INTO NANO-NOTHINGNESS, LEAVING ALL THE PRETTIES STANDING AROUND THEIR FANCY PARTY TOTALLY NAKEFIED!
FRECKLES!
LOUD MUCH?

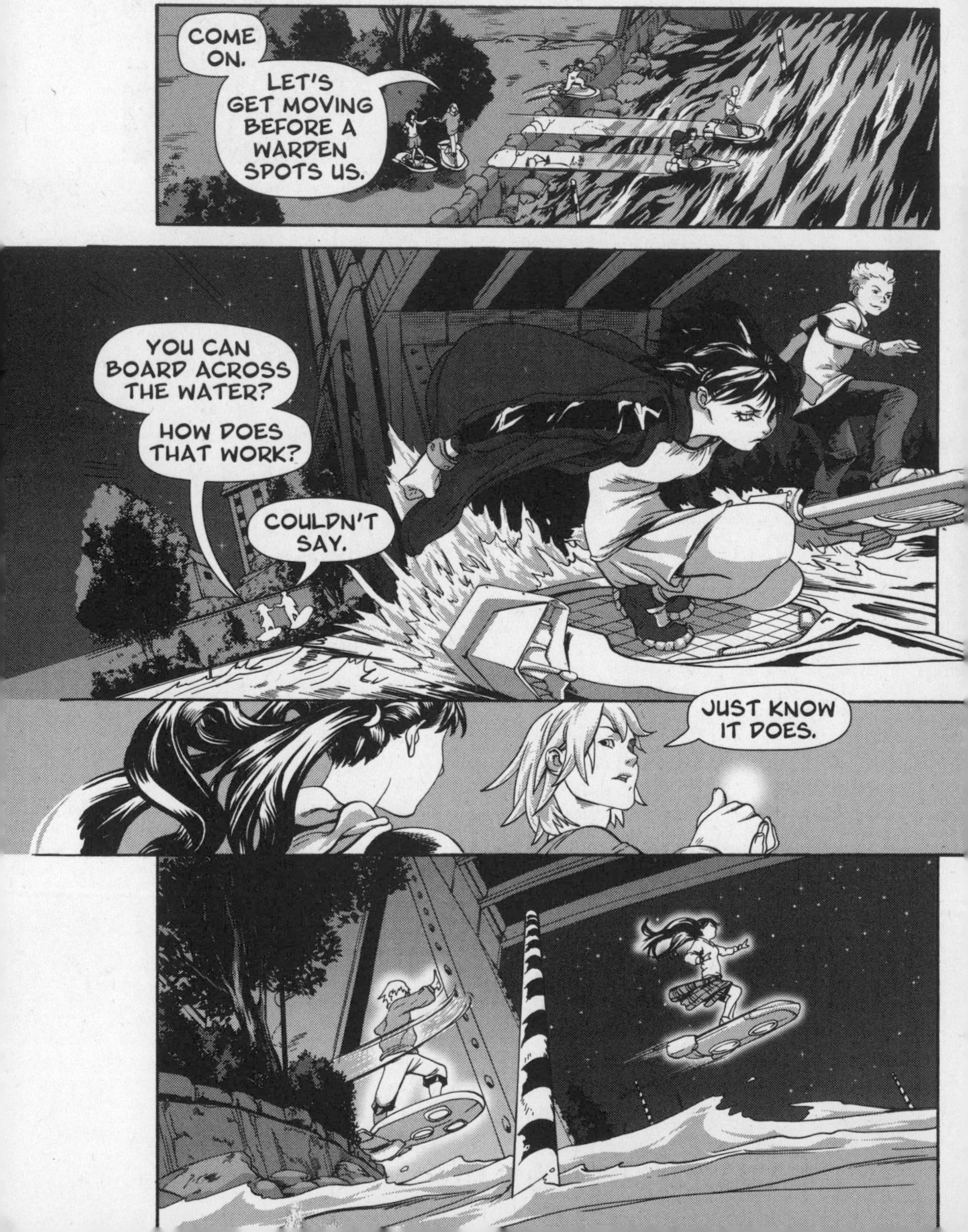
COME ON.
LET'S GET MOVING BEFORE A WARDEN SPOTS US.
YOU CAN BOARD ACROSS THE WATER?
HOW DOES THAT WORK?
COULDN'T SAY.
JUST KNOW IT DOES.

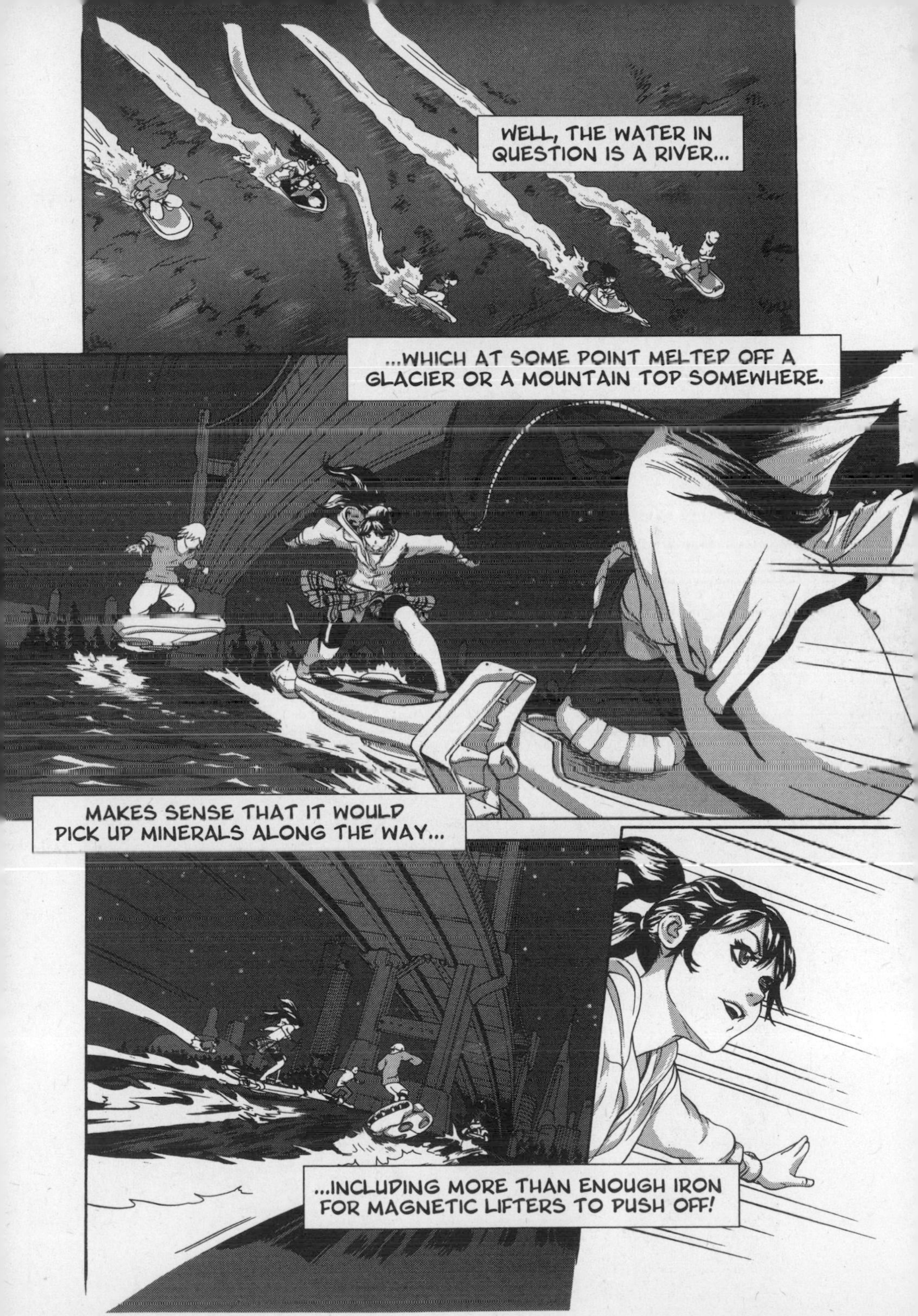
WELL, THE WATER IN QUESTION IS A RIVER...
...WHICH AT SOME POINT MELTED OFF A GLACIER OR A MOUNTAIN TOP SOMEWHERE.
MAKES SENSE THAT IT WOULD PICK UP MINERALS ALONG THE WAY...
...INCLUDING MORE THAN ENOUGH IRON FOR MAGNETIC LIFTERS TO PUSH OFF!

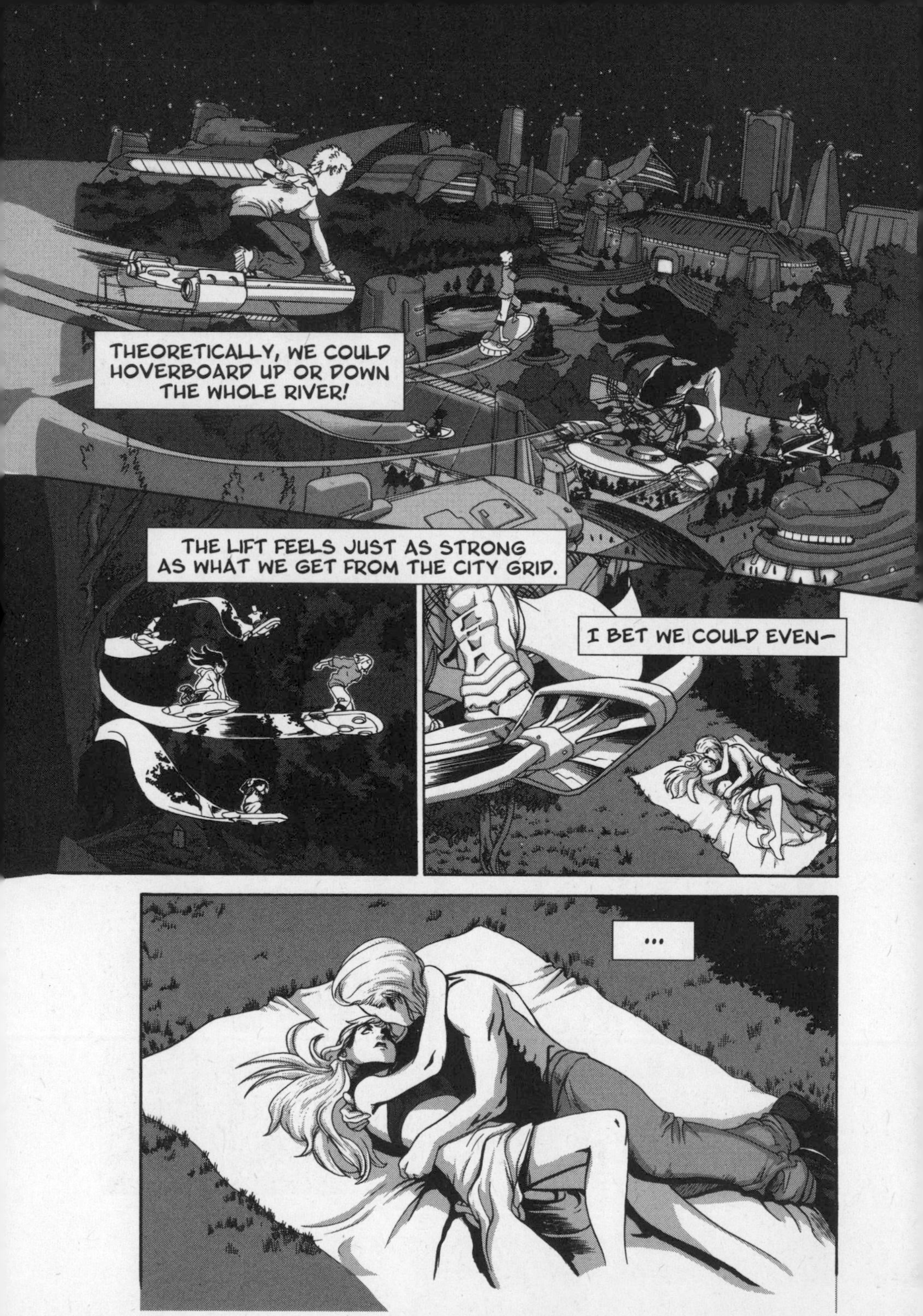
THEORETICALLY, WE COULD HOVERBOARD UP OR DOWN THE WHOLE RIVER!
THE LIFT FEELS JUST AS STRONG AS WHAT WE GET FROM THE CITY GRID.
I BET WE COULD EVEN—
...

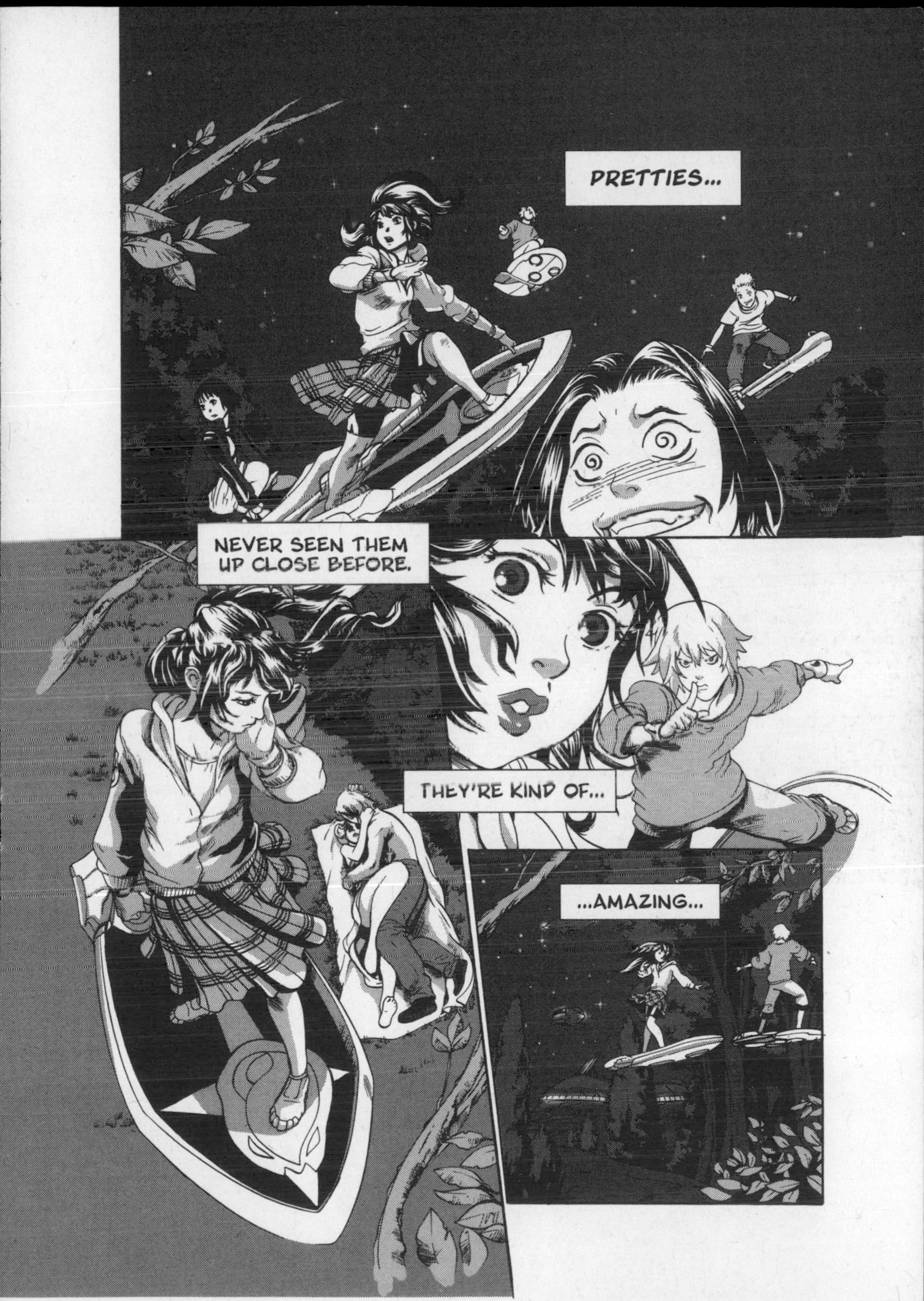
PRETTIES...
NEVER SEEN THEM UP CLOSE BEFORE.
THEY'RE KIND OF...
...AMAZING...

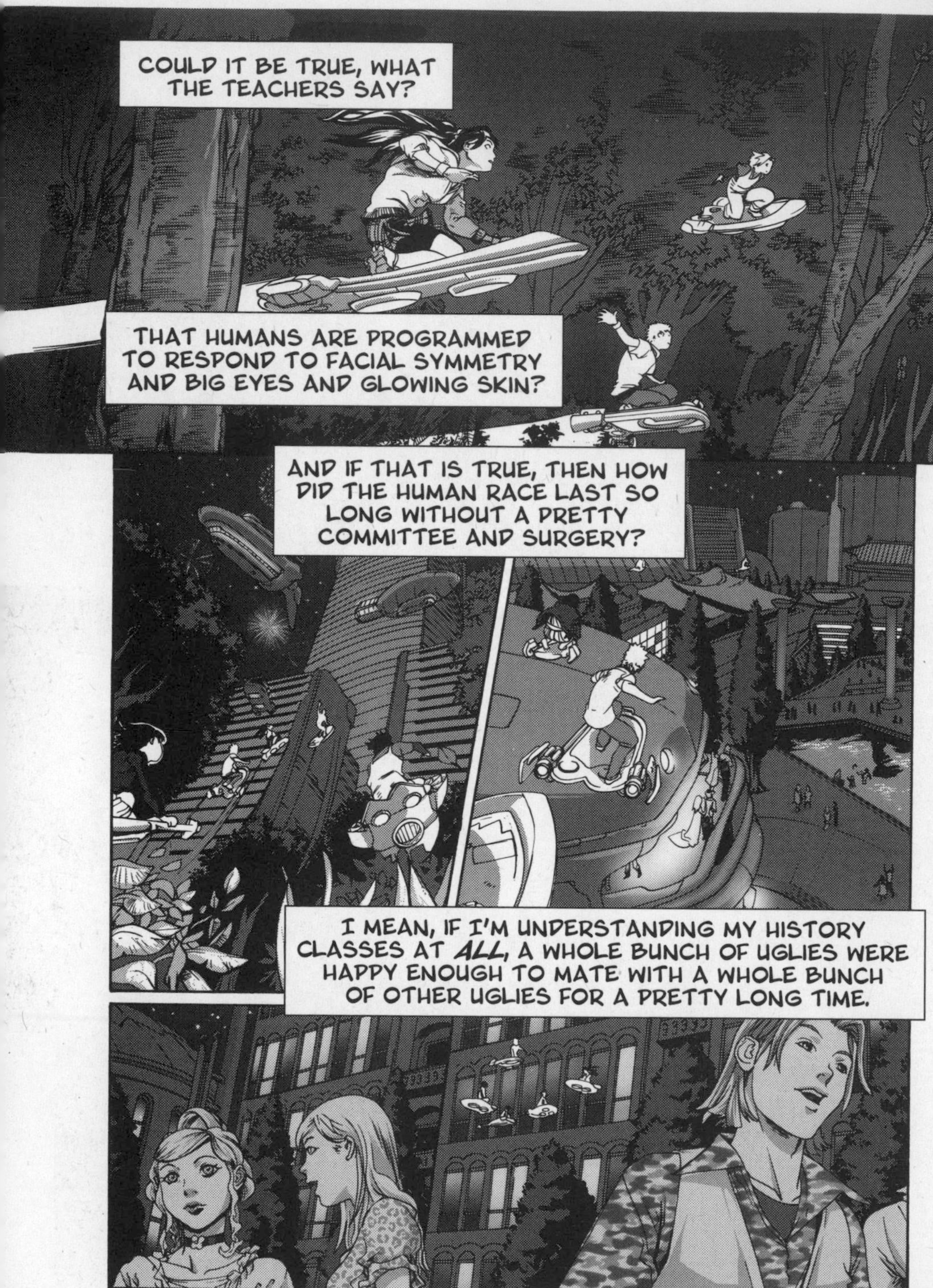
COULD IT BE TRUE, WHAT THE TEACHERS SAY?
THAT HUMANS ARE PROGRAMMED TO RESPOND TO FACIAL SYMMETRY AND BIG EYES AND GLOWING SKIN?
AND IF THAT IS TRUE, THEN HOW DID THE HUMAN RACE LAST SO LONG WITHOUT A PRETTY COMMITTEE AND SURGERY?
I MEAN, IF I'M UNDERSTANDING MY HISTORY CLASSES AT *ALL*, A WHOLE BUNCH OF UGLIES WERE HAPPY ENOUGH TO MATE WITH A WHOLE BUNCH OF OTHER UGLIES FOR A PRETTY LONG TIME.

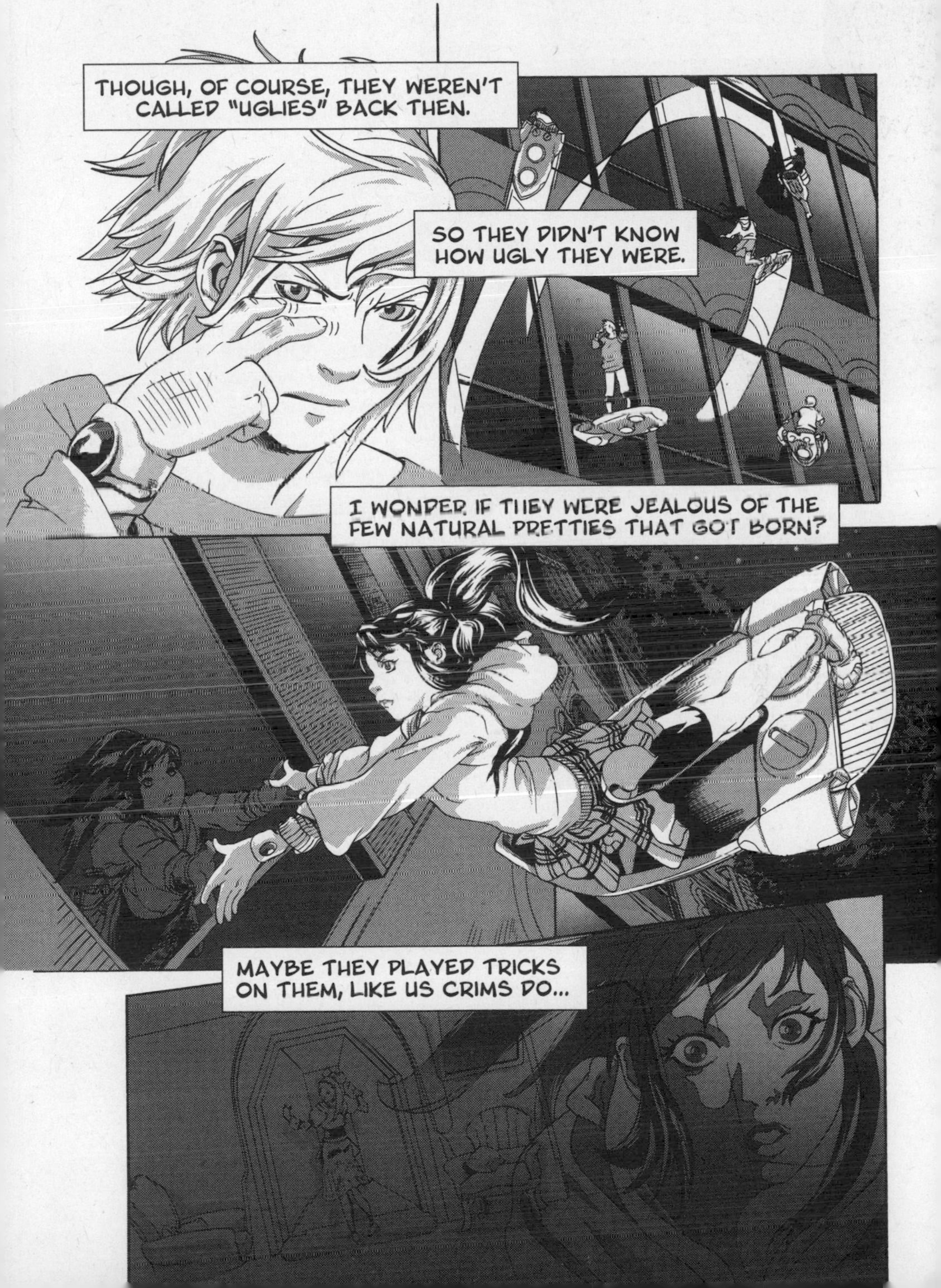
THOUGH, OF COURSE, THEY WEREN'T CALLED "UGLIES" BACK THEN.
SO THEY DIDN'T KNOW HOW UGLY THEY WERE.
I WONDER IF THEY WERE JEALOUS OF THE FEW NATURAL PRETTIES THAT GOT BORN?
MAYBE THEY PLAYED TRICKS ON THEM, LIKE US CRIMS DO...

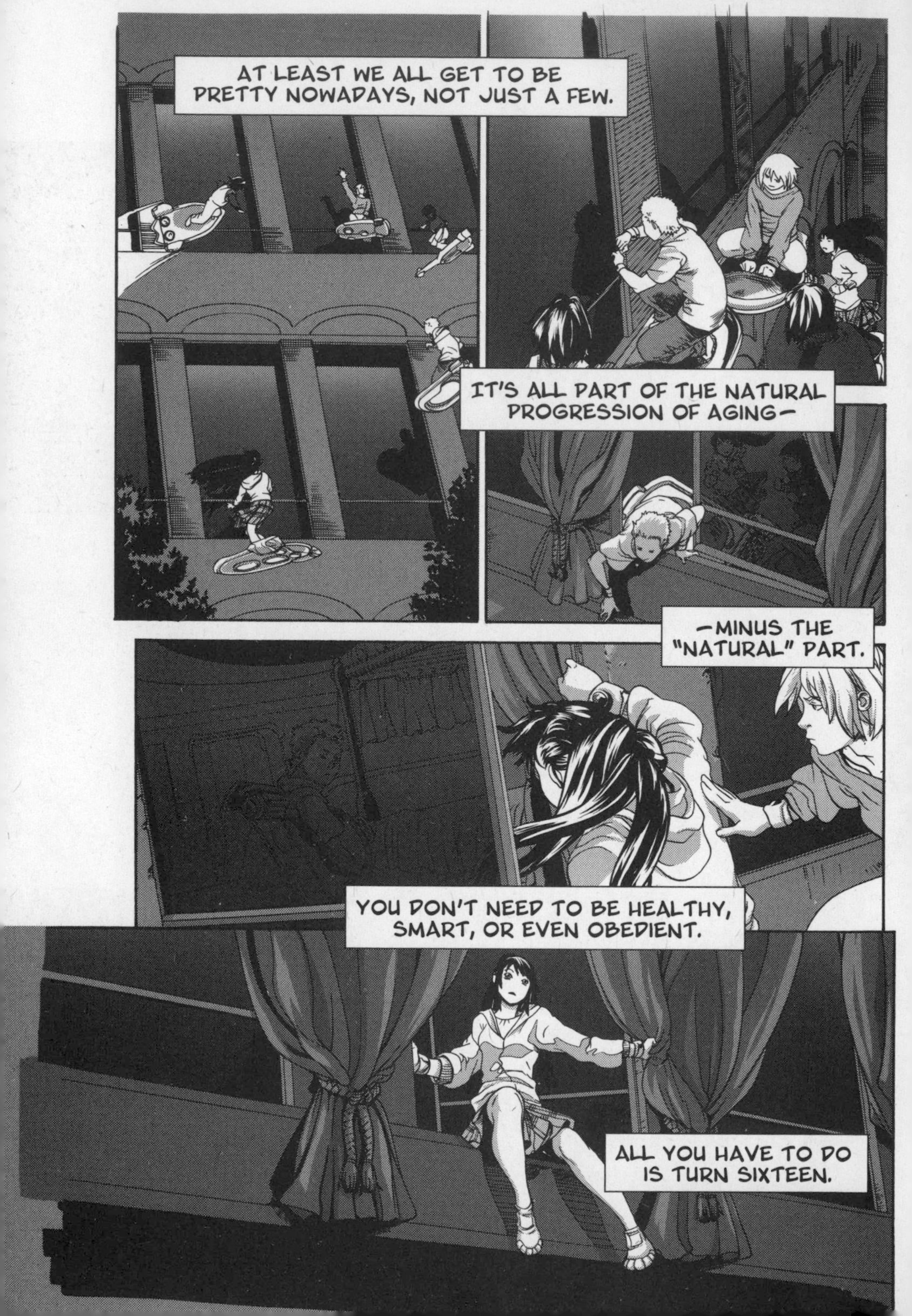
AT LEAST WE ALL GET TO BE PRETTY NOWADAYS, NOT JUST A FEW.
IT'S ALL PART OF THE NATURAL PROGRESSION OF AGING—
—MINUS THE "NATURAL" PART.
YOU DON'T NEED TO BE HEALTHY, SMART, OR EVEN OBEDIENT.
ALL YOU HAVE TO DO IS TURN SIXTEEN.

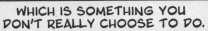
WHICH IS SOMETHING YOU DON'T REALLY CHOOSE TO DO.

WHOA!

SWOOOSH

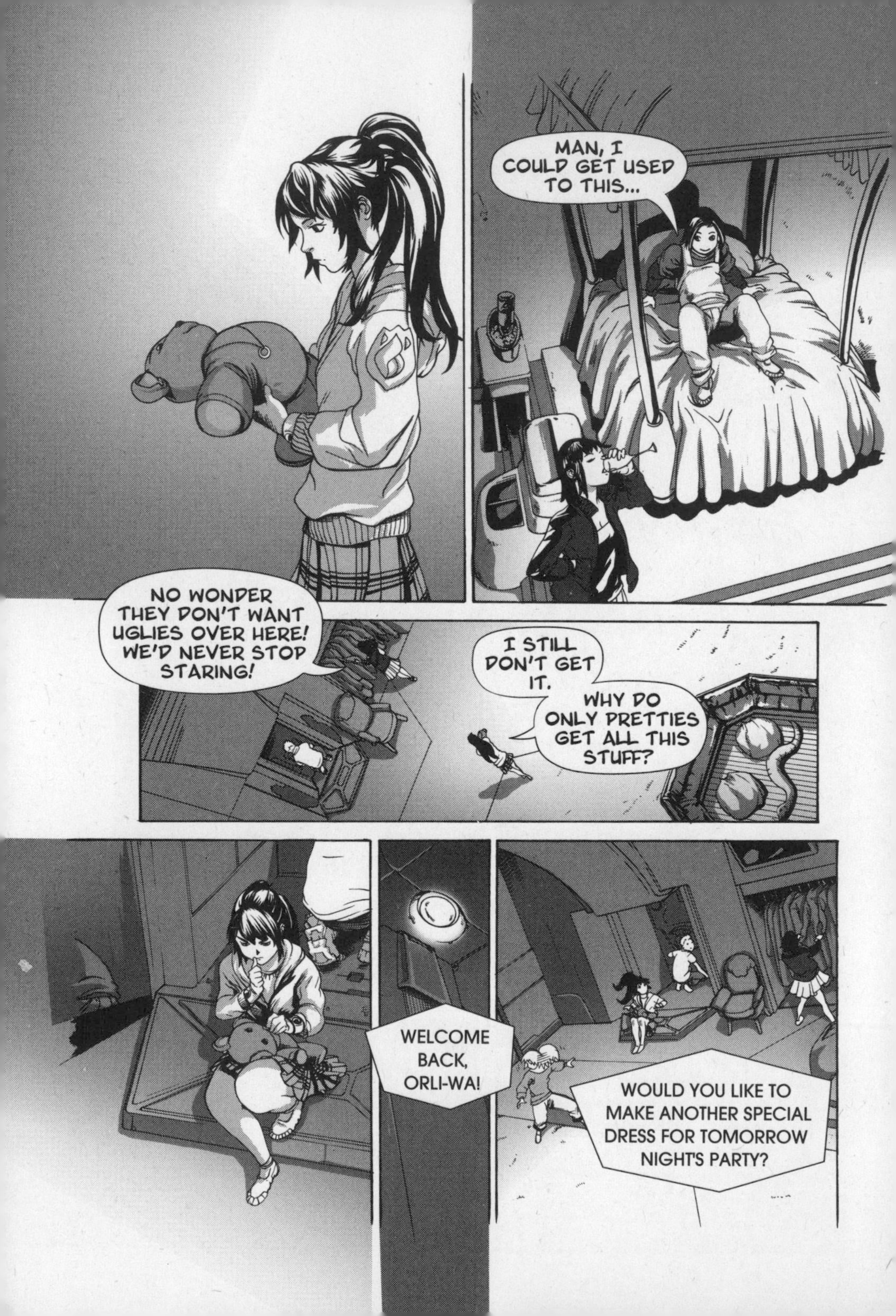
MAN, I COULD GET USED TO THIS...
NO WONDER THEY DON'T WANT UGLIES OVER HERE! WE'D NEVER STOP STARING!
I STILL DON'T GET IT.
WHY DO ONLY PRETTIES GET ALL THIS STUFF?
WELCOME BACK, ORLI-WA!
WOULD YOU LIKE TO MAKE ANOTHER SPECIAL DRESS FOR TOMORROW NIGHT'S PARTY?

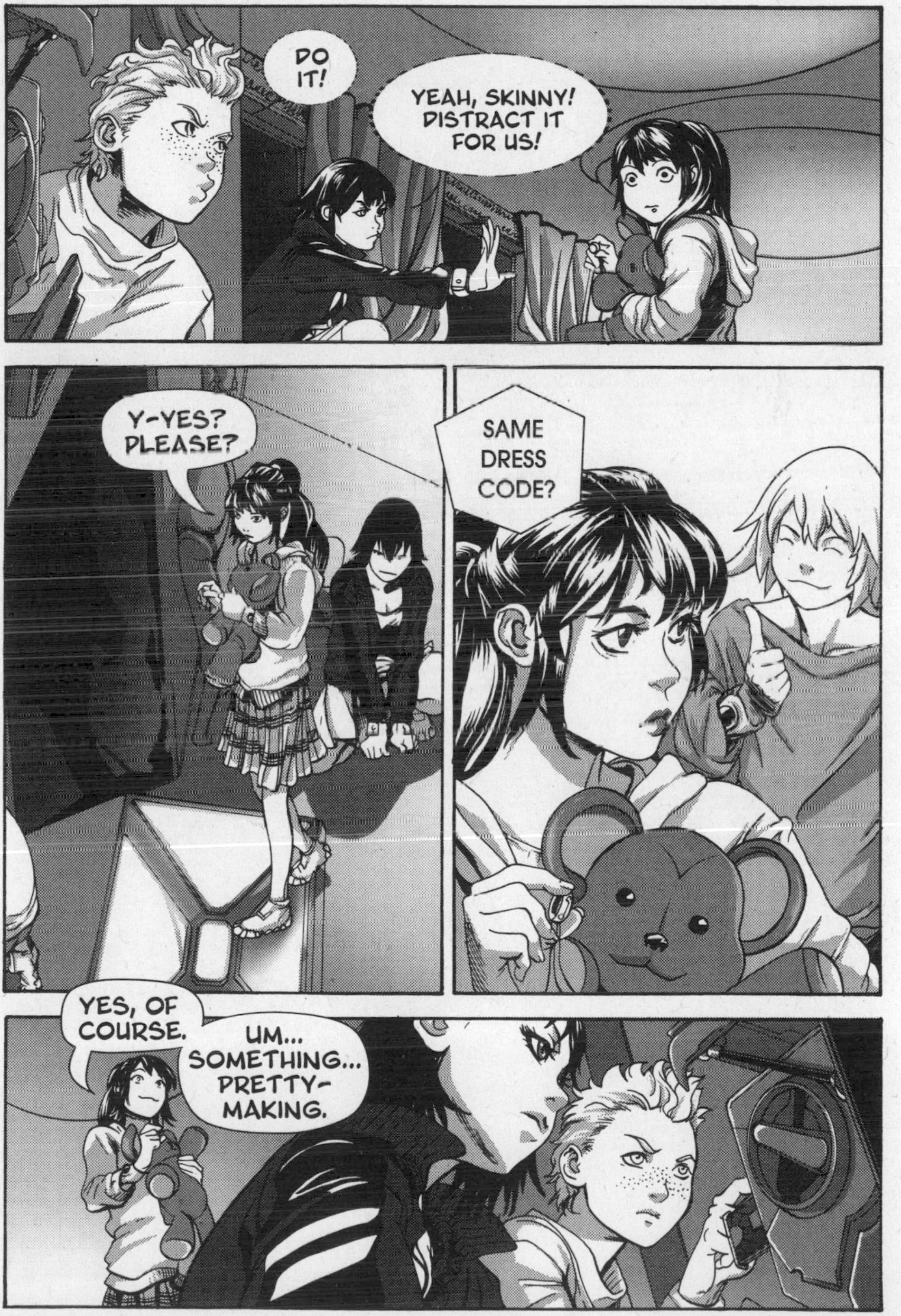
DO IT!
YEAH, SKINNY! DISTRACT IT FOR US!
Y-YES? PLEASE?
SAME DRESS CODE?
YES, OF COURSE.
UM... SOMETHING... PRETTY-MAKING.

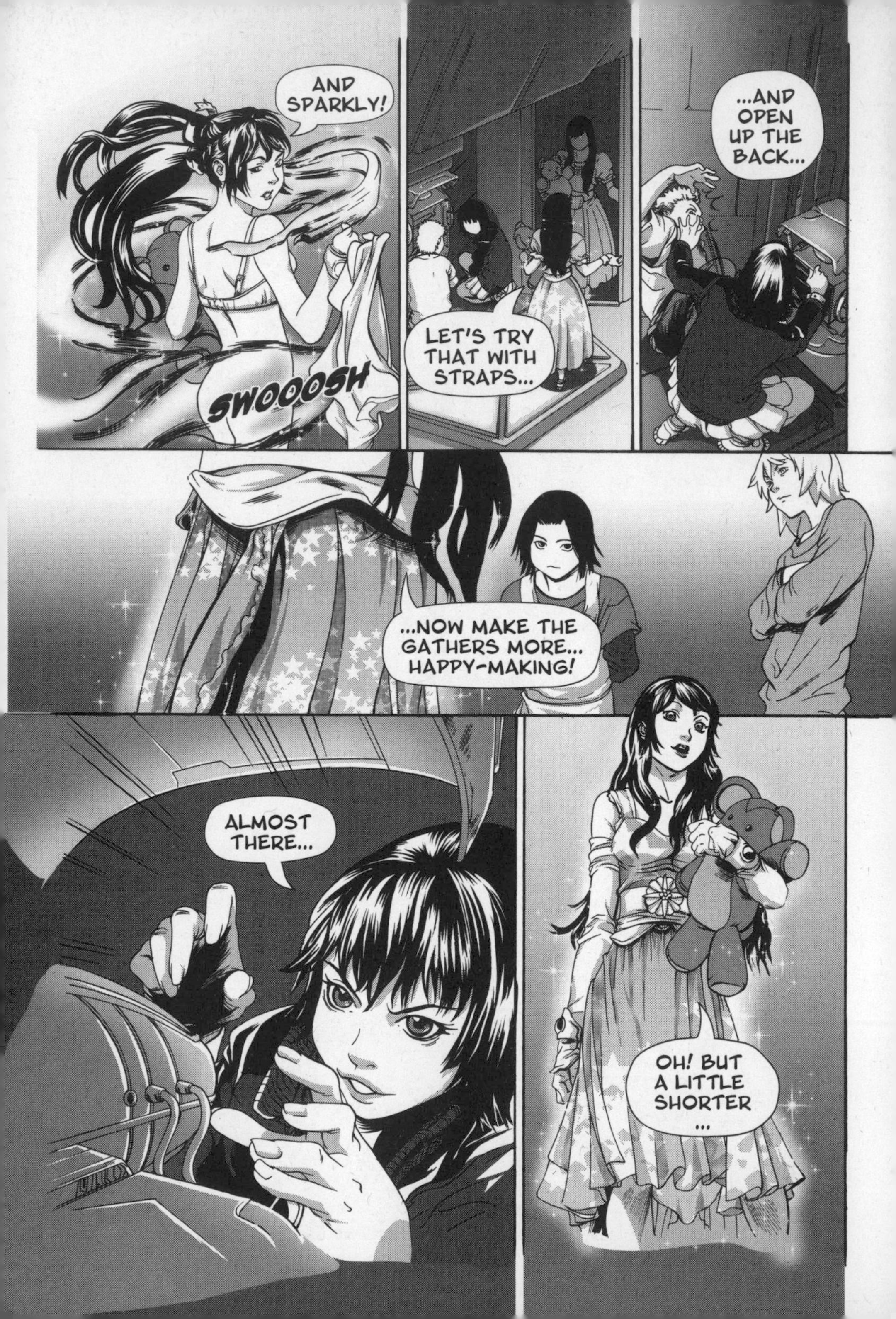
AND SPARKLY!
SWOOOSH
LET'S TRY THAT WITH STRAPS...
...AND OPEN UP THE BACK...
...NOW MAKE THE GATHERS MORE... HAPPY-MAKING!
ALMOST THERE...
OH! BUT A LITTLE SHORTER ...

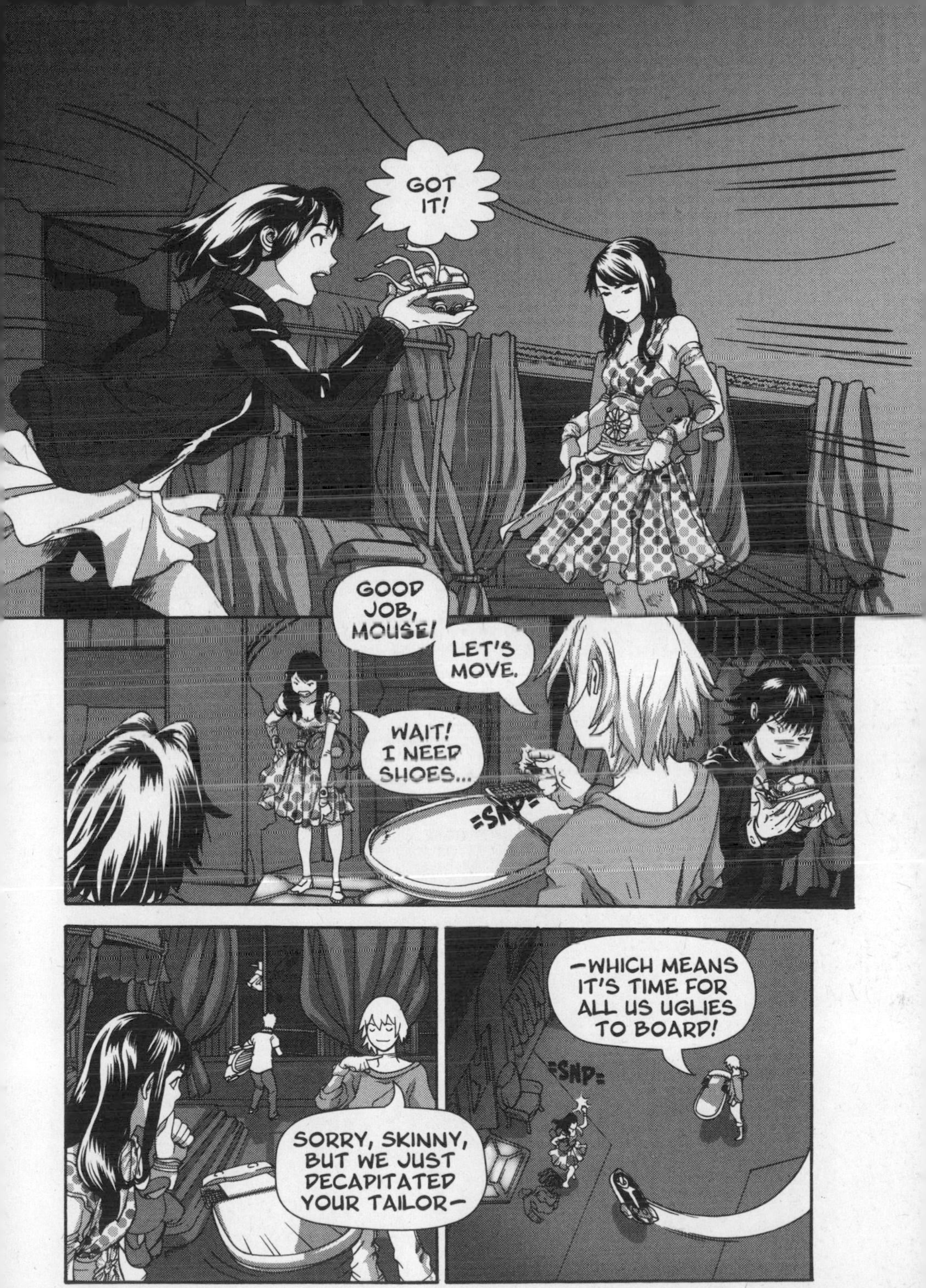
GOT IT!
GOOD JOB, MOUSE!
LET'S MOVE.
WAIT! I NEED SHOES...
=SNP=
SORRY, SKINNY, BUT WE JUST DECAPITATED YOUR TAILOR—
—WHICH MEANS IT'S TIME FOR ALL US UGLIES TO BOARD!
=SNP=

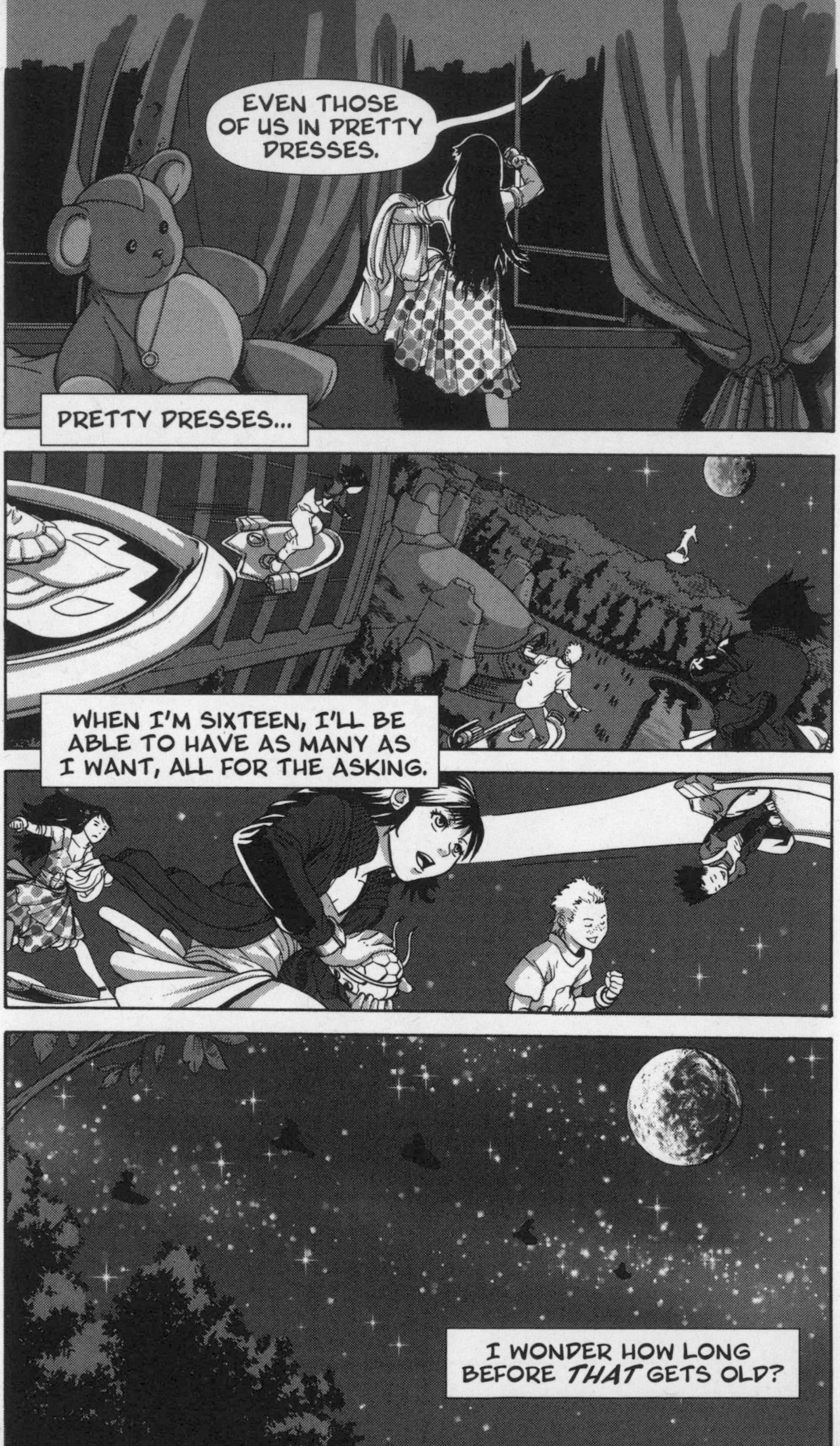
EVEN THOSE OF US IN PRETTY DRESSES.
PRETTY DRESSES...
WHEN I'M SIXTEEN, I'LL BE ABLE TO HAVE AS MANY AS I WANT, ALL FOR THE ASKING.
I WONDER HOW LONG BEFORE *THAT* GETS OLD?

# CHAPTER 4

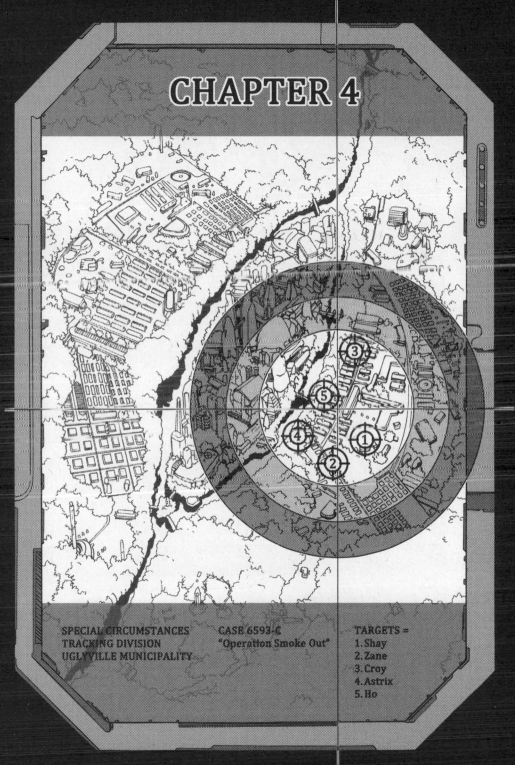

SPECIAL CIRCUMSTANCES
TRACKING DIVISION
UGLYVILLE MUNICIPALITY

CASE 6593-C
"Operation Smoke Out"

TARGETS =
1. Shay
2. Zane
3. Croy
4. Astrix
5. Ho

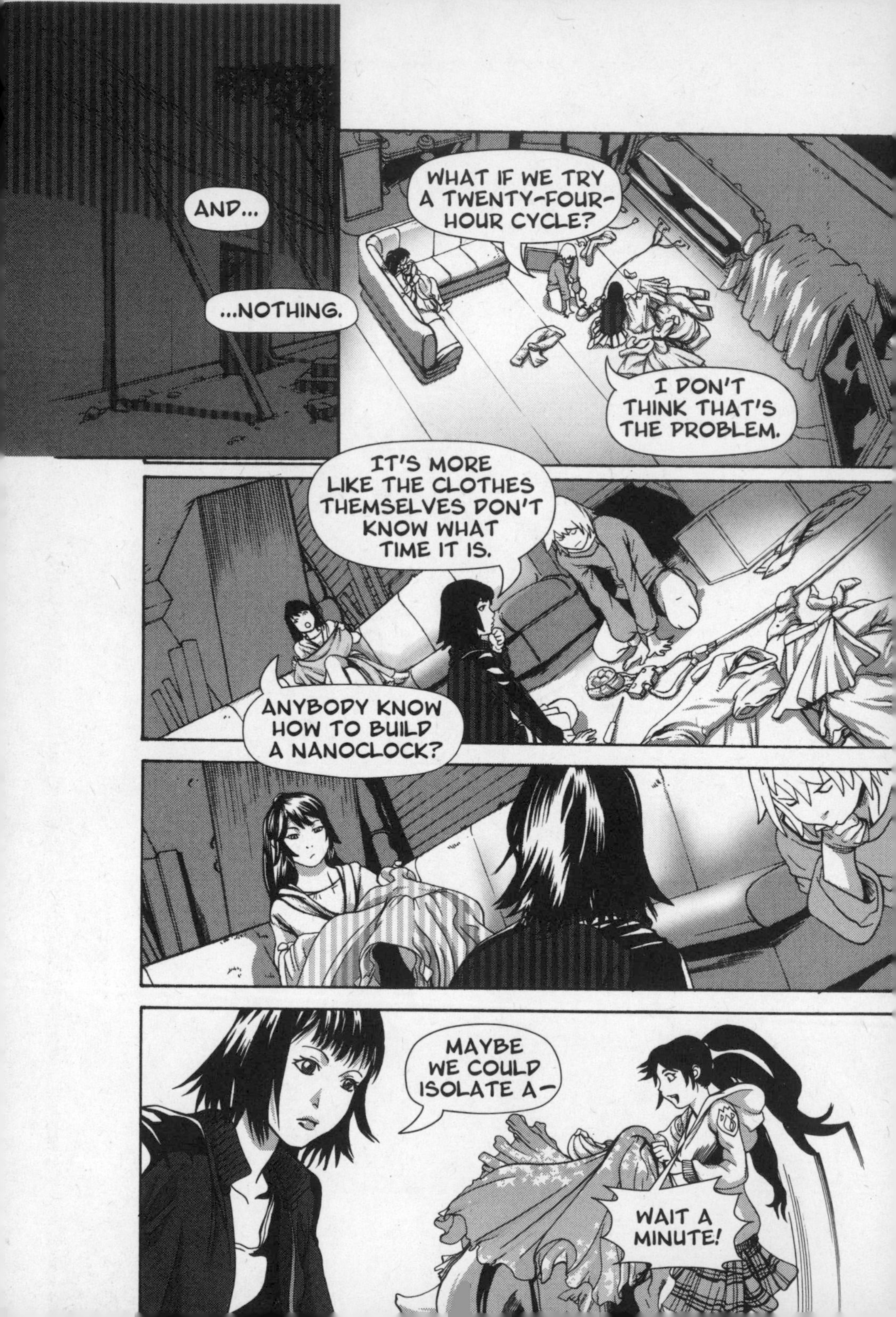
AND...
...NOTHING.
WHAT IF WE TRY A TWENTY-FOUR-HOUR CYCLE?
I DON'T THINK THAT'S THE PROBLEM.
IT'S MORE LIKE THE CLOTHES THEMSELVES DON'T KNOW WHAT TIME IT IS.
ANYBODY KNOW HOW TO BUILD A NANOCLOCK?
MAYBE WE COULD ISOLATE A—
WAIT A MINUTE!

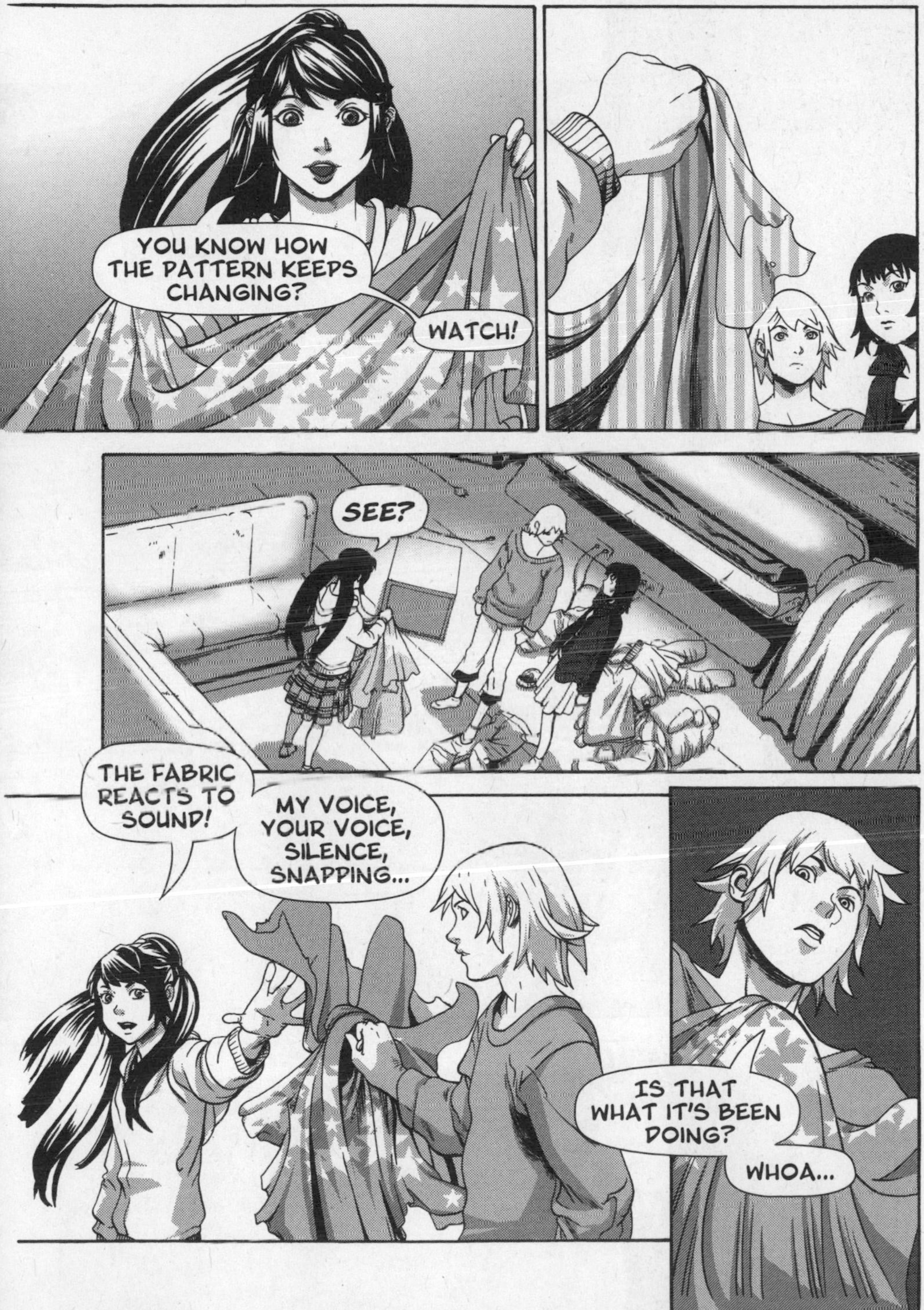
YOU KNOW HOW THE PATTERN KEEPS CHANGING?
WATCH!
SEE?
THE FABRIC REACTS TO SOUND!
MY VOICE, YOUR VOICE, SILENCE, SNAPPING...
IS THAT WHAT IT'S BEEN DOING?
WHOA...

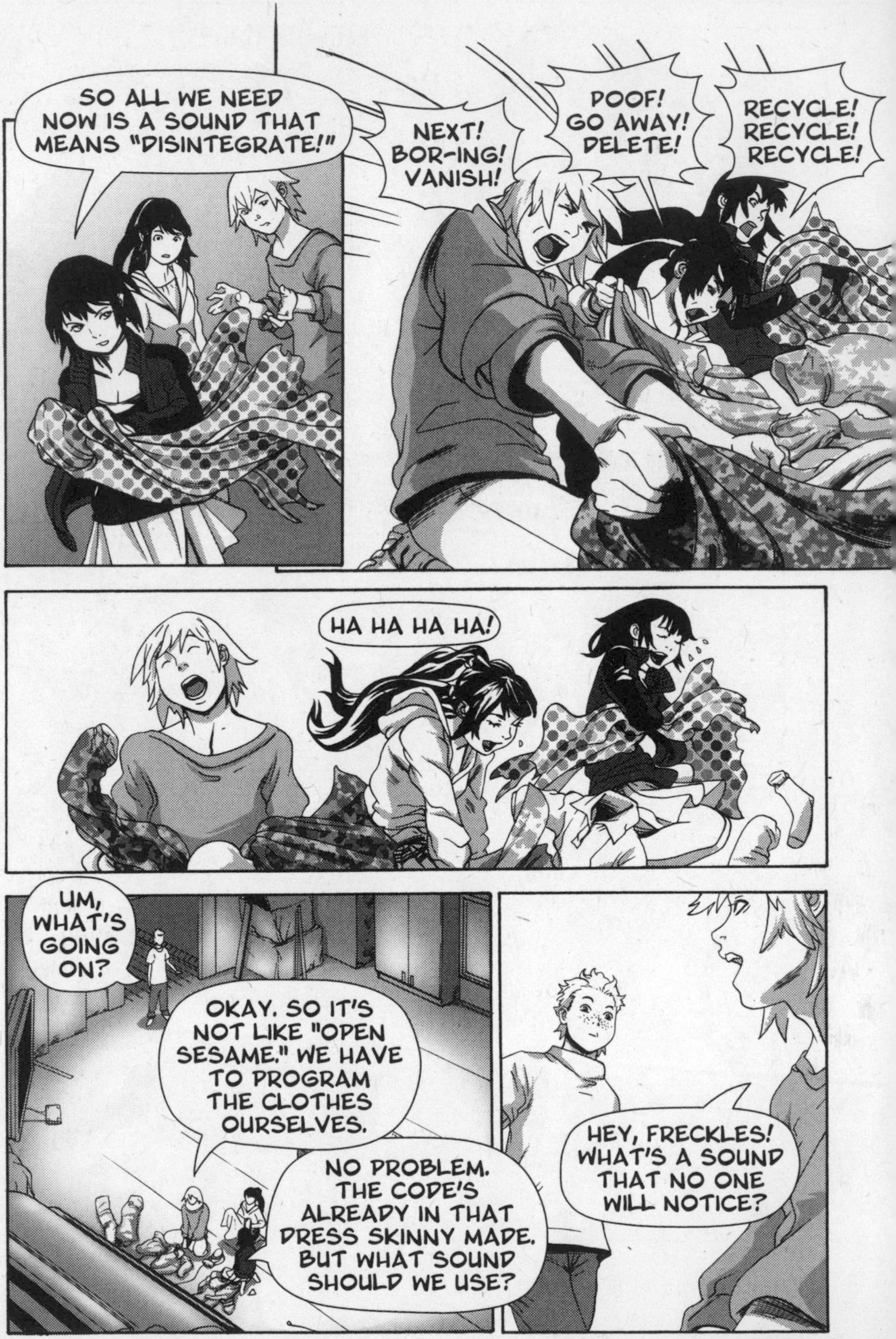
SO ALL WE NEED NOW IS A SOUND THAT MEANS "DISINTEGRATE!"
NEXT! BOR-ING! VANISH!
POOF! GO AWAY! DELETE!
RECYCLE! RECYCLE! RECYCLE!
HA HA HA HA!
UM, WHAT'S GOING ON?
OKAY. SO IT'S NOT LIKE "OPEN SESAME." WE HAVE TO PROGRAM THE CLOTHES OURSELVES.
NO PROBLEM. THE CODE'S ALREADY IN THAT DRESS SKINNY MADE. BUT WHAT SOUND SHOULD WE USE?
HEY, FRECKLES! WHAT'S A SOUND THAT NO ONE WILL NOTICE?

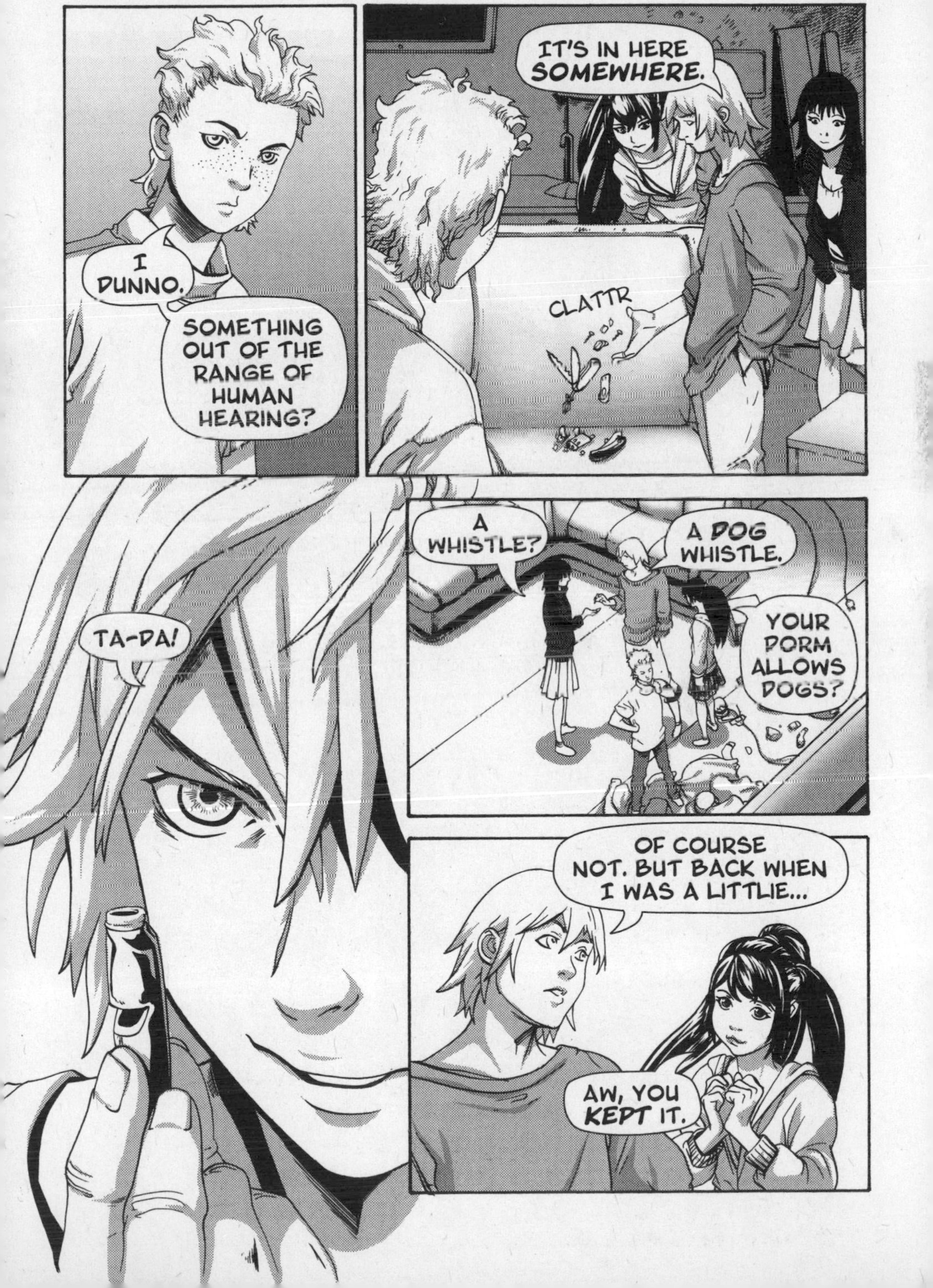
I DUNNO.
SOMETHING OUT OF THE RANGE OF HUMAN HEARING?
IT'S IN HERE SOMEWHERE.
CLATTR
TA-DA!
A WHISTLE?
A DOG WHISTLE.
YOUR DORM ALLOWS DOGS?
OF COURSE NOT. BUT BACK WHEN I WAS A LITTLIE...
AW, YOU KEPT IT.

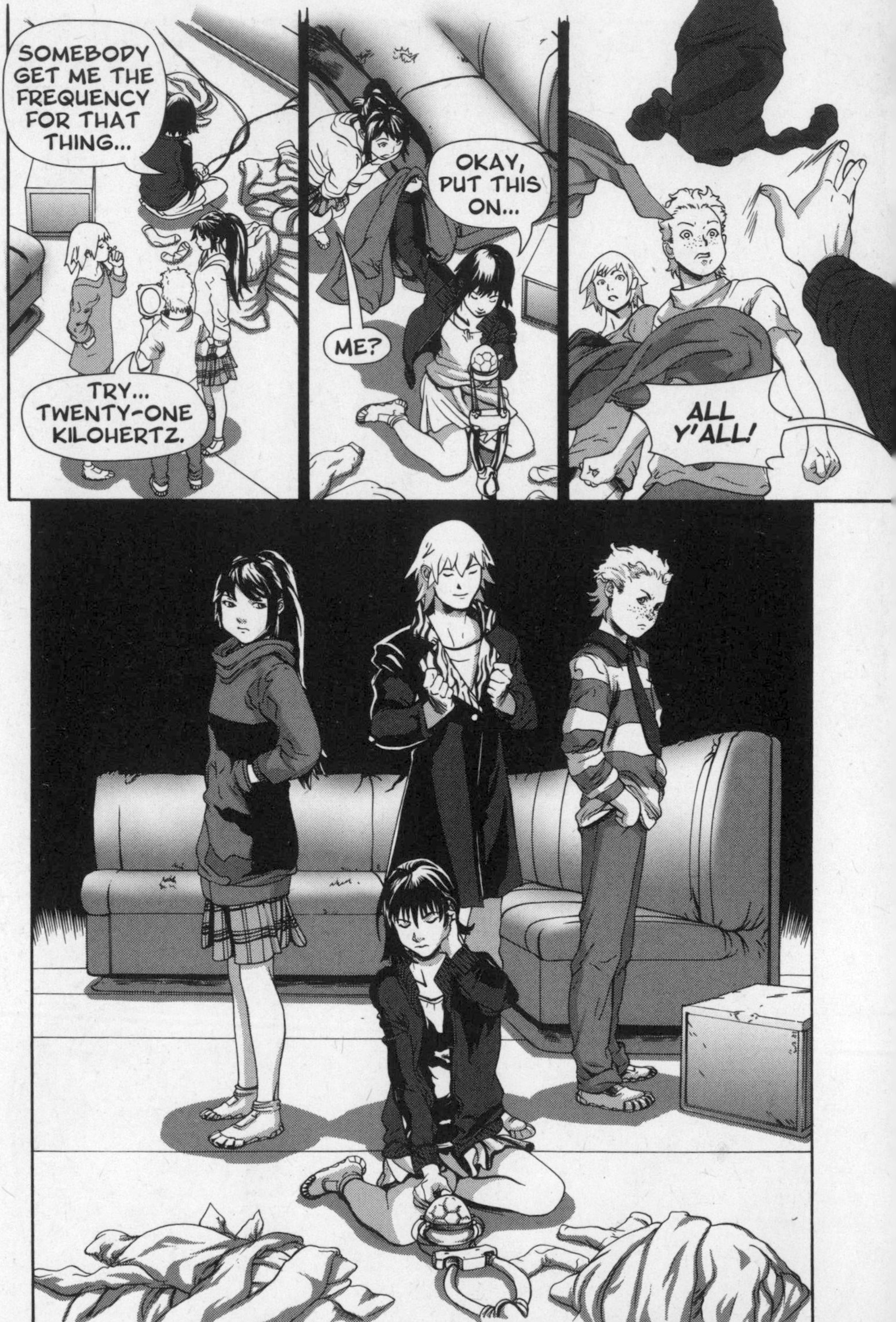
SOMEBODY GET ME THE FREQUENCY FOR THAT THING...
TRY... TWENTY-ONE KILOHERTZ.
OKAY, PUT THIS ON...
ME?
ALL Y'ALL!

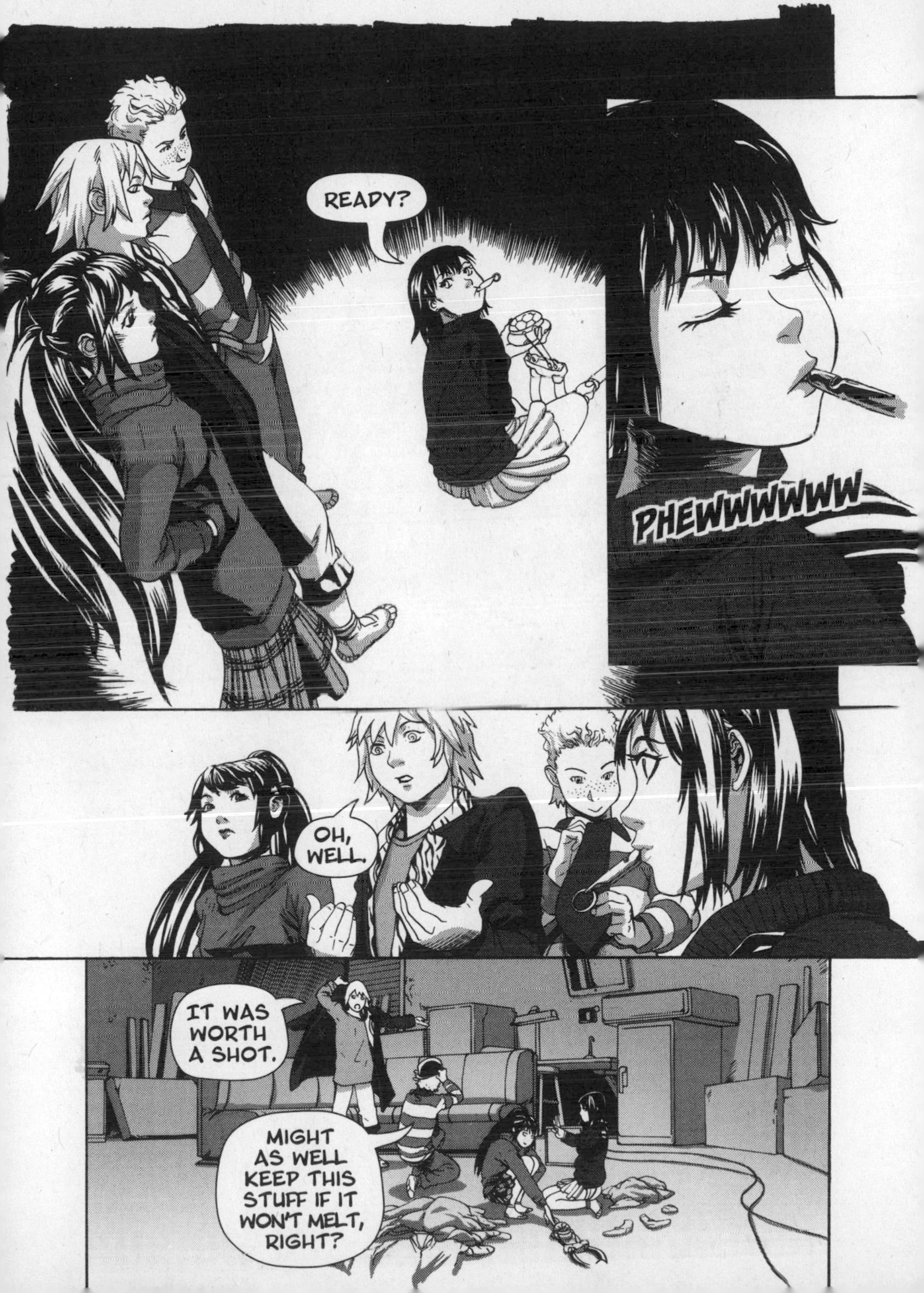
READY?
PHEWWWWWW
OH, WELL.
IT WAS WORTH A SHOT.
MIGHT AS WELL KEEP THIS STUFF IF IT WON'T MELT, RIGHT?

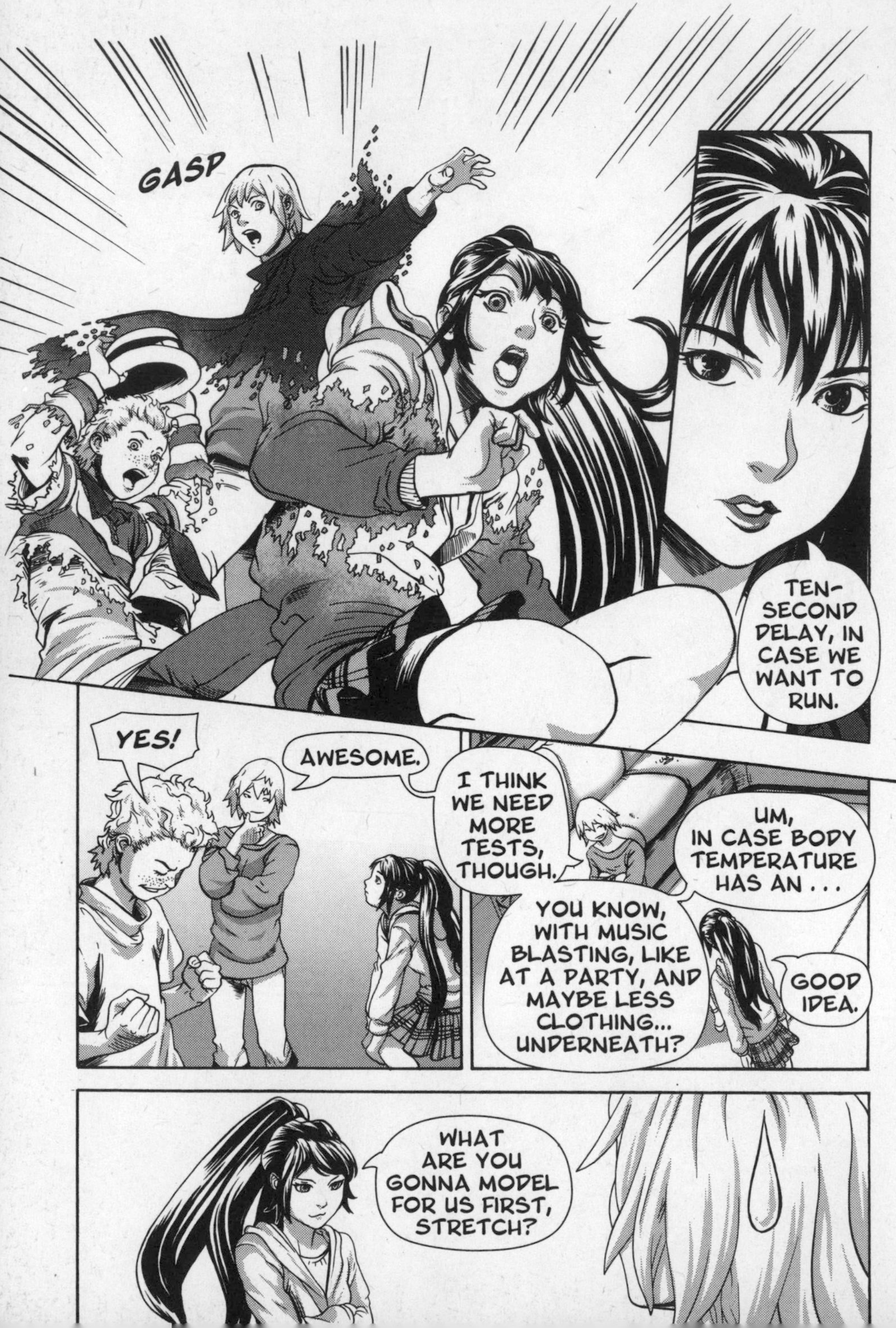
GASP
TEN-SECOND DELAY, IN CASE WE WANT TO RUN.
YES!
AWESOME.
I THINK WE NEED MORE TESTS, THOUGH.
UM, IN CASE BODY TEMPERATURE HAS AN . . .
YOU KNOW, WITH MUSIC BLASTING, LIKE AT A PARTY, AND MAYBE LESS CLOTHING... UNDERNEATH?
GOOD IDEA.
WHAT ARE YOU GONNA MODEL FOR US FIRST, STRETCH?

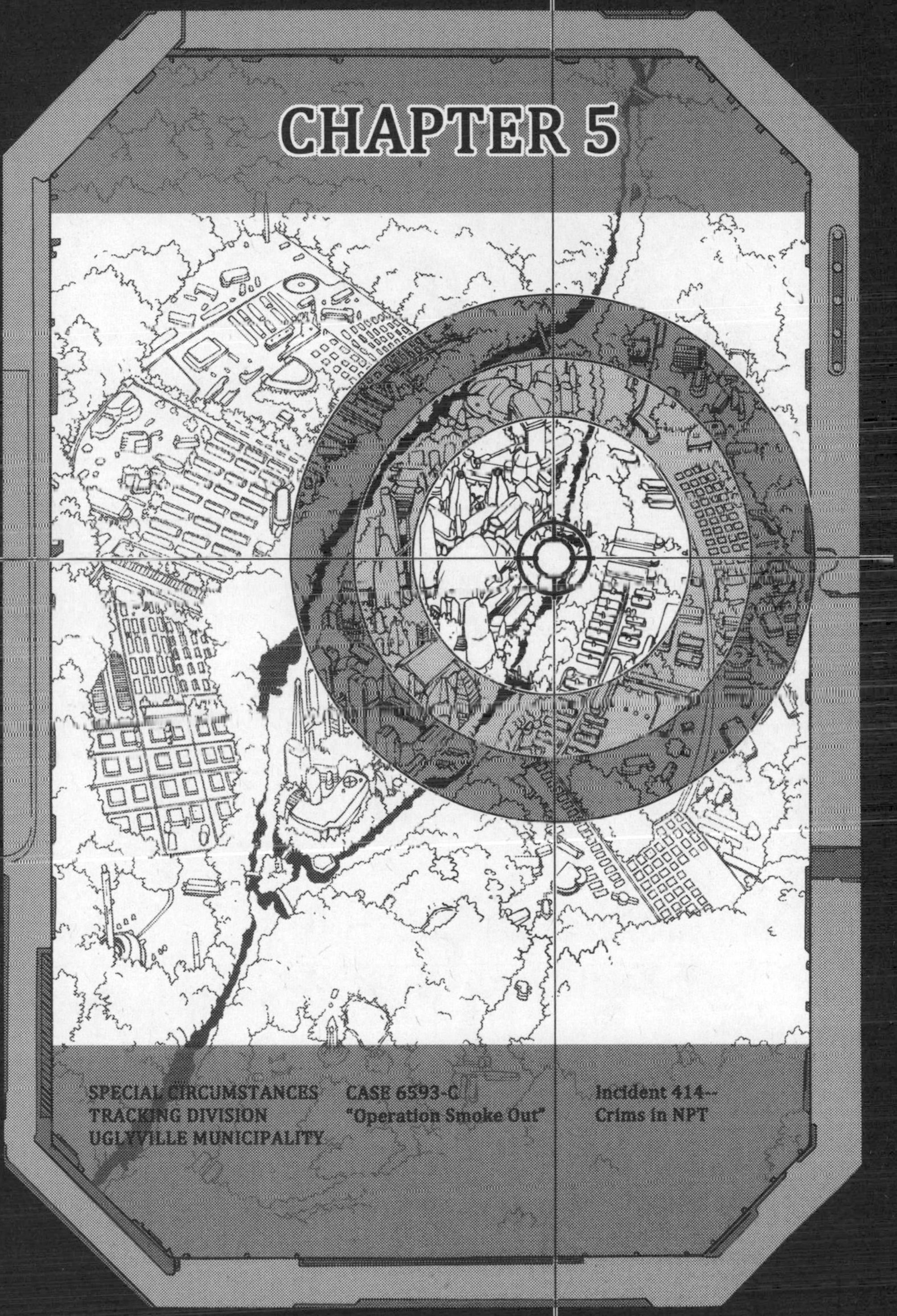
CHAPTER 5
SPECIAL CIRCUMSTANCES
TRACKING DIVISION
UGLYVILLE MUNICIPALITY
CASE 6593-G
"Operation Smoke Out"
Incident 414--
Crims in NPT

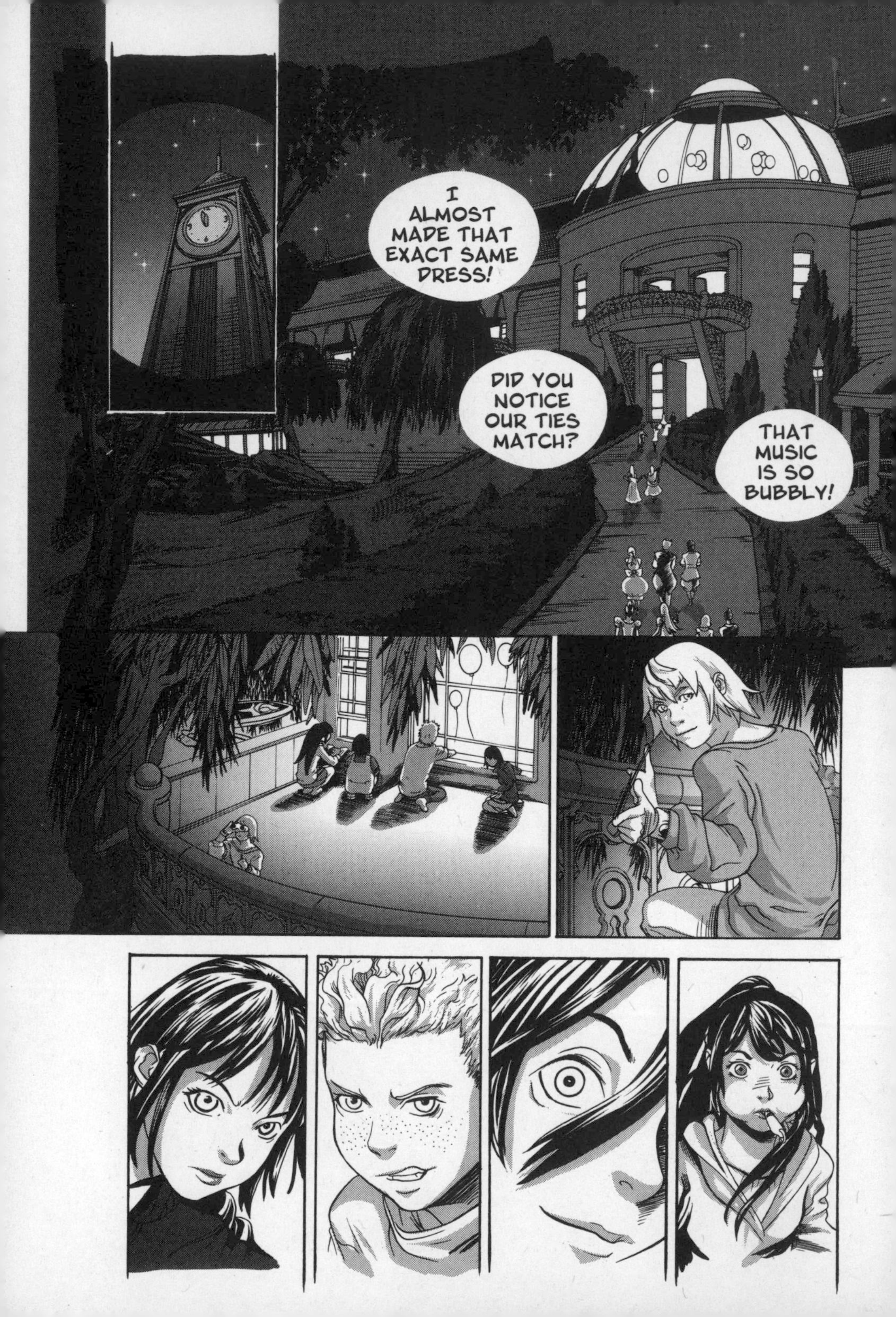
I ALMOST MADE THAT EXACT SAME DRESS!
DID YOU NOTICE OUR TIES MATCH?
THAT MUSIC IS SO BUBBLY!

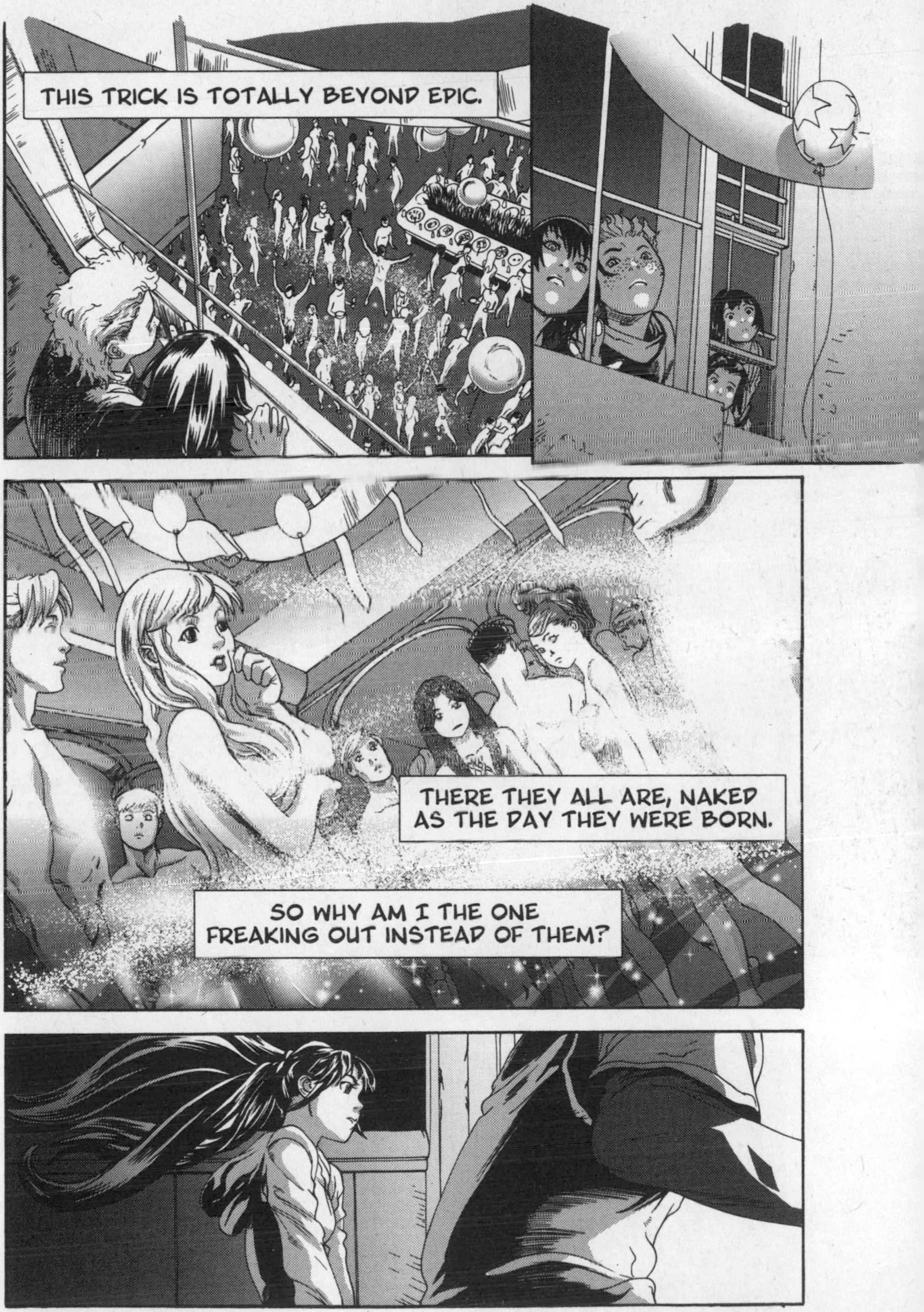
THIS TRICK IS TOTALLY BEYOND EPIC.
THERE THEY ALL ARE, NAKED AS THE DAY THEY WERE BORN.
SO WHY AM I THE ONE FREAKING OUT INSTEAD OF THEM?

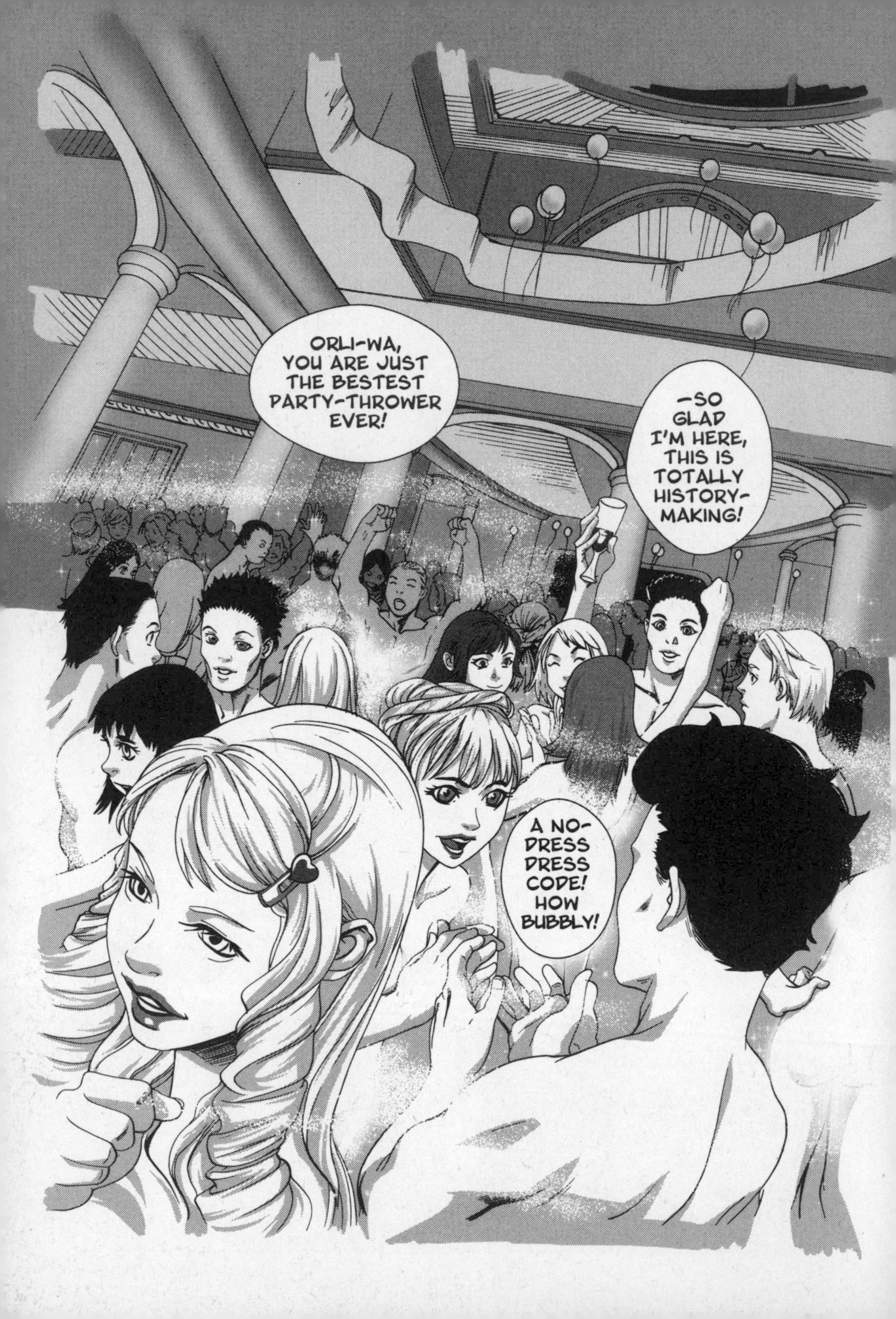
ORLI-WA, YOU ARE JUST THE BESTEST PARTY-THROWER EVER!
—SO GLAD I'M HERE, THIS IS TOTALLY HISTORY-MAKING!
A NO-DRESS DRESS CODE! HOW BUBBLY!

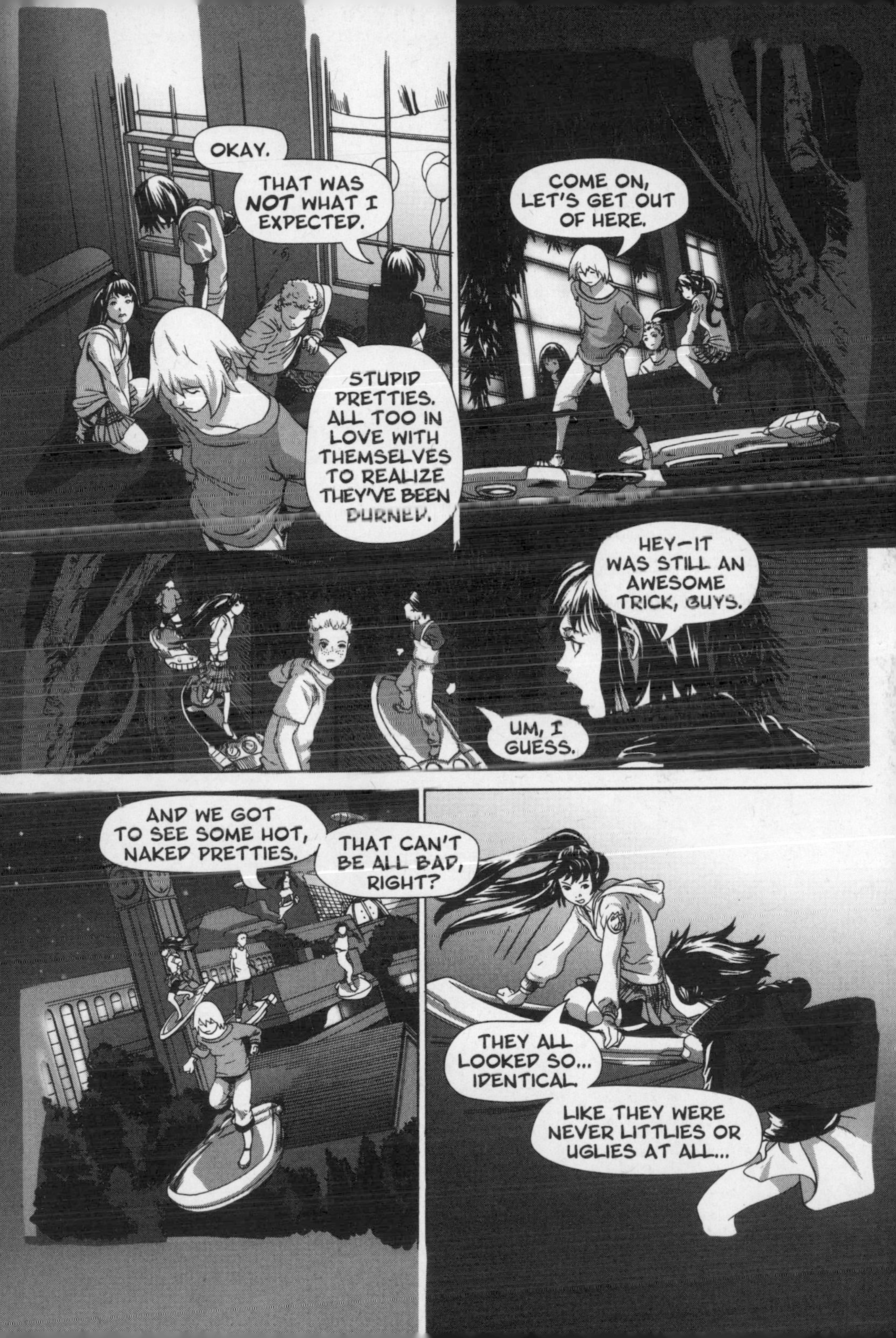
OKAY.
THAT WAS NOT WHAT I EXPECTED.
STUPID PRETTIES. ALL TOO IN LOVE WITH THEMSELVES TO REALIZE THEY'VE BEEN BURNED.
COME ON, LET'S GET OUT OF HERE.
HEY—IT WAS STILL AN AWESOME TRICK, GUYS.
UM, I GUESS.
AND WE GOT TO SEE SOME HOT, NAKED PRETTIES.
THAT CAN'T BE ALL BAD, RIGHT?
THEY ALL LOOKED SO... IDENTICAL.
LIKE THEY WERE NEVER LITTLIES OR UGLIES AT ALL...

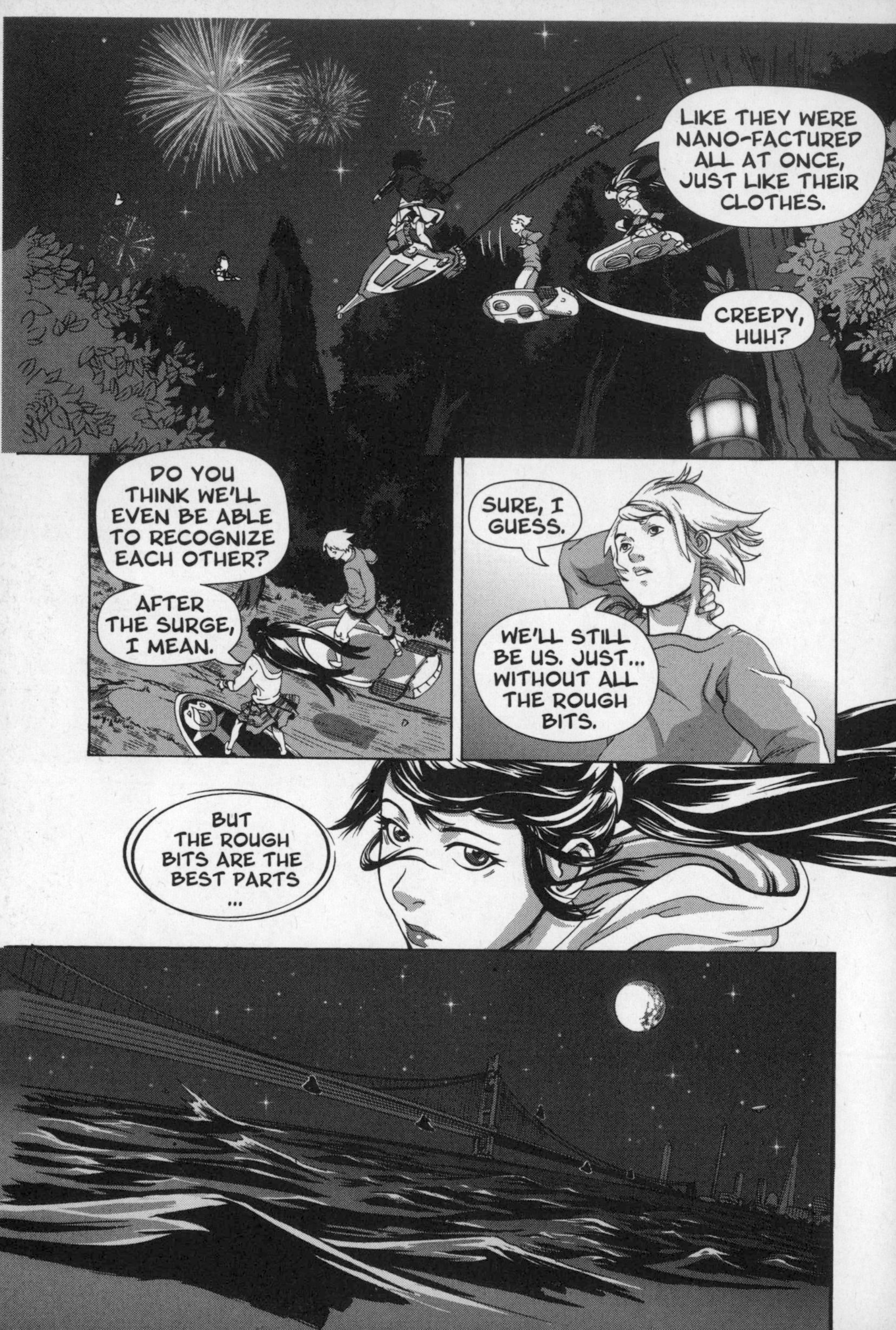
LIKE THEY WERE NANO-FACTURED ALL AT ONCE, JUST LIKE THEIR CLOTHES.
CREEPY, HUH?
DO YOU THINK WE'LL EVEN BE ABLE TO RECOGNIZE EACH OTHER?
AFTER THE SURGE, I MEAN.
SURE, I GUESS.
WE'LL STILL BE US. JUST... WITHOUT ALL THE ROUGH BITS.
BUT THE ROUGH BITS ARE THE BEST PARTS ...

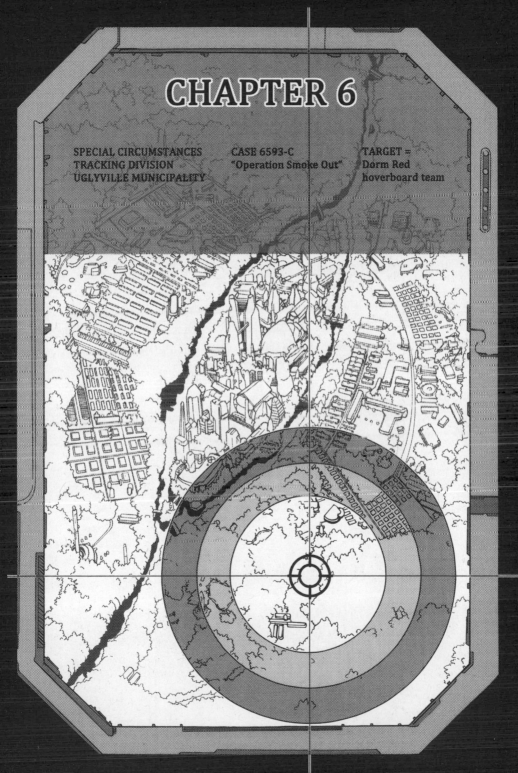

# CHAPTER 6

SPECIAL CIRCUMSTANCES
TRACKING DIVISION
UGLYVILLE MUNICIPALITY

CASE 6593-C
"Operation Smoke Out"

TARGET =
Dorm Red
hoverboard team

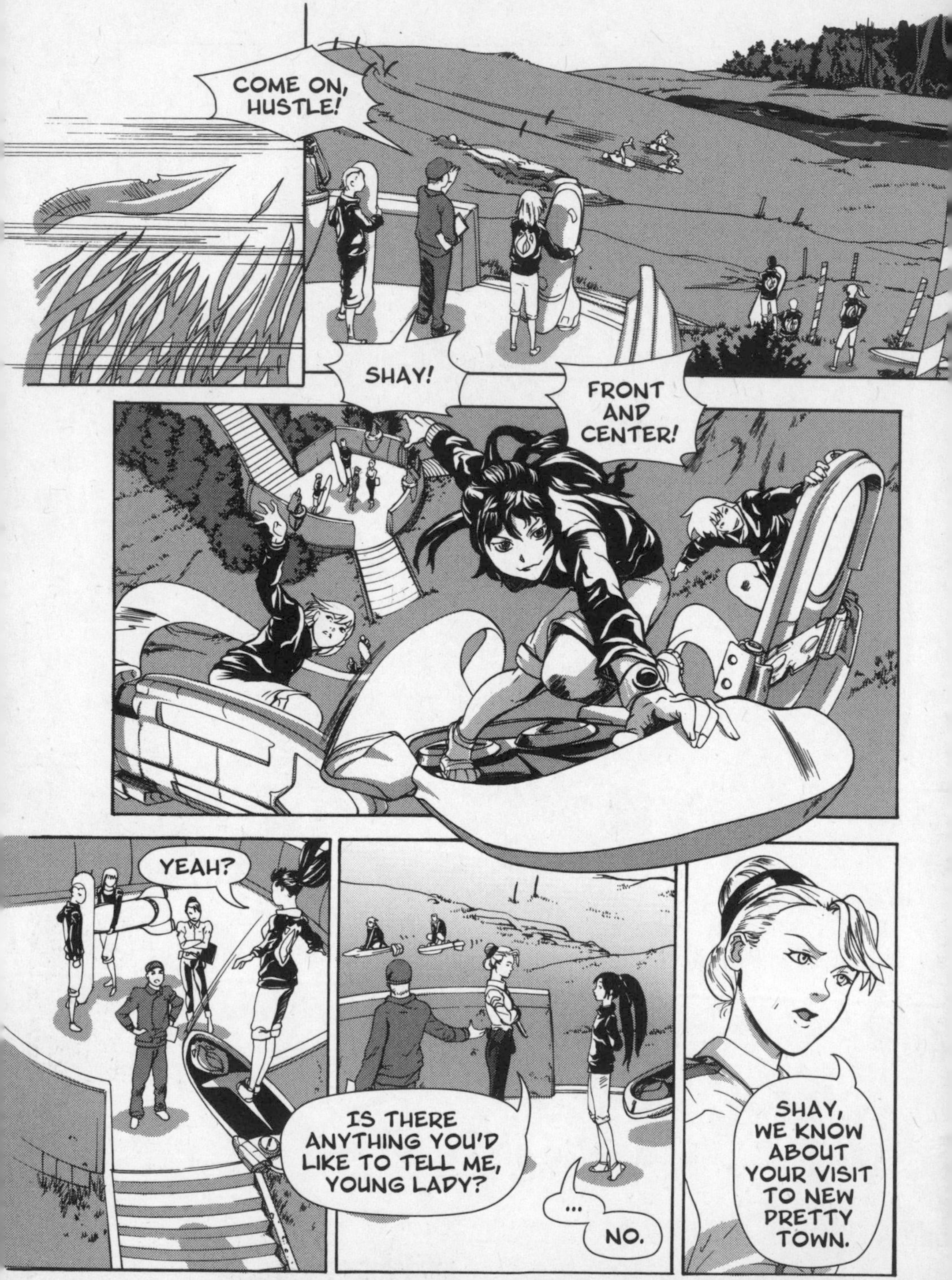
COME ON, HUSTLE!
SHAY!
FRONT AND CENTER!
YEAH?
IS THERE ANYTHING YOU'D LIKE TO TELL ME, YOUNG LADY?
...
NO.
SHAY, WE KNOW ABOUT YOUR VISIT TO NEW PRETTY TOWN.

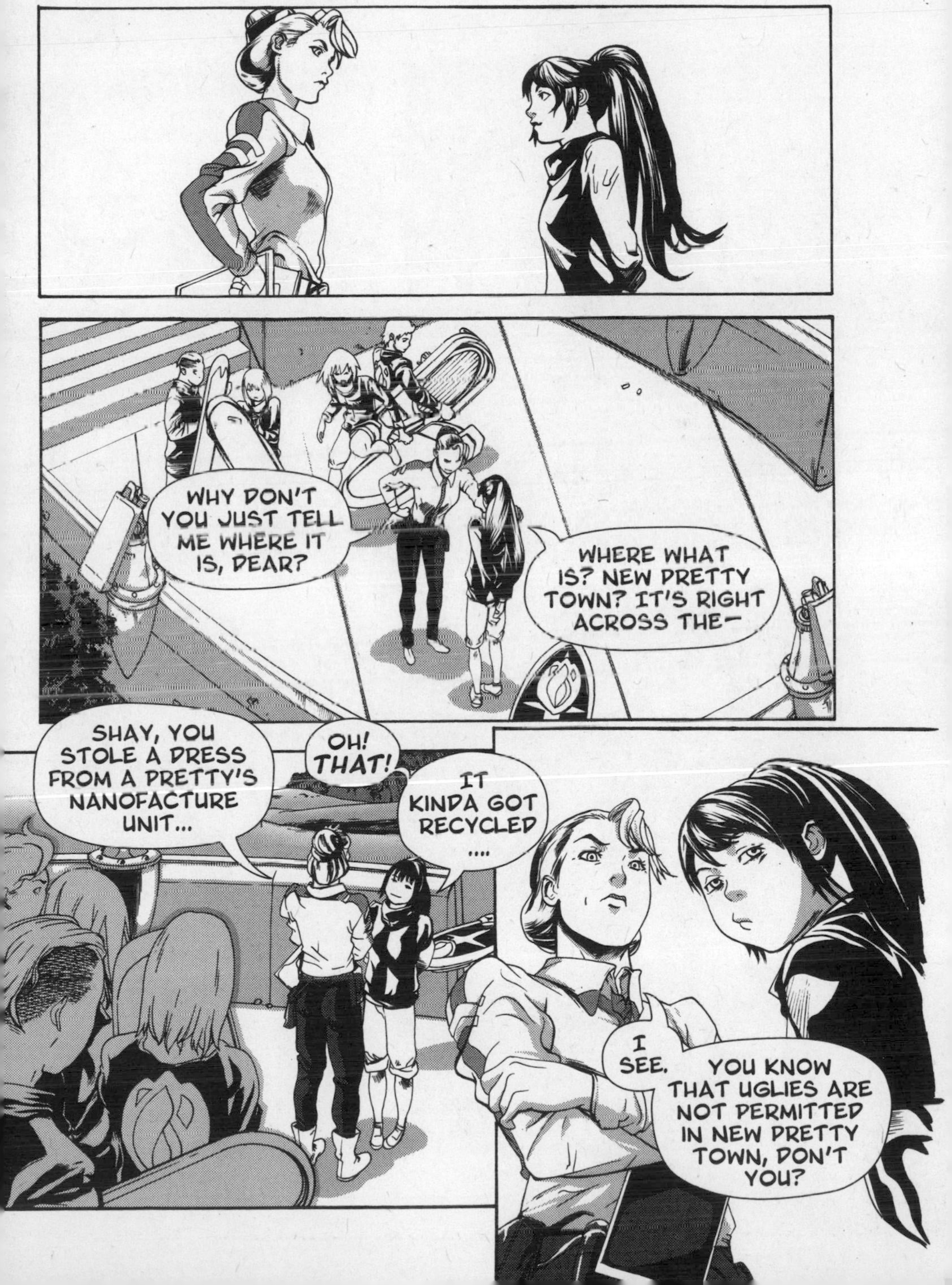
WHY DON'T YOU JUST TELL ME WHERE IT IS, DEAR?
WHERE WHAT IS? NEW PRETTY TOWN? IT'S RIGHT ACROSS THE—
SHAY, YOU STOLE A DRESS FROM A PRETTY'S NANOFACTURE UNIT...
OH! THAT!
IT KINDA GOT RECYCLED ....
I SEE.
YOU KNOW THAT UGLIES ARE NOT PERMITTED IN NEW PRETTY TOWN, DON'T YOU?

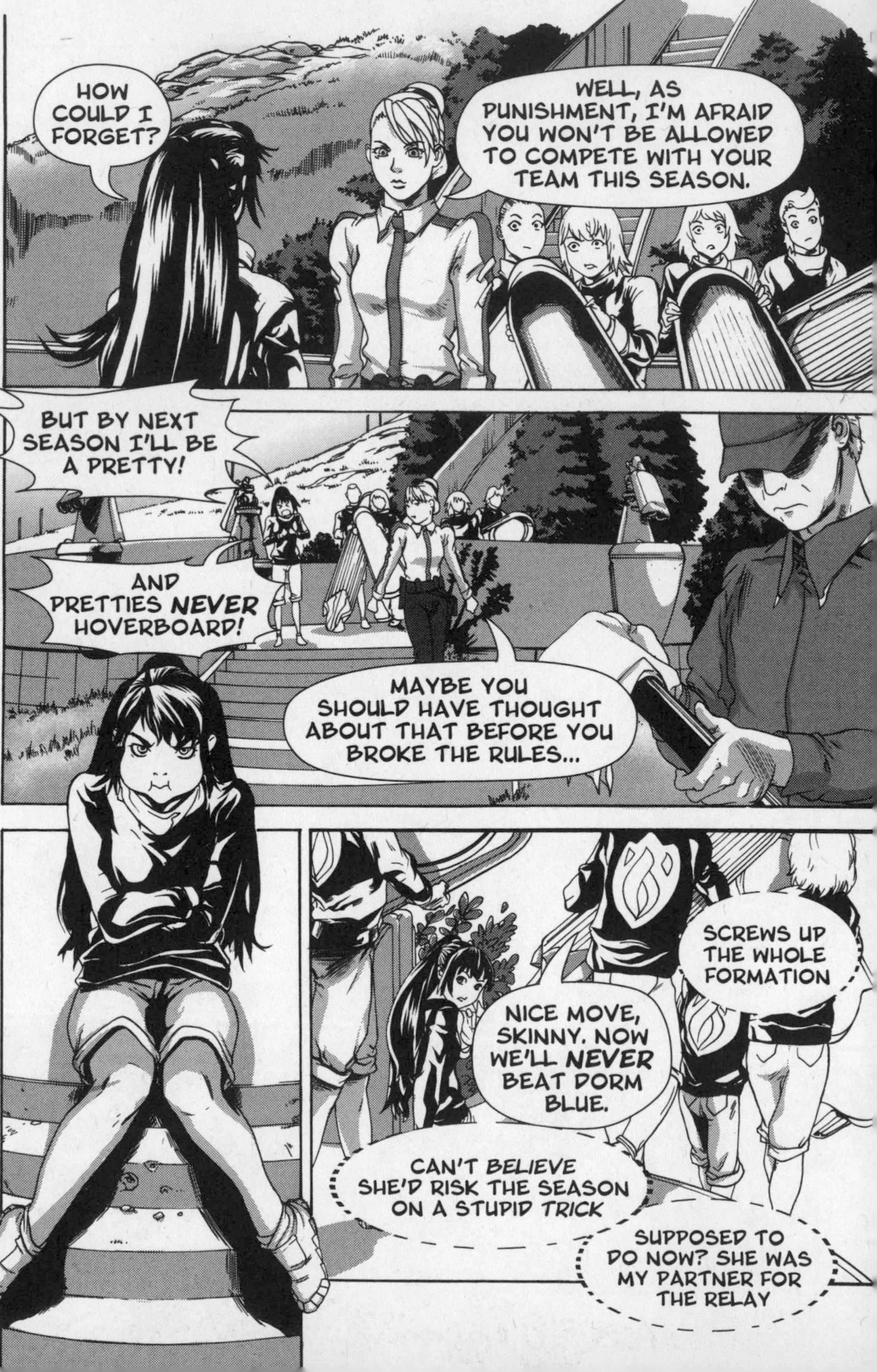
HOW COULD I FORGET?
WELL, AS PUNISHMENT, I'M AFRAID YOU WON'T BE ALLOWED TO COMPETE WITH YOUR TEAM THIS SEASON.
BUT BY NEXT SEASON I'LL BE A PRETTY!
AND PRETTIES NEVER HOVERBOARD!
MAYBE YOU SHOULD HAVE THOUGHT ABOUT THAT BEFORE YOU BROKE THE RULES...
SCREWS UP THE WHOLE FORMATION
NICE MOVE, SKINNY. NOW WE'LL NEVER BEAT DORM BLUE.
CAN'T BELIEVE SHE'D RISK THE SEASON ON A STUPID TRICK
SUPPOSED TO DO NOW? SHE WAS MY PARTNER FOR THE RELAY

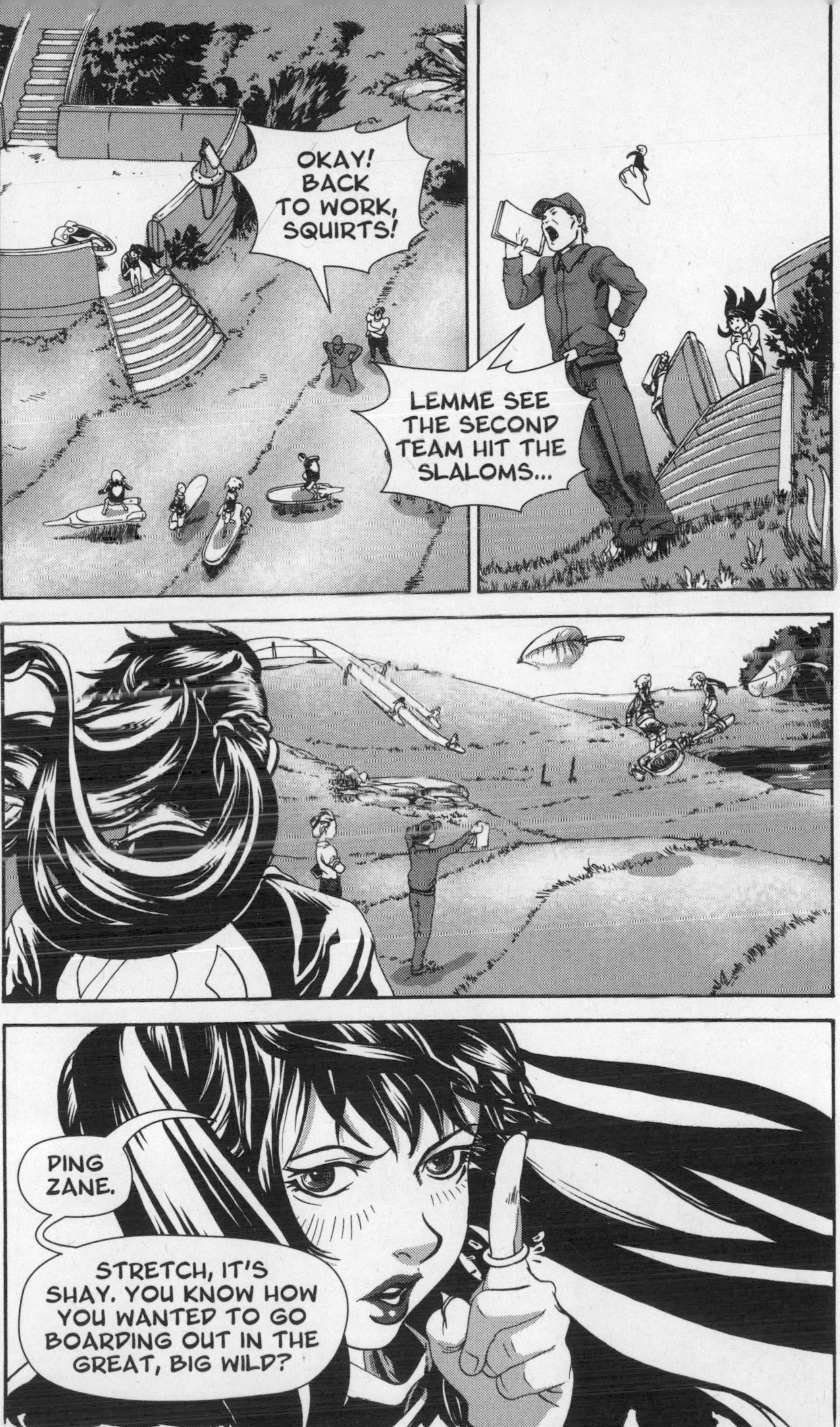
OKAY! BACK TO WORK, SQUIRTS!
LEMME SEE THE SECOND TEAM HIT THE SLALOMS...
PING ZANE.
STRETCH, IT'S SHAY. YOU KNOW HOW YOU WANTED TO GO BOARDING OUT IN THE GREAT, BIG WILD?

# CHAPTER 7

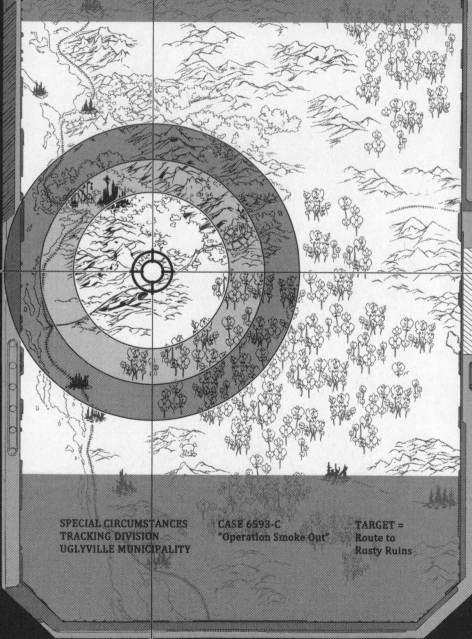

SPECIAL CIRCUMSTANCES
TRACKING DIVISION
UGLYVILLE MUNICIPALITY

CASE 6593-C
"Operation Smoke Out"

TARGET =
Route to
Rusty Ruins

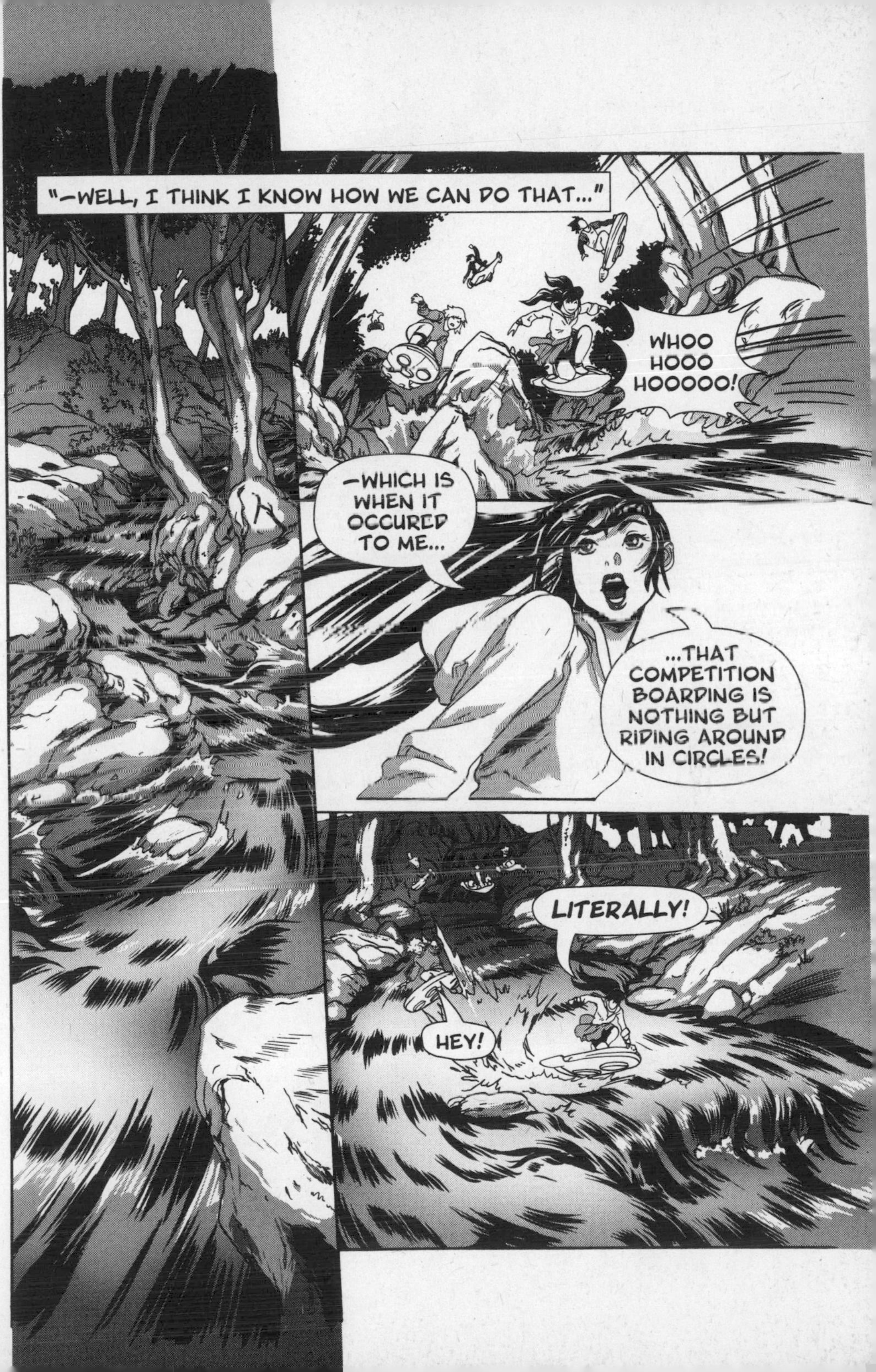
"–WELL, I THINK I KNOW HOW WE CAN DO THAT..."
WHOO HOOO HOOOOO!
–WHICH IS WHEN IT OCCURED TO ME...
...THAT COMPETITION BOARDING IS NOTHING BUT RIDING AROUND IN CIRCLES!
LITERALLY!
HEY!

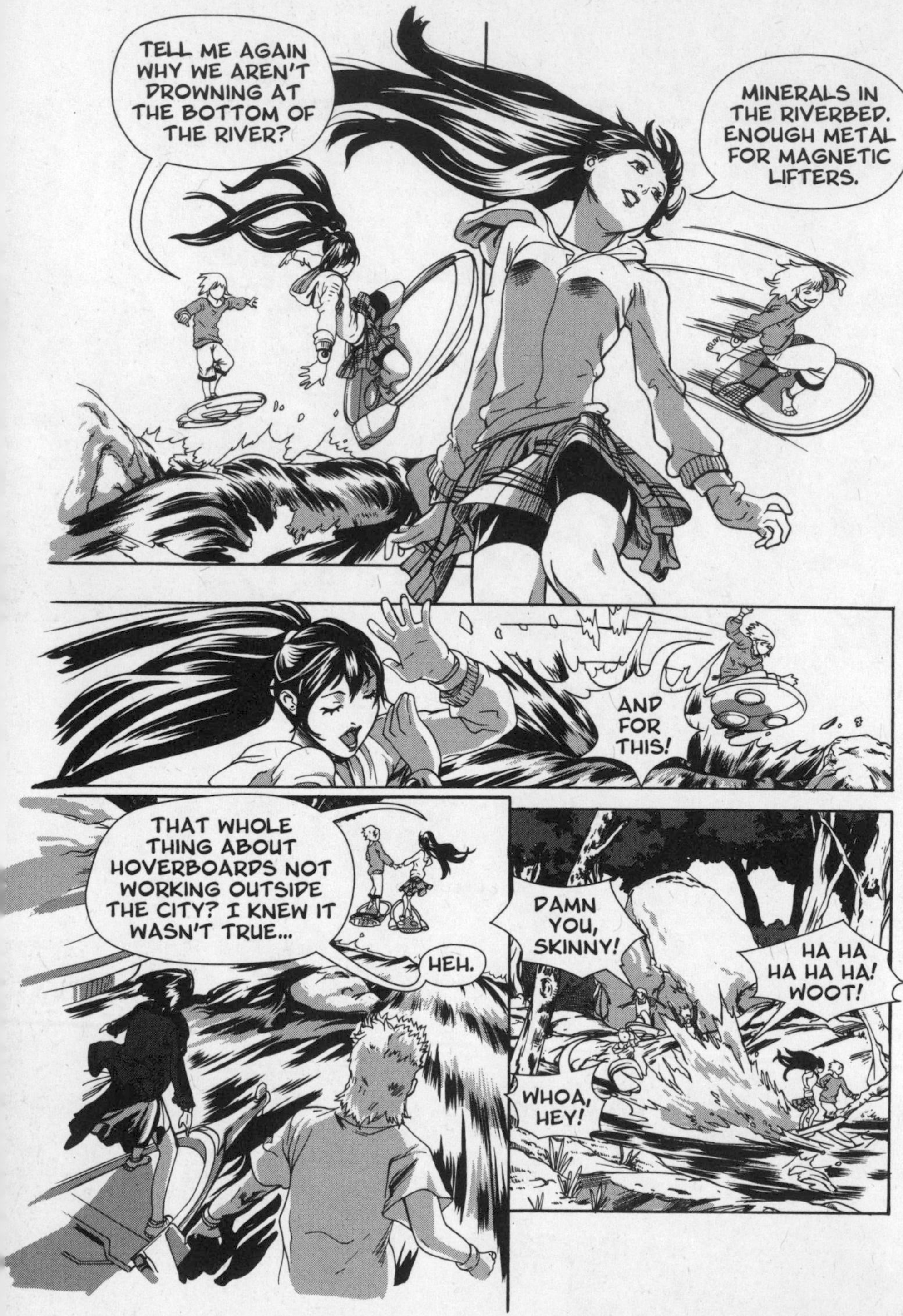
TELL ME AGAIN WHY WE AREN'T DROWNING AT THE BOTTOM OF THE RIVER?
MINERALS IN THE RIVERBED. ENOUGH METAL FOR MAGNETIC LIFTERS.
AND FOR THIS!
THAT WHOLE THING ABOUT HOVERBOARDS NOT WORKING OUTSIDE THE CITY? I KNEW IT WASN'T TRUE...
HEH.
DAMN YOU, SKINNY!
HA HA HA HA HA! WOOT!
WHOA, HEY!

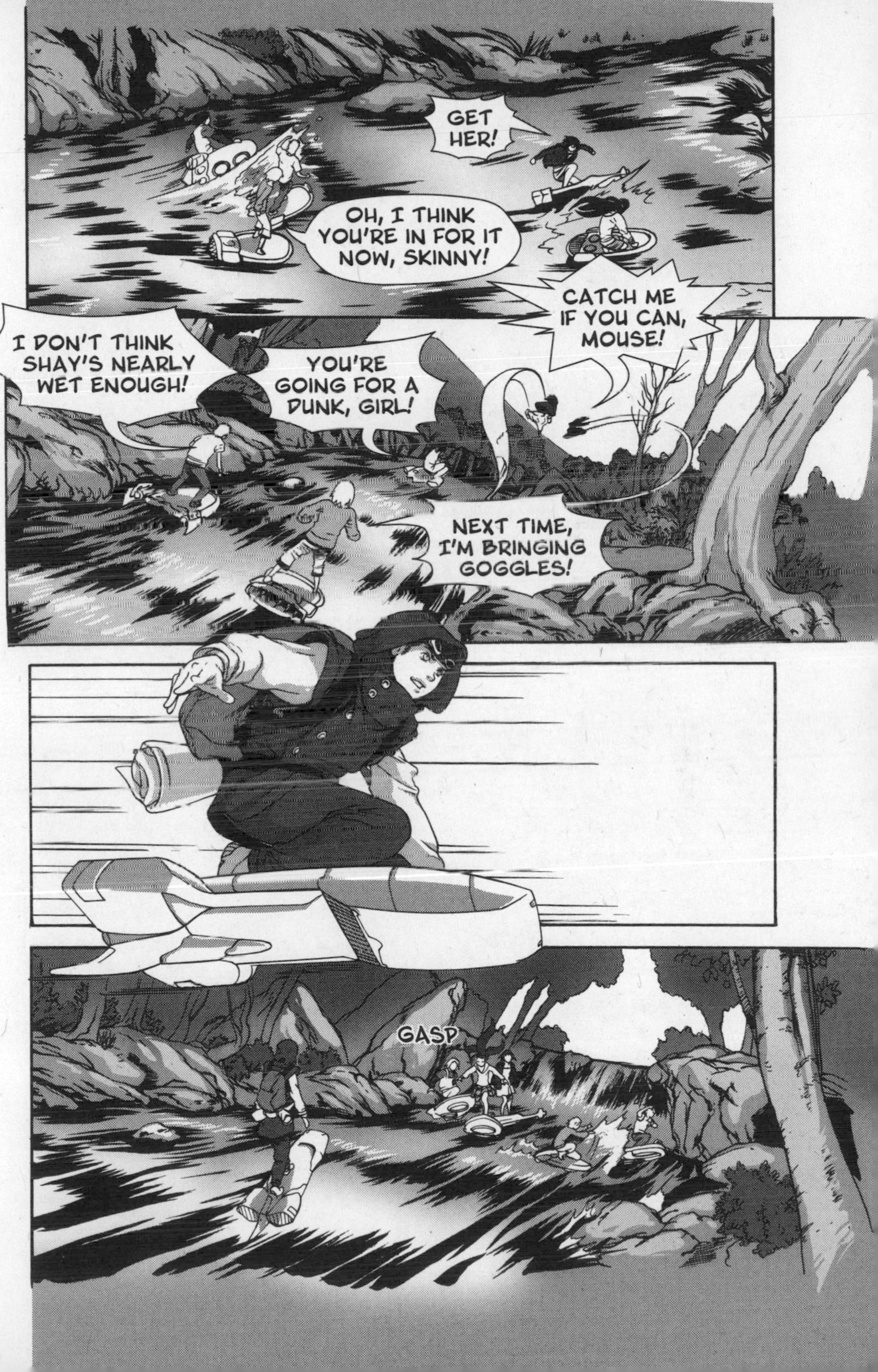
GET HER!
OH, I THINK YOU'RE IN FOR IT NOW, SKINNY!
I DON'T THINK SHAY'S NEARLY WET ENOUGH!
YOU'RE GOING FOR A DUNK, GIRL!
CATCH ME IF YOU CAN, MOUSE!
NEXT TIME, I'M BRINGING GOGGLES!
GASP

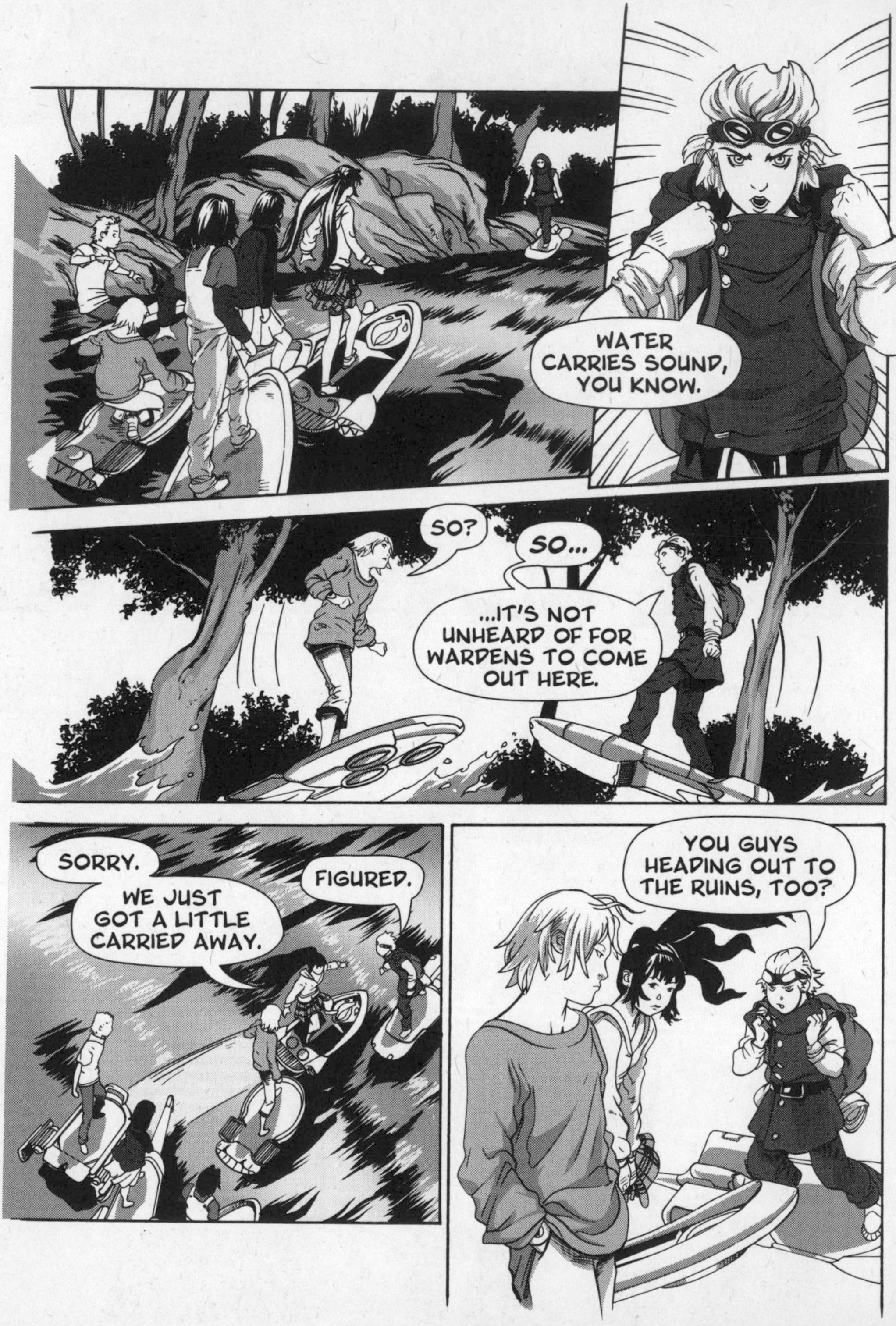
WATER CARRIES SOUND, YOU KNOW.
SO?
SO...
...IT'S NOT UNHEARD OF FOR WARDENS TO COME OUT HERE.
SORRY.
WE JUST GOT A LITTLE CARRIED AWAY.
FIGURED.
YOU GUYS HEADING OUT TO THE RUINS, TOO?

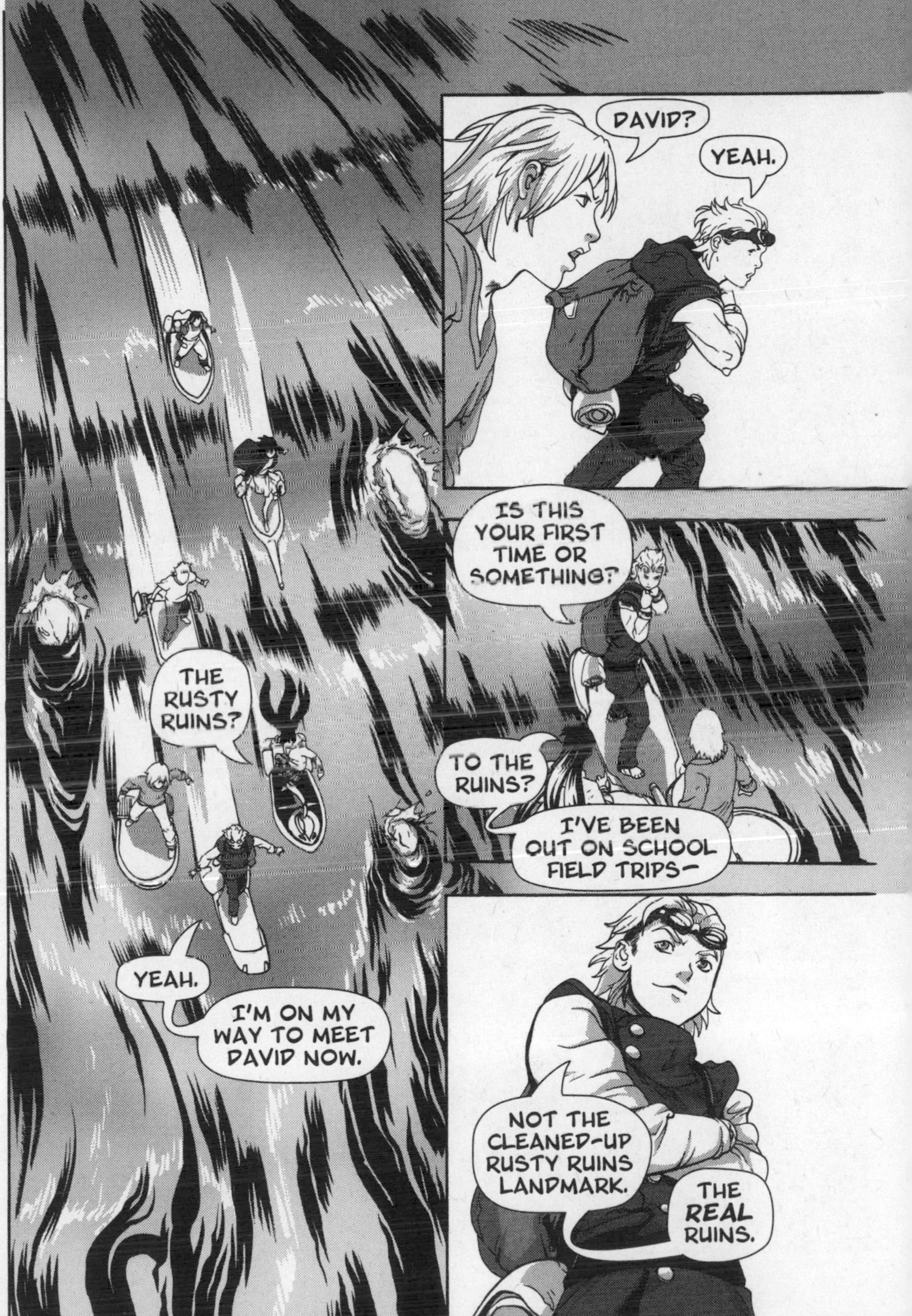
THE RUSTY RUINS?
YEAH.
I'M ON MY WAY TO MEET DAVID NOW.
DAVID?
YEAH.
IS THIS YOUR FIRST TIME OR SOMETHING?
TO THE RUINS?
I'VE BEEN OUT ON SCHOOL FIELD TRIPS—
NOT THE CLEANED-UP RUSTY RUINS LANDMARK.
THE *REAL* RUINS.

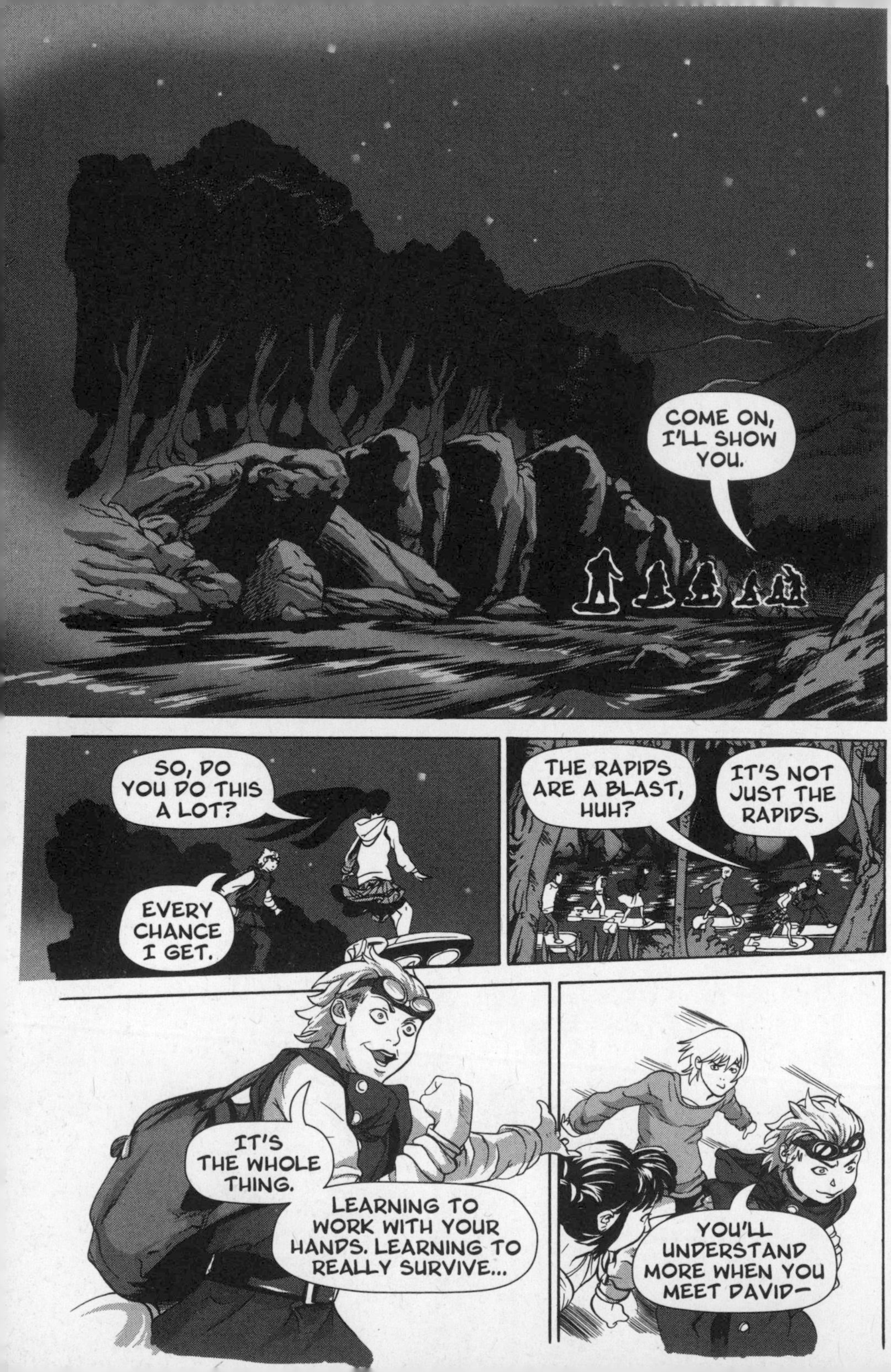
COME ON, I'LL SHOW YOU.
SO, DO YOU DO THIS A LOT?
EVERY CHANCE I GET.
THE RAPIDS ARE A BLAST, HUH?
IT'S NOT JUST THE RAPIDS.
IT'S THE WHOLE THING.
LEARNING TO WORK WITH YOUR HANDS. LEARNING TO REALLY SURVIVE...
YOU'LL UNDERSTAND MORE WHEN YOU MEET DAVID—

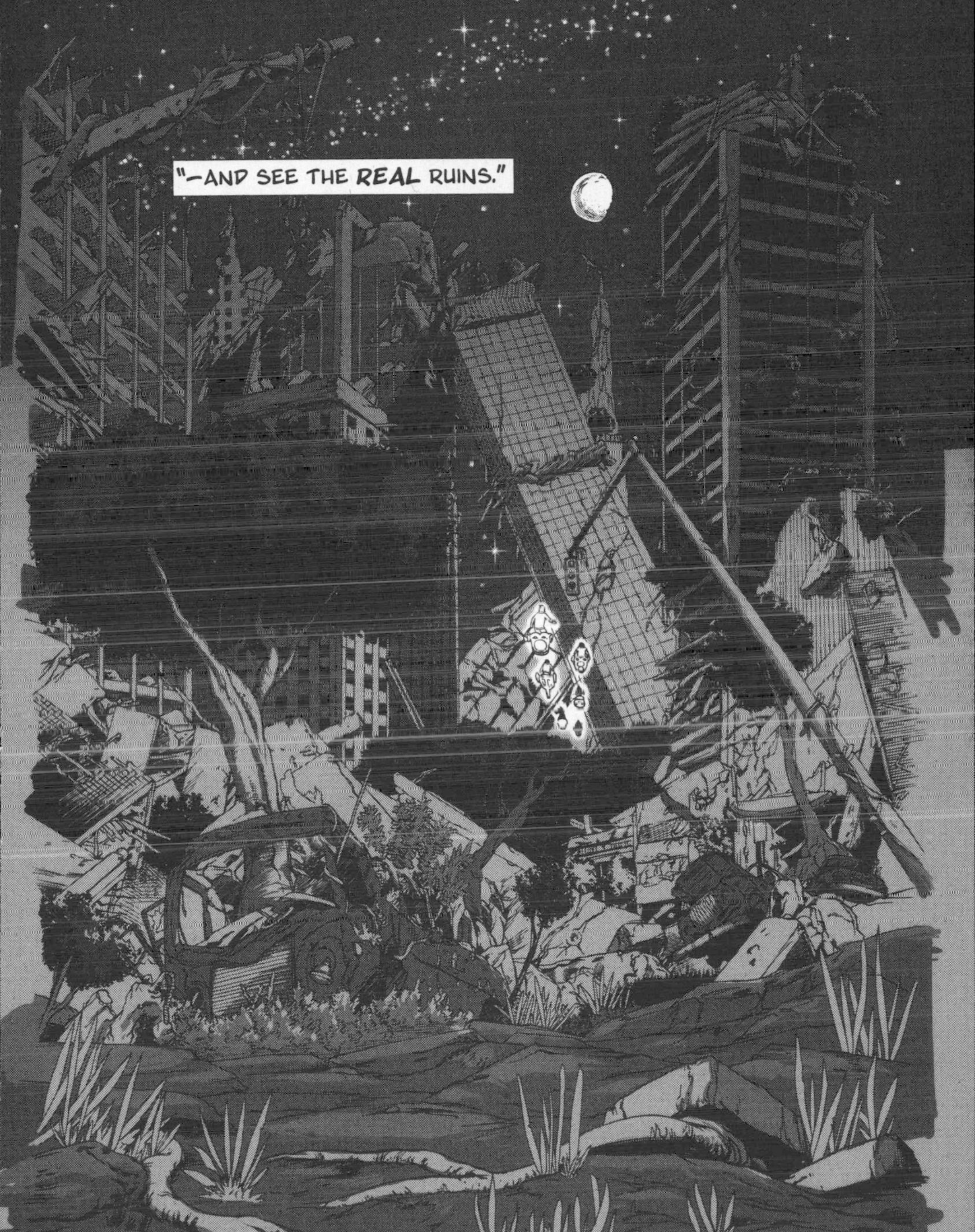
"—AND SEE THE REAL RUINS."

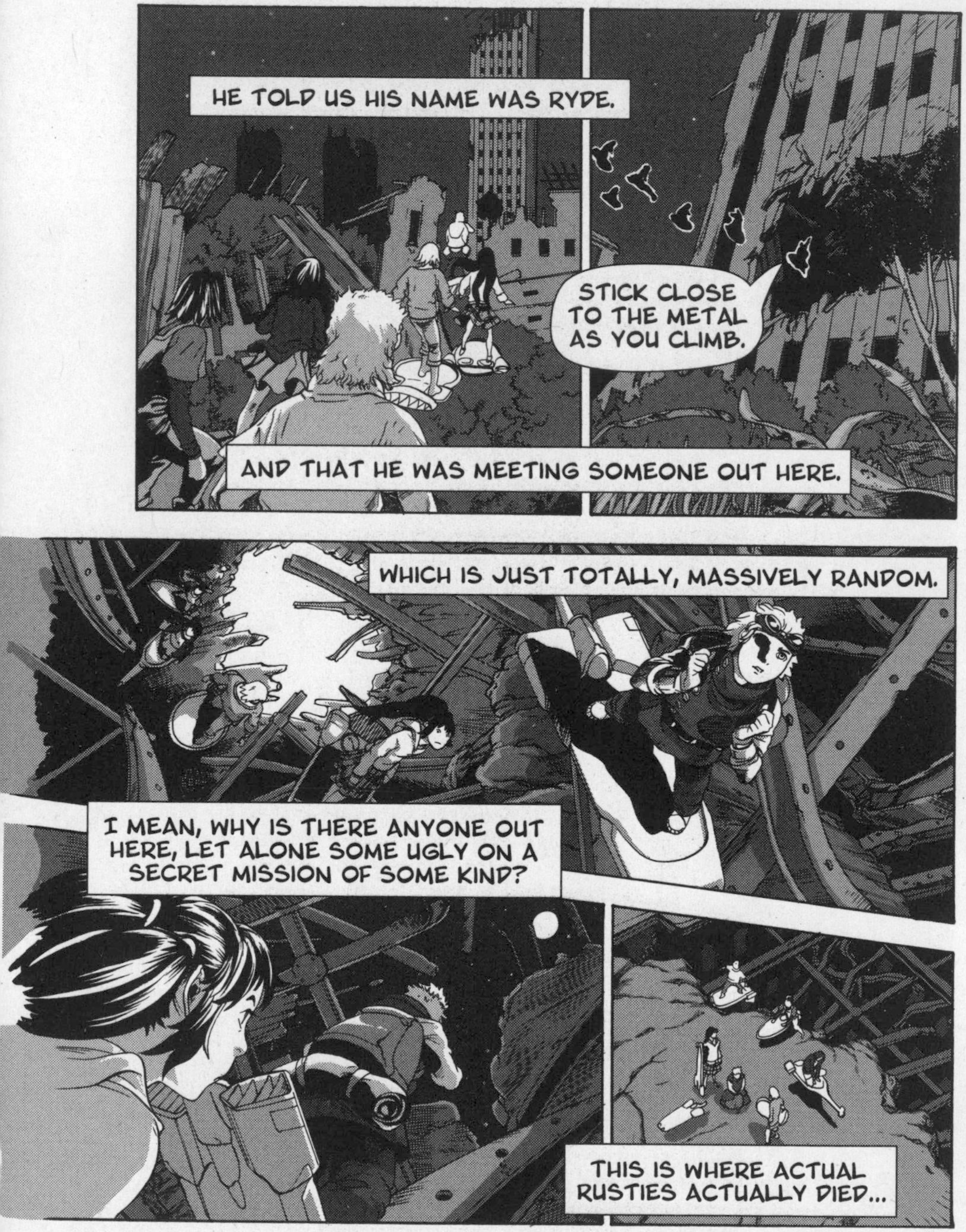
HE TOLD US HIS NAME WAS RYDE.
STICK CLOSE TO THE METAL AS YOU CLIMB.
AND THAT HE WAS MEETING SOMEONE OUT HERE.
WHICH IS JUST TOTALLY, MASSIVELY RANDOM.
I MEAN, WHY IS THERE ANYONE OUT HERE, LET ALONE SOME UGLY ON A SECRET MISSION OF SOME KIND?
THIS IS WHERE ACTUAL RUSTIES ACTUALLY DIED...

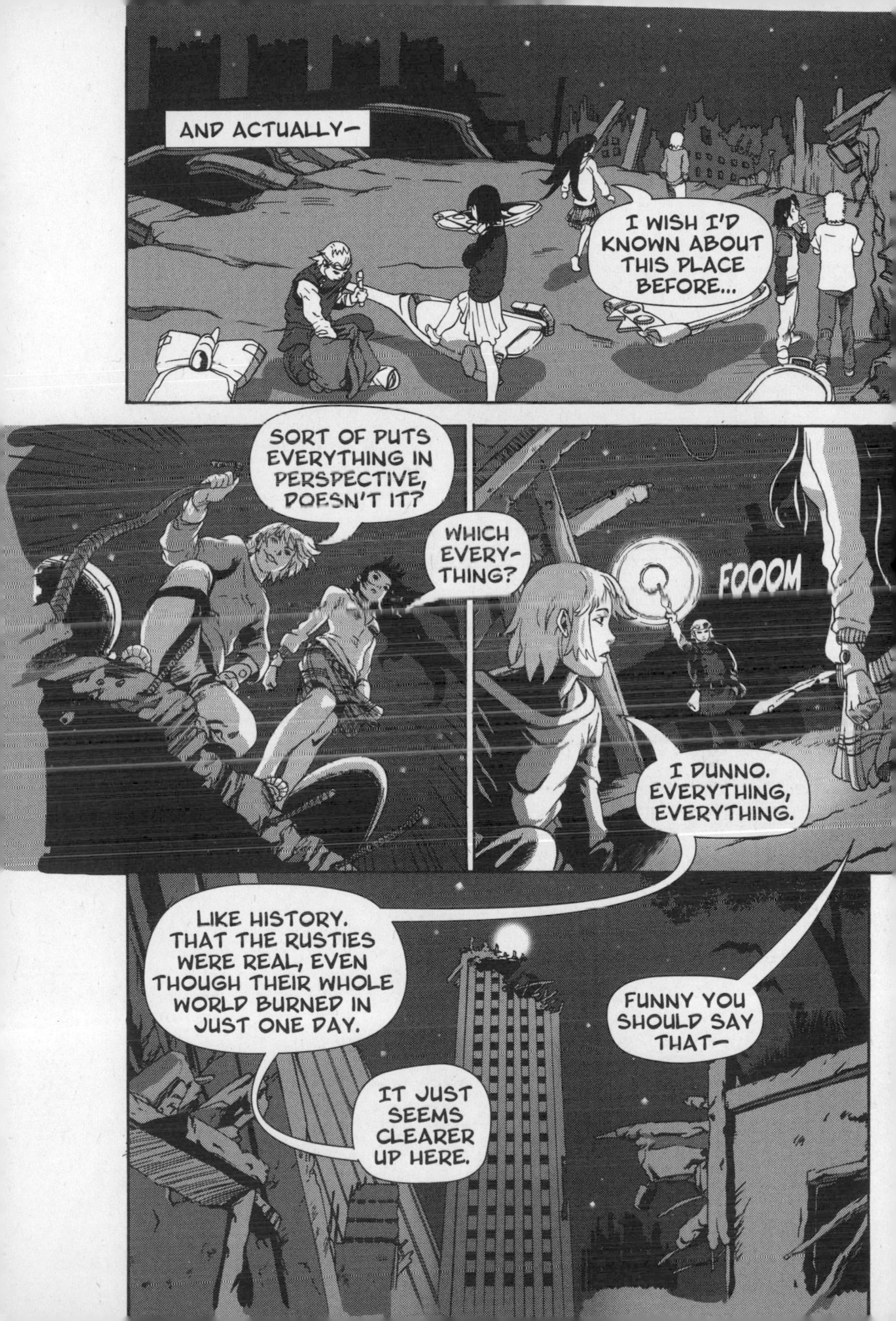
AND ACTUALLY—
I WISH I'D KNOWN ABOUT THIS PLACE BEFORE...
SORT OF PUTS EVERYTHING IN PERSPECTIVE, DOESN'T IT?
WHICH EVERY-THING?
FOOOM
I DUNNO. EVERYTHING, EVERYTHING.
LIKE HISTORY. THAT THE RUSTIES WERE REAL, EVEN THOUGH THEIR WHOLE WORLD BURNED IN JUST ONE DAY.
IT JUST SEEMS CLEARER UP HERE.
FUNNY YOU SHOULD SAY THAT—

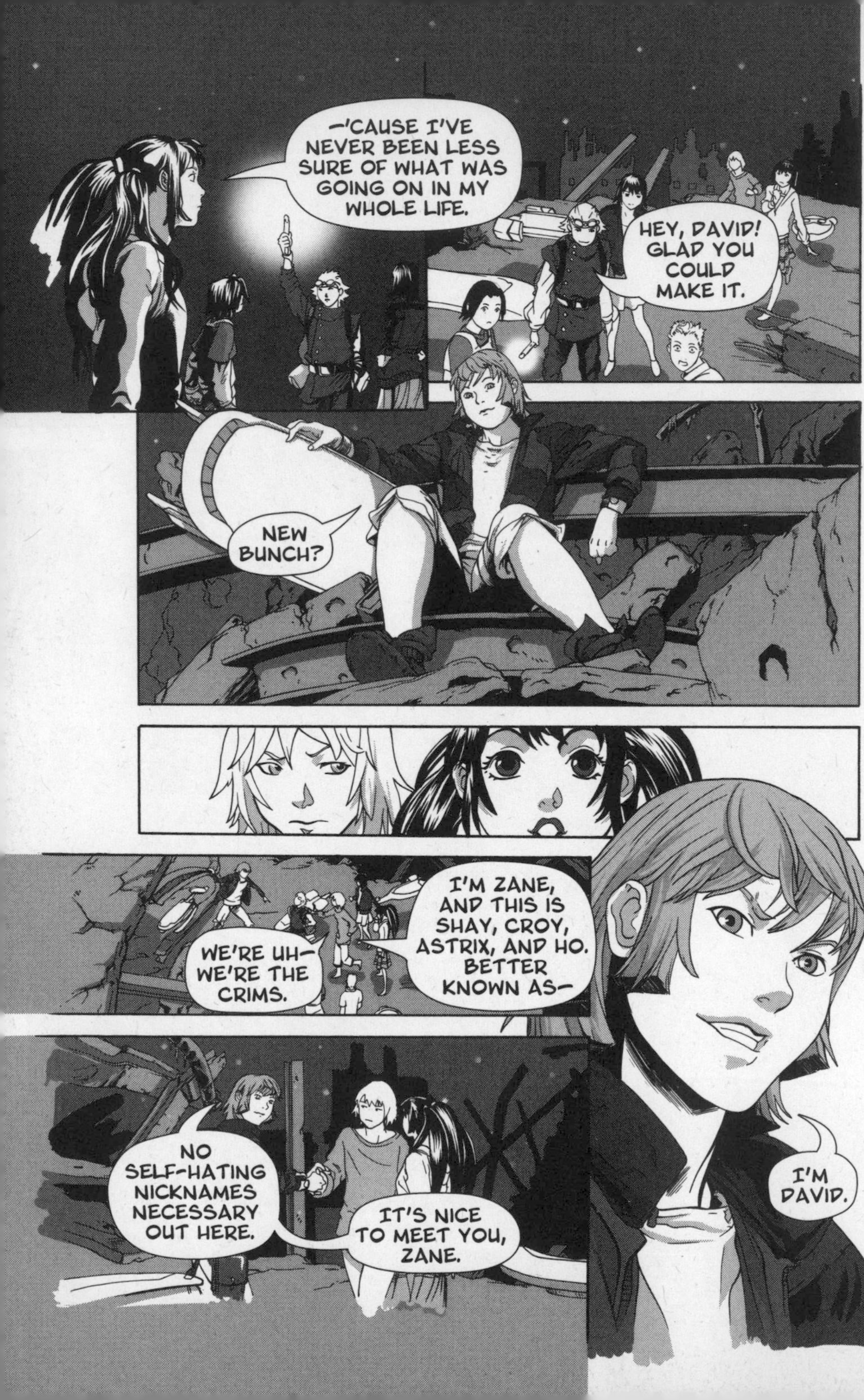
—'CAUSE I'VE NEVER BEEN LESS SURE OF WHAT WAS GOING ON IN MY WHOLE LIFE.
HEY, DAVID! GLAD YOU COULD MAKE IT.
NEW BUNCH?
WE'RE UH— WE'RE THE CRIMS.
I'M ZANE, AND THIS IS SHAY, CROY, ASTRIX, AND HO. BETTER KNOWN AS—
NO SELF-HATING NICKNAMES NECESSARY OUT HERE.
IT'S NICE TO MEET YOU, ZANE.
I'M DAVID.

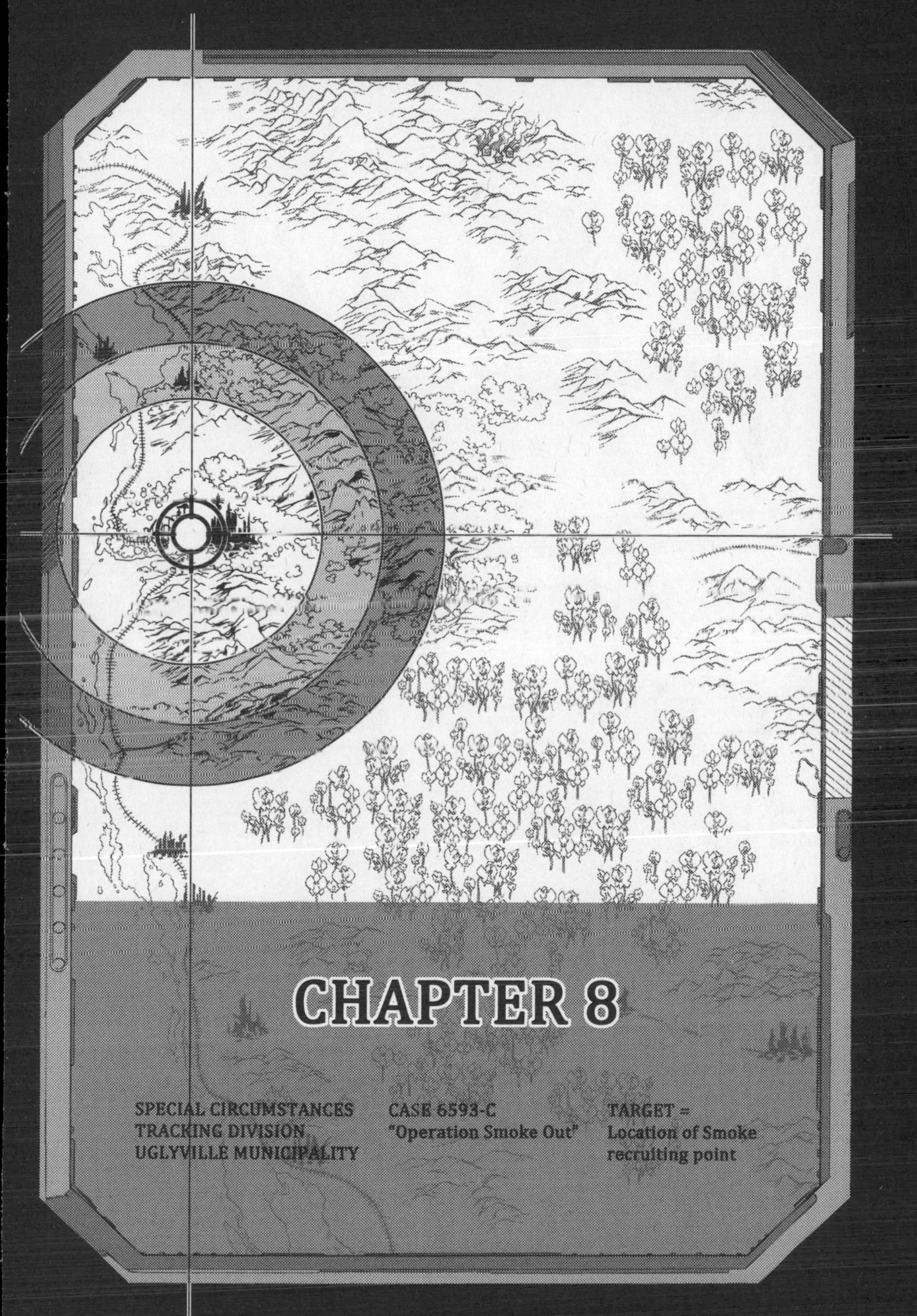

# CHAPTER 8

SPECIAL CIRCUMSTANCES
TRACKING DIVISION
UGLYVILLE MUNICIPALITY

CASE 6593-C
"Operation Smoke Out"

TARGET =
Location of Smoke
recruiting point

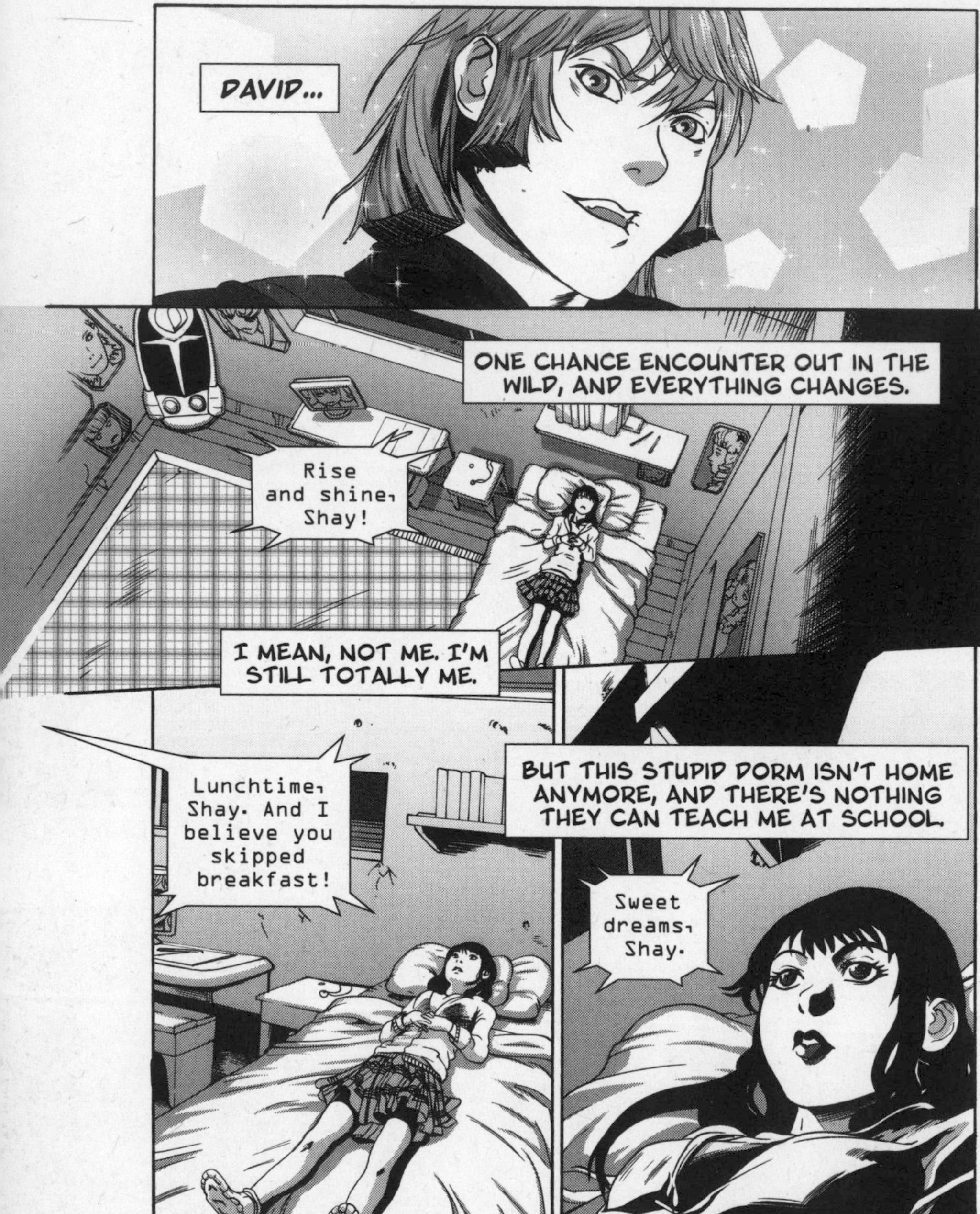
DAVID...
ONE CHANCE ENCOUNTER OUT IN THE WILD, AND EVERYTHING CHANGES.
Rise and shine, Shay!
I MEAN, NOT ME. I'M STILL TOTALLY ME.
Lunchtime, Shay. And I believe you skipped breakfast!
BUT THIS STUPID DORM ISN'T HOME ANYMORE, AND THERE'S NOTHING THEY CAN TEACH ME AT SCHOOL.
Sweet dreams, Shay.

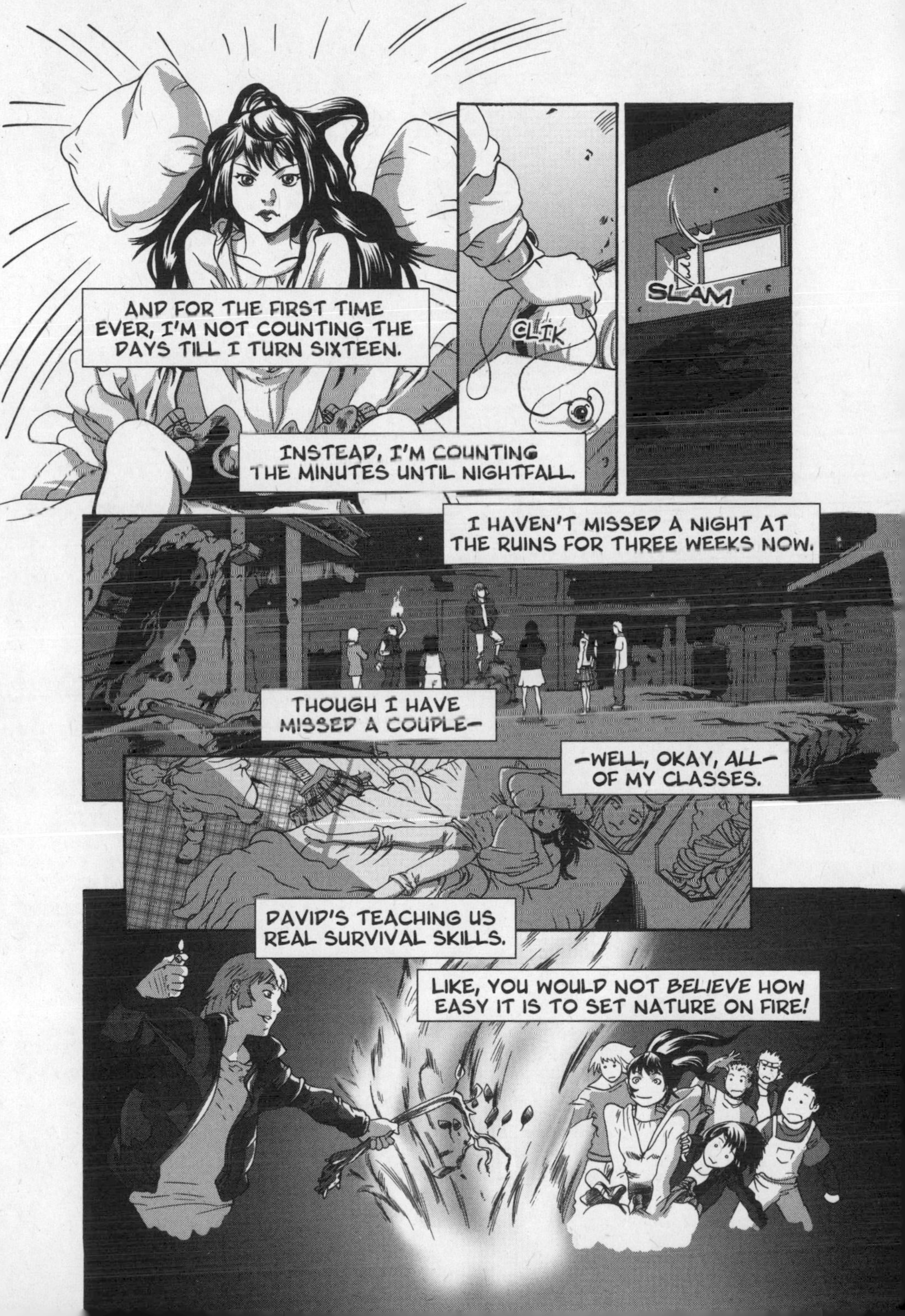
AND FOR THE FIRST TIME EVER, I'M NOT COUNTING THE DAYS TILL I TURN SIXTEEN.
CLIK
INSTEAD, I'M COUNTING THE MINUTES UNTIL NIGHTFALL.
SLAM
I HAVEN'T MISSED A NIGHT AT THE RUINS FOR THREE WEEKS NOW.
THOUGH I HAVE MISSED A COUPLE—
—WELL, OKAY, ALL— OF MY CLASSES.
DAVID'S TEACHING US REAL SURVIVAL SKILLS.
LIKE, YOU WOULD NOT *BELIEVE* HOW EASY IT IS TO SET NATURE ON FIRE!

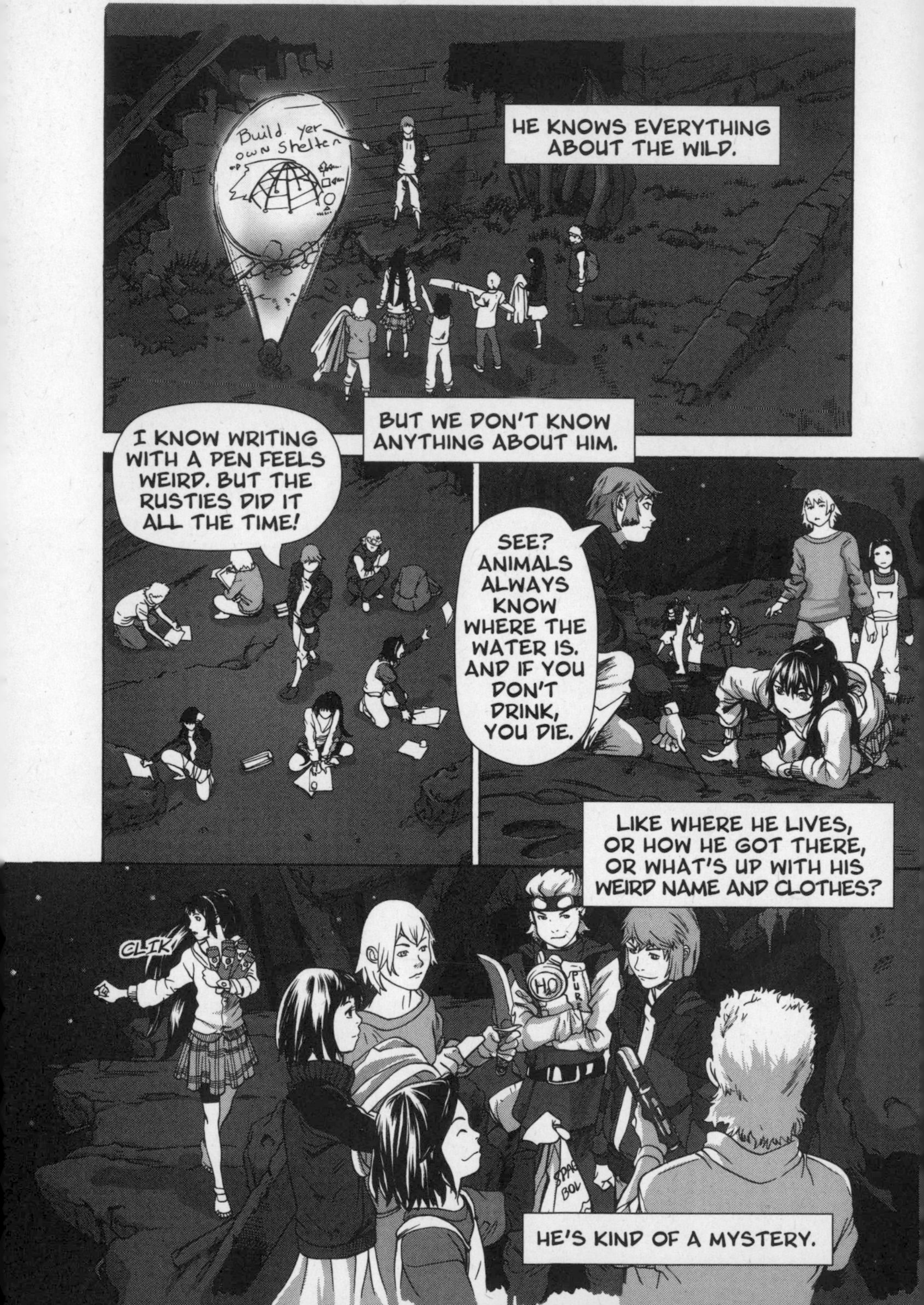
Build yer own Shelter
HE KNOWS EVERYTHING ABOUT THE WILD.
BUT WE DON'T KNOW ANYTHING ABOUT HIM.
I KNOW WRITING WITH A PEN FEELS WEIRD. BUT THE RUSTIES DID IT ALL THE TIME!
SEE? ANIMALS ALWAYS KNOW WHERE THE WATER IS. AND IF YOU DON'T DRINK, YOU DIE.
LIKE WHERE HE LIVES, OR HOW HE GOT THERE, OR WHAT'S UP WITH HIS WEIRD NAME AND CLOTHES?
CLIK
HE'S KIND OF A MYSTERY.

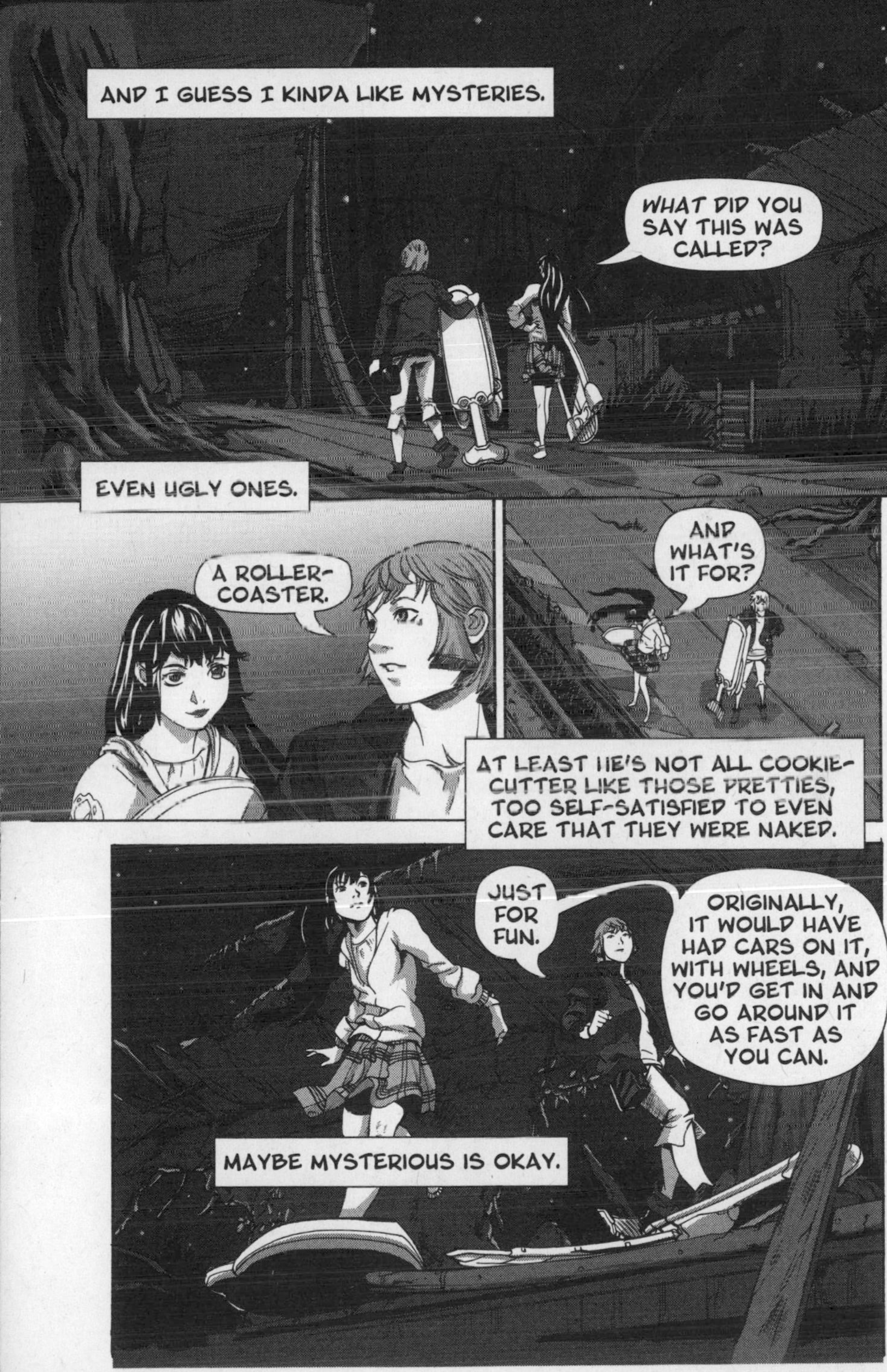
AND I GUESS I KINDA LIKE MYSTERIES.
WHAT DID YOU SAY THIS WAS CALLED?
EVEN UGLY ONES.
A ROLLER-COASTER.
AND WHAT'S IT FOR?
AT LEAST HE'S NOT ALL COOKIE-CUTTER LIKE THOSE PRETTIES, TOO SELF-SATISFIED TO EVEN CARE THAT THEY WERE NAKED.
JUST FOR FUN.
ORIGINALLY, IT WOULD HAVE HAD CARS ON IT, WITH WHEELS, AND YOU'D GET IN AND GO AROUND IT AS FAST AS YOU CAN.
MAYBE MYSTERIOUS IS OKAY.

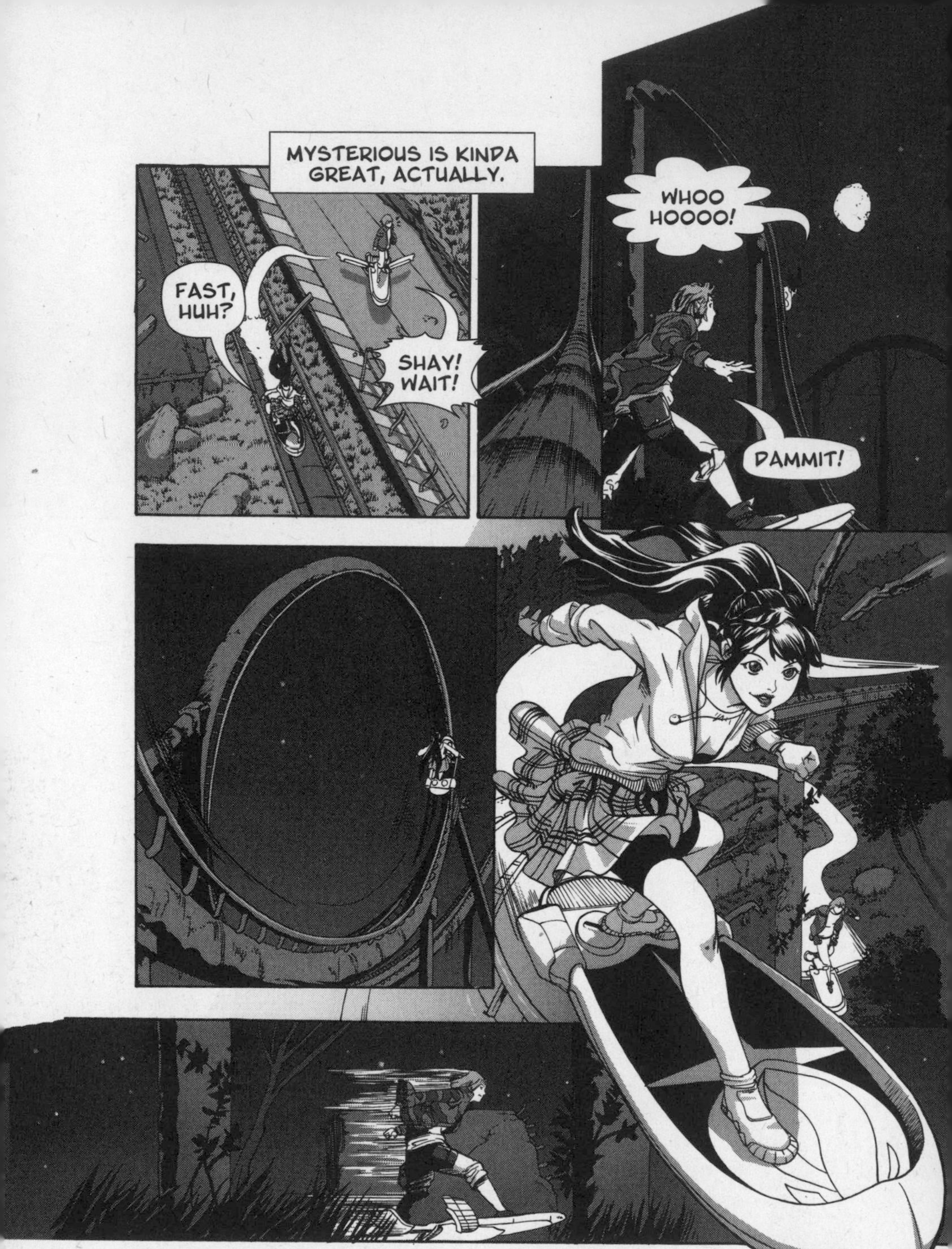
MYSTERIOUS IS KINDA GREAT, ACTUALLY.
FAST, HUH?
SHAY! WAIT!
WHOO HOOOO!
DAMMIT!

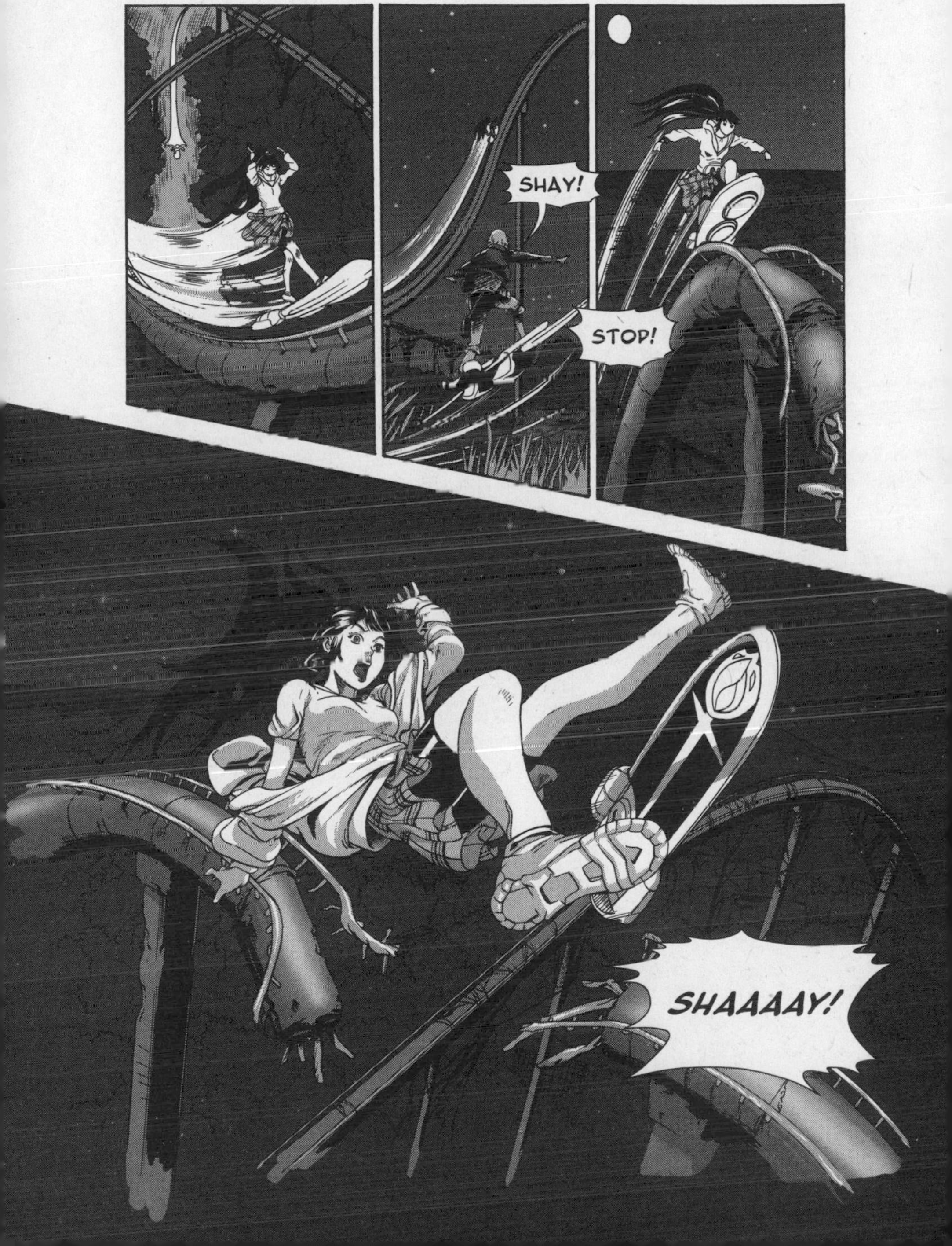
SHAY!
STOP!
SHAAAAY!

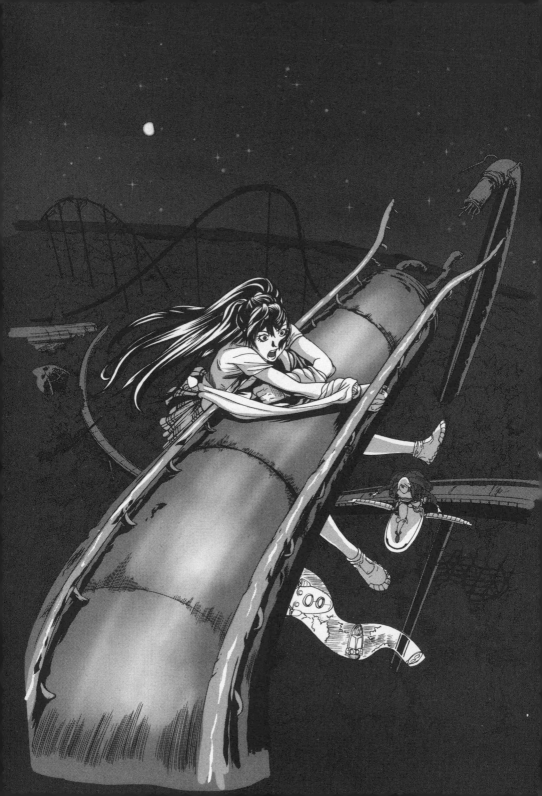

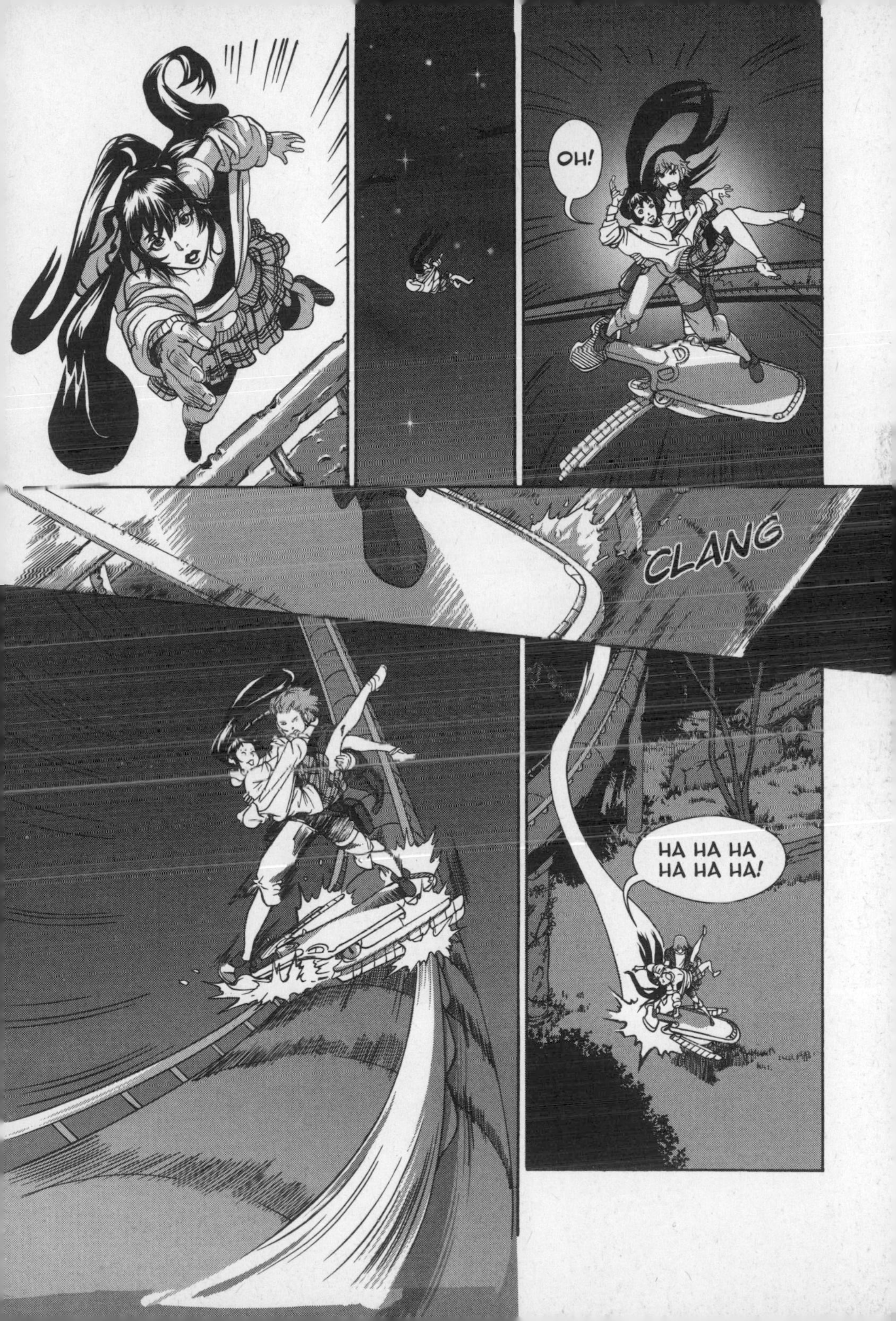
OH!
CLANG
HA HA HA
HA HA HA!

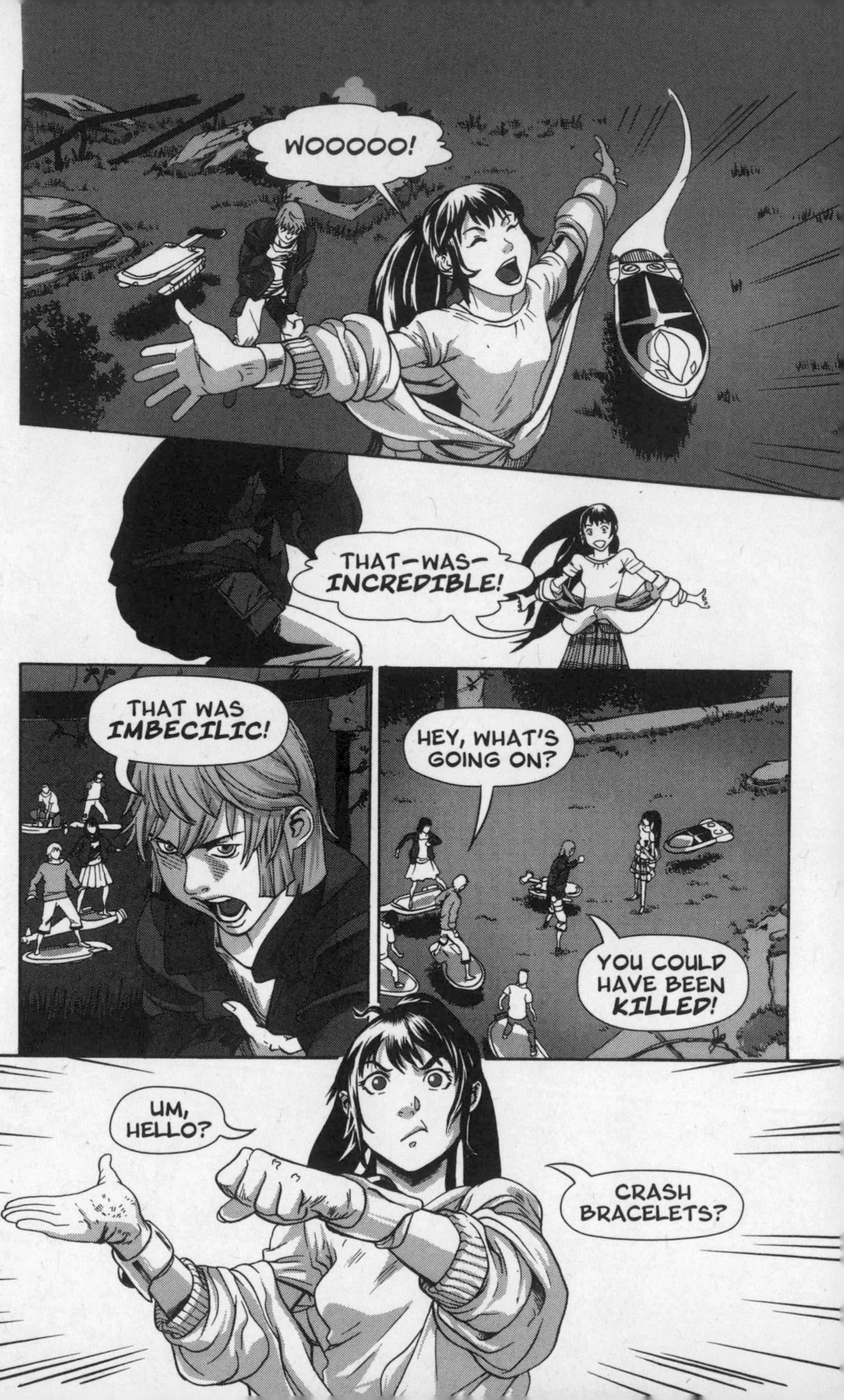
WOOOOO!
THAT—WAS—INCREDIBLE!
THAT WAS IMBECILIC!
HEY, WHAT'S GOING ON?
YOU COULD HAVE BEEN KILLED!
UM, HELLO?
CRASH BRACELETS?

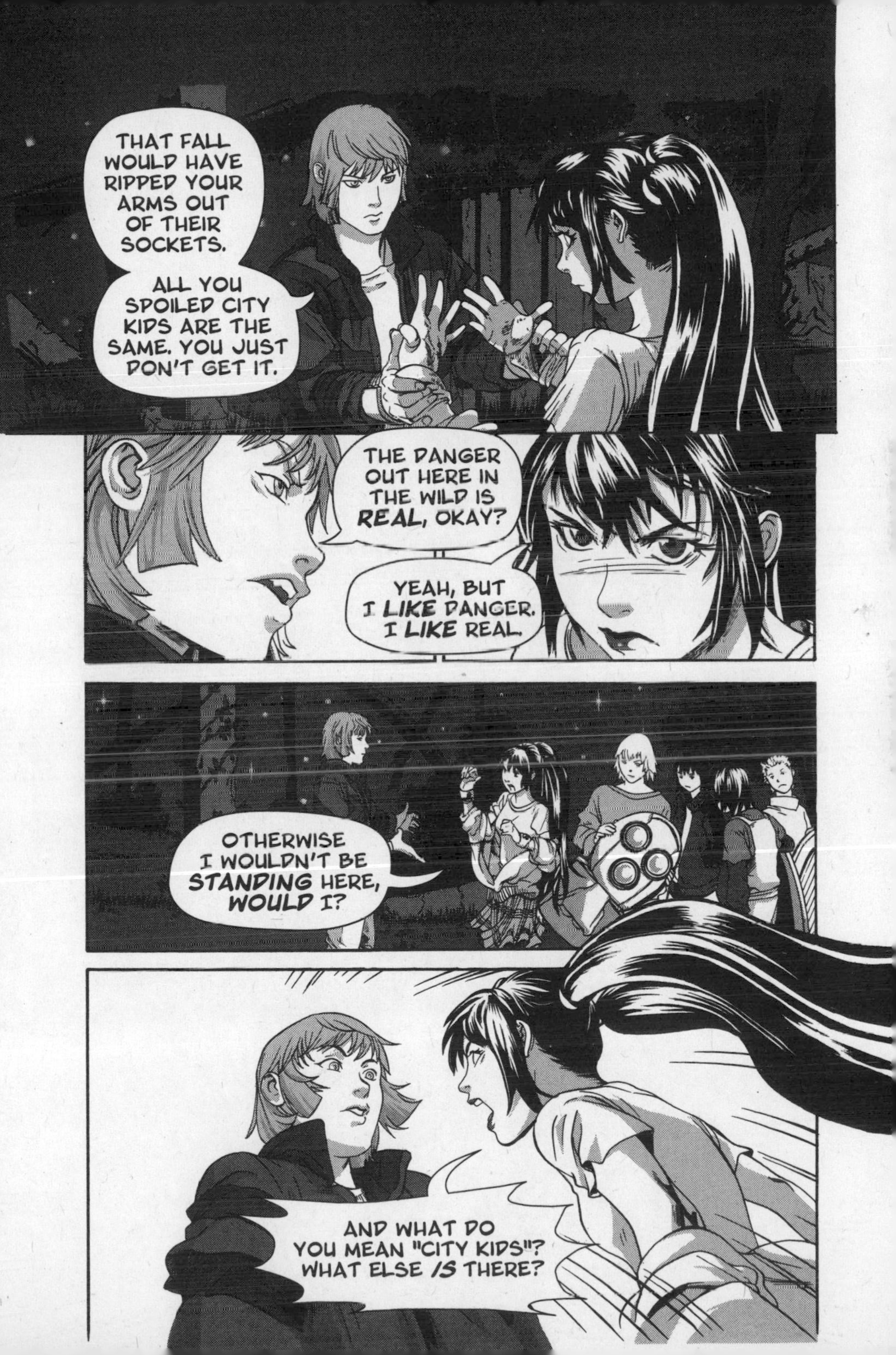
THAT FALL WOULD HAVE RIPPED YOUR ARMS OUT OF THEIR SOCKETS.
ALL YOU SPOILED CITY KIDS ARE THE SAME. YOU JUST DON'T GET IT.
THE DANGER OUT HERE IN THE WILD IS REAL, OKAY?
YEAH, BUT I LIKE DANGER. I LIKE REAL.
OTHERWISE I WOULDN'T BE STANDING HERE, WOULD I?
AND WHAT DO YOU MEAN "CITY KIDS"? WHAT ELSE IS THERE?

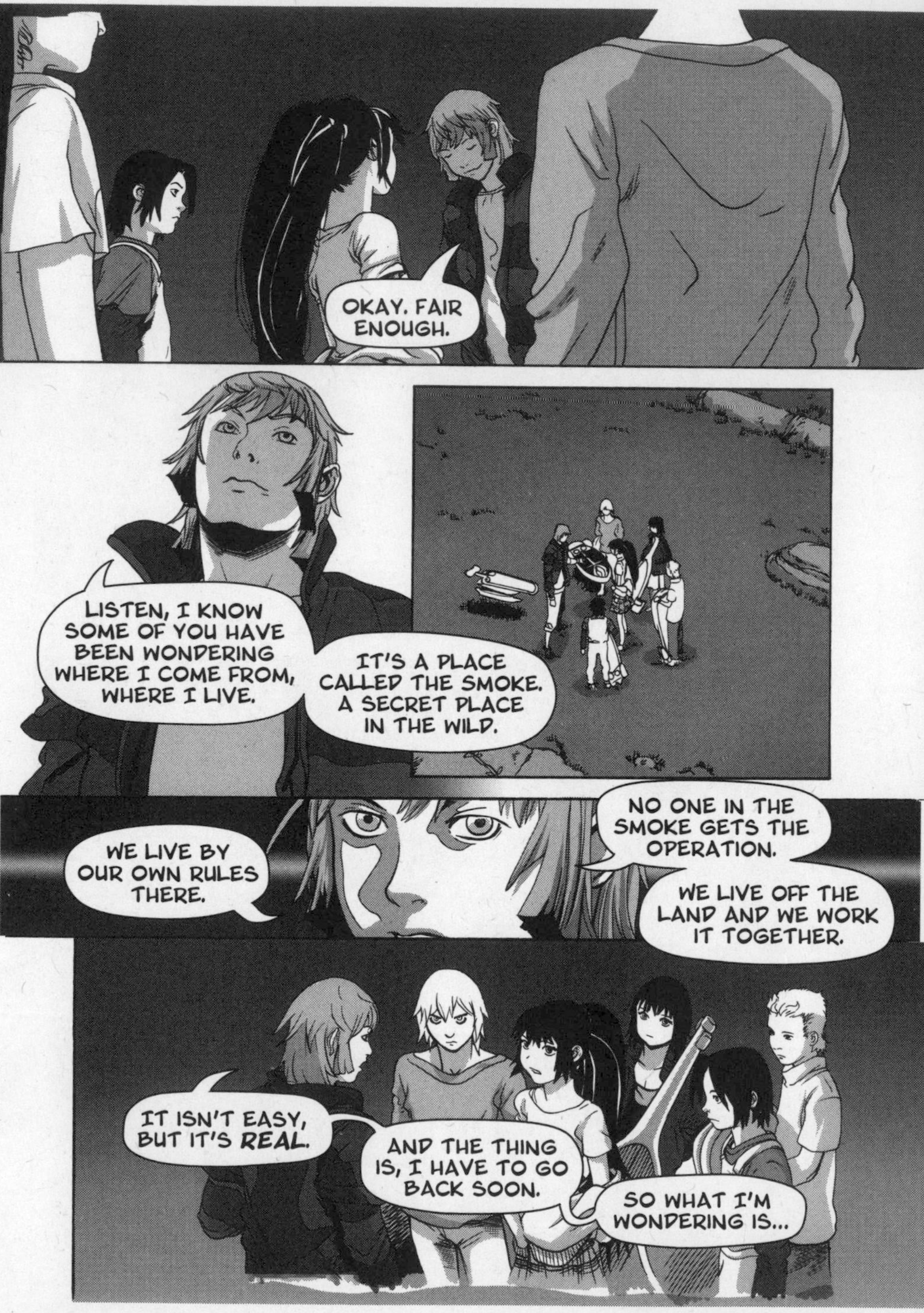
OKAY. FAIR ENOUGH.
LISTEN, I KNOW SOME OF YOU HAVE BEEN WONDERING WHERE I COME FROM, WHERE I LIVE.
IT'S A PLACE CALLED THE SMOKE. A SECRET PLACE IN THE WILD.
WE LIVE BY OUR OWN RULES THERE.
NO ONE IN THE SMOKE GETS THE OPERATION.
WE LIVE OFF THE LAND AND WE WORK IT TOGETHER.
IT ISN'T EASY, BUT IT'S REAL.
AND THE THING IS, I HAVE TO GO BACK SOON.
SO WHAT I'M WONDERING IS...

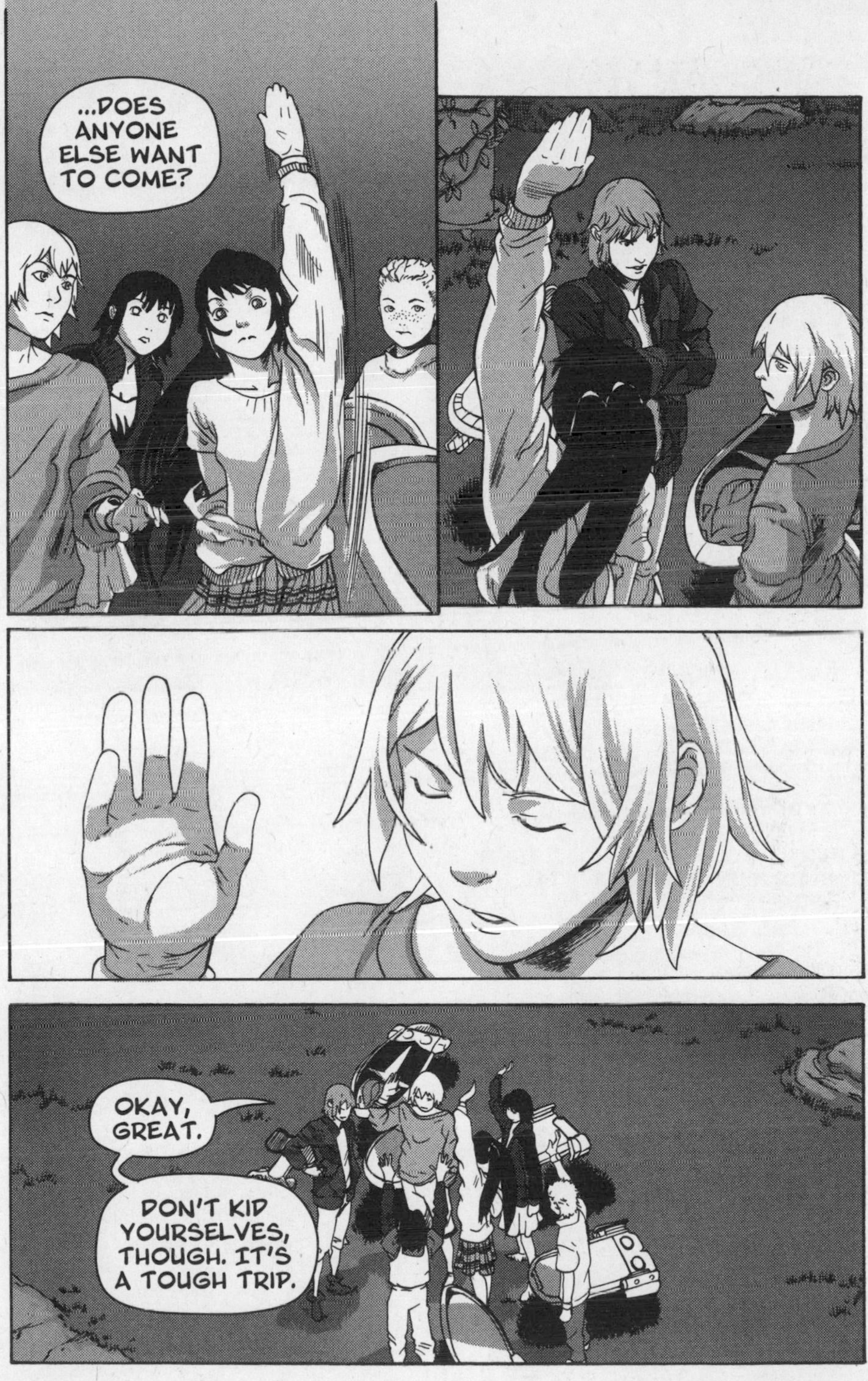
...DOES ANYONE ELSE WANT TO COME?
OKAY, GREAT.
DON'T KID YOURSELVES, THOUGH. IT'S A TOUGH TRIP.

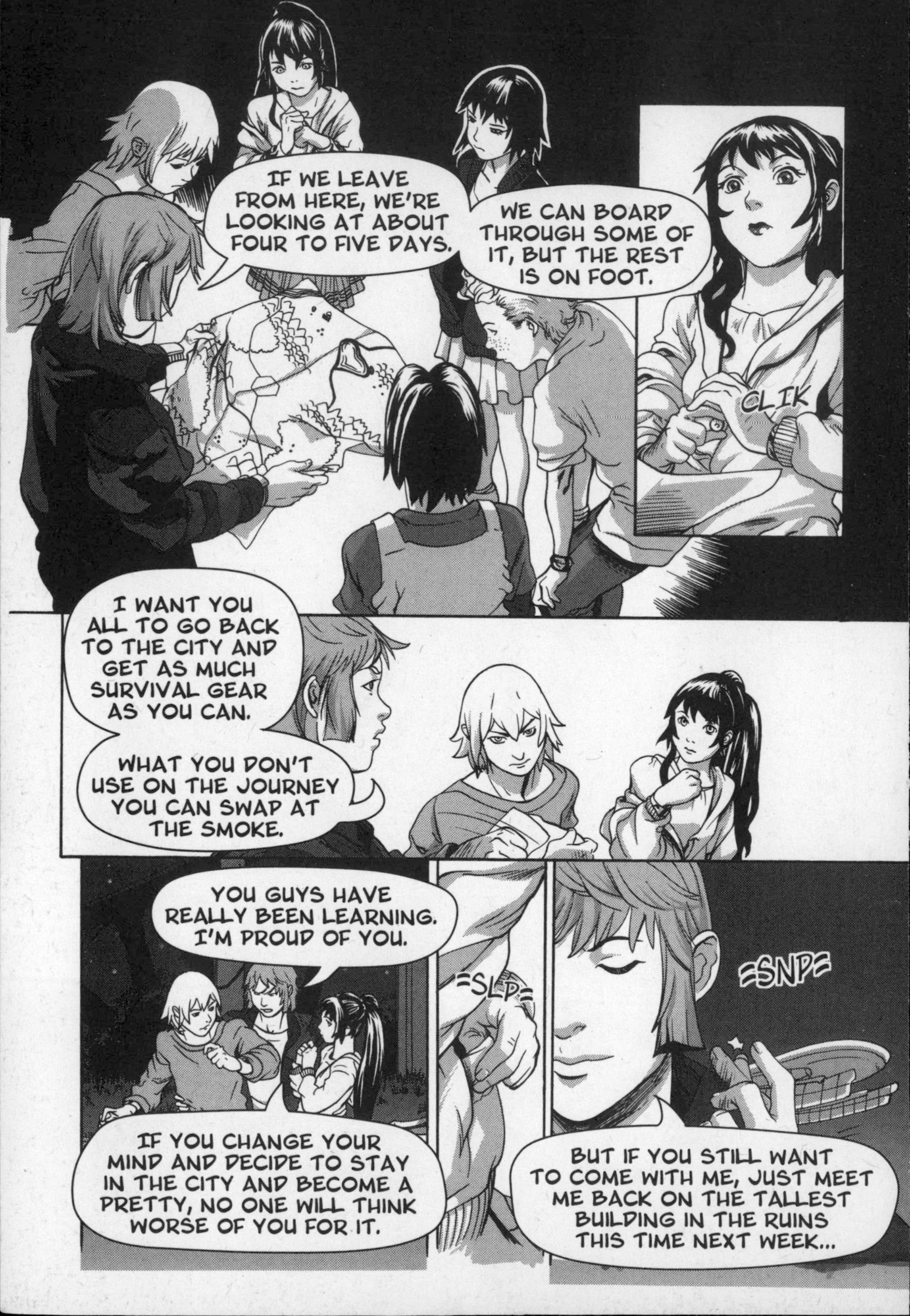
IF WE LEAVE FROM HERE, WE'RE LOOKING AT ABOUT FOUR TO FIVE DAYS.
WE CAN BOARD THROUGH SOME OF IT, BUT THE REST IS ON FOOT.
CLIK
I WANT YOU ALL TO GO BACK TO THE CITY AND GET AS MUCH SURVIVAL GEAR AS YOU CAN.
WHAT YOU DON'T USE ON THE JOURNEY YOU CAN SWAP AT THE SMOKE.
YOU GUYS HAVE REALLY BEEN LEARNING. I'M PROUD OF YOU.
IF YOU CHANGE YOUR MIND AND DECIDE TO STAY IN THE CITY AND BECOME A PRETTY, NO ONE WILL THINK WORSE OF YOU FOR IT.
=SLP=
=SNP=
BUT IF YOU STILL WANT TO COME WITH ME, JUST MEET ME BACK ON THE TALLEST BUILDING IN THE RUINS THIS TIME NEXT WEEK...

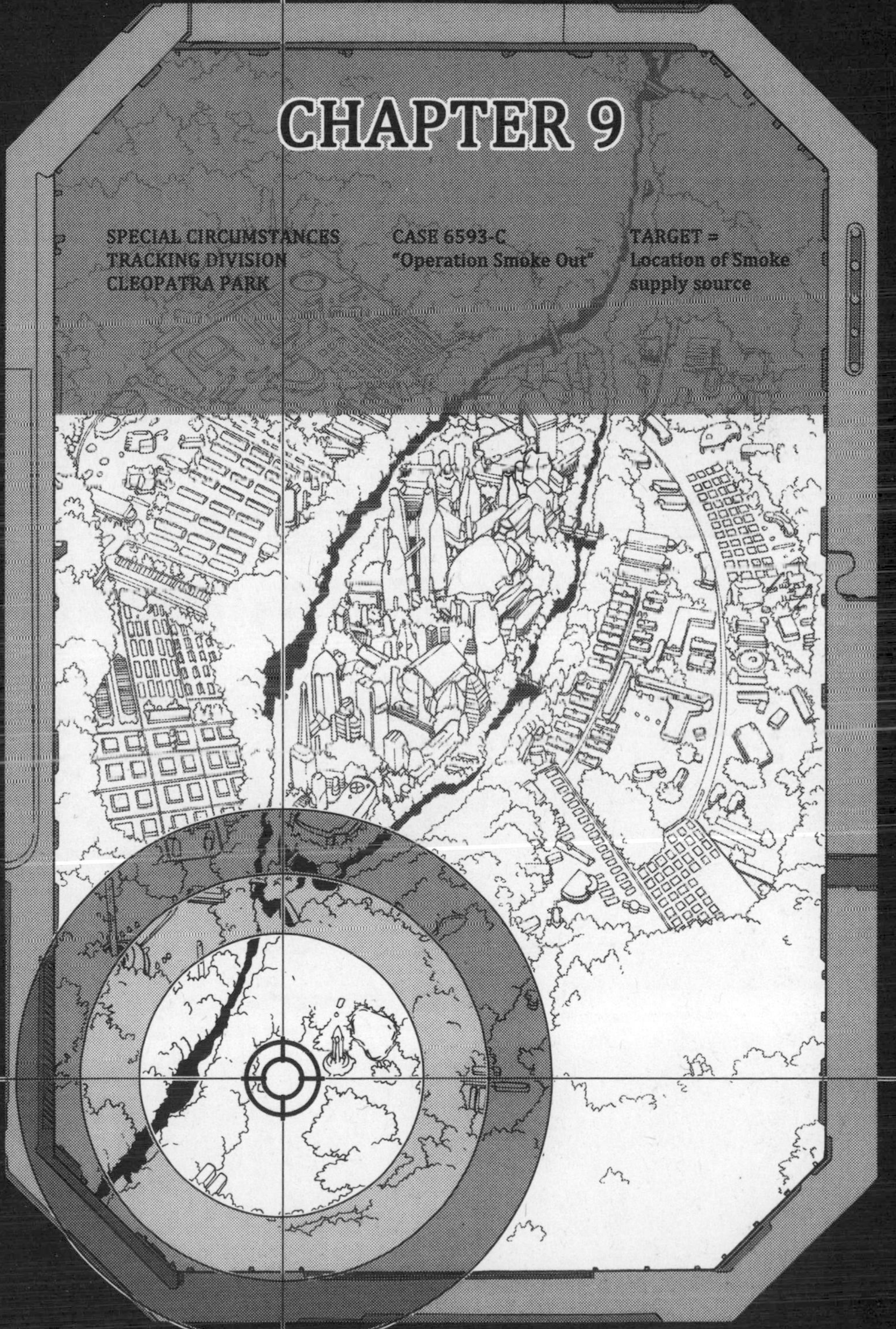
CHAPTER 9
SPECIAL CIRCUMSTANCES
TRACKING DIVISION
CLEOPATRA PARK
CASE 6593-C
"Operation Smoke Out"
TARGET =
Location of Smoke
supply source

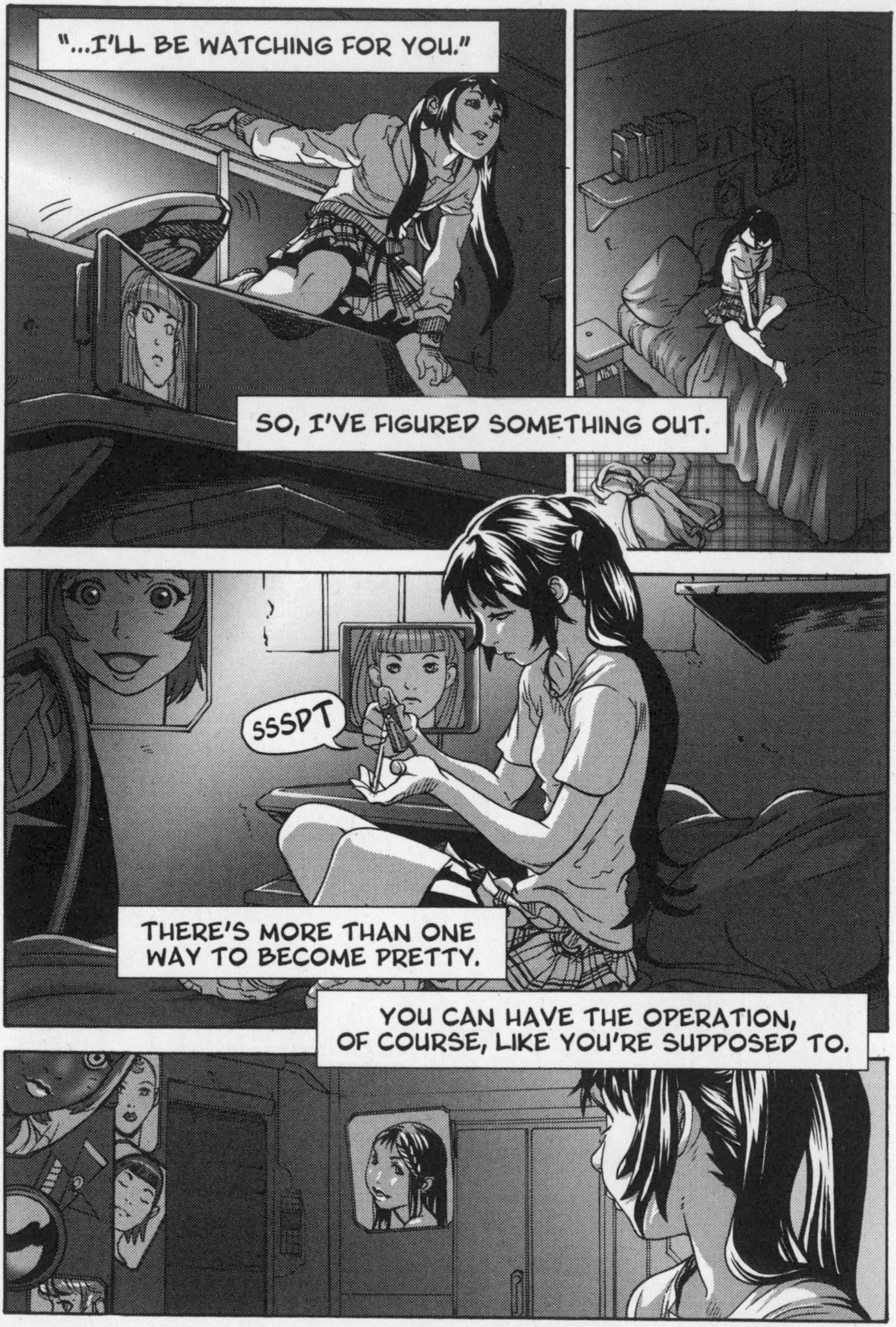
"...I'LL BE WATCHING FOR YOU."
SO, I'VE FIGURED SOMETHING OUT.
SSSPT
THERE'S MORE THAN ONE WAY TO BECOME PRETTY.
YOU CAN HAVE THE OPERATION, OF COURSE, LIKE YOU'RE SUPPOSED TO.

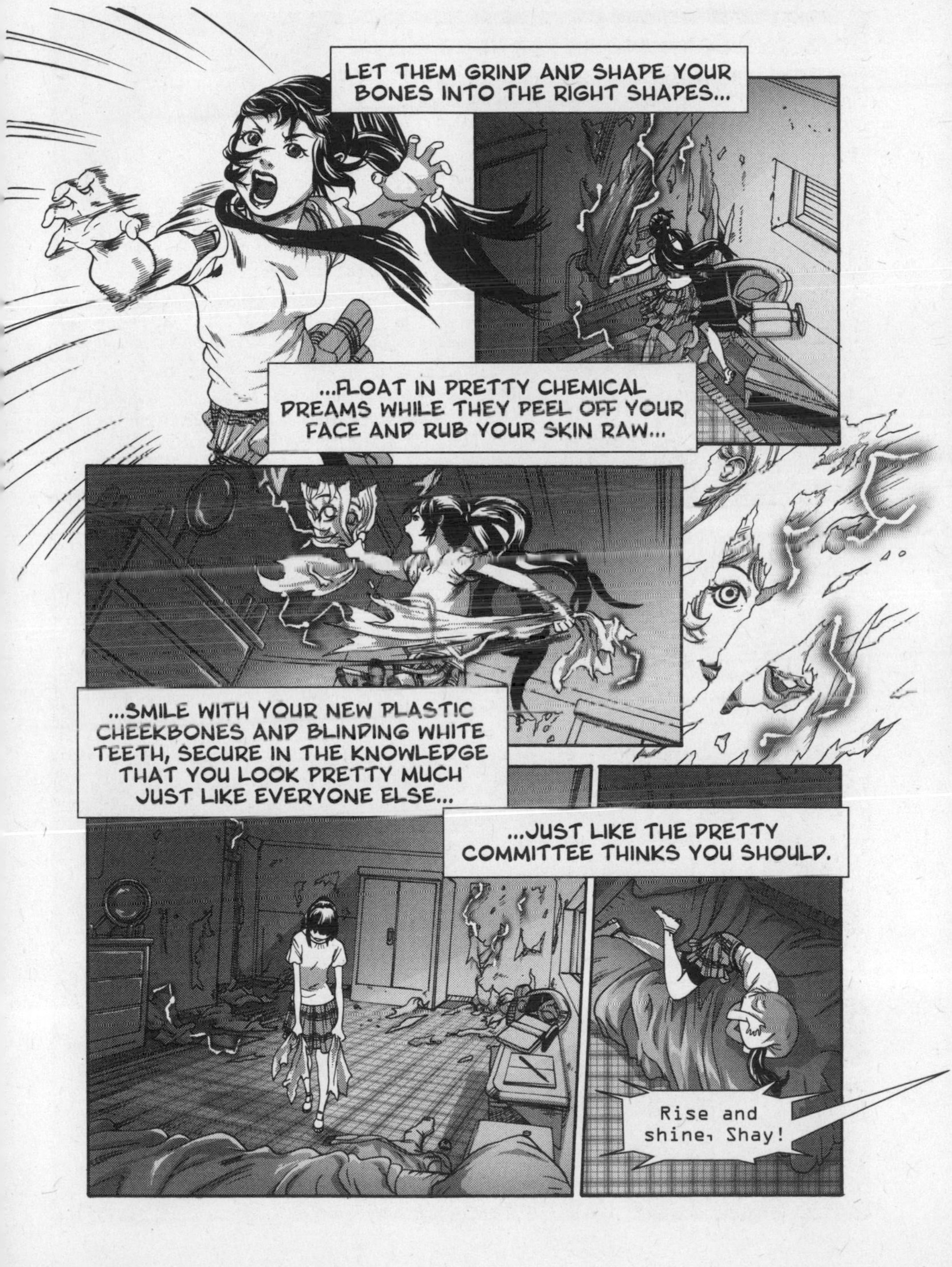
LET THEM GRIND AND SHAPE YOUR BONES INTO THE RIGHT SHAPES...
...FLOAT IN PRETTY CHEMICAL DREAMS WHILE THEY PEEL OFF YOUR FACE AND RUB YOUR SKIN RAW...
...SMILE WITH YOUR NEW PLASTIC CHEEKBONES AND BLINDING WHITE TEETH, SECURE IN THE KNOWLEDGE THAT YOU LOOK PRETTY MUCH JUST LIKE EVERYONE ELSE...
...JUST LIKE THE PRETTY COMMITTEE THINKS YOU SHOULD.
Rise and shine, Shay!

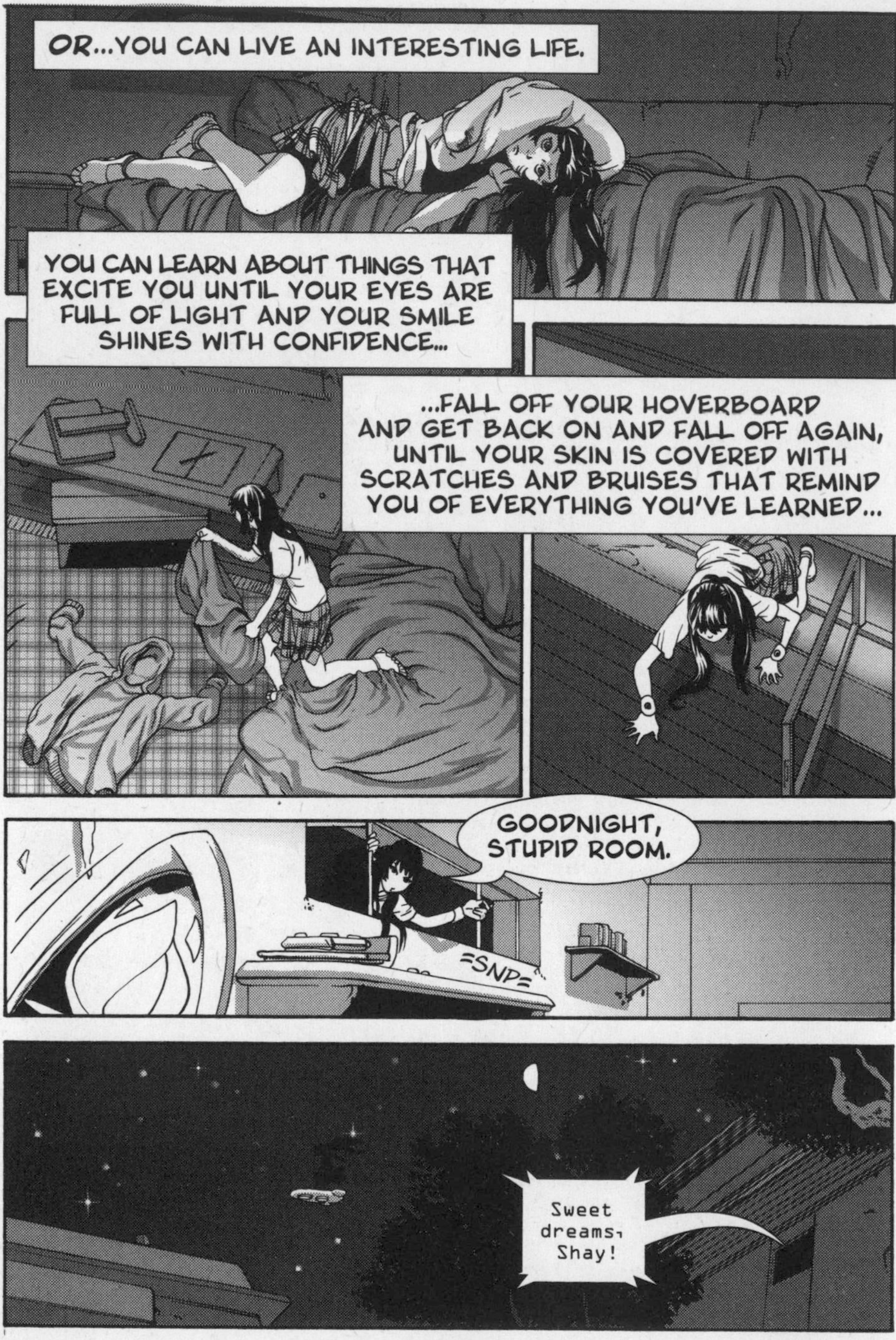
OR...YOU CAN LIVE AN INTERESTING LIFE.
YOU CAN LEARN ABOUT THINGS THAT EXCITE YOU UNTIL YOUR EYES ARE FULL OF LIGHT AND YOUR SMILE SHINES WITH CONFIDENCE...
...FALL OFF YOUR HOVERBOARD AND GET BACK ON AND FALL OFF AGAIN, UNTIL YOUR SKIN IS COVERED WITH SCRATCHES AND BRUISES THAT REMIND YOU OF EVERYTHING YOU'VE LEARNED...
GOODNIGHT, STUPID ROOM.
=SNP=
Sweet dreams, Shay!

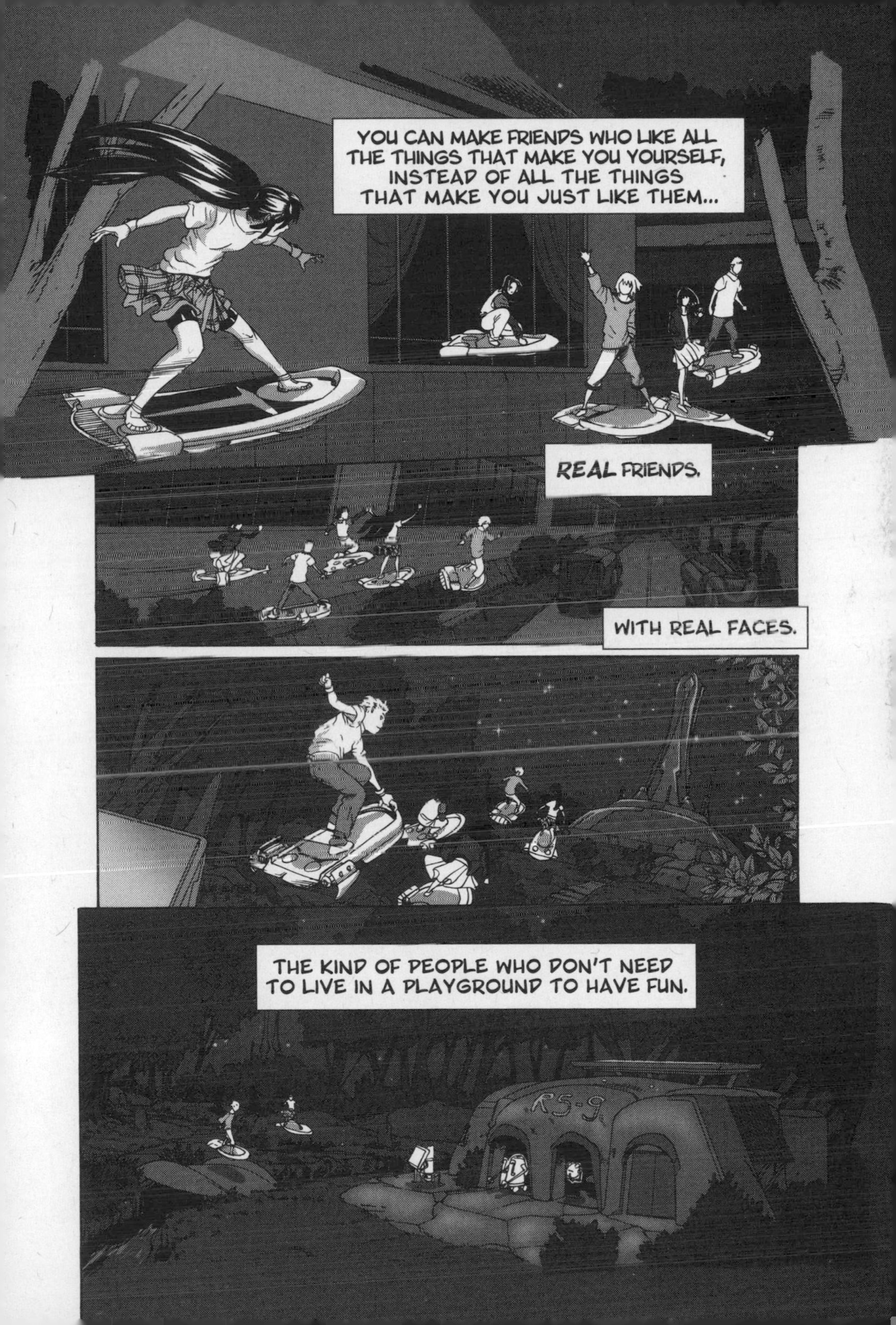
YOU CAN MAKE FRIENDS WHO LIKE ALL THE THINGS THAT MAKE YOU YOURSELF, INSTEAD OF ALL THE THINGS THAT MAKE YOU JUST LIKE THEM...
REAL FRIENDS.
WITH REAL FACES.
THE KIND OF PEOPLE WHO DON'T NEED TO LIVE IN A PLAYGROUND TO HAVE FUN.
RS-9

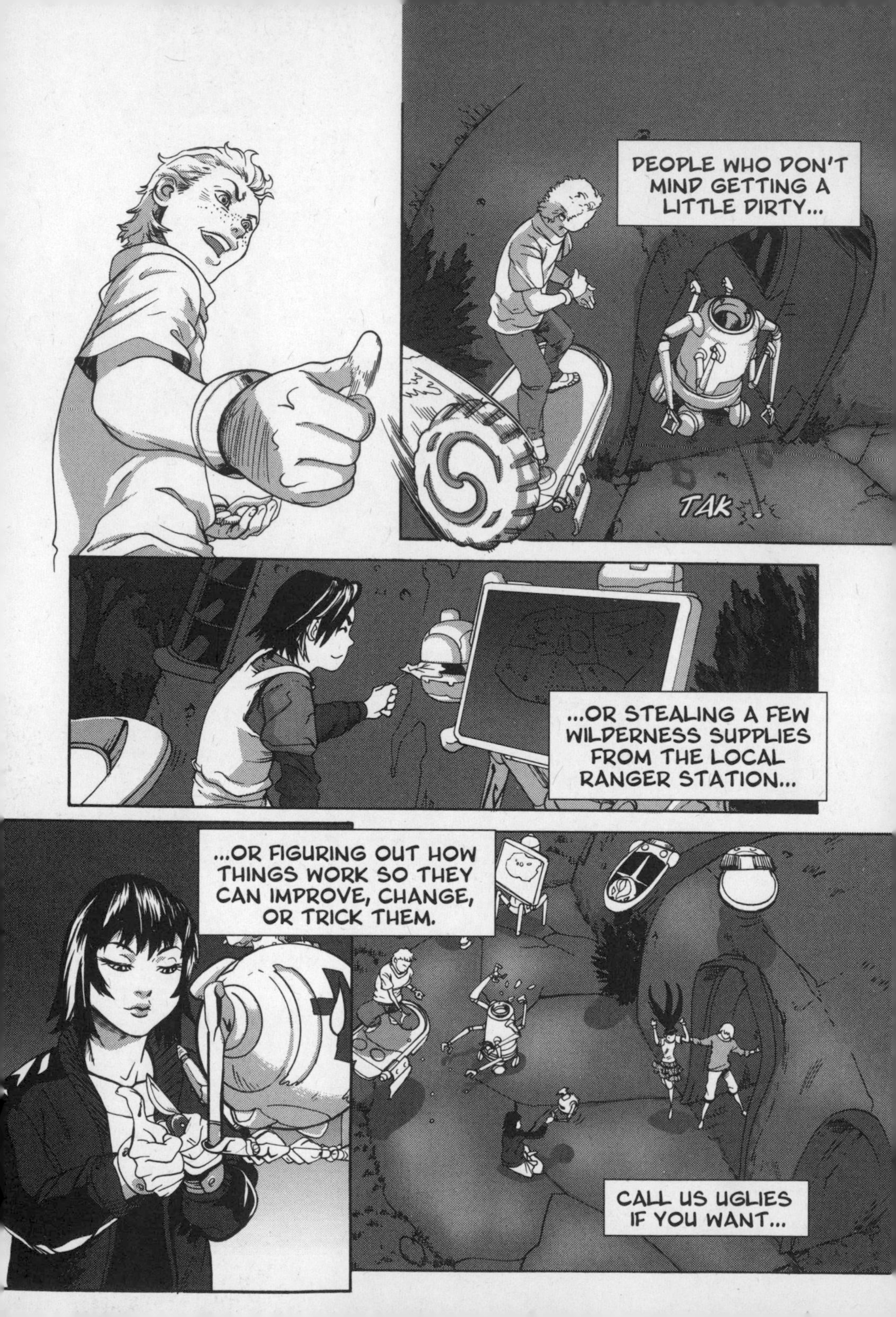
PEOPLE WHO DON'T MIND GETTING A LITTLE DIRTY...
TAK
...OR STEALING A FEW WILDERNESS SUPPLIES FROM THE LOCAL RANGER STATION...
...OR FIGURING OUT HOW THINGS WORK SO THEY CAN IMPROVE, CHANGE, OR TRICK THEM.
CALL US UGLIES IF YOU WANT...

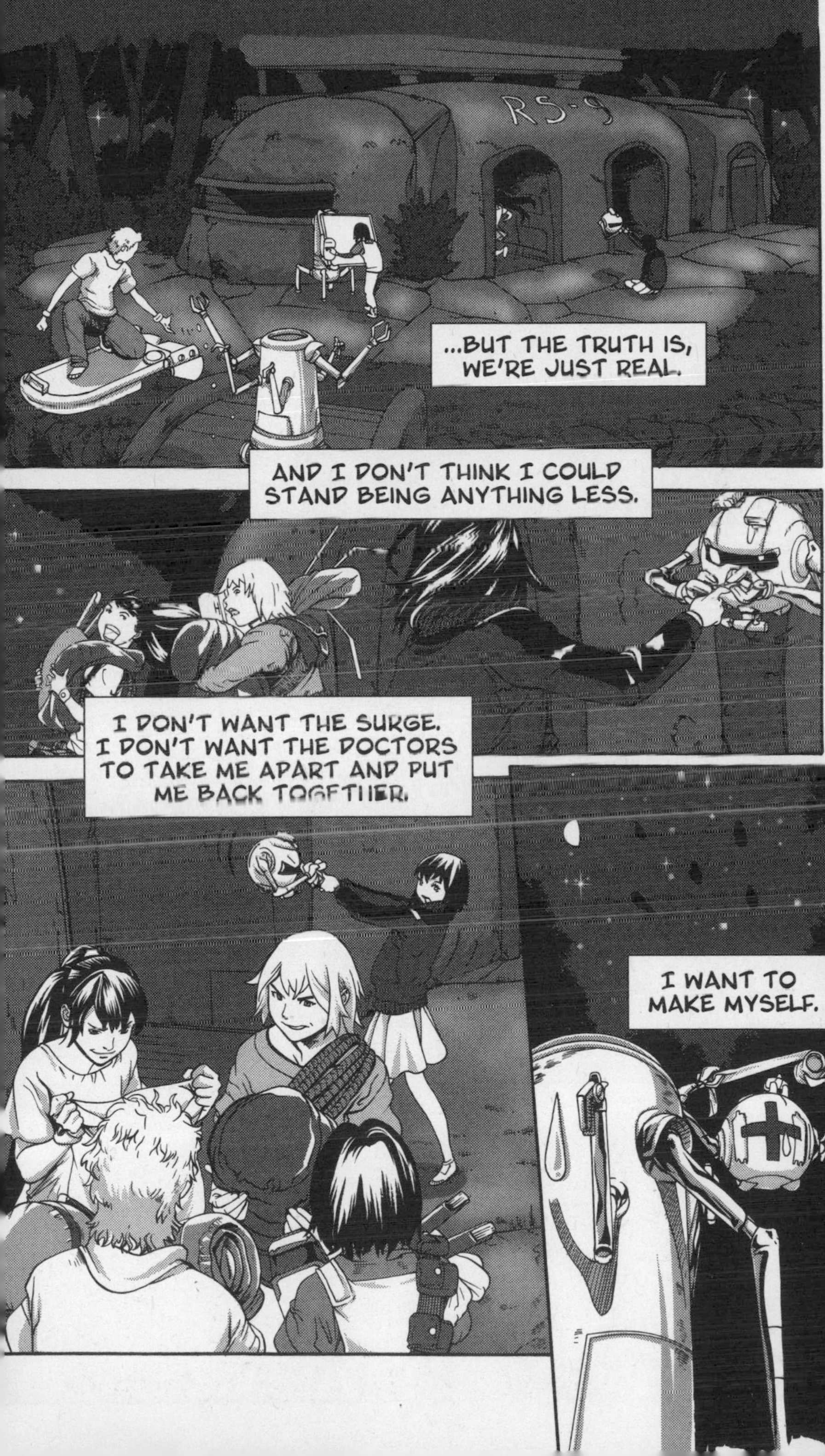
RS-9
...BUT THE TRUTH IS, WE'RE JUST REAL.
AND I DON'T THINK I COULD STAND BEING ANYTHING LESS.
I DON'T WANT THE SURGE. I DON'T WANT THE DOCTORS TO TAKE ME APART AND PUT ME BACK TOGETHER.
I WANT TO MAKE MYSELF.

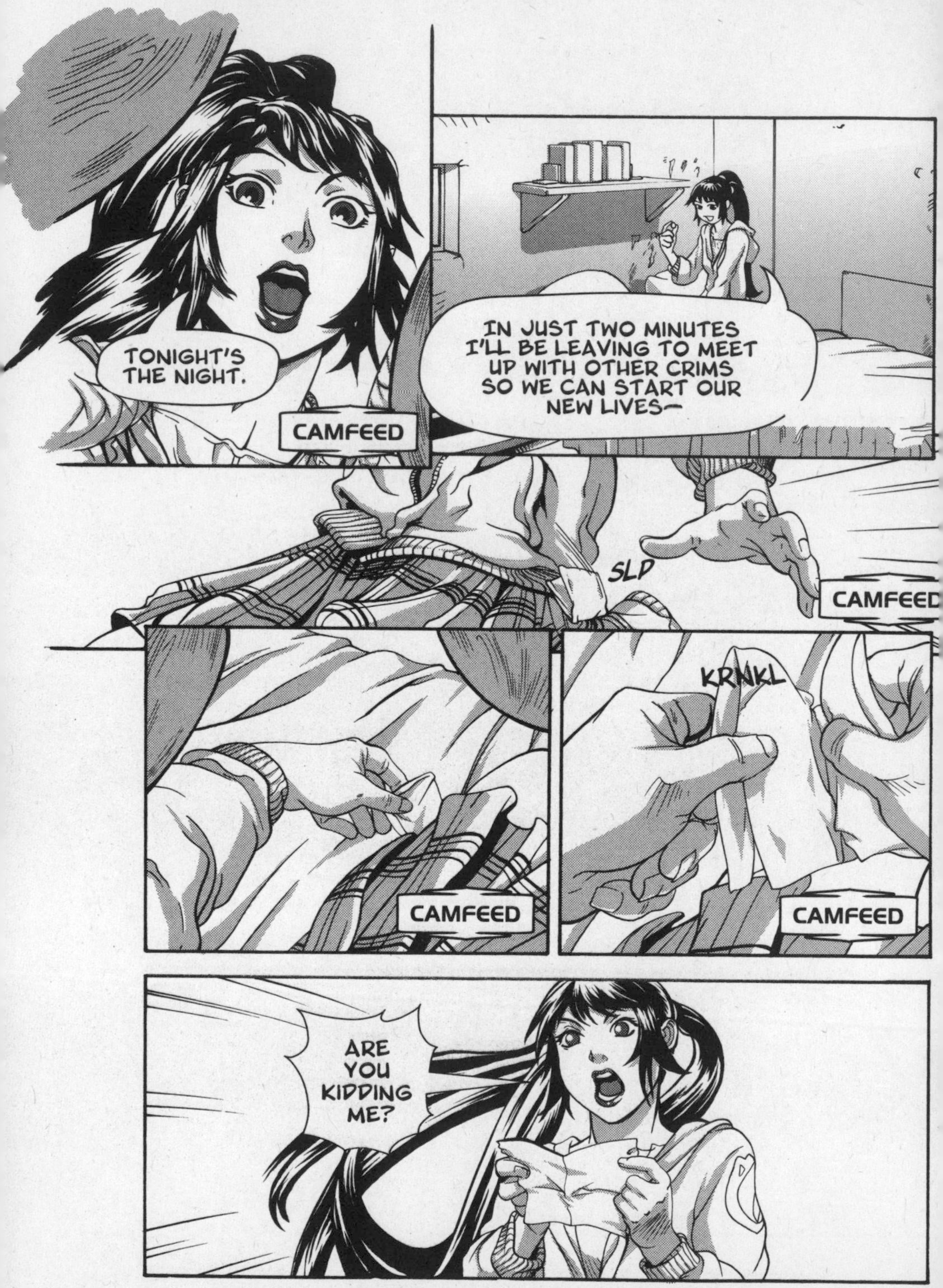
TONIGHT'S THE NIGHT.
CAMFEED
IN JUST TWO MINUTES I'LL BE LEAVING TO MEET UP WITH OTHER CRIMS SO WE CAN START OUR NEW LIVES—
SLP
CAMFEED
CAMFEED
KRNKL
CAMFEED
ARE YOU KIDDING ME?

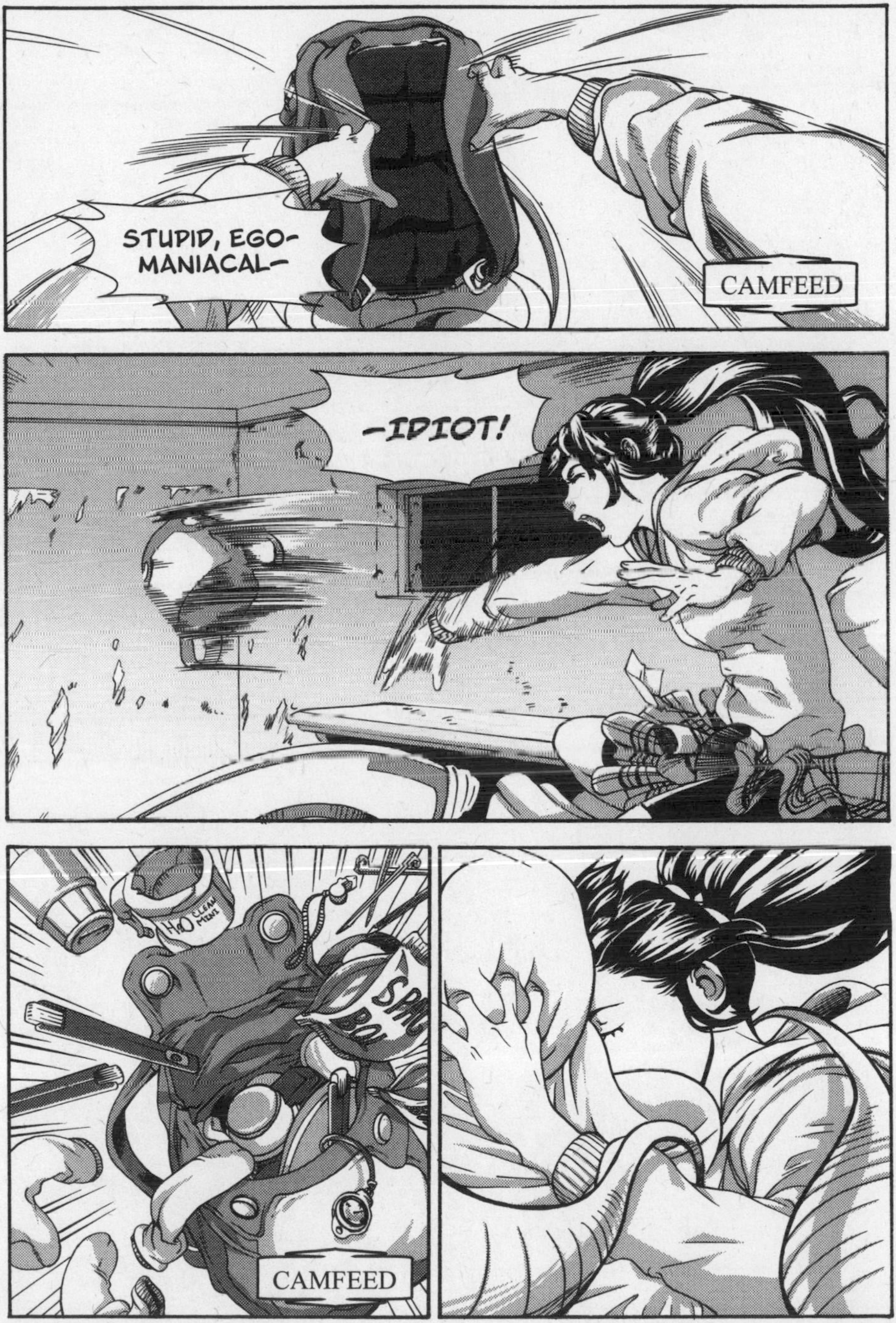
STUPID, EGO-MANIACAL—
CAMFEED
—IDIOT!
CAMFEED

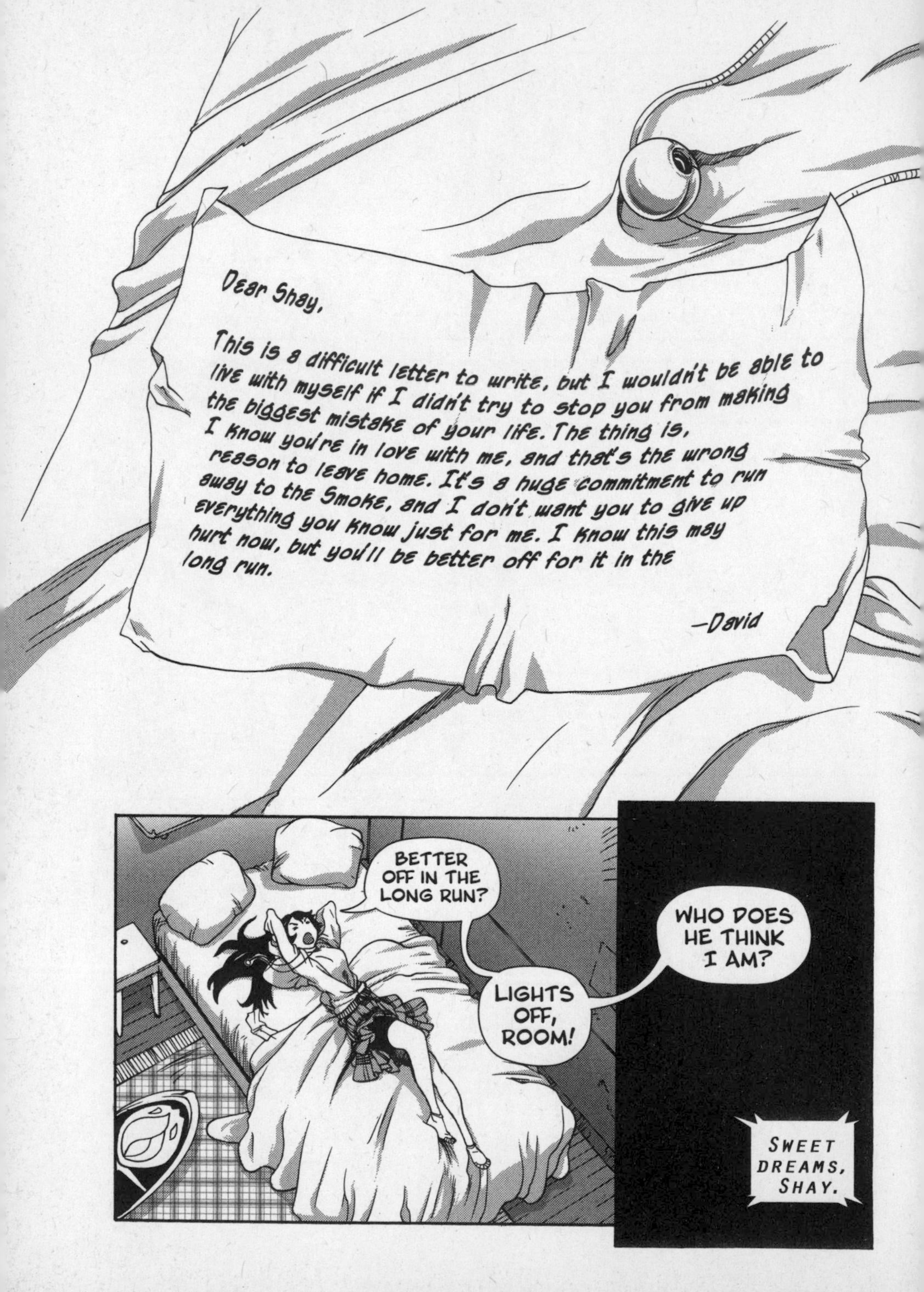
Dear Shay,
This is a difficult letter to write, but I wouldn't be able to live with myself if I didn't try to stop you from making the biggest mistake of your life. The thing is, I know you're in love with me, and that's the wrong reason to leave home. It's a huge commitment to run away to the Smoke, and I don't want you to give up everything you know just for me. I know this may hurt now, but you'll be better off for it in the long run.
—David
BETTER OFF IN THE LONG RUN?
LIGHTS OFF, ROOM!
WHO DOES HE THINK I AM?
SWEET DREAMS, SHAY.

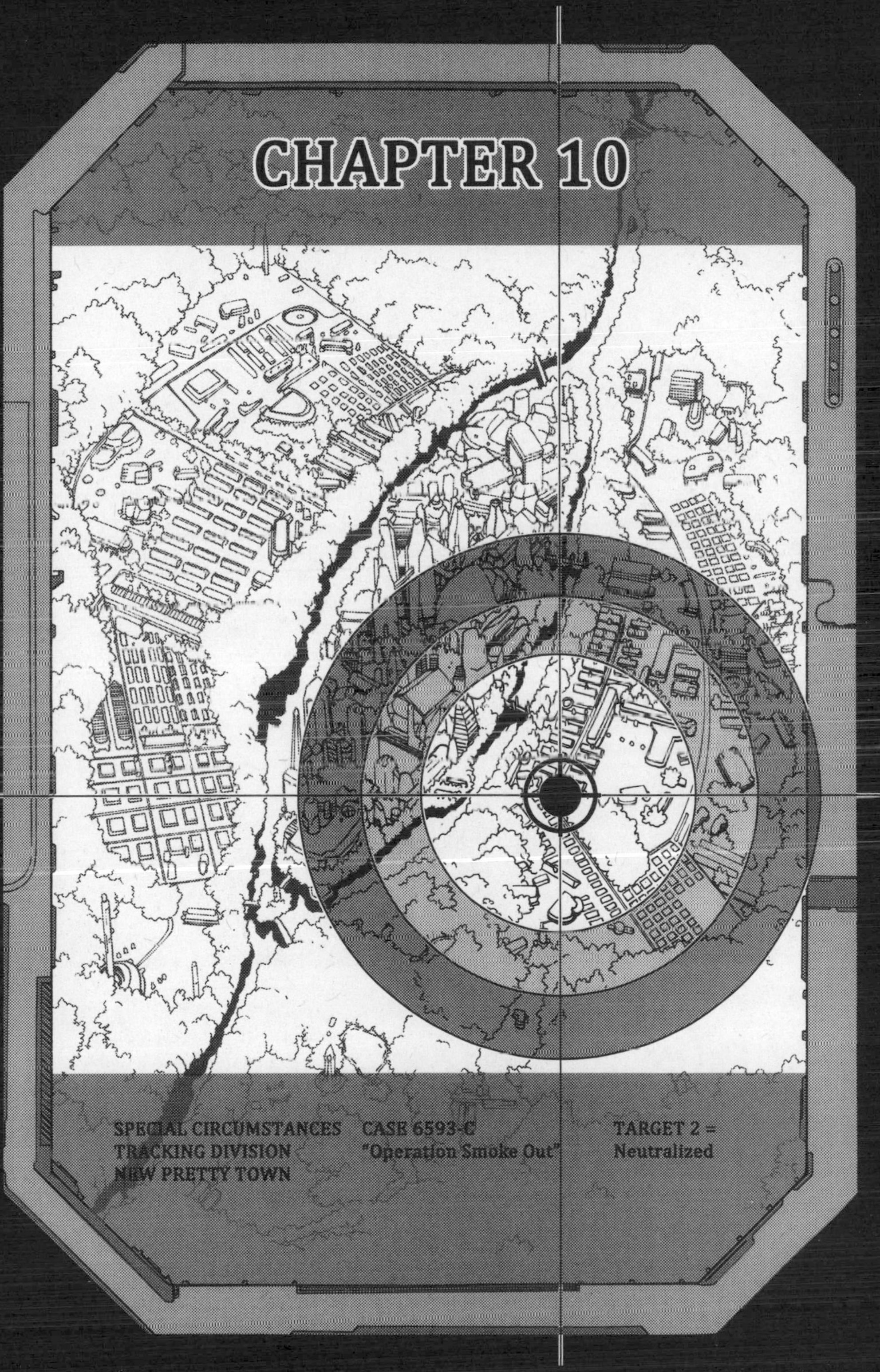
CHAPTER 10
SPECIAL CIRCUMSTANCES
TRACKING DIVISION
NEW PRETTY TOWN
CASE 6593-C
"Operation Smoke Out"
TARGET 2 =
Neutralized

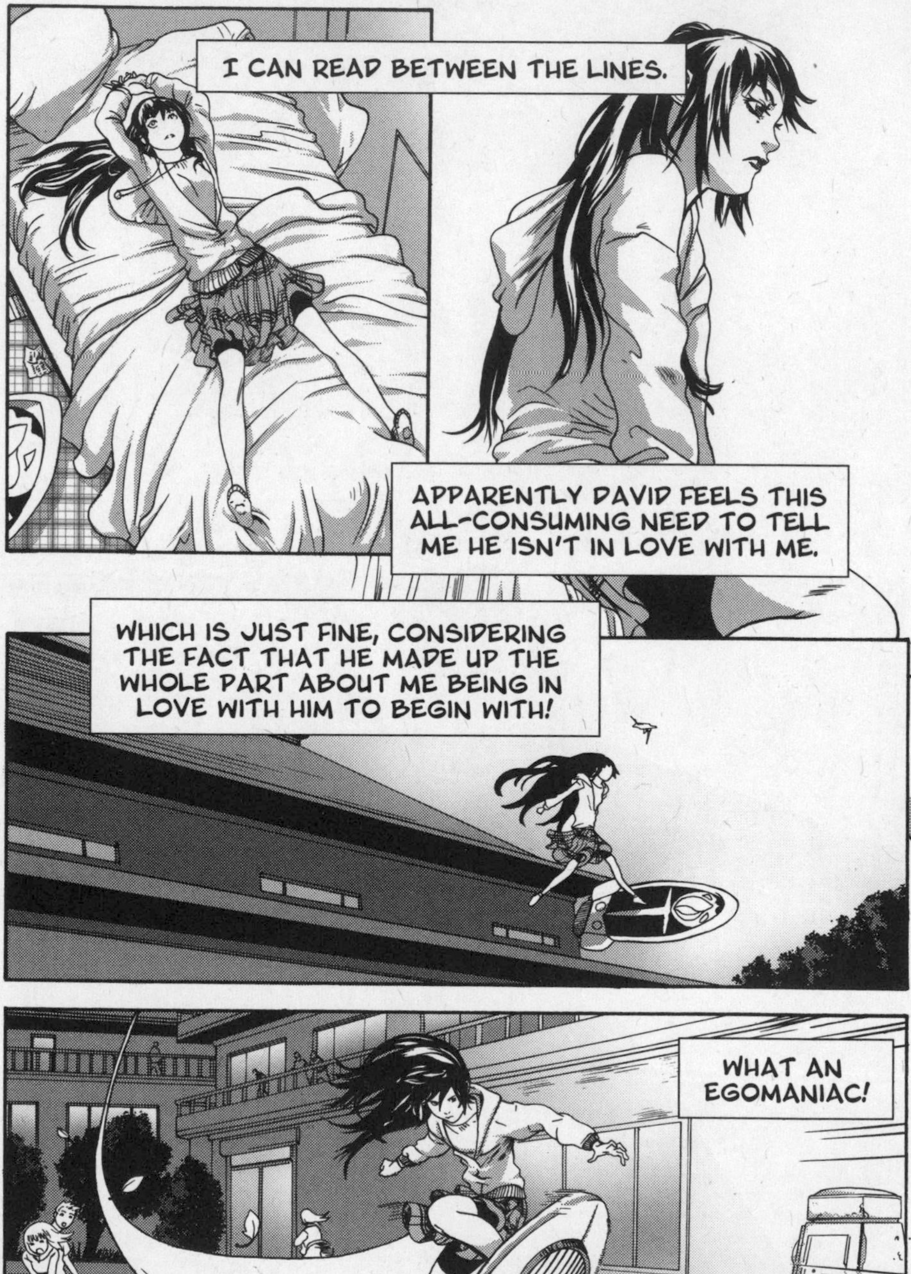
I CAN READ BETWEEN THE LINES.
APPARENTLY DAVID FEELS THIS ALL-CONSUMING NEED TO TELL ME HE ISN'T IN LOVE WITH ME.
WHICH IS JUST FINE, CONSIDERING THE FACT THAT HE MADE UP THE WHOLE PART ABOUT ME BEING IN LOVE WITH HIM TO BEGIN WITH!
WHAT AN EGOMANIAC!

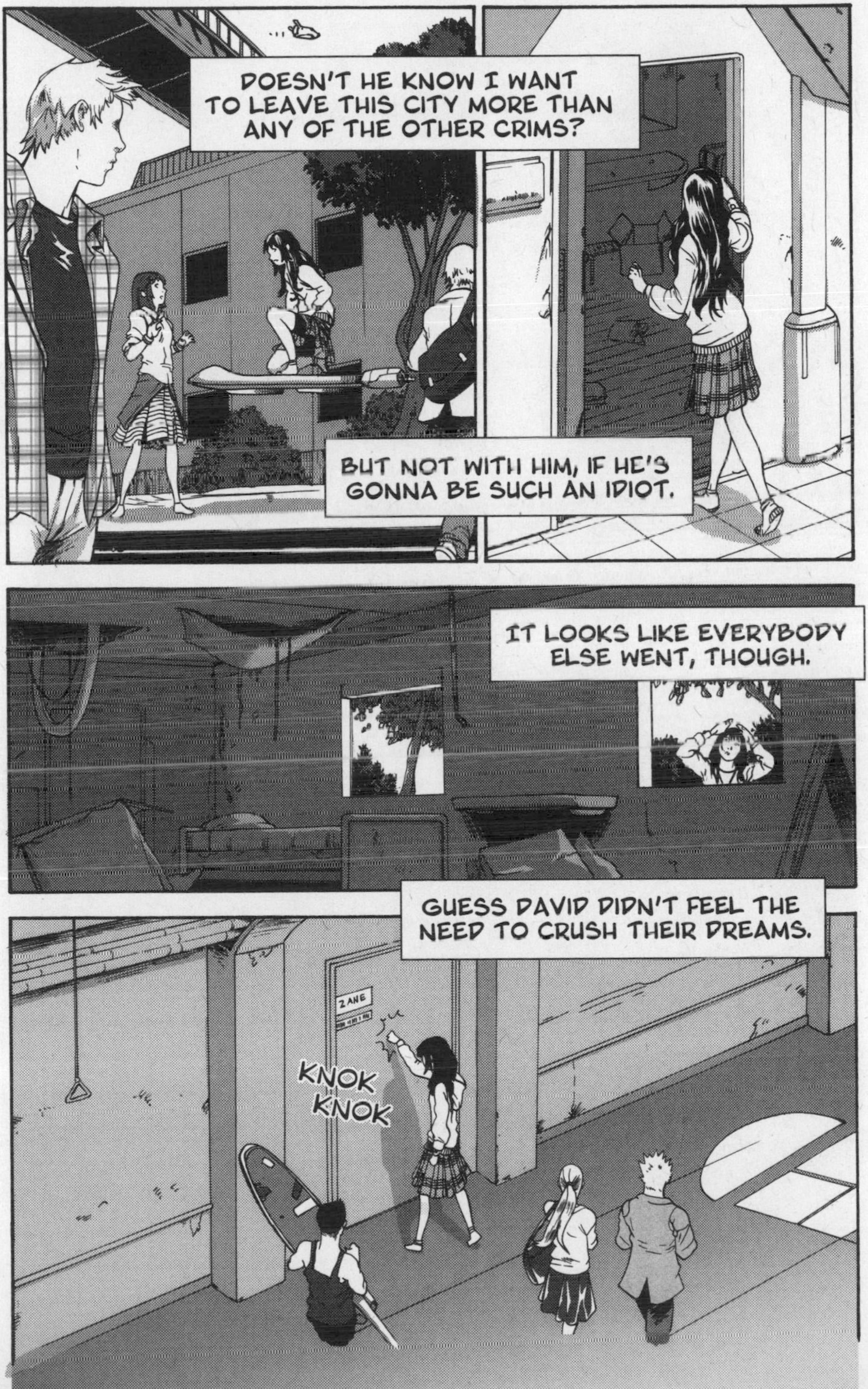
DOESN'T HE KNOW I WANT TO LEAVE THIS CITY MORE THAN ANY OF THE OTHER CRIMS?
BUT NOT WITH HIM, IF HE'S GONNA BE SUCH AN IDIOT.
IT LOOKS LIKE EVERYBODY ELSE WENT, THOUGH.
GUESS DAVID DIDN'T FEEL THE NEED TO CRUSH THEIR DREAMS.
ZANE
KNOK KNOK

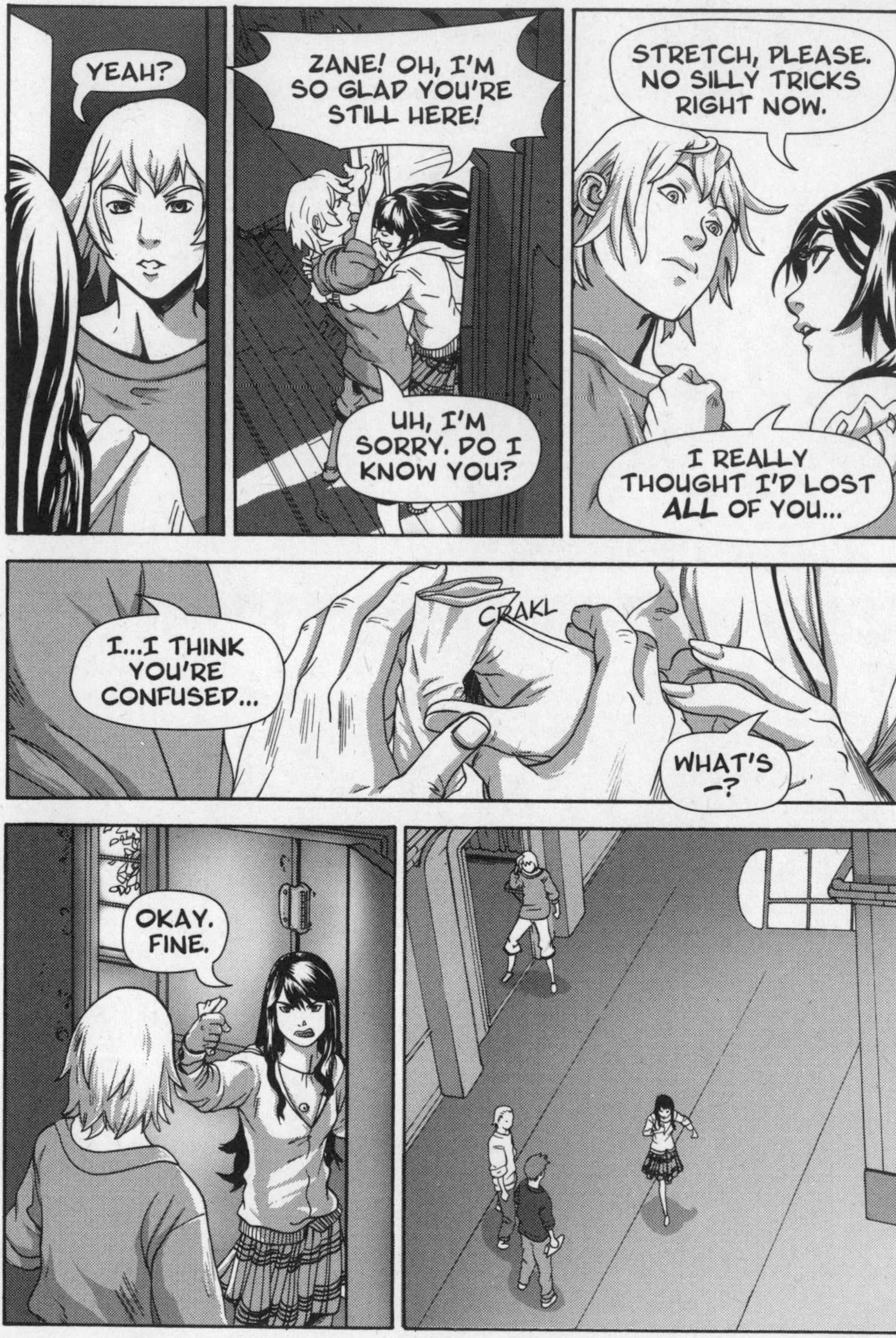
YEAH?
ZANE! OH, I'M SO GLAD YOU'RE STILL HERE!
UH, I'M SORRY. DO I KNOW YOU?
STRETCH, PLEASE. NO SILLY TRICKS RIGHT NOW.
I REALLY THOUGHT I'D LOST ALL OF YOU...
I...I THINK YOU'RE CONFUSED...
CRAKL
WHAT'S —?
OKAY. FINE.

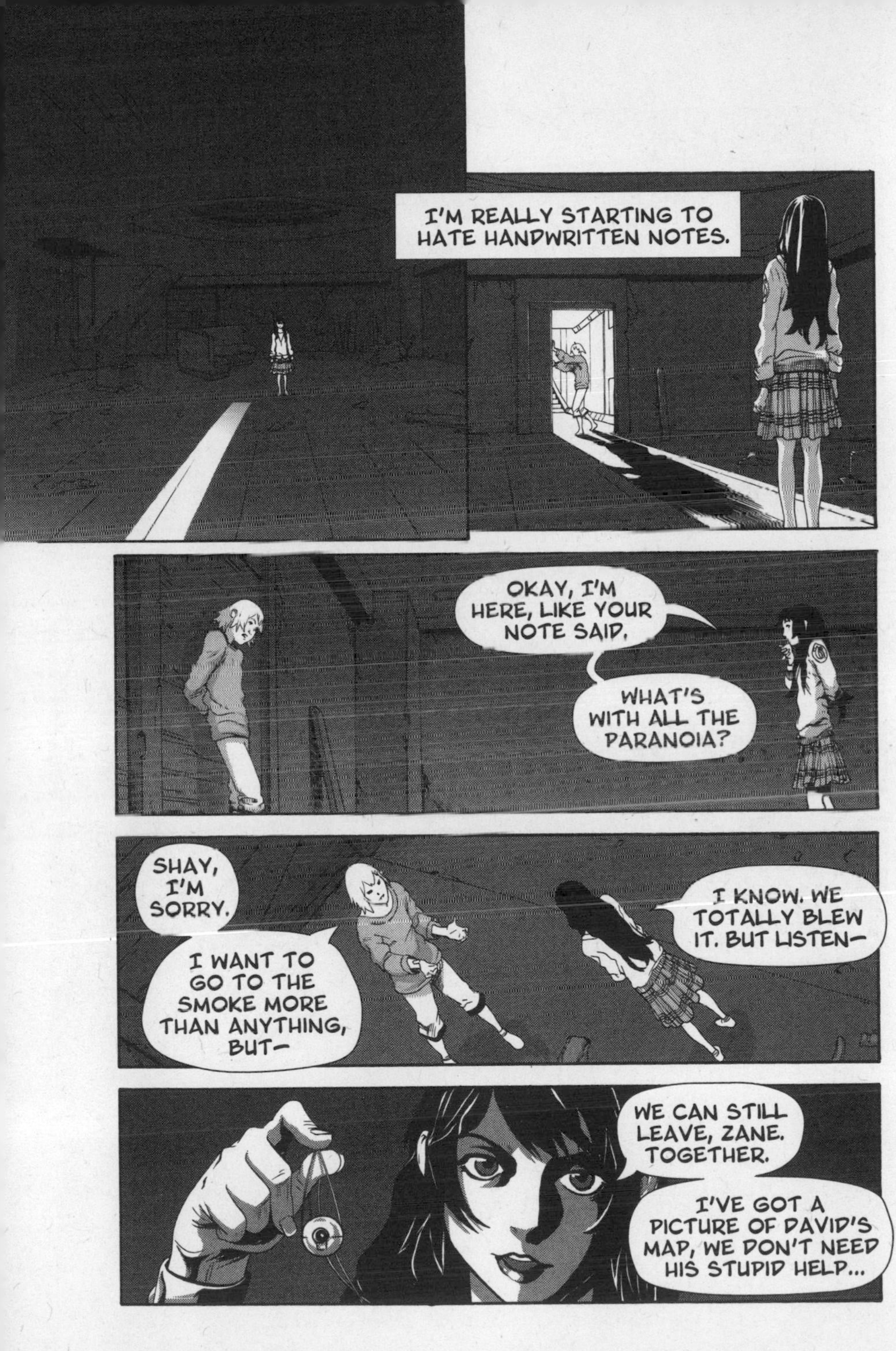
I'M REALLY STARTING TO HATE HANDWRITTEN NOTES.
OKAY, I'M HERE, LIKE YOUR NOTE SAID.
WHAT'S WITH ALL THE PARANOIA?
SHAY, I'M SORRY.
I WANT TO GO TO THE SMOKE MORE THAN ANYTHING, BUT–
I KNOW. WE TOTALLY BLEW IT. BUT LISTEN–
WE CAN STILL LEAVE, ZANE. TOGETHER.
I'VE GOT A PICTURE OF DAVID'S MAP, WE DON'T NEED HIS STUPID HELP...

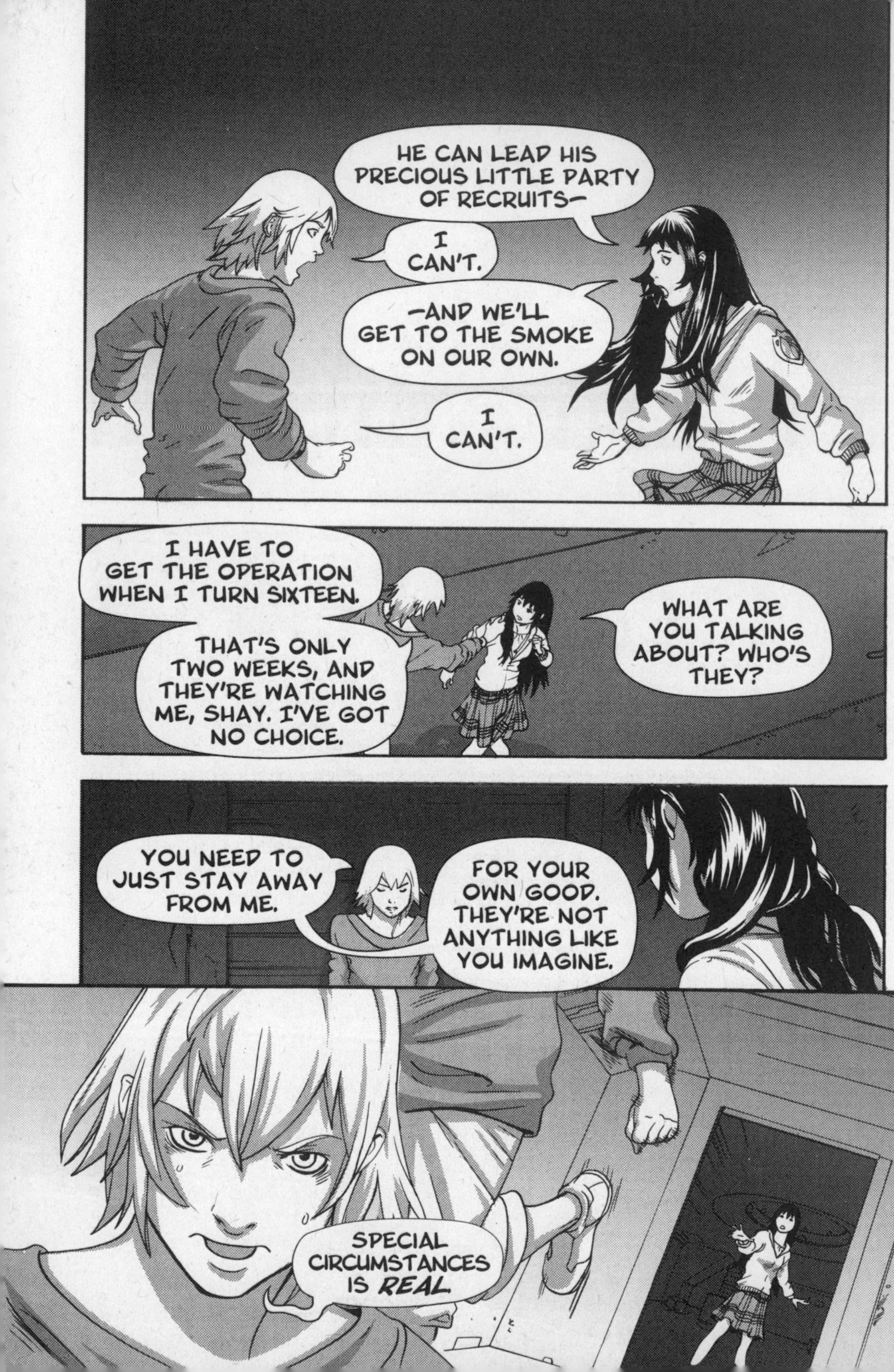
HE CAN LEAD HIS PRECIOUS LITTLE PARTY OF RECRUITS—
I CAN'T.
—AND WE'LL GET TO THE SMOKE ON OUR OWN.
I CAN'T.
I HAVE TO GET THE OPERATION WHEN I TURN SIXTEEN.
THAT'S ONLY TWO WEEKS, AND THEY'RE WATCHING ME, SHAY. I'VE GOT NO CHOICE.
WHAT ARE YOU TALKING ABOUT? WHO'S THEY?
YOU NEED TO JUST STAY AWAY FROM ME.
FOR YOUR OWN GOOD. THEY'RE NOT ANYTHING LIKE YOU IMAGINE.
SPECIAL CIRCUMSTANCES IS *REAL*

# CHAPTER 11

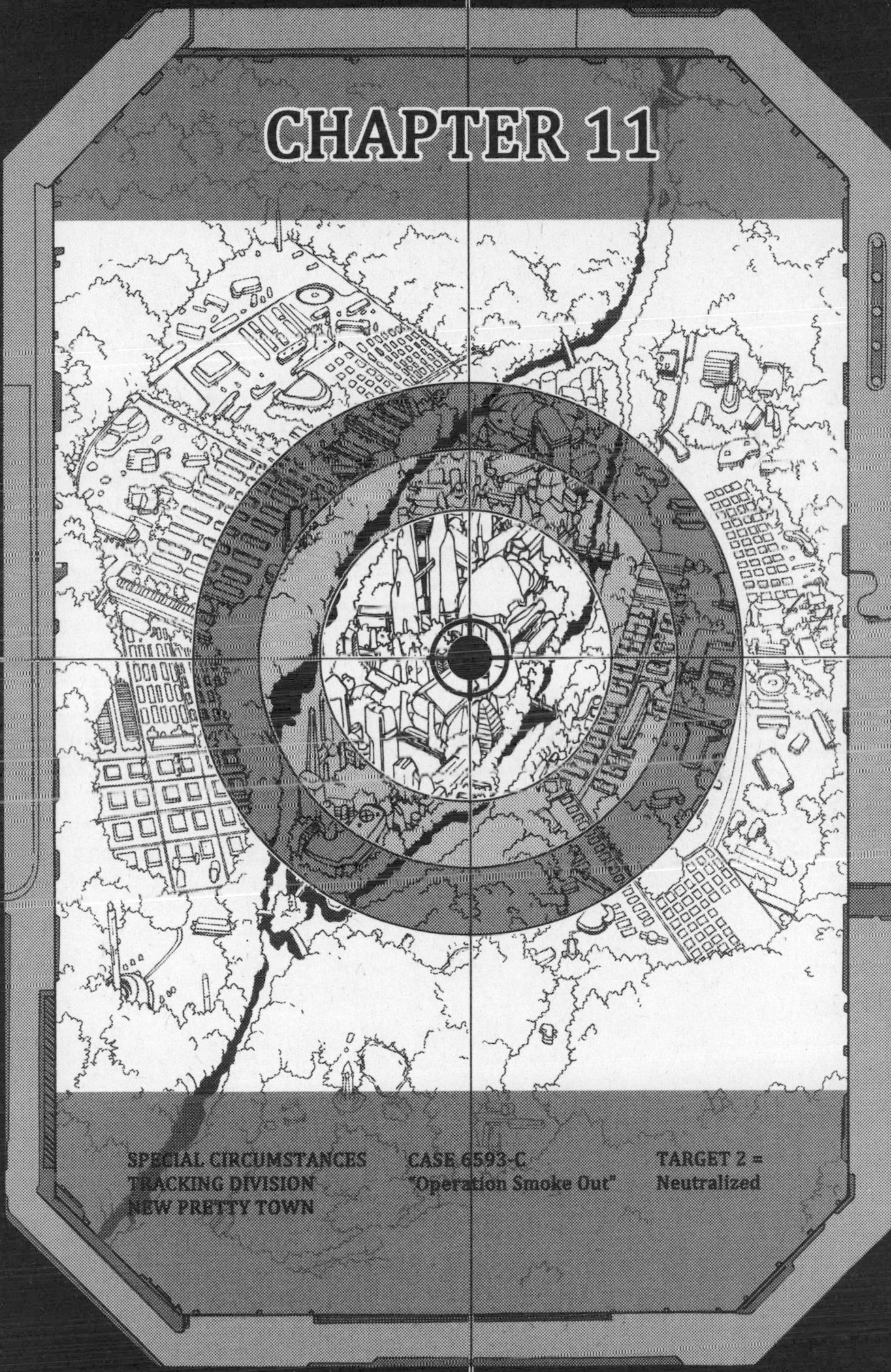
SPECIAL CIRCUMSTANCES
TRACKING DIVISION
NEW PRETTY TOWN
CASE 6593-C
"Operation Smoke Out"
TARGET 2 =
Neutralized

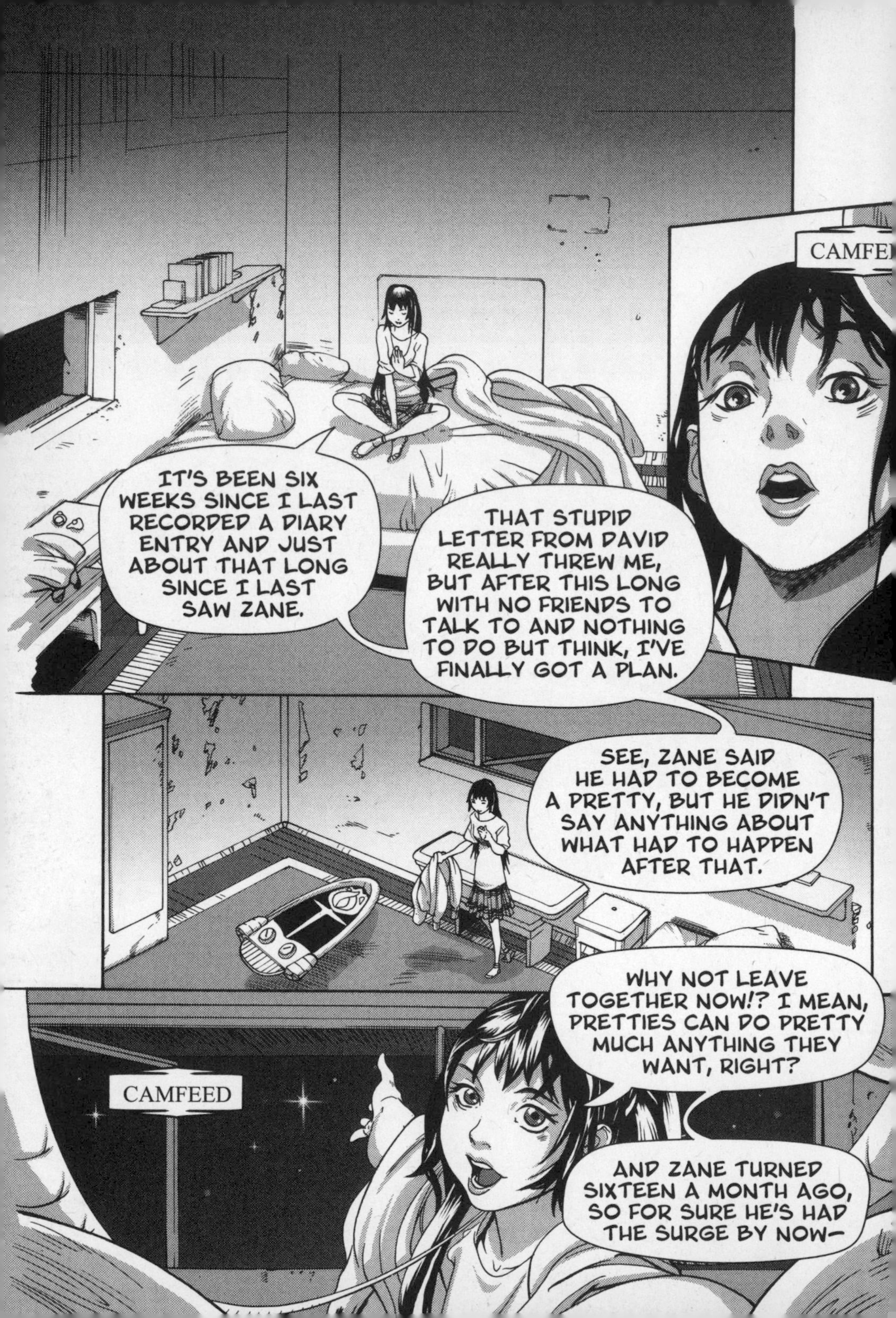
IT'S BEEN SIX WEEKS SINCE I LAST RECORDED A DIARY ENTRY AND JUST ABOUT THAT LONG SINCE I LAST SAW ZANE.
THAT STUPID LETTER FROM DAVID REALLY THREW ME, BUT AFTER THIS LONG WITH NO FRIENDS TO TALK TO AND NOTHING TO DO BUT THINK, I'VE FINALLY GOT A PLAN.
CAMFE
SEE, ZANE SAID HE HAD TO BECOME A PRETTY, BUT HE DIDN'T SAY ANYTHING ABOUT WHAT HAD TO HAPPEN AFTER THAT.
CAMFEED
WHY NOT LEAVE TOGETHER NOW!? I MEAN, PRETTIES CAN DO PRETTY MUCH ANYTHING THEY WANT, RIGHT?
AND ZANE TURNED SIXTEEN A MONTH AGO, SO FOR SURE HE'S HAD THE SURGE BY NOW—

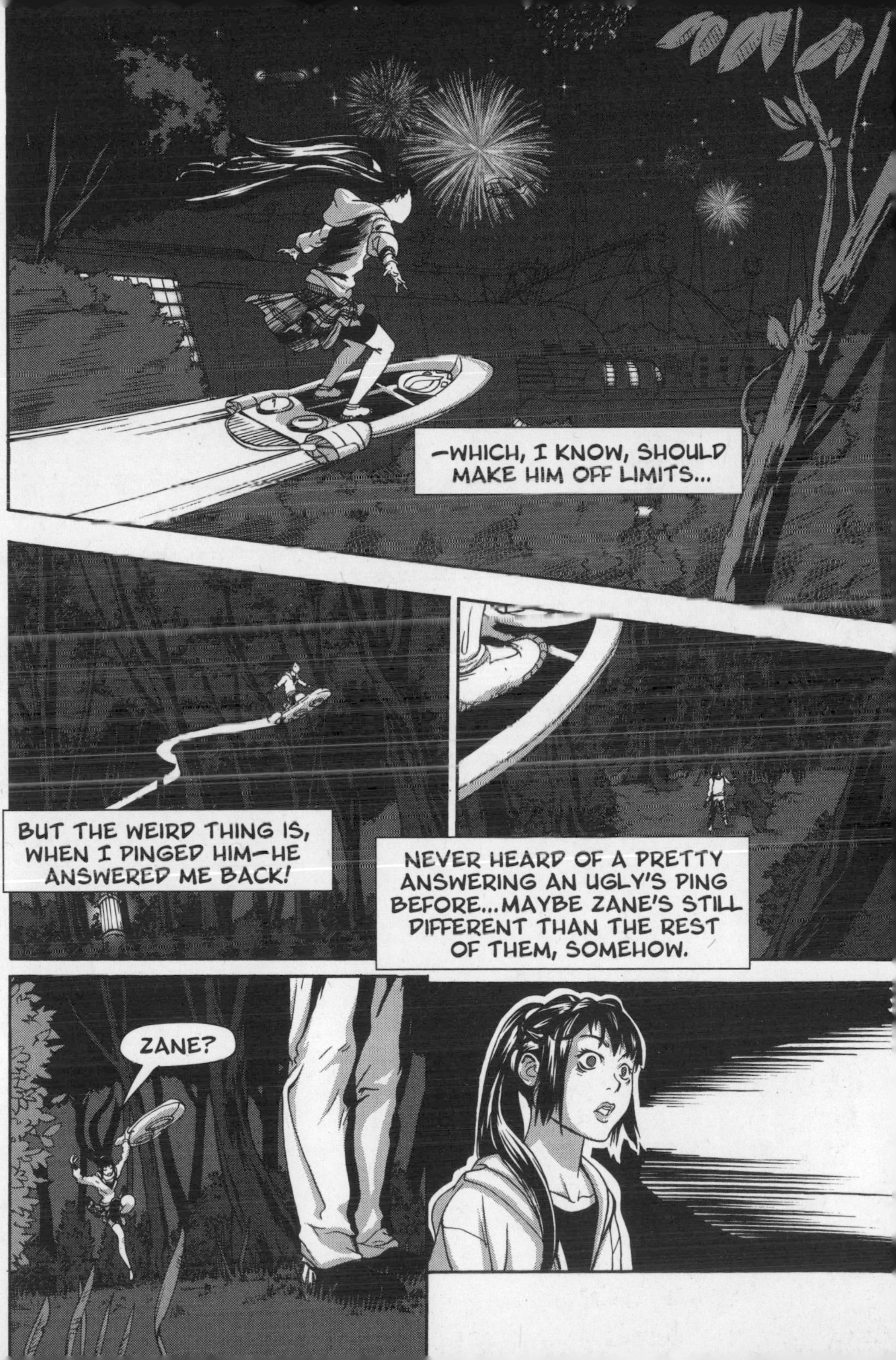
—WHICH, I KNOW, SHOULD MAKE HIM OFF LIMITS...
BUT THE WEIRD THING IS, WHEN I PINGED HIM—HE ANSWERED ME BACK!
NEVER HEARD OF A PRETTY ANSWERING AN UGLY'S PING BEFORE...MAYBE ZANE'S STILL DIFFERENT THAN THE REST OF THEM, SOMEHOW.
ZANE?

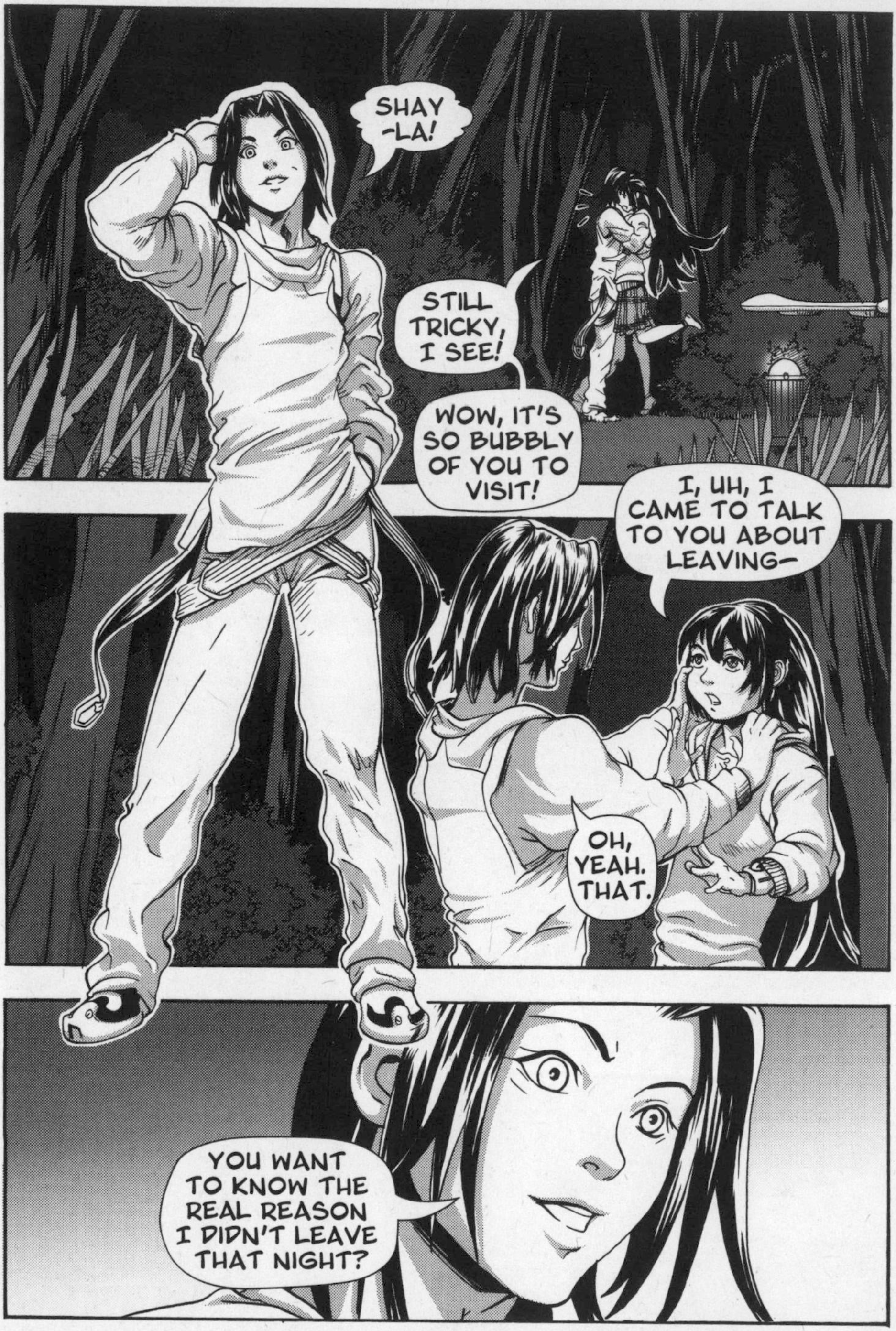
SHAY -LA!
STILL TRICKY, I SEE!
WOW, IT'S SO BUBBLY OF YOU TO VISIT!
I, UH, I CAME TO TALK TO YOU ABOUT LEAVING–
OH, YEAH. THAT.
YOU WANT TO KNOW THE REAL REASON I DIDN'T LEAVE THAT NIGHT?

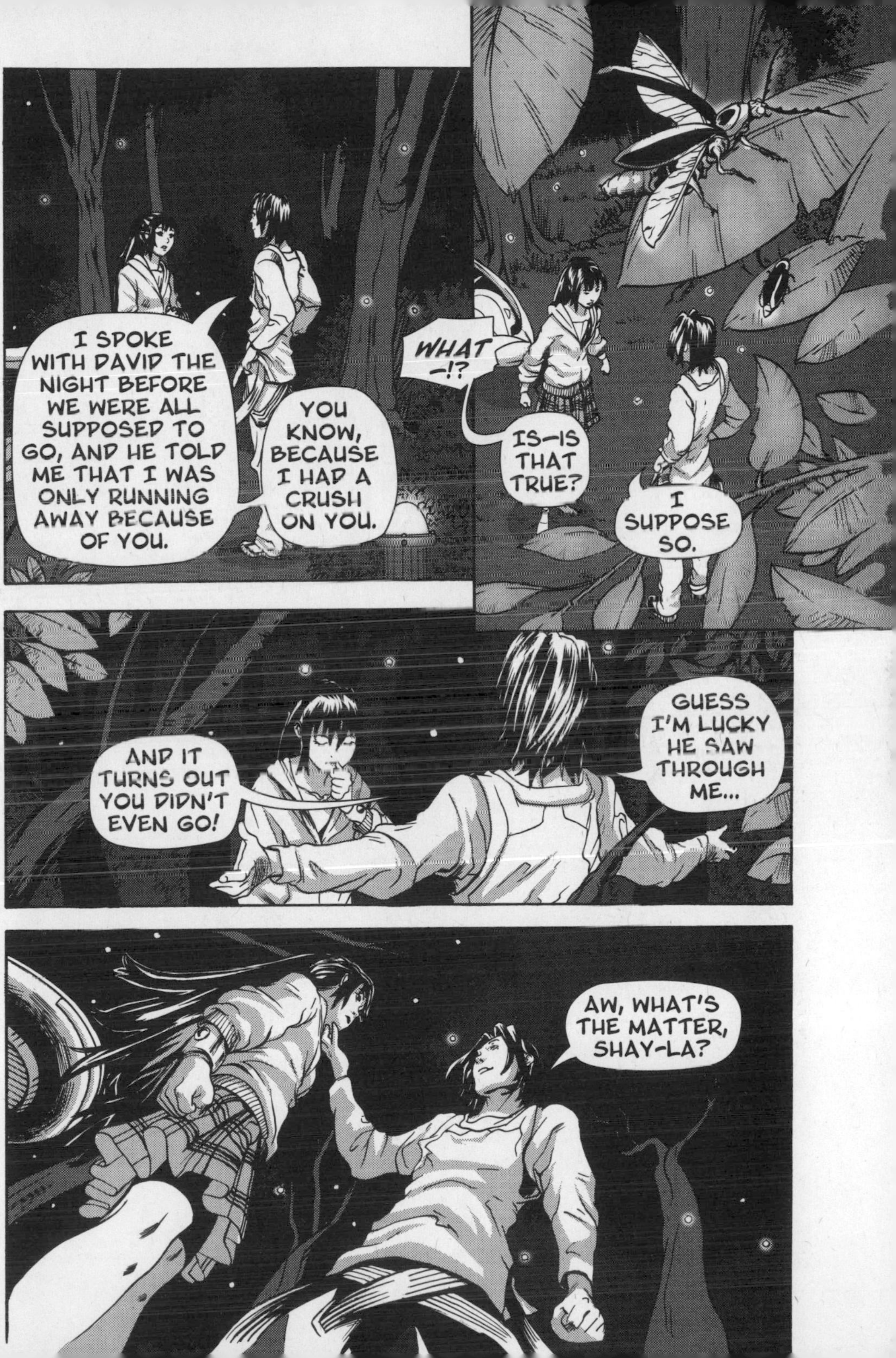
I SPOKE WITH DAVID THE NIGHT BEFORE WE WERE ALL SUPPOSED TO GO, AND HE TOLD ME THAT I WAS ONLY RUNNING AWAY BECAUSE OF YOU.
YOU KNOW, BECAUSE I HAD A CRUSH ON YOU.
WHAT —!?
IS—IS THAT TRUE?
I SUPPOSE SO.
AND IT TURNS OUT YOU DIDN'T EVEN GO!
GUESS I'M LUCKY HE SAW THROUGH ME...
AW, WHAT'S THE MATTER, SHAY-LA?

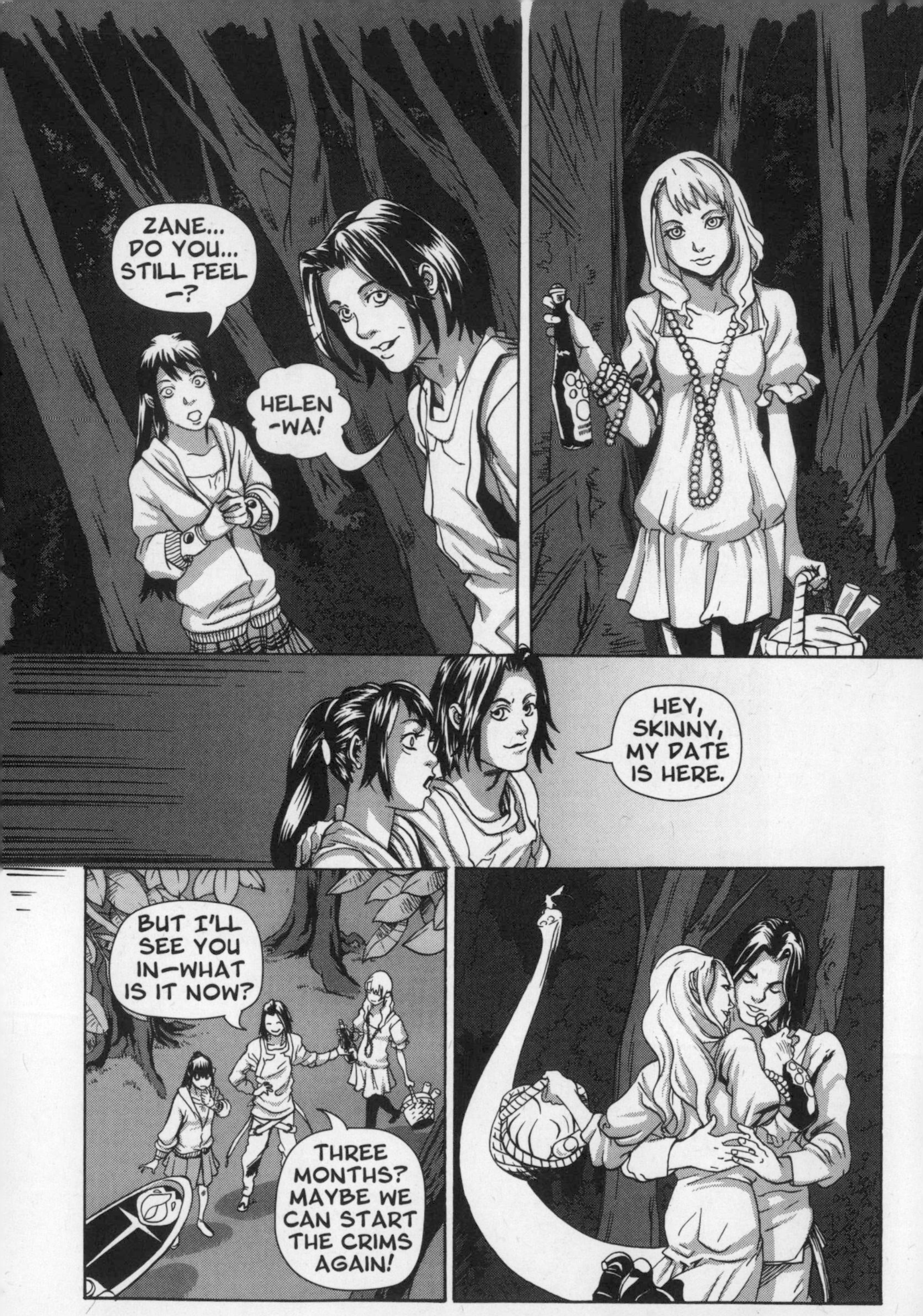
ZANE... DO YOU... STILL FEEL —?
HELEN -WA!
HEY, SKINNY, MY DATE IS HERE.
BUT I'LL SEE YOU IN—WHAT IS IT NOW?
THREE MONTHS? MAYBE WE CAN START THE CRIMS AGAIN!

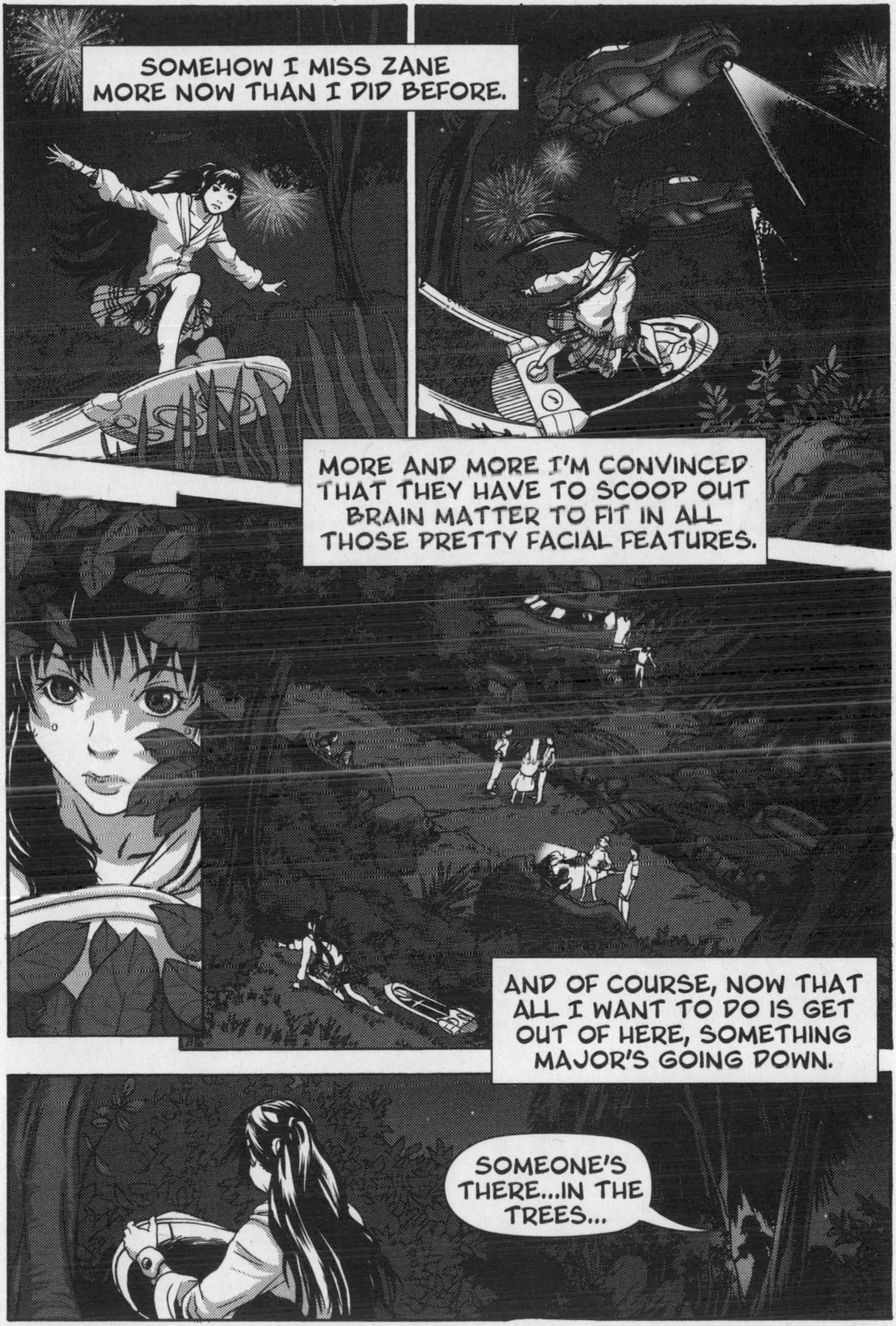
SOMEHOW I MISS ZANE MORE NOW THAN I DID BEFORE.
MORE AND MORE I'M CONVINCED THAT THEY HAVE TO SCOOP OUT BRAIN MATTER TO FIT IN ALL THOSE PRETTY FACIAL FEATURES.
AND OF COURSE, NOW THAT ALL I WANT TO DO IS GET OUT OF HERE, SOMETHING MAJOR'S GOING DOWN.
SOMEONE'S THERE...IN THE TREES...

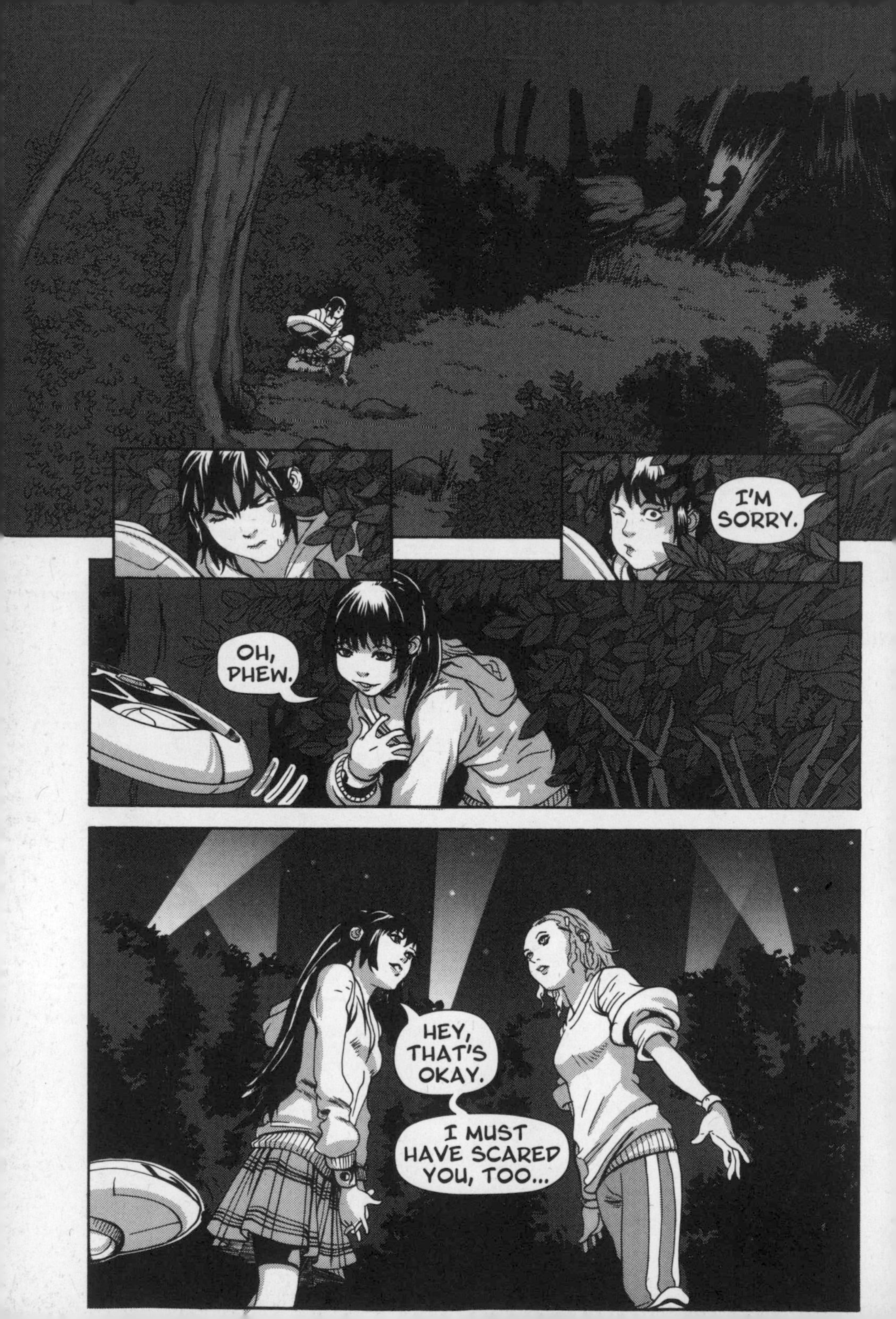
I'M SORRY.
OH, PHEW.
HEY, THAT'S OKAY.
I MUST HAVE SCARED YOU, TOO...

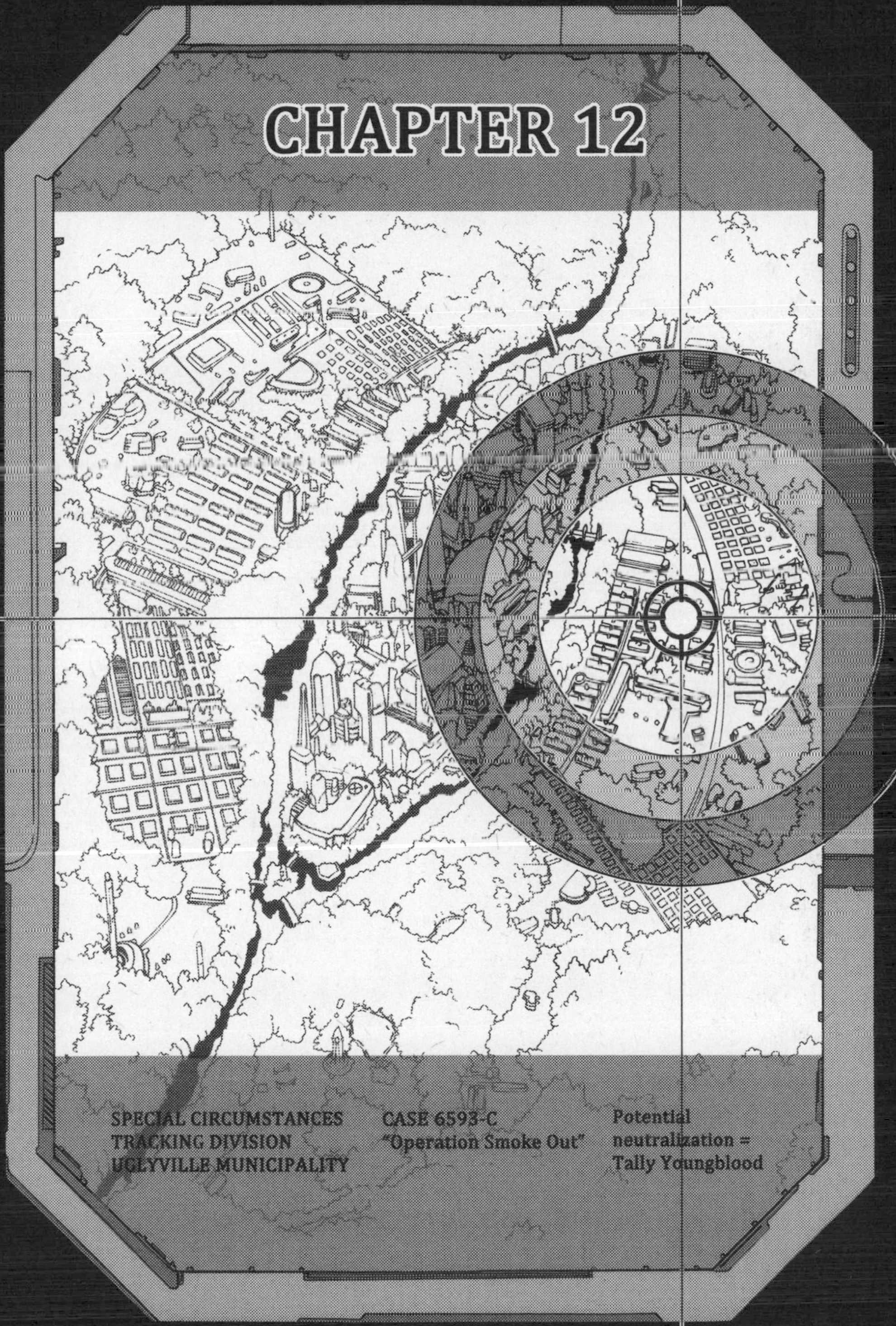
CHAPTER 12
SPECIAL CIRCUMSTANCES
TRACKING DIVISION
UGLYVILLE MUNICIPALITY
CASE 6593-C
"Operation Smoke Out"
Potential
neutralization =
Tally Youngblood

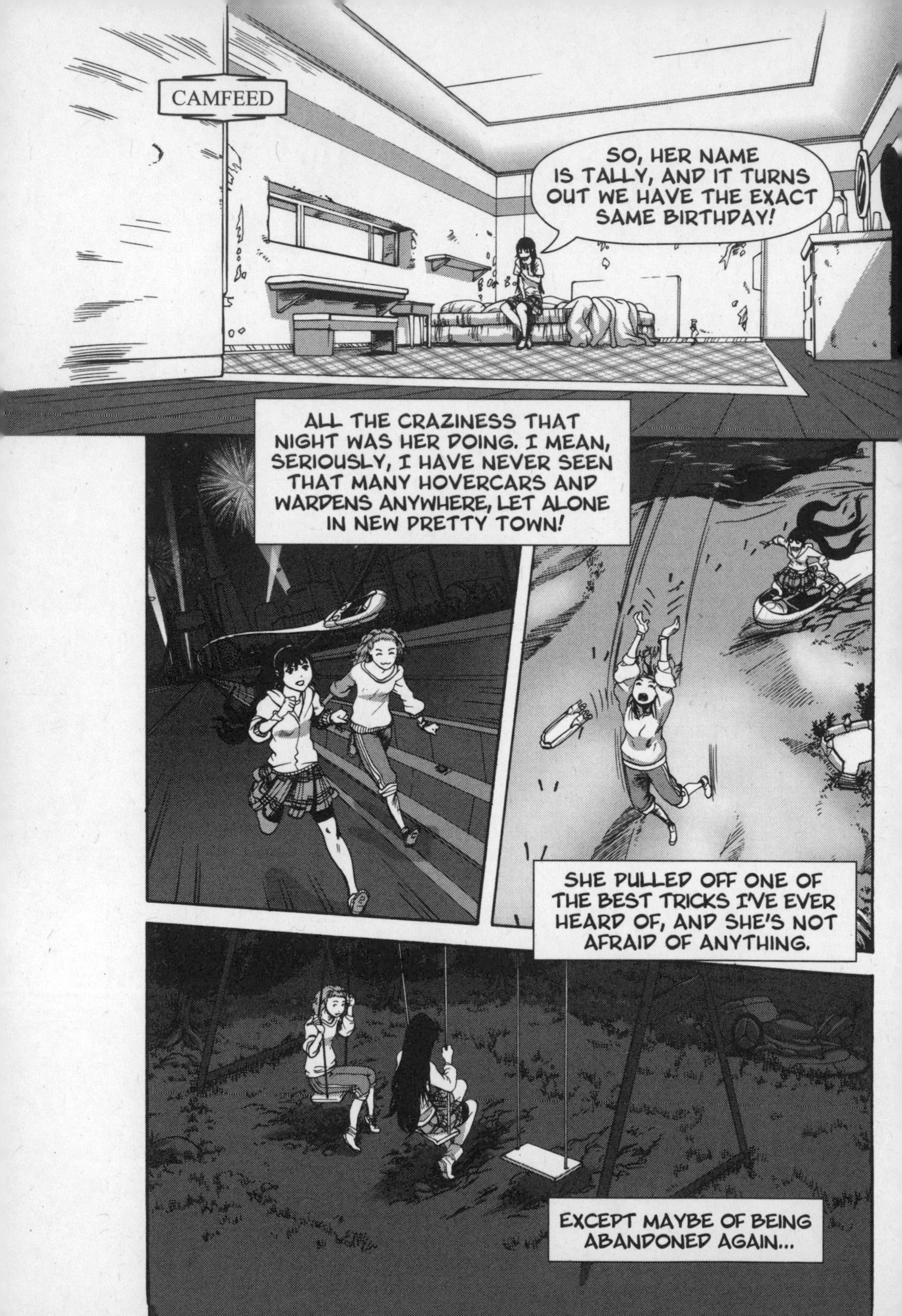
CAMFEED
SO, HER NAME IS TALLY, AND IT TURNS OUT WE HAVE THE EXACT SAME BIRTHDAY!
ALL THE CRAZINESS THAT NIGHT WAS HER DOING. I MEAN, SERIOUSLY, I HAVE NEVER SEEN THAT MANY HOVERCARS AND WARDENS ANYWHERE, LET ALONE IN NEW PRETTY TOWN!
SHE PULLED OFF ONE OF THE BEST TRICKS I'VE EVER HEARD OF, AND SHE'S NOT AFRAID OF ANYTHING.
EXCEPT MAYBE OF BEING ABANDONED AGAIN...

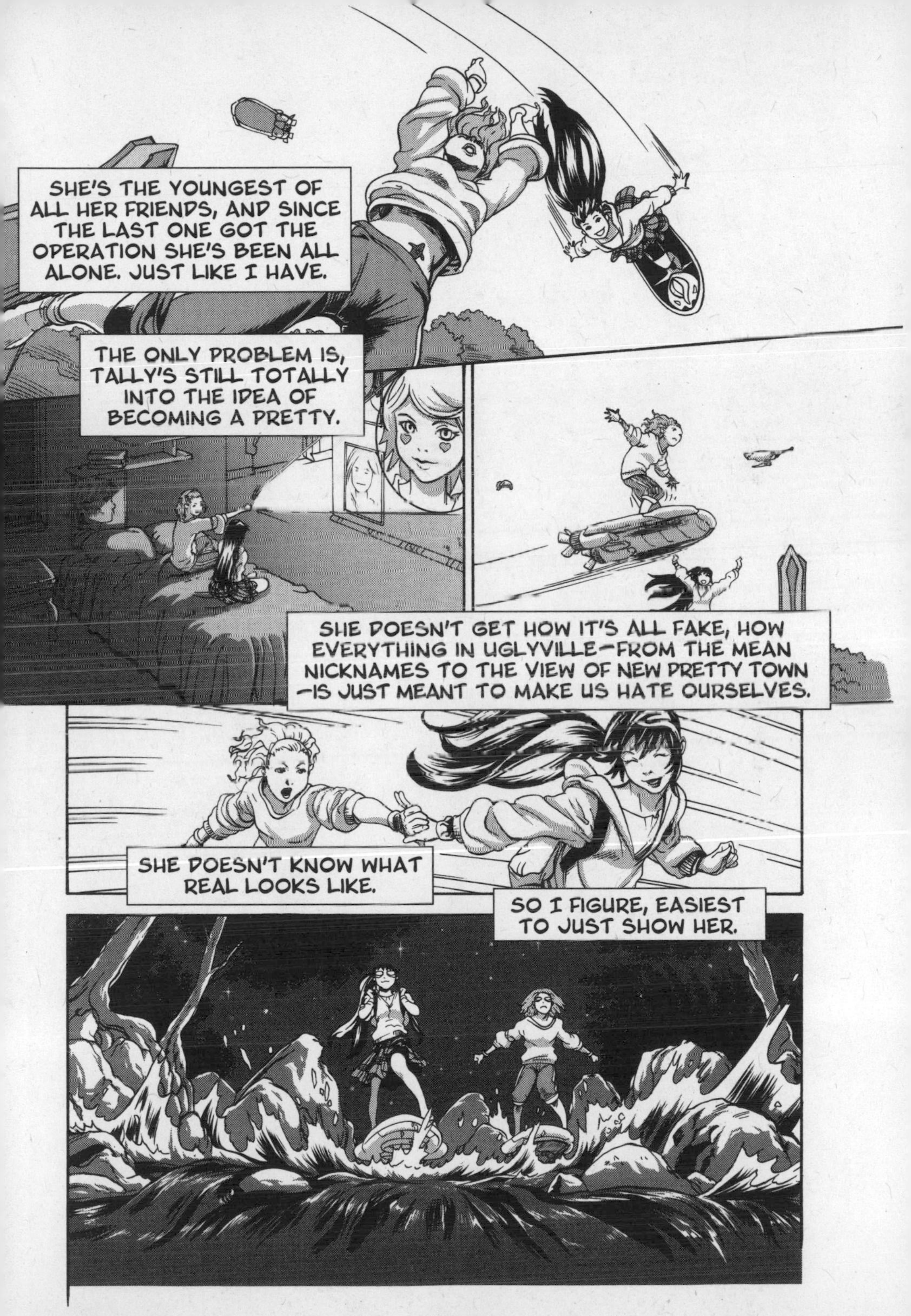
SHE'S THE YOUNGEST OF ALL HER FRIENDS, AND SINCE THE LAST ONE GOT THE OPERATION SHE'S BEEN ALL ALONE. JUST LIKE I HAVE.
THE ONLY PROBLEM IS, TALLY'S STILL TOTALLY INTO THE IDEA OF BECOMING A PRETTY.
SHE DOESN'T GET HOW IT'S ALL FAKE, HOW EVERYTHING IN UGLYVILLE—FROM THE MEAN NICKNAMES TO THE VIEW OF NEW PRETTY TOWN—IS JUST MEANT TO MAKE US HATE OURSELVES.
SHE DOESN'T KNOW WHAT REAL LOOKS LIKE.
SO I FIGURE, EASIEST TO JUST SHOW HER.

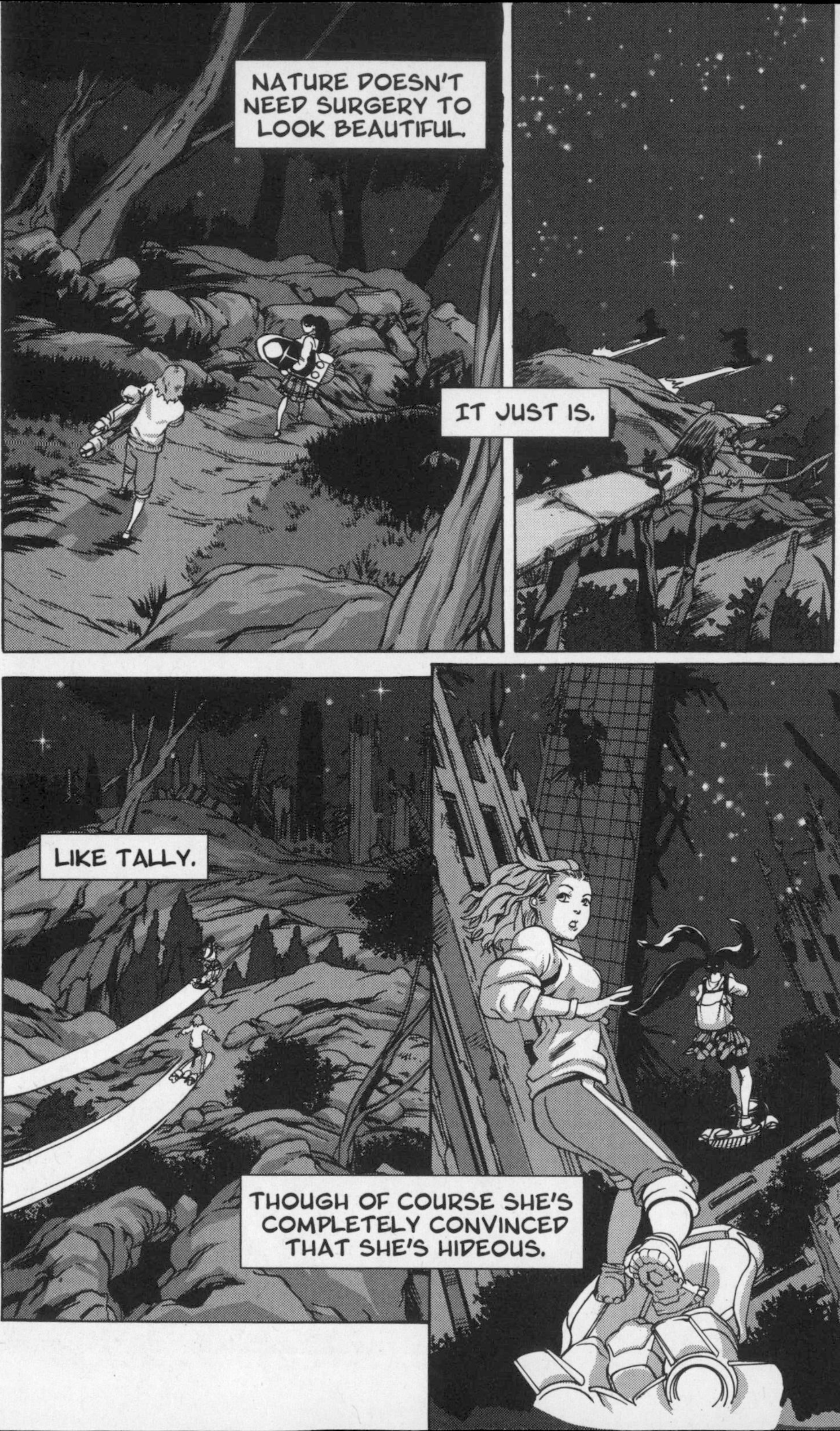
NATURE DOESN'T NEED SURGERY TO LOOK BEAUTIFUL.
IT JUST IS.
LIKE TALLY.
THOUGH OF COURSE SHE'S COMPLETELY CONVINCED THAT SHE'S HIDEOUS.

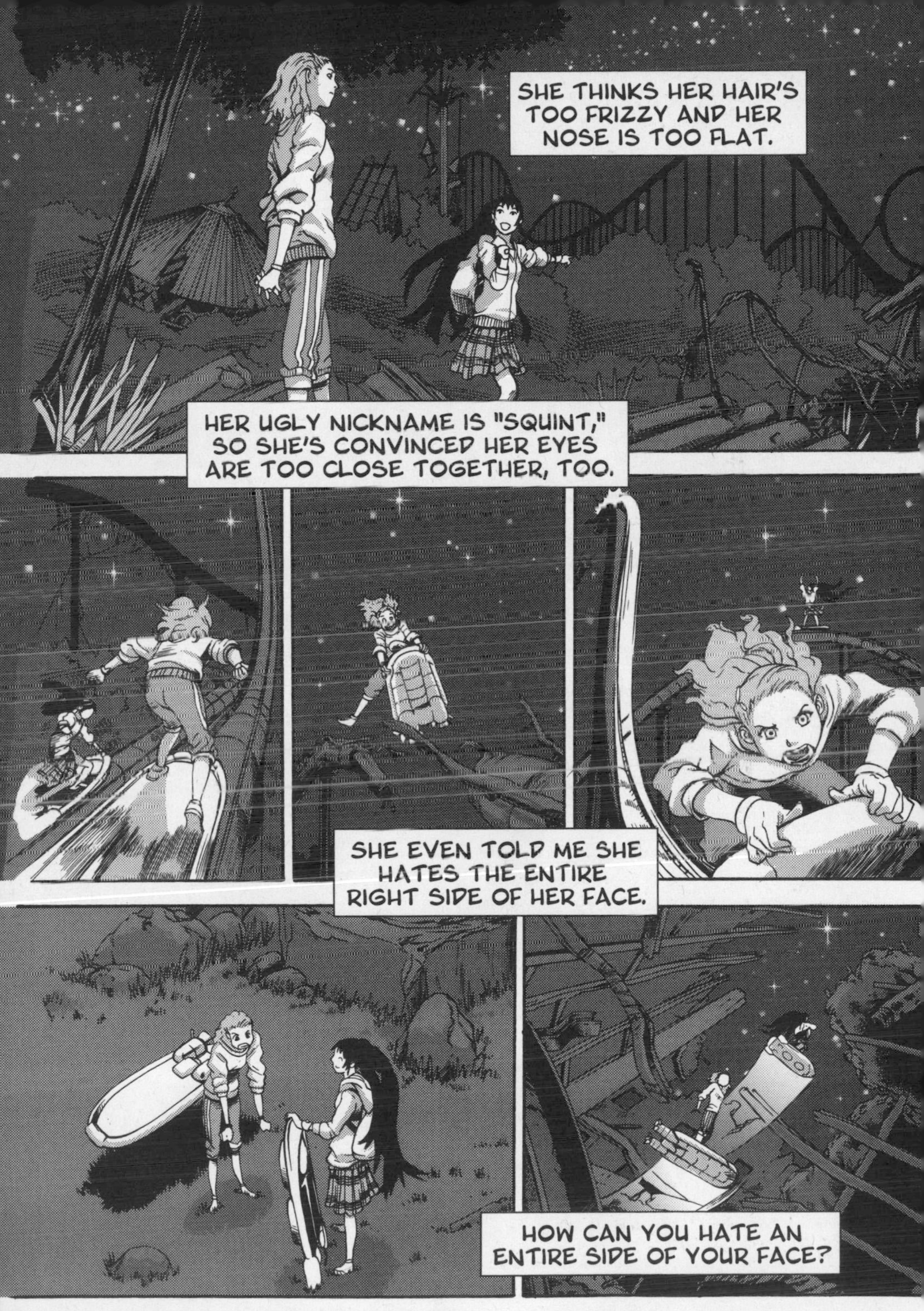
SHE THINKS HER HAIR'S TOO FRIZZY AND HER NOSE IS TOO FLAT.
HER UGLY NICKNAME IS "SQUINT," SO SHE'S CONVINCED HER EYES ARE TOO CLOSE TOGETHER, TOO.
SHE EVEN TOLD ME SHE HATES THE ENTIRE RIGHT SIDE OF HER FACE.
HOW CAN YOU HATE AN ENTIRE SIDE OF YOUR FACE?

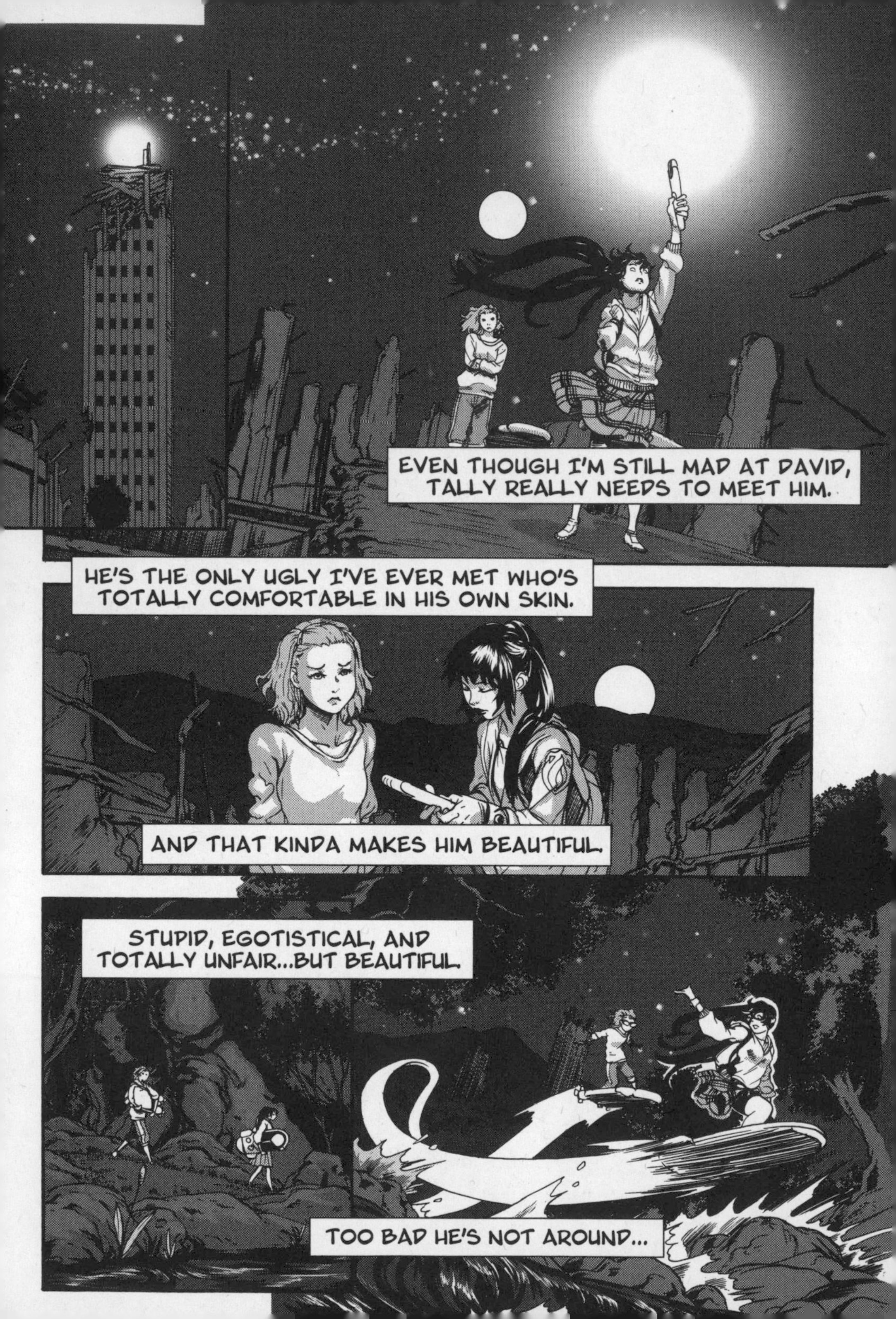
EVEN THOUGH I'M STILL MAD AT DAVID, TALLY REALLY NEEDS TO MEET HIM.
HE'S THE ONLY UGLY I'VE EVER MET WHO'S TOTALLY COMFORTABLE IN HIS OWN SKIN.
AND THAT KINDA MAKES HIM BEAUTIFUL.
STUPID, EGOTISTICAL, AND TOTALLY UNFAIR...BUT BEAUTIFUL.
TOO BAD HE'S NOT AROUND...

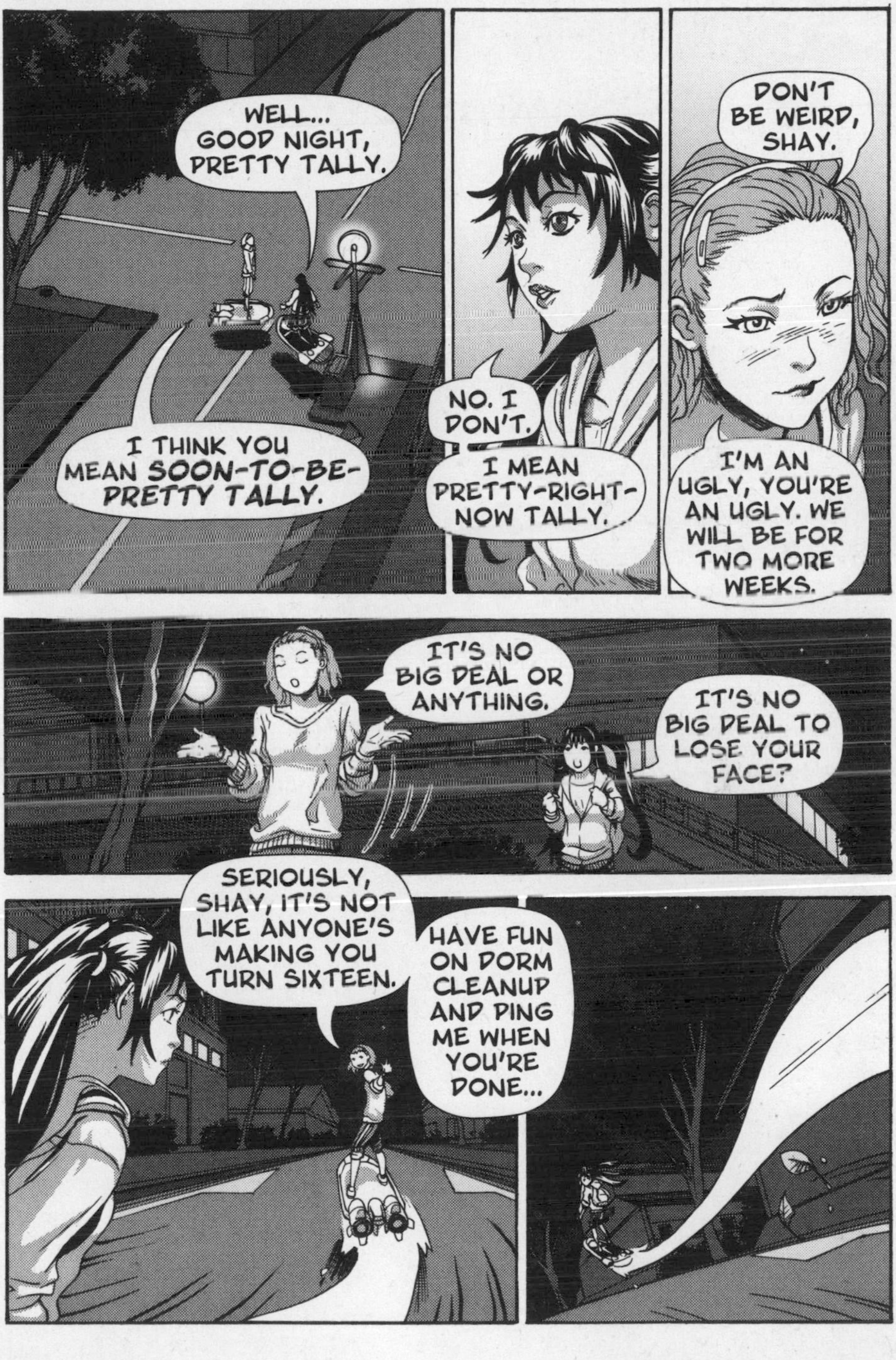
WELL... GOOD NIGHT, PRETTY TALLY.
I THINK YOU MEAN SOON-TO-BE-PRETTY TALLY.
NO. I DON'T.
I MEAN PRETTY-RIGHT-NOW TALLY.
DON'T BE WEIRD, SHAY.
I'M AN UGLY, YOU'RE AN UGLY. WE WILL BE FOR TWO MORE WEEKS.
IT'S NO BIG DEAL OR ANYTHING.
IT'S NO BIG DEAL TO LOSE YOUR FACE?
SERIOUSLY, SHAY, IT'S NOT LIKE ANYONE'S MAKING YOU TURN SIXTEEN.
HAVE FUN ON DORM CLEANUP AND PING ME WHEN YOU'RE DONE...

# CHAPTER 13

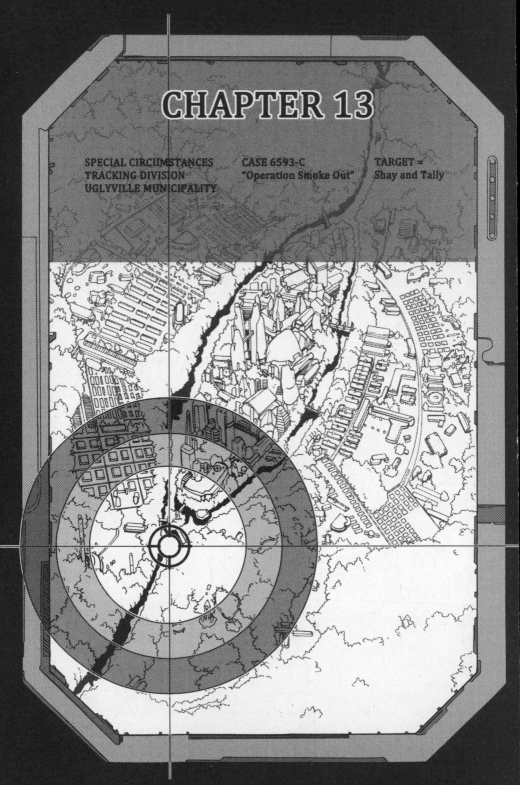

SPECIAL CIRCUMSTANCES
TRACKING DIVISION
UGLYVILLE MUNICIPALITY

CASE 6593-C
"Operation Smoke Out"

TARGET =
Shay and Tally

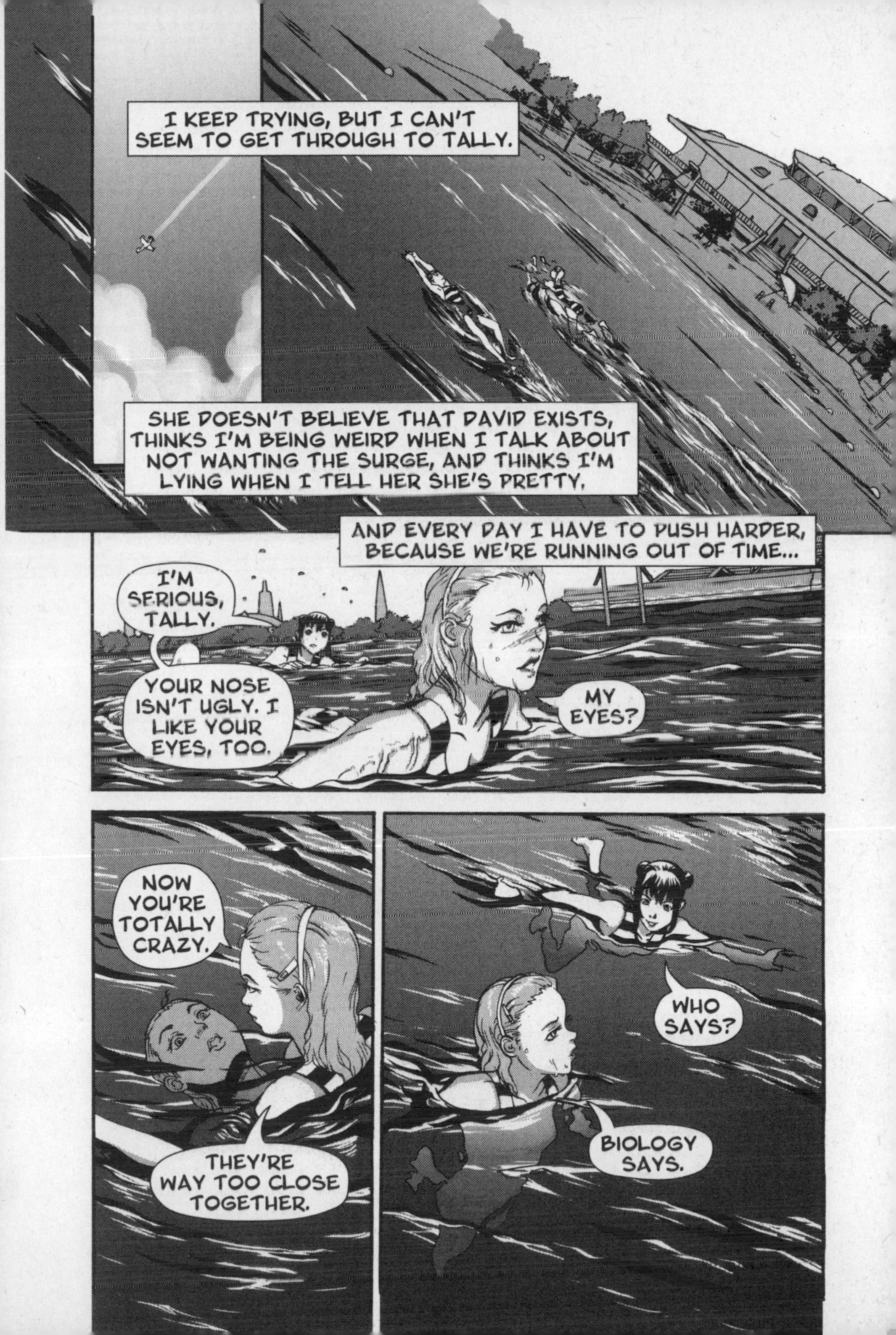
I KEEP TRYING, BUT I CAN'T SEEM TO GET THROUGH TO TALLY.
SHE DOESN'T BELIEVE THAT DAVID EXISTS, THINKS I'M BEING WEIRD WHEN I TALK ABOUT NOT WANTING THE SURGE, AND THINKS I'M LYING WHEN I TELL HER SHE'S PRETTY.
AND EVERY DAY I HAVE TO PUSH HARDER, BECAUSE WE'RE RUNNING OUT OF TIME...
I'M SERIOUS, TALLY.
YOUR NOSE ISN'T UGLY. I LIKE YOUR EYES, TOO.
MY EYES?
NOW YOU'RE TOTALLY CRAZY.
THEY'RE WAY TOO CLOSE TOGETHER.
WHO SAYS?
BIOLOGY SAYS.

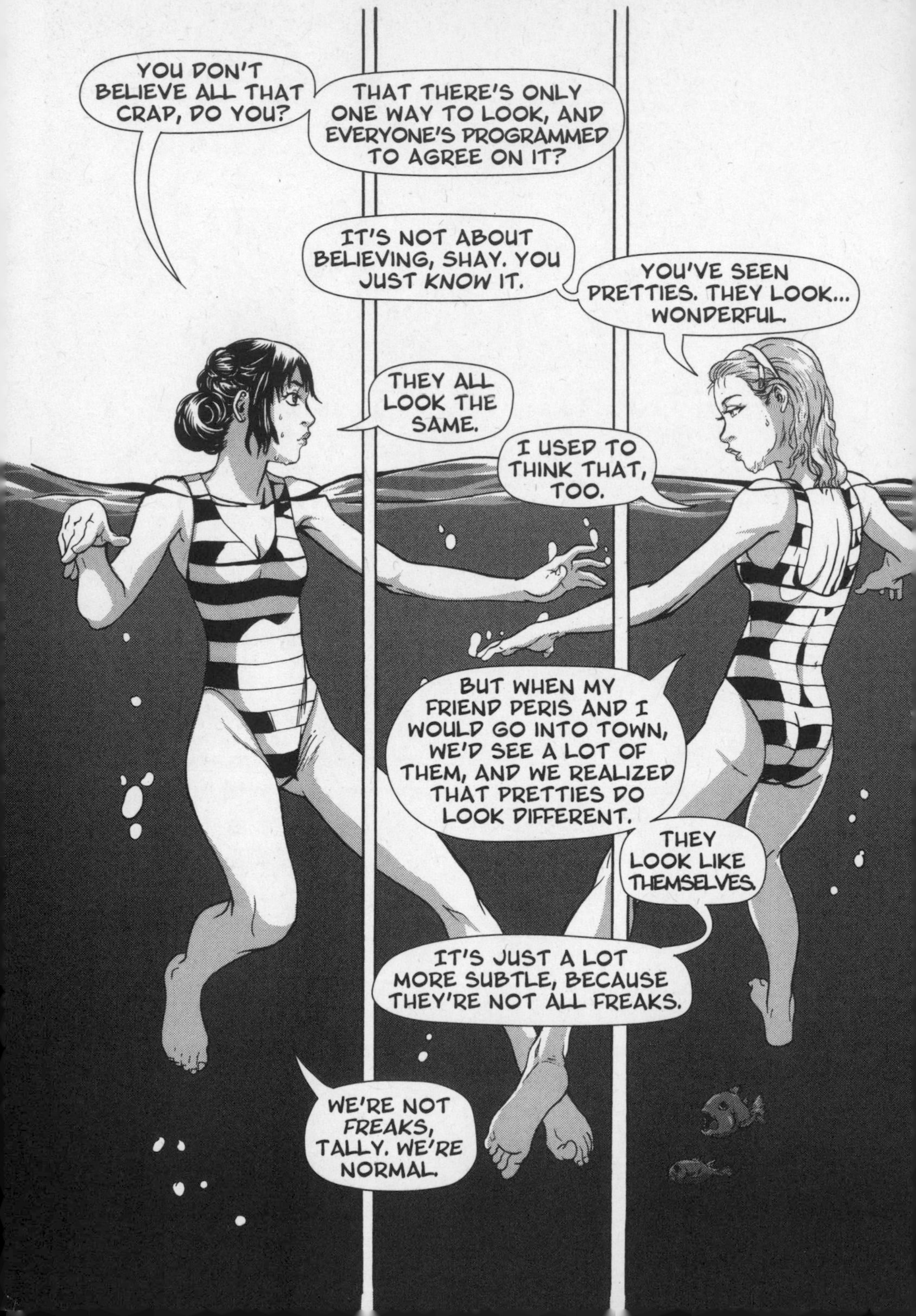
YOU DON'T BELIEVE ALL THAT CRAP, DO YOU?
THAT THERE'S ONLY ONE WAY TO LOOK, AND EVERYONE'S PROGRAMMED TO AGREE ON IT?
IT'S NOT ABOUT BELIEVING, SHAY. YOU JUST KNOW IT.
YOU'VE SEEN PRETTIES. THEY LOOK... WONDERFUL.
THEY ALL LOOK THE SAME.
I USED TO THINK THAT, TOO.
BUT WHEN MY FRIEND PERIS AND I WOULD GO INTO TOWN, WE'D SEE A LOT OF THEM, AND WE REALIZED THAT PRETTIES DO LOOK DIFFERENT.
THEY LOOK LIKE THEMSELVES.
IT'S JUST A LOT MORE SUBTLE, BECAUSE THEY'RE NOT ALL FREAKS.
WE'RE NOT FREAKS, TALLY. WE'RE NORMAL.

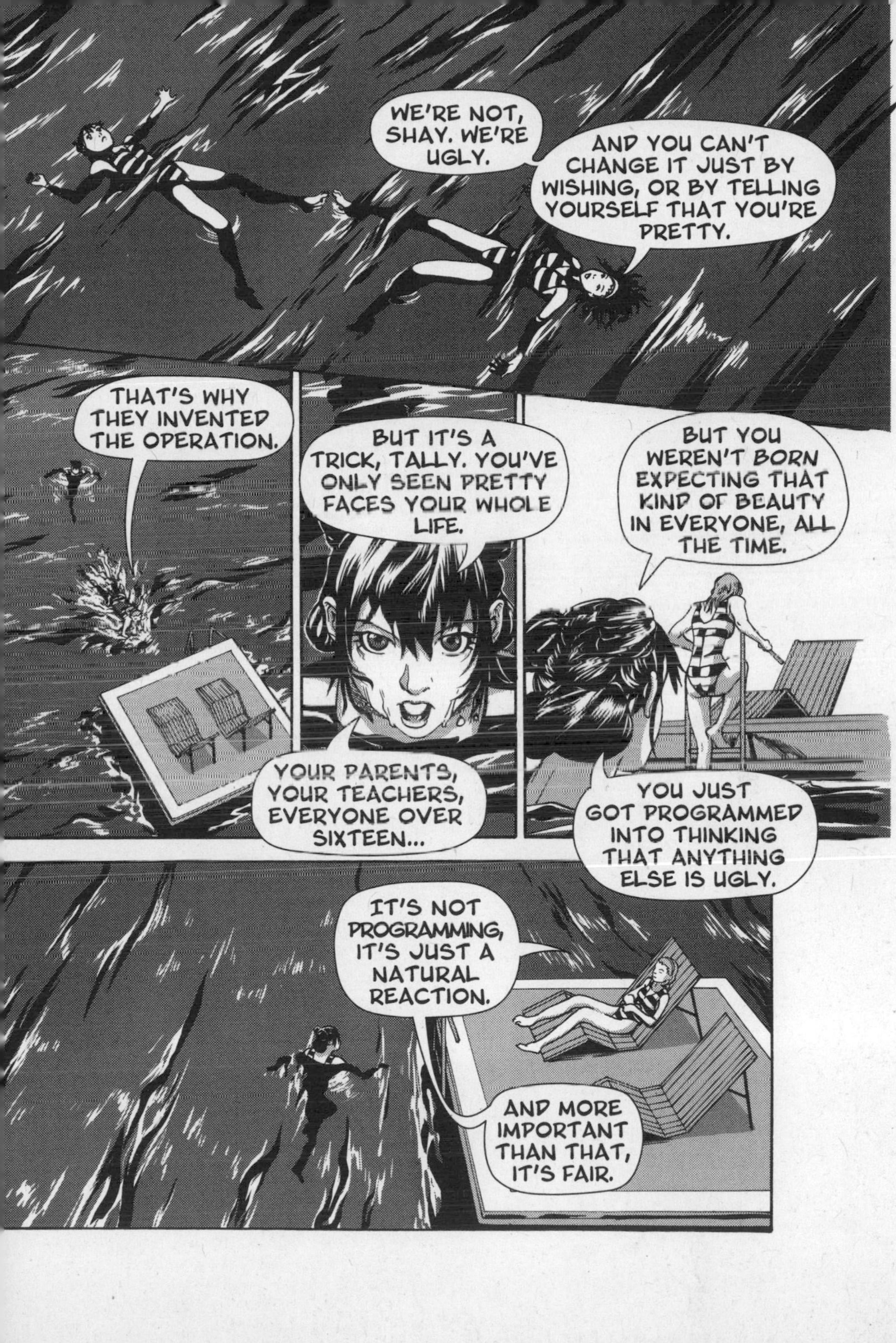
WE'RE NOT, SHAY. WE'RE UGLY.
AND YOU CAN'T CHANGE IT JUST BY WISHING, OR BY TELLING YOURSELF THAT YOU'RE PRETTY.
THAT'S WHY THEY INVENTED THE OPERATION.
BUT IT'S A TRICK, TALLY. YOU'VE ONLY SEEN PRETTY FACES YOUR WHOLE LIFE.
YOUR PARENTS, YOUR TEACHERS, EVERYONE OVER SIXTEEN...
BUT YOU WEREN'T BORN EXPECTING THAT KIND OF BEAUTY IN EVERYONE, ALL THE TIME.
YOU JUST GOT PROGRAMMED INTO THINKING THAT ANYTHING ELSE IS UGLY.
IT'S NOT PROGRAMMING, IT'S JUST A NATURAL REACTION.
AND MORE IMPORTANT THAN THAT, IT'S FAIR.

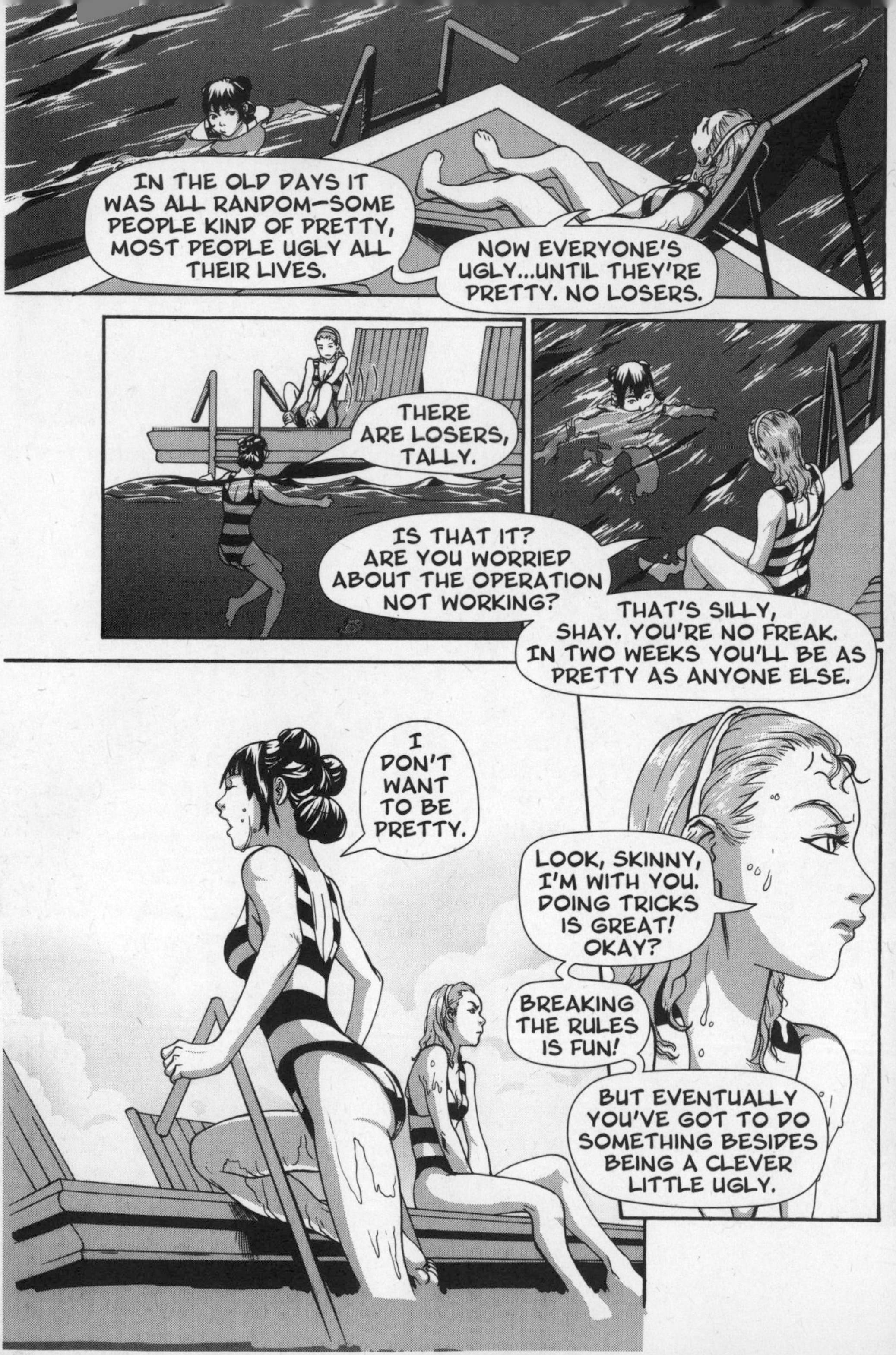
IN THE OLD DAYS IT WAS ALL RANDOM—SOME PEOPLE KIND OF PRETTY, MOST PEOPLE UGLY ALL THEIR LIVES.
NOW EVERYONE'S UGLY...UNTIL THEY'RE PRETTY. NO LOSERS.
THERE ARE LOSERS, TALLY.
IS THAT IT? ARE YOU WORRIED ABOUT THE OPERATION NOT WORKING?
THAT'S SILLY, SHAY. YOU'RE NO FREAK. IN TWO WEEKS YOU'LL BE AS PRETTY AS ANYONE ELSE.
I DON'T WANT TO BE PRETTY.
LOOK, SKINNY, I'M WITH YOU. DOING TRICKS IS GREAT! OKAY?
BREAKING THE RULES IS FUN!
BUT EVENTUALLY YOU'VE GOT TO DO SOMETHING BESIDES BEING A CLEVER LITTLE UGLY.

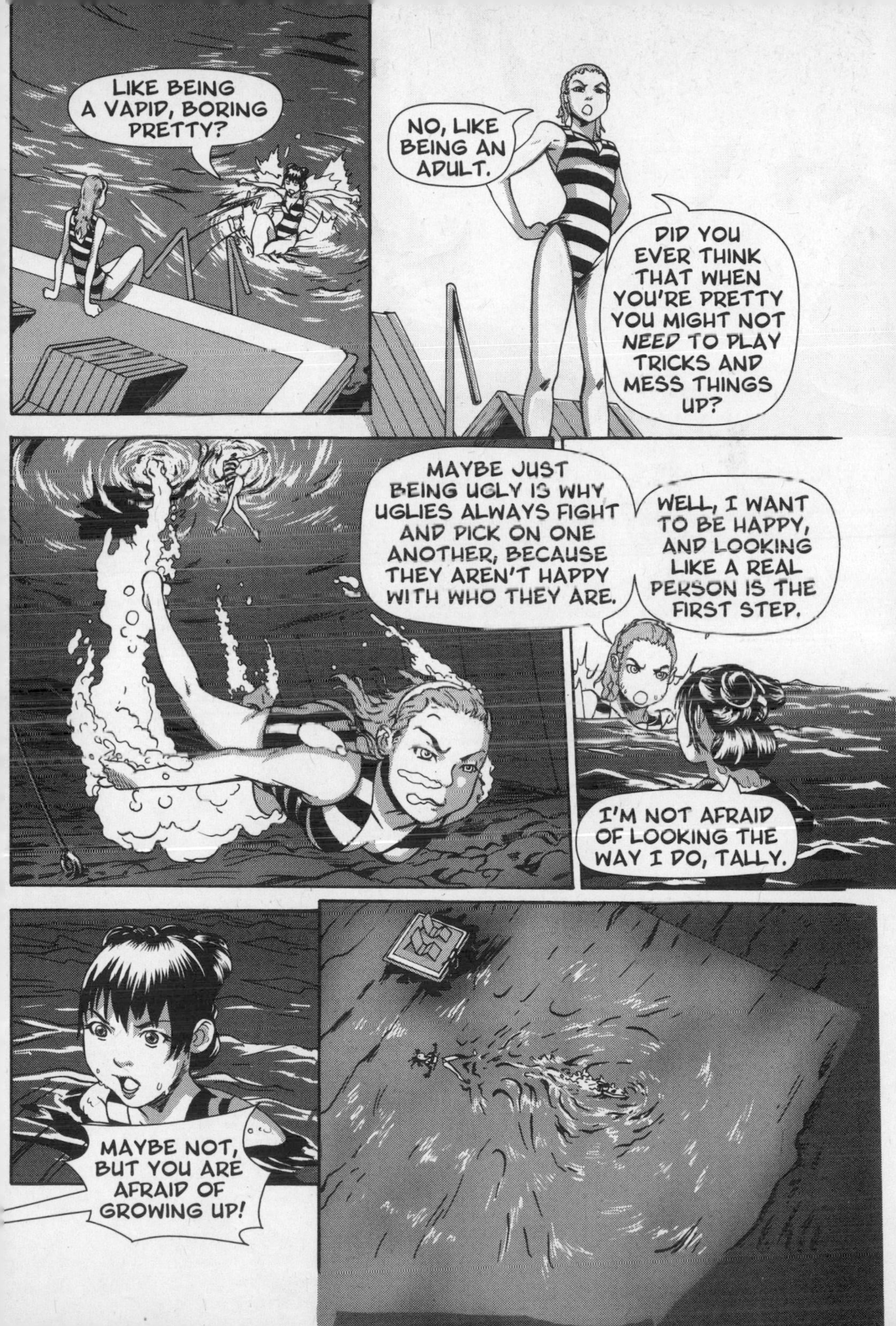
LIKE BEING A VAPID, BORING PRETTY?
NO, LIKE BEING AN ADULT.
DID YOU EVER THINK THAT WHEN YOU'RE PRETTY YOU MIGHT NOT NEED TO PLAY TRICKS AND MESS THINGS UP?
MAYBE JUST BEING UGLY IS WHY UGLIES ALWAYS FIGHT AND PICK ON ONE ANOTHER, BECAUSE THEY AREN'T HAPPY WITH WHO THEY ARE.
WELL, I WANT TO BE HAPPY, AND LOOKING LIKE A REAL PERSON IS THE FIRST STEP.
I'M NOT AFRAID OF LOOKING THE WAY I DO, TALLY.
MAYBE NOT, BUT YOU ARE AFRAID OF GROWING UP!

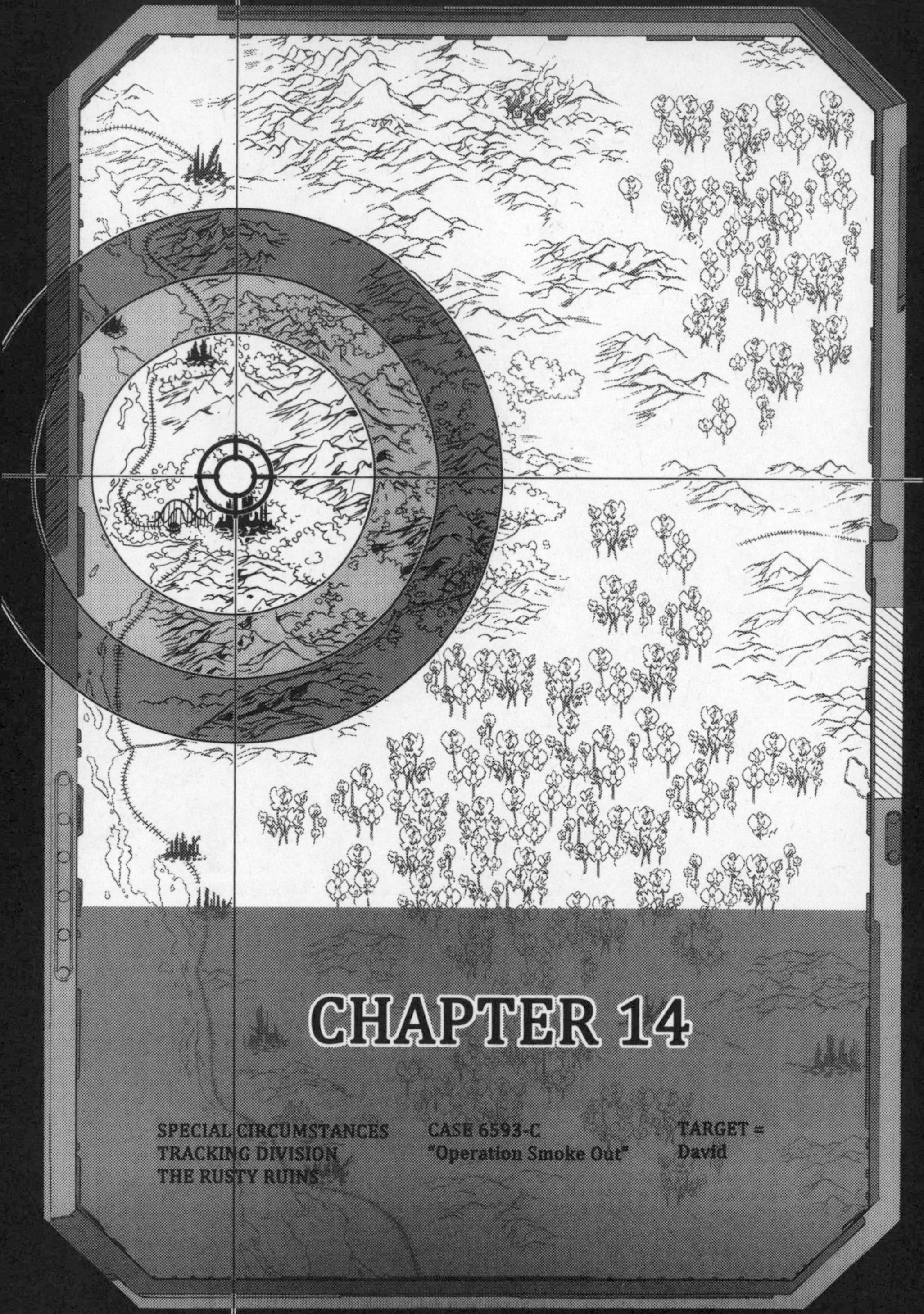
CHAPTER 14
SPECIAL CIRCUMSTANCES
TRACKING DIVISION
THE RUSTY RUINS
CASE 6593-C
"Operation Smoke Out"
TARGET =
David

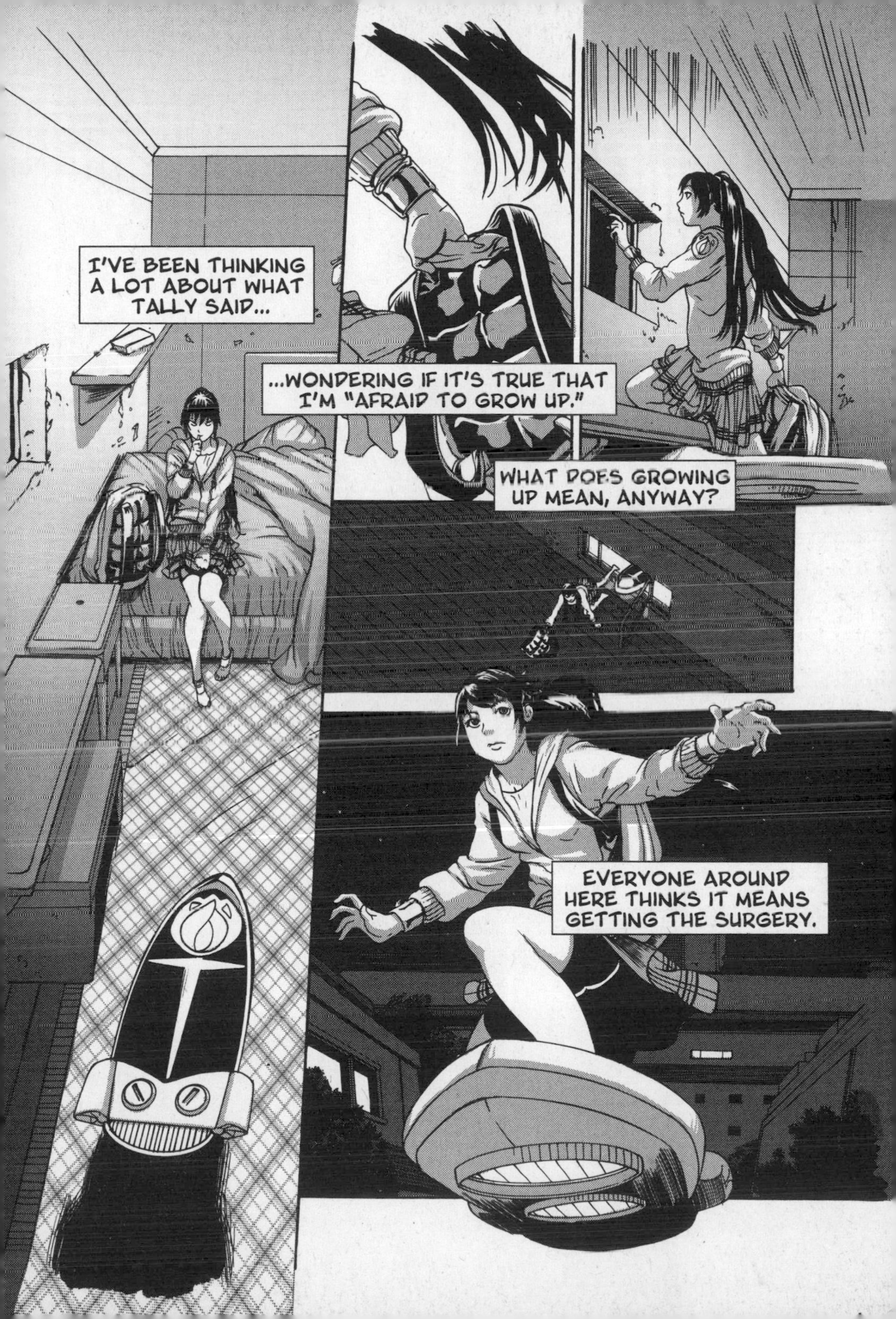
I'VE BEEN THINKING A LOT ABOUT WHAT TALLY SAID...
...WONDERING IF IT'S TRUE THAT I'M "AFRAID TO GROW UP."
WHAT DOES GROWING UP MEAN, ANYWAY?
EVERYONE AROUND HERE THINKS IT MEANS GETTING THE SURGERY.

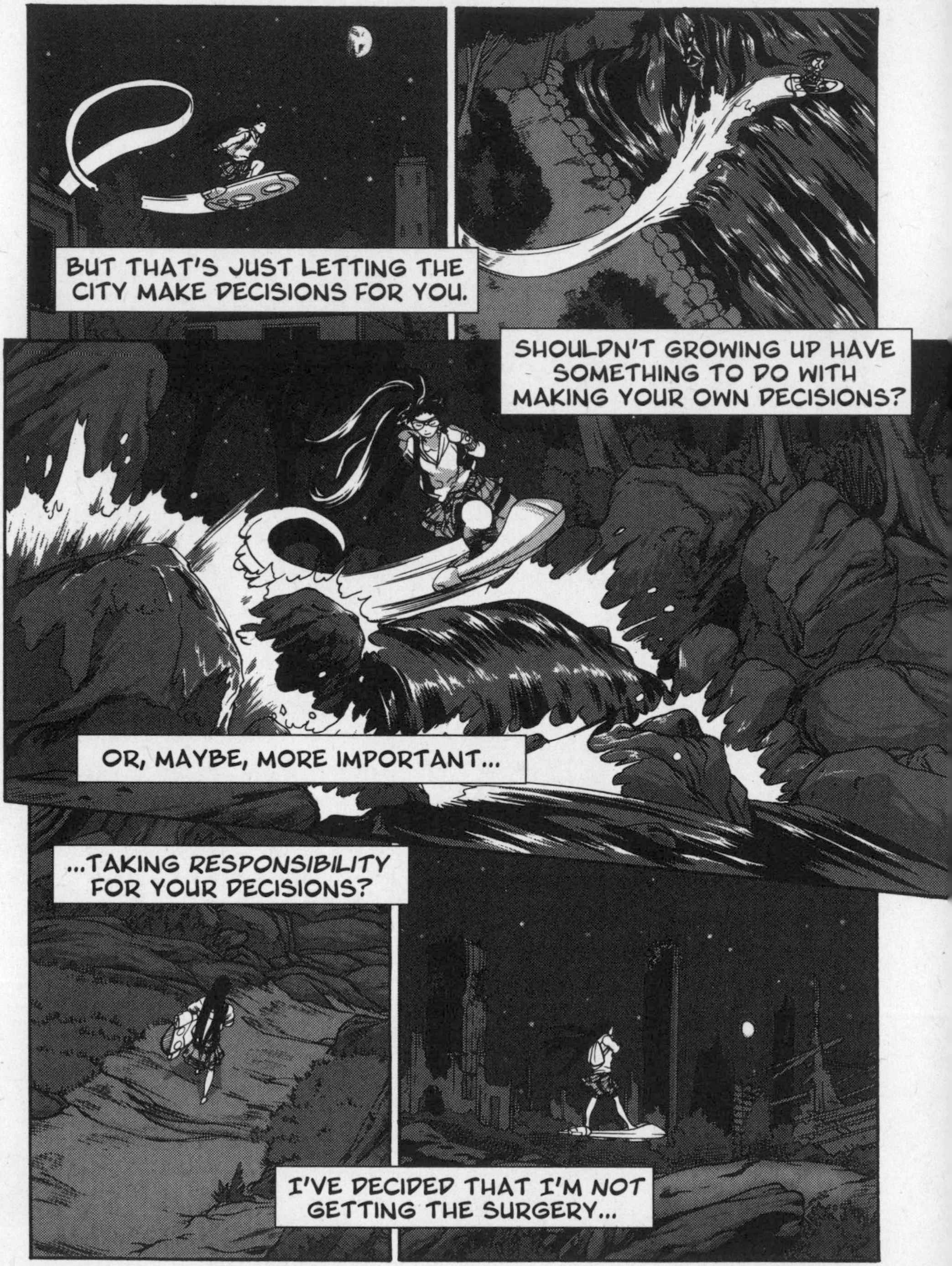
BUT THAT'S JUST LETTING THE CITY MAKE DECISIONS FOR YOU.
SHOULDN'T GROWING UP HAVE SOMETHING TO DO WITH MAKING YOUR OWN DECISIONS?
OR, MAYBE, MORE IMPORTANT...
...TAKING *RESPONSIBILITY* FOR YOUR DECISIONS?
I'VE DECIDED THAT I'M NOT GETTING THE SURGERY...

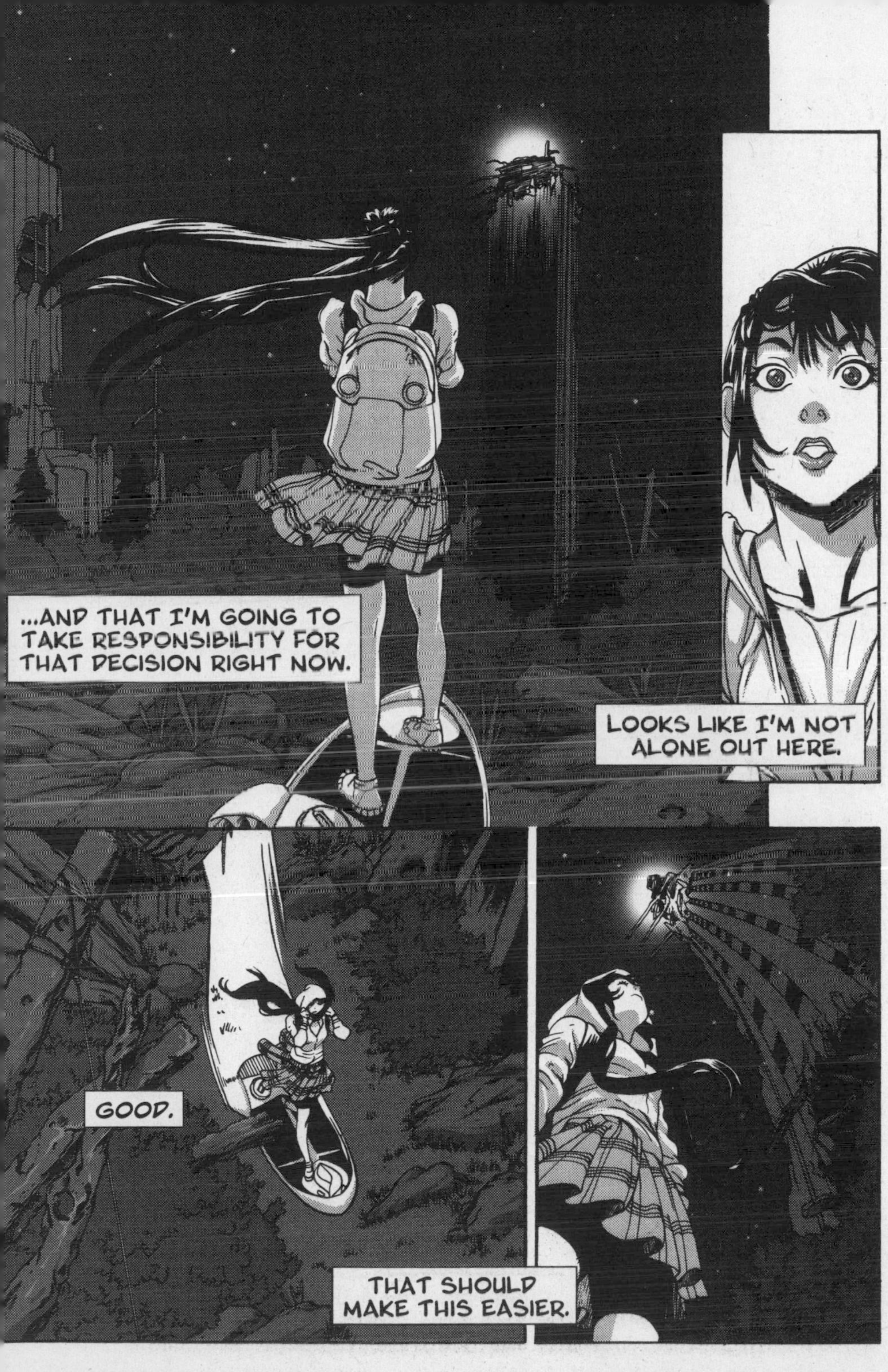
...AND THAT I'M GOING TO TAKE RESPONSIBILITY FOR THAT DECISION RIGHT NOW.
LOOKS LIKE I'M NOT ALONE OUT HERE.
GOOD.
THAT SHOULD MAKE THIS EASIER.

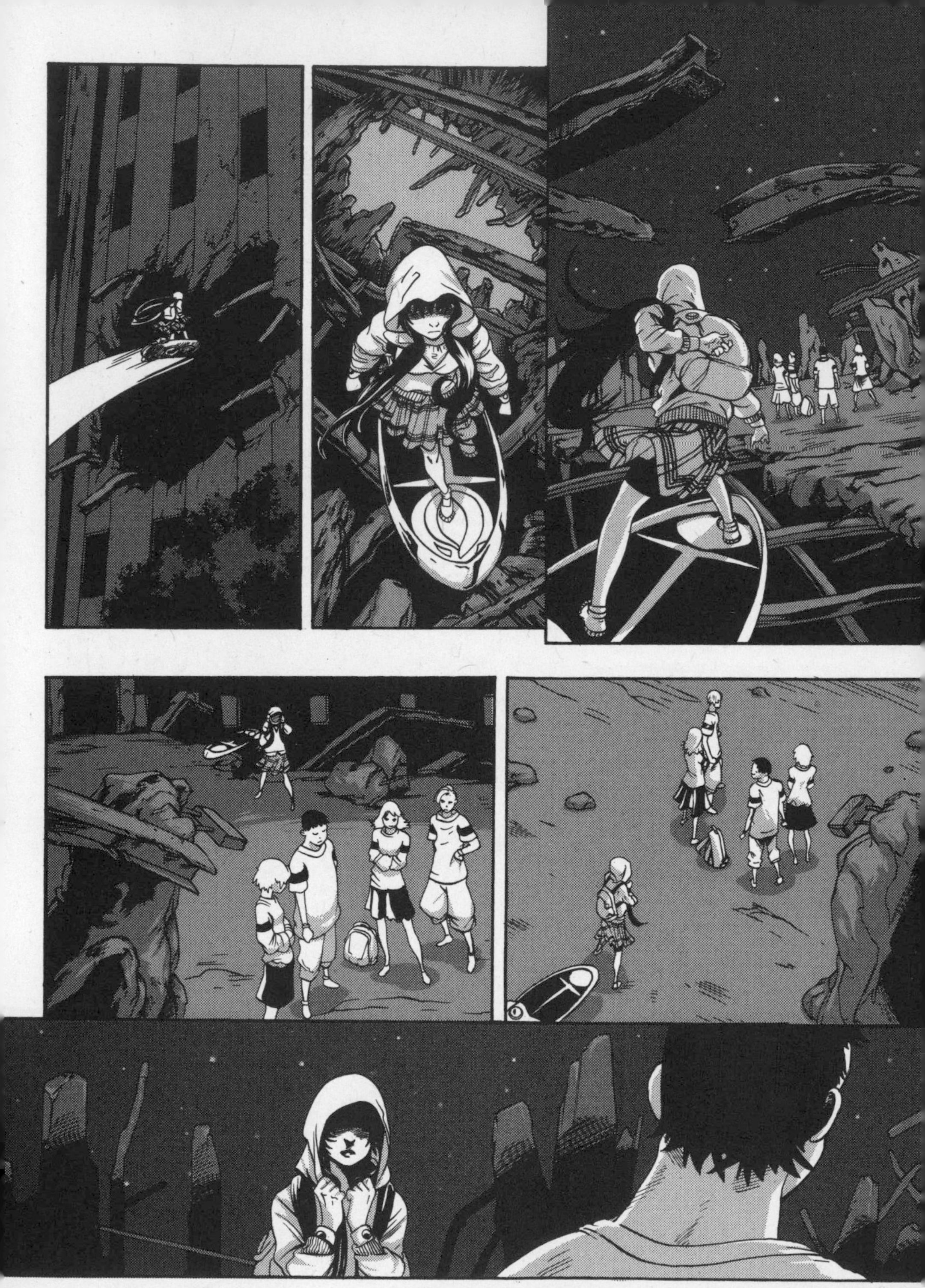

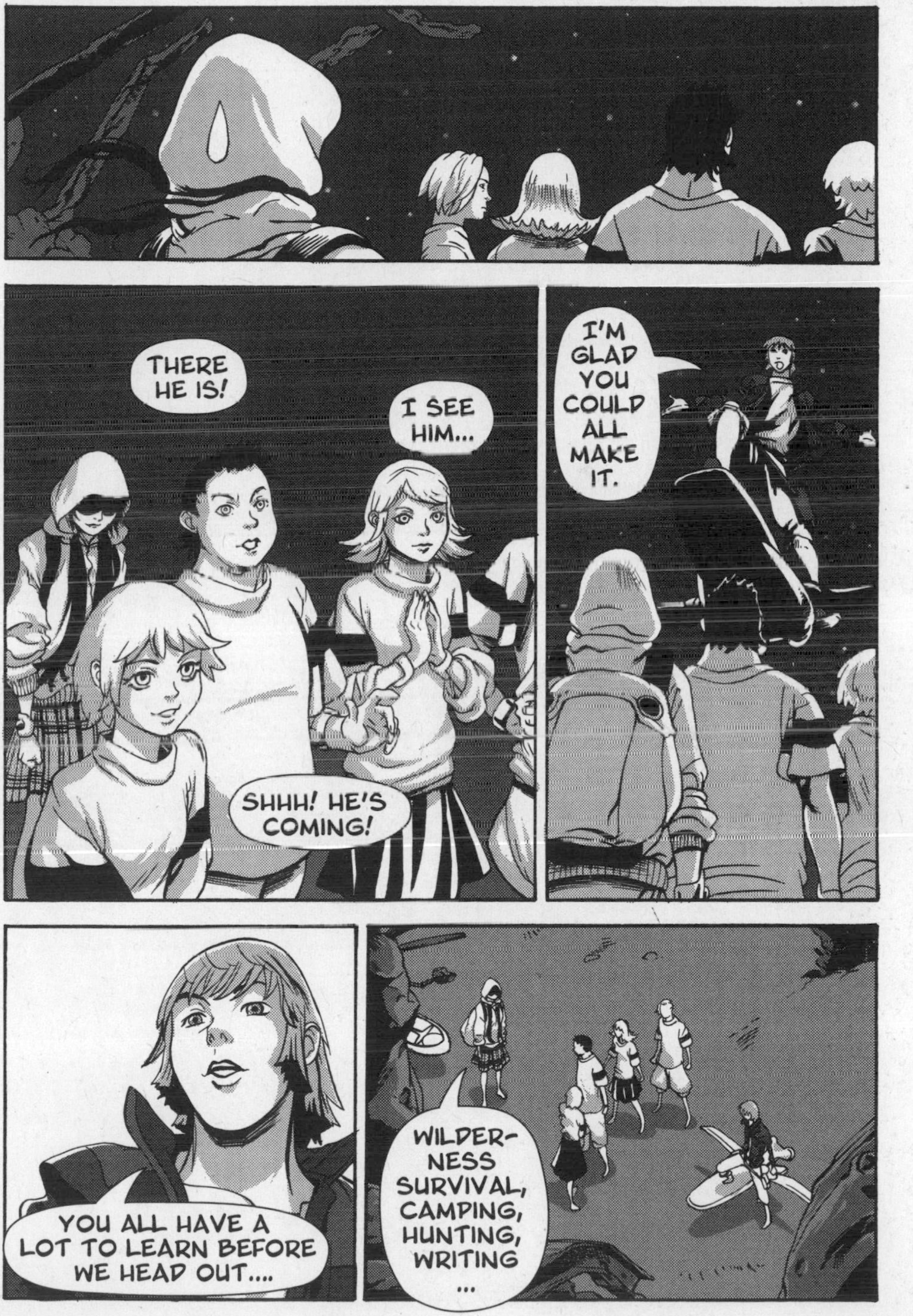
THERE HE IS!
I SEE HIM...
SHHH! HE'S COMING!
I'M GLAD YOU COULD ALL MAKE IT.
YOU ALL HAVE A LOT TO LEARN BEFORE WE HEAD OUT....
WILDER-NESS SURVIVAL, CAMPING, HUNTING, WRITING ...

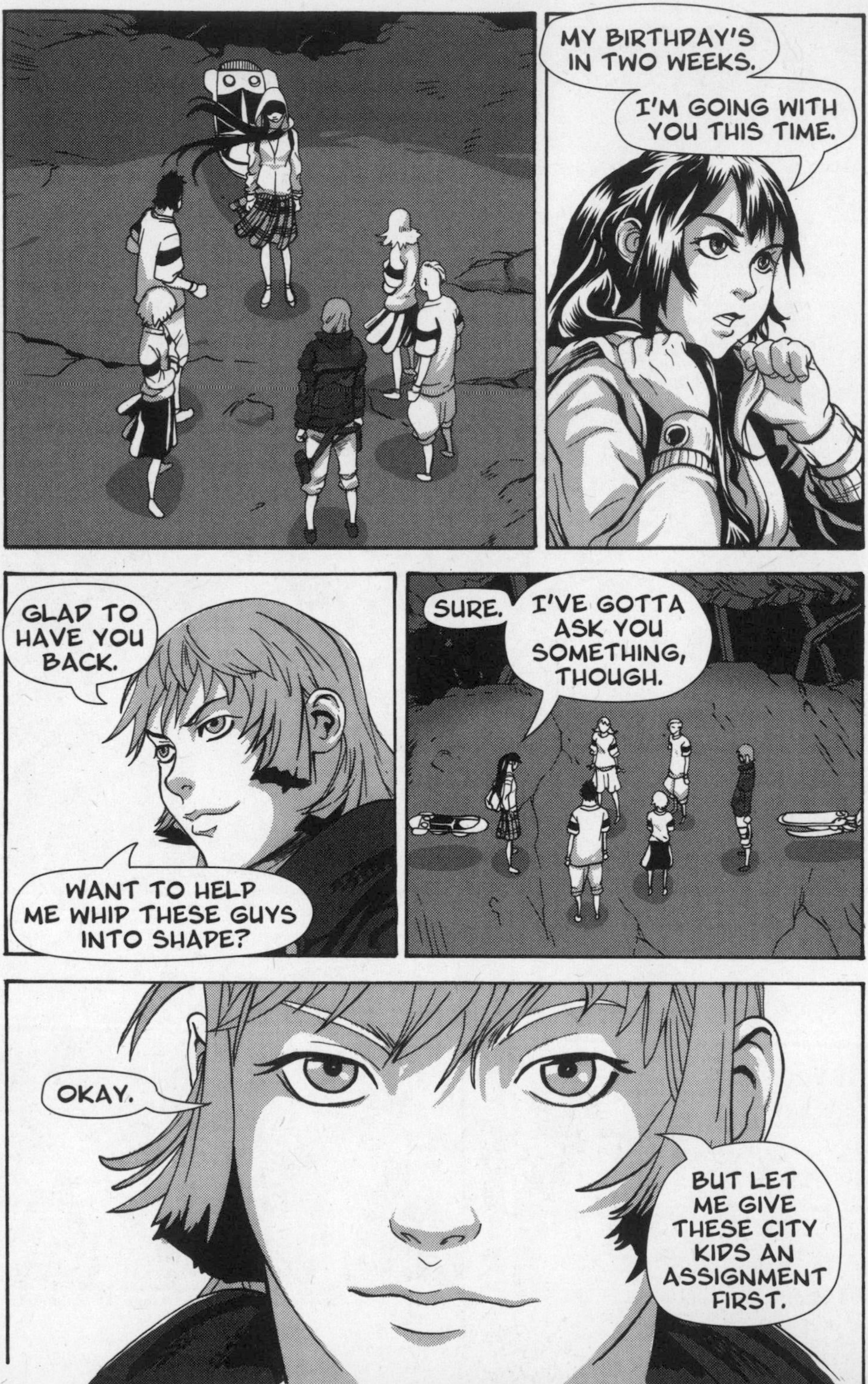
MY BIRTHDAY'S IN TWO WEEKS.
I'M GOING WITH YOU THIS TIME.
GLAD TO HAVE YOU BACK.
WANT TO HELP ME WHIP THESE GUYS INTO SHAPE?
SURE.
I'VE GOTTA ASK YOU SOMETHING, THOUGH.
OKAY.
BUT LET ME GIVE THESE CITY KIDS AN ASSIGNMENT FIRST.

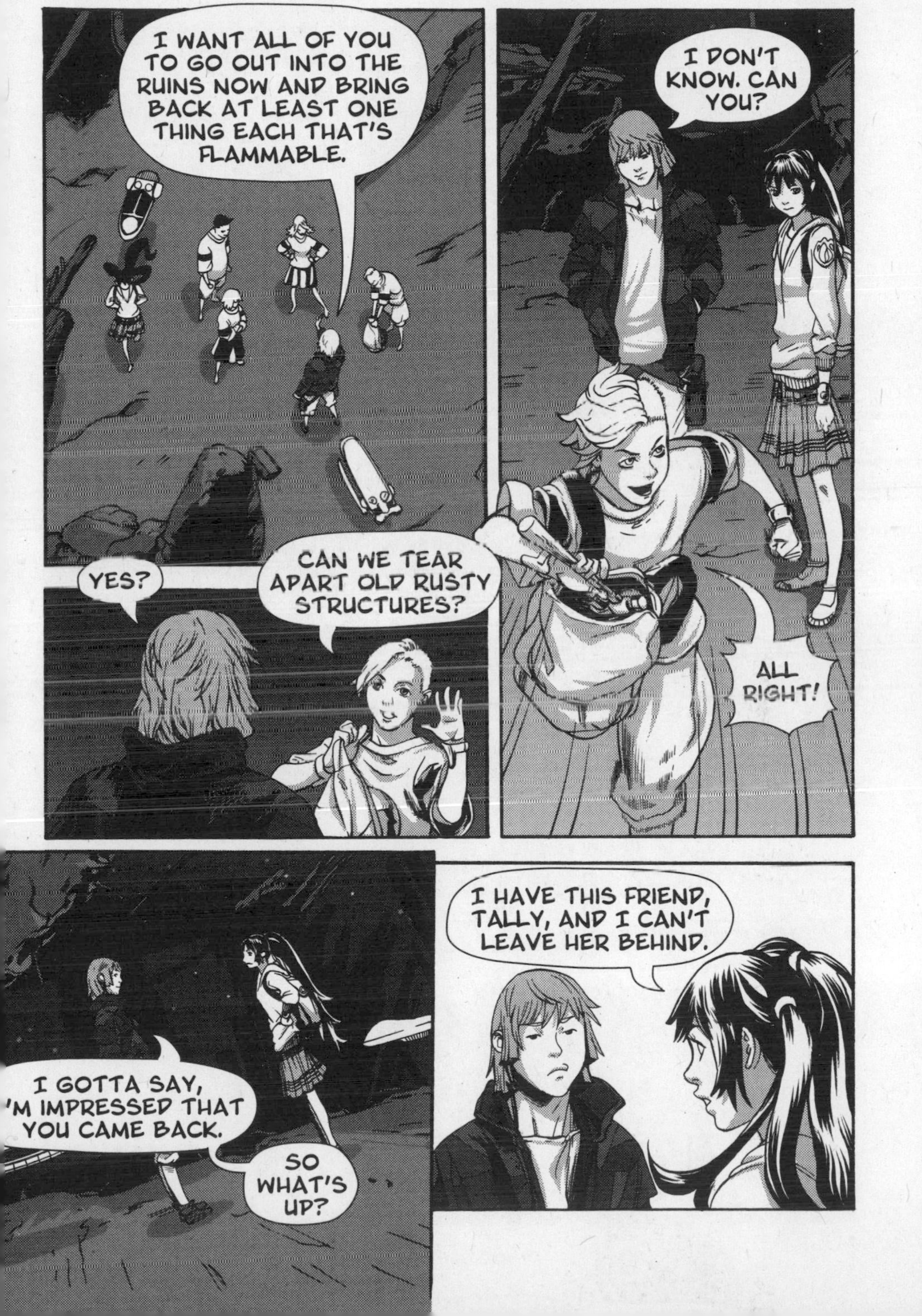

I WANT ALL OF YOU TO GO OUT INTO THE RUINS NOW AND BRING BACK AT LEAST ONE THING EACH THAT'S FLAMMABLE.
YES?
CAN WE TEAR APART OLD RUSTY STRUCTURES?
I DON'T KNOW. CAN YOU?
ALL RIGHT!
I GOTTA SAY, 'M IMPRESSED THAT YOU CAME BACK.
SO WHAT'S UP?
I HAVE THIS FRIEND, TALLY, AND I CAN'T LEAVE HER BEHIND.

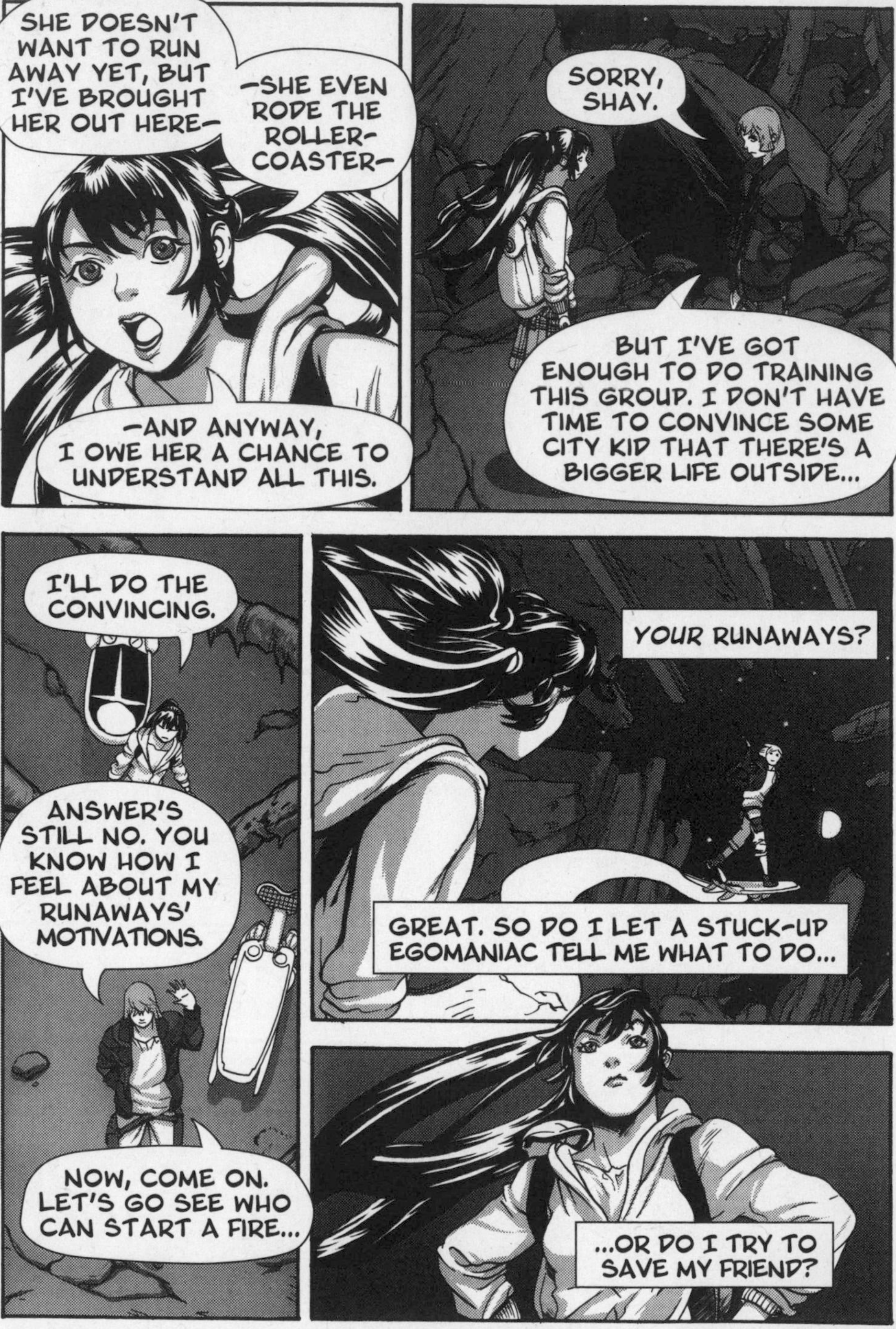
SHE DOESN'T WANT TO RUN AWAY YET, BUT I'VE BROUGHT HER OUT HERE—
—SHE EVEN RODE THE ROLLER-COASTER—
—AND ANYWAY, I OWE HER A CHANCE TO UNDERSTAND ALL THIS.
SORRY, SHAY.
BUT I'VE GOT ENOUGH TO DO TRAINING THIS GROUP. I DON'T HAVE TIME TO CONVINCE SOME CITY KID THAT THERE'S A BIGGER LIFE OUTSIDE...
I'LL DO THE CONVINCING.
ANSWER'S STILL NO. YOU KNOW HOW I FEEL ABOUT MY RUNAWAYS' MOTIVATIONS.
NOW, COME ON. LET'S GO SEE WHO CAN START A FIRE...
YOUR RUNAWAYS?
GREAT. SO DO I LET A STUCK-UP EGOMANIAC TELL ME WHAT TO DO...
...OR DO I TRY TO SAVE MY FRIEND?

# CHAPTER 15

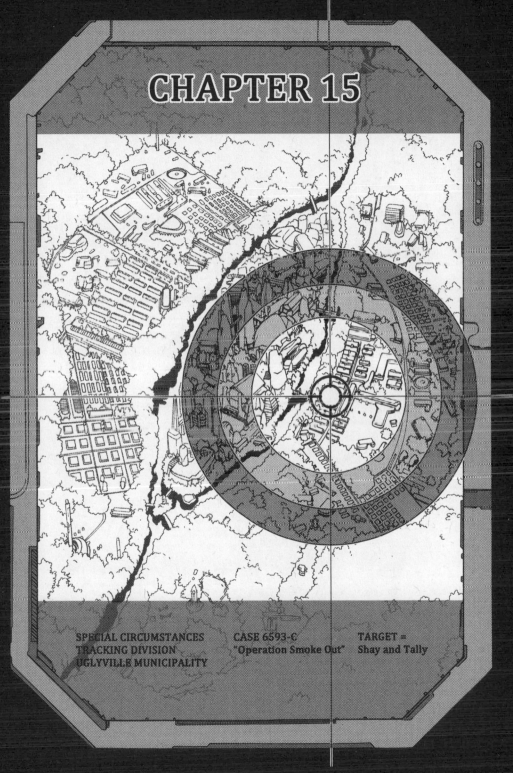

SPECIAL CIRCUMSTANCES
TRACKING DIVISION
UGLYVILLE MUNICIPALITY

CASE 6593-C
"Operation Smoke Out"

TARGET =
Shay and Tally

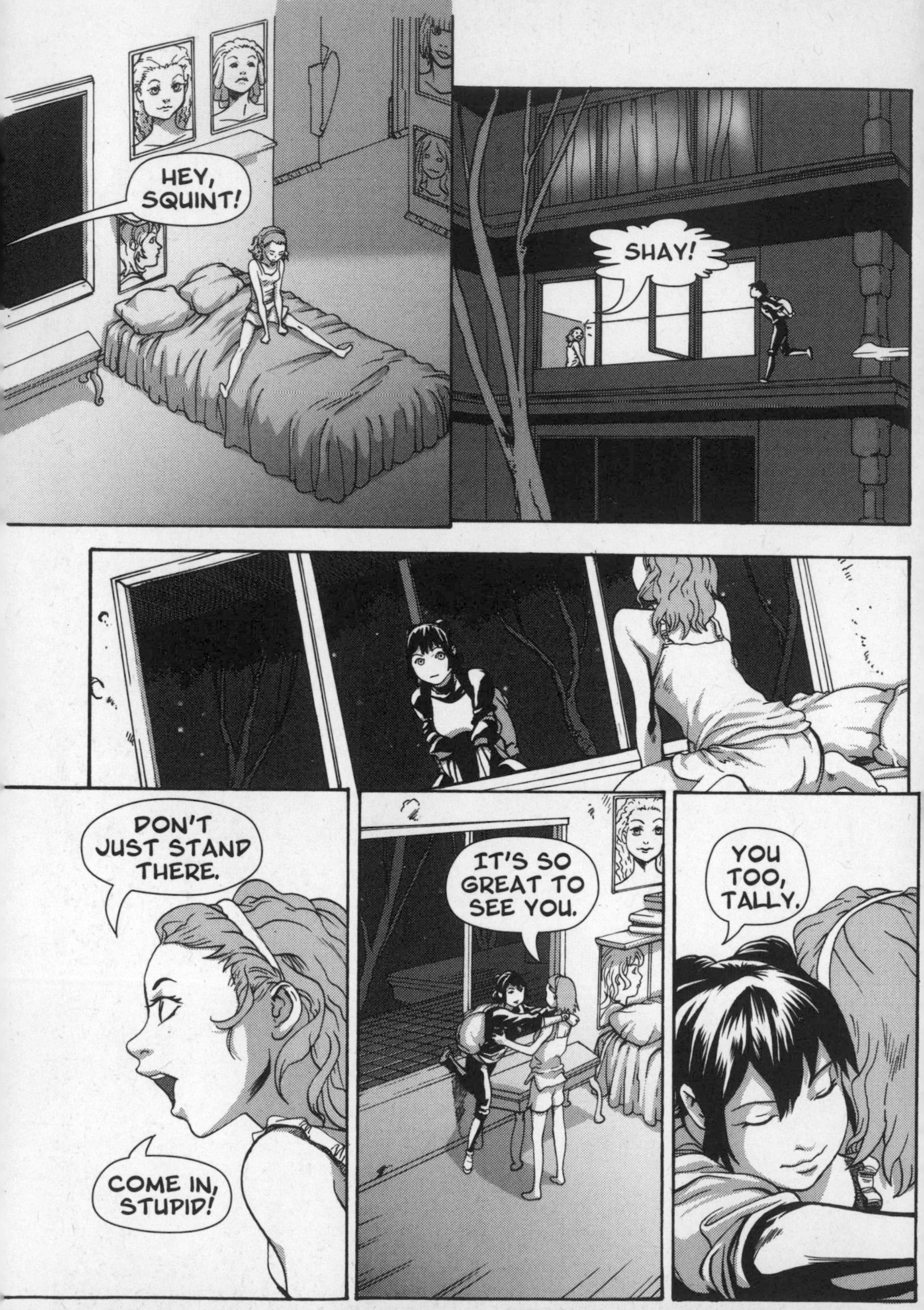
HEY, SQUINT!
SHAY!
DON'T JUST STAND THERE.
COME IN, STUPID!
IT'S SO GREAT TO SEE YOU.
YOU TOO, TALLY.

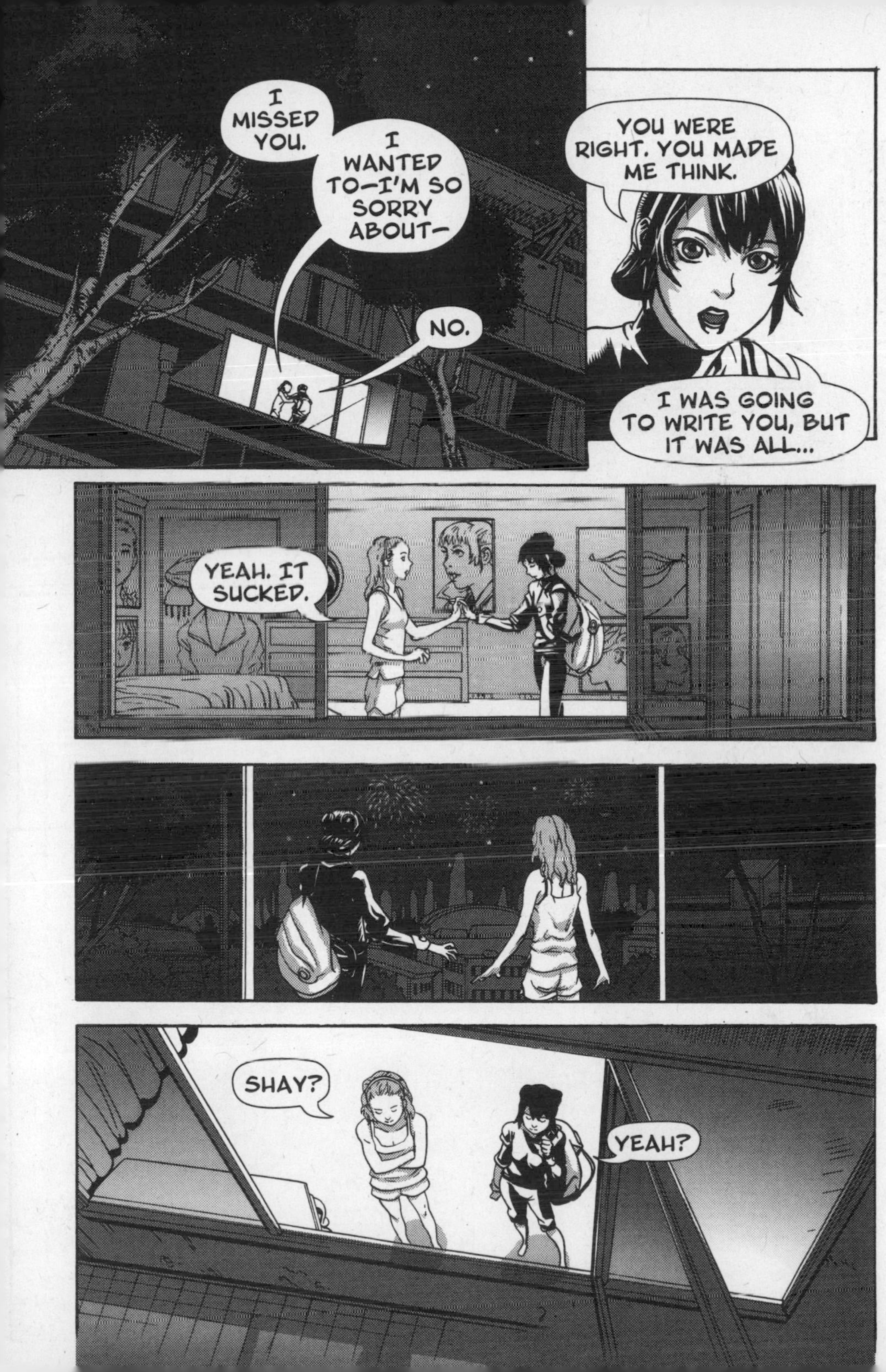
I MISSED YOU.
I WANTED TO—I'M SO SORRY ABOUT—
NO.
YOU WERE RIGHT. YOU MADE ME THINK.
I WAS GOING TO WRITE YOU, BUT IT WAS ALL...
YEAH. IT SUCKED.
SHAY?
YEAH?

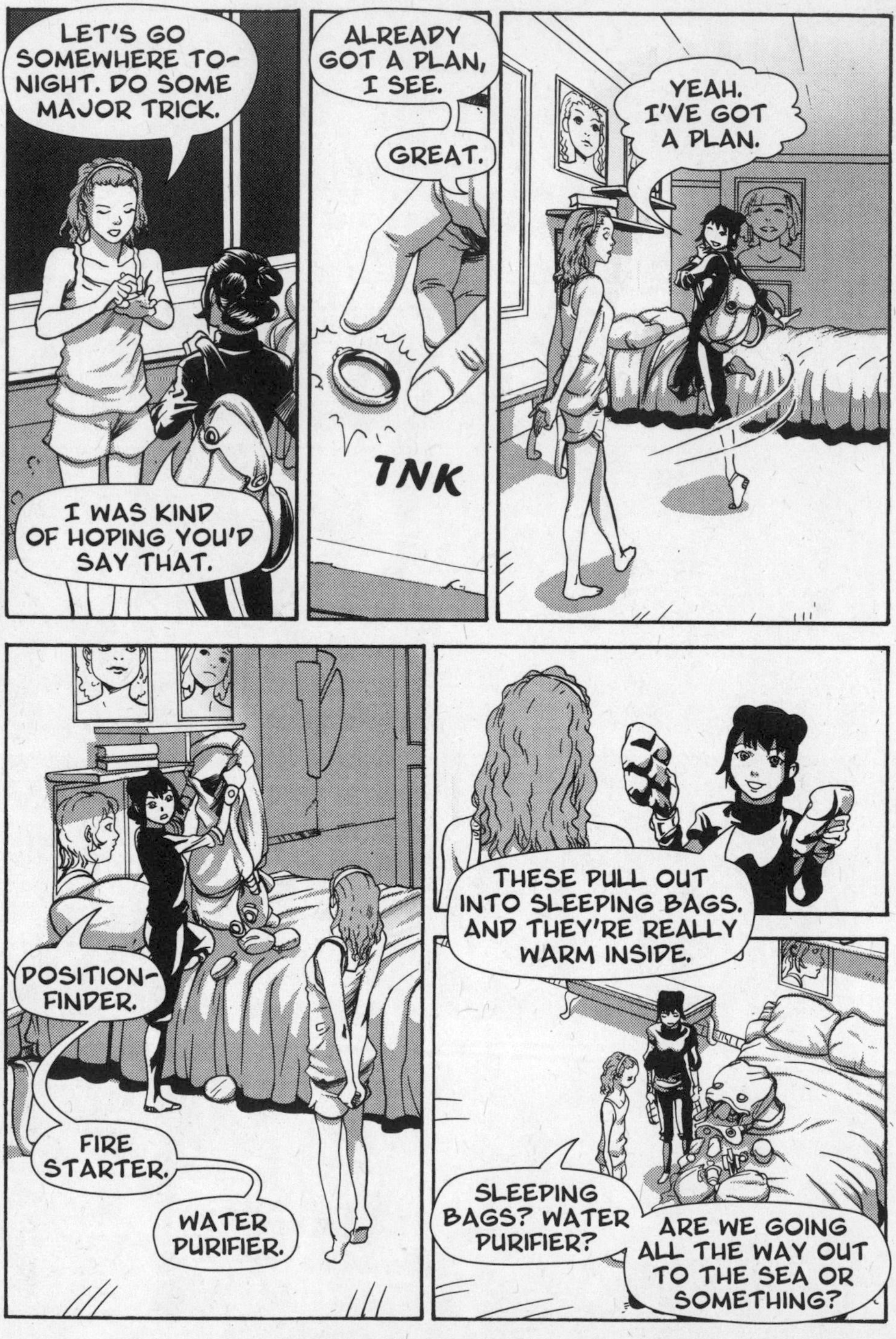
LET'S GO SOMEWHERE TO-NIGHT. DO SOME MAJOR TRICK.
I WAS KIND OF HOPING YOU'D SAY THAT.
ALREADY GOT A PLAN, I SEE.
GREAT.
TNK
YEAH. I'VE GOT A PLAN.
POSITION-FINDER.
FIRE STARTER.
WATER PURIFIER.
THESE PULL OUT INTO SLEEPING BAGS. AND THEY'RE REALLY WARM INSIDE.
SLEEPING BAGS? WATER PURIFIER?
ARE WE GOING ALL THE WAY OUT TO THE SEA OR SOMETHING?

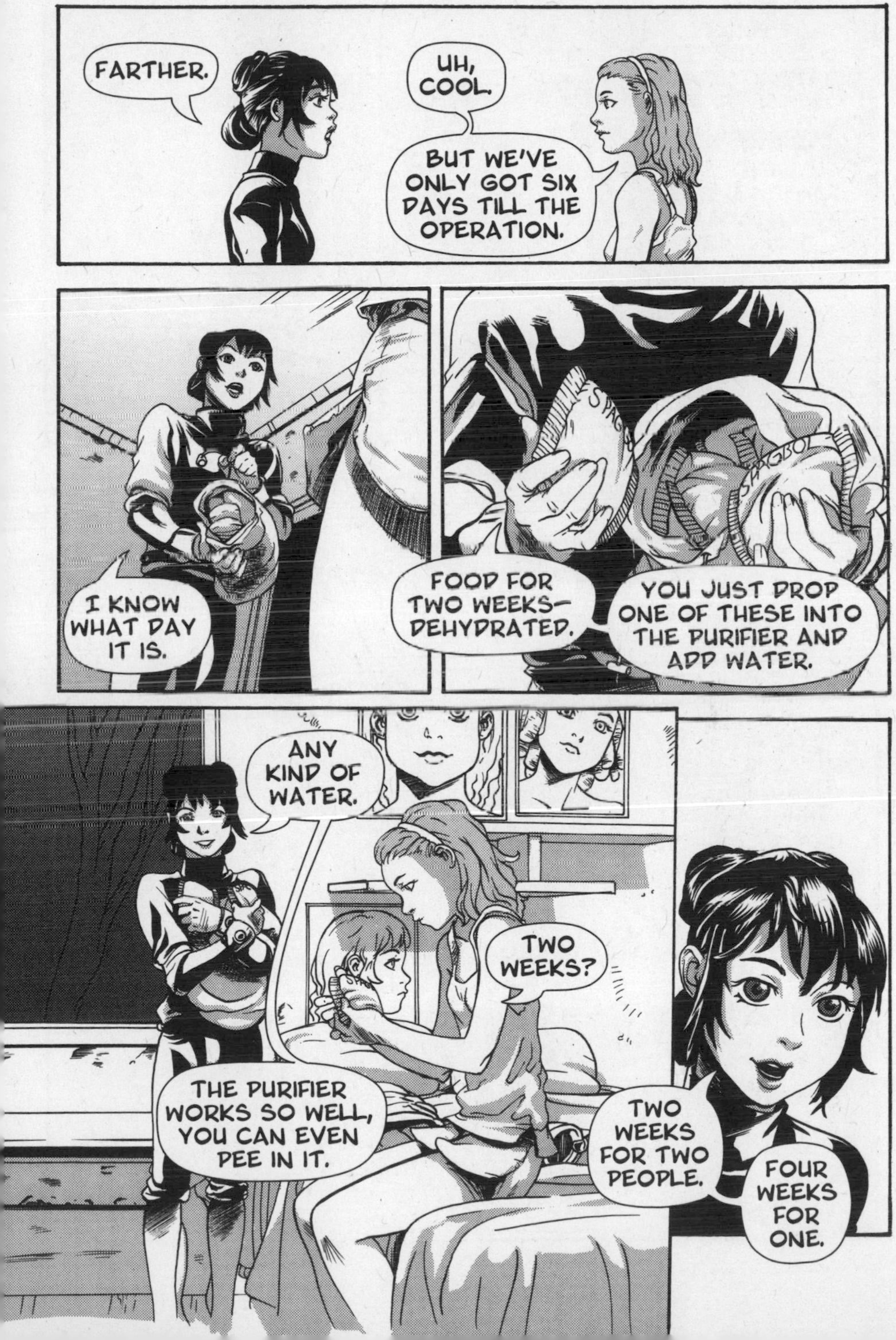
FARTHER.
UH, COOL.
BUT WE'VE ONLY GOT SIX DAYS TILL THE OPERATION.
I KNOW WHAT DAY IT IS.
SPAGBOL
SPAGBOL
FOOD FOR TWO WEEKS-DEHYDRATED.
YOU JUST DROP ONE OF THESE INTO THE PURIFIER AND ADD WATER.
ANY KIND OF WATER.
TWO WEEKS?
THE PURIFIER WORKS SO WELL, YOU CAN EVEN PEE IN IT.
TWO WEEKS FOR TWO PEOPLE.
FOUR WEEKS FOR ONE.

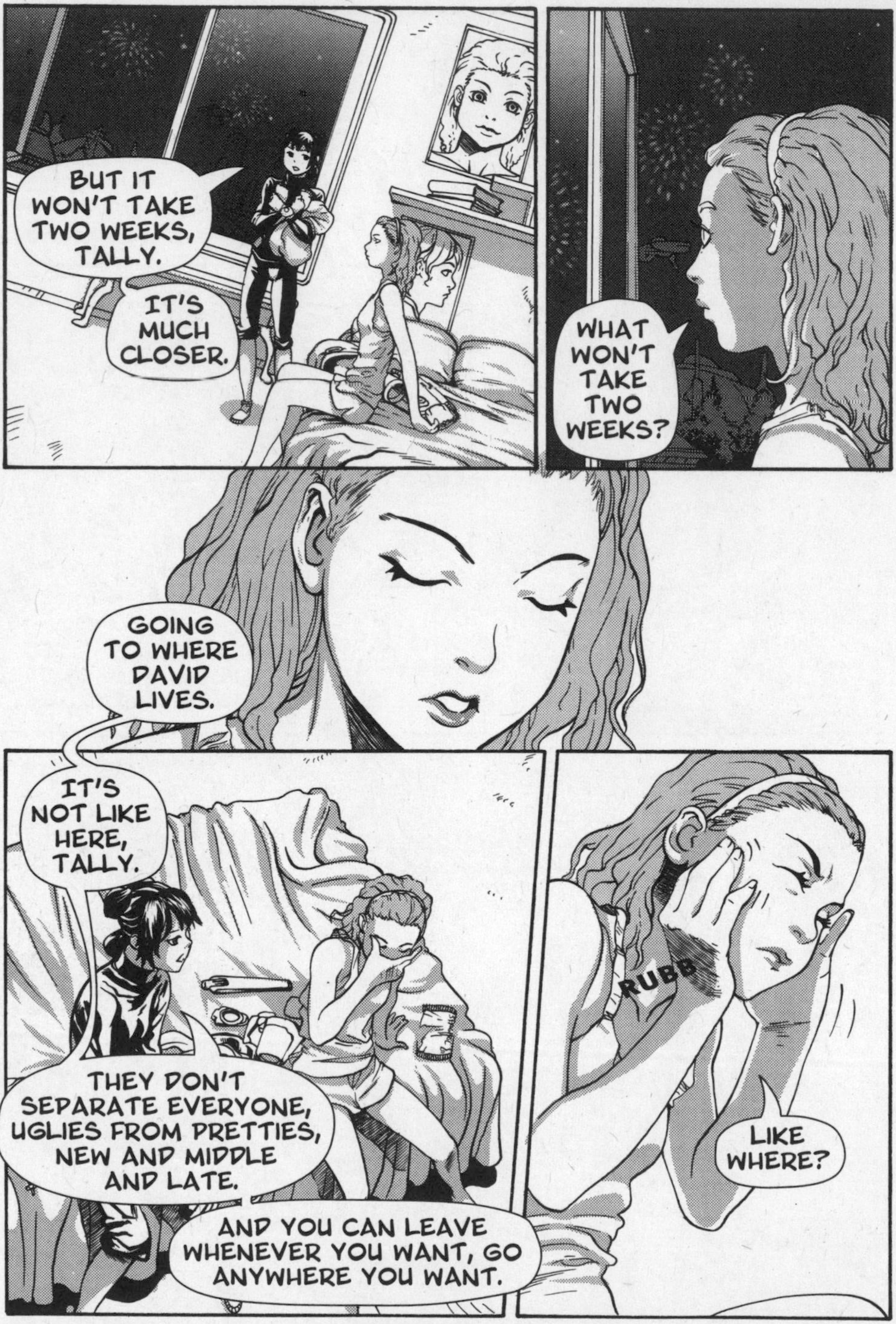
BUT IT WON'T TAKE TWO WEEKS, TALLY.
IT'S MUCH CLOSER.
WHAT WON'T TAKE TWO WEEKS?
GOING TO WHERE DAVID LIVES.
IT'S NOT LIKE HERE, TALLY.
THEY DON'T SEPARATE EVERYONE, UGLIES FROM PRETTIES, NEW AND MIDDLE AND LATE.
AND YOU CAN LEAVE WHENEVER YOU WANT, GO ANYWHERE YOU WANT.
RUBB
LIKE WHERE?

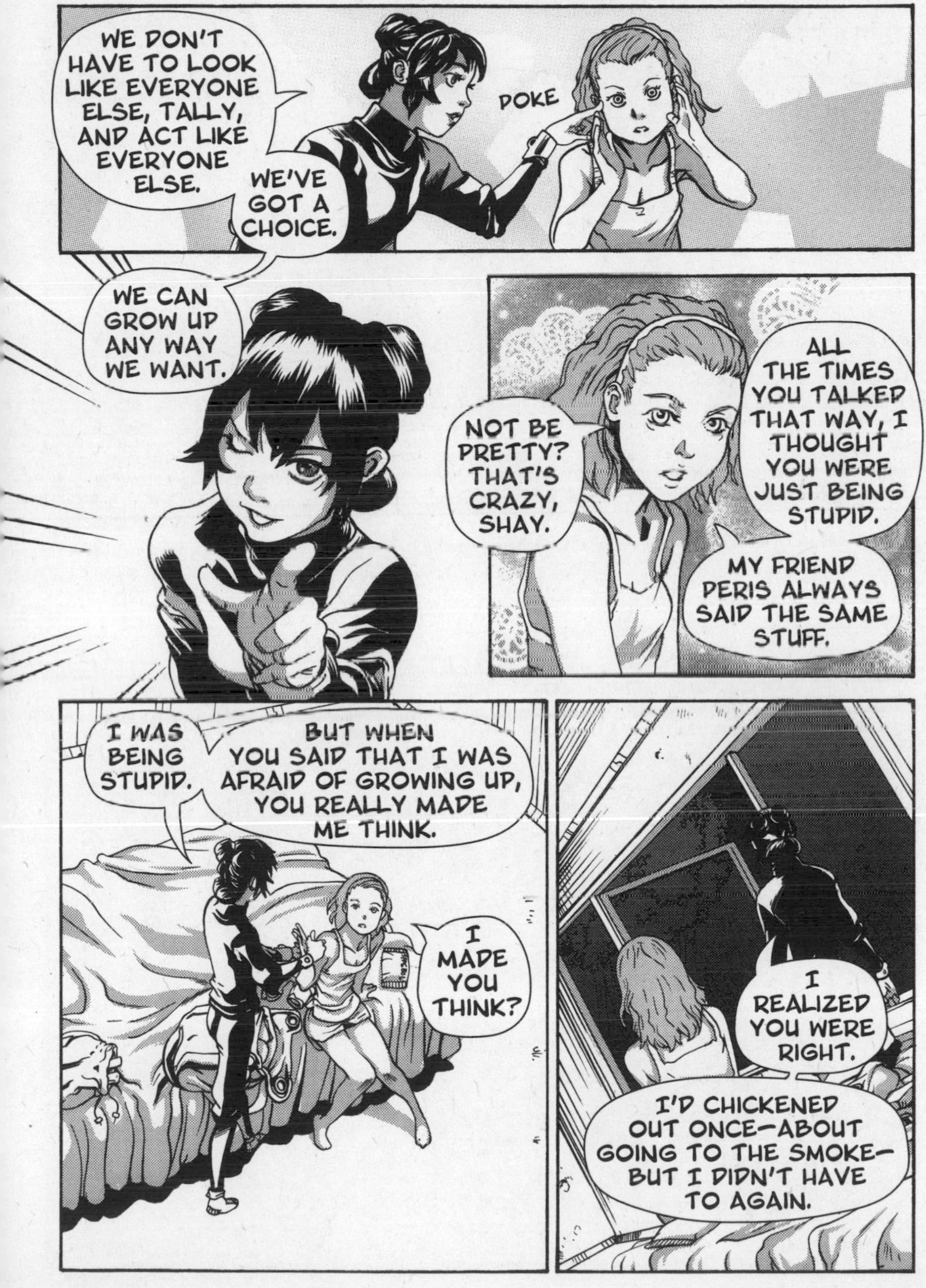
WE DON'T HAVE TO LOOK LIKE EVERYONE ELSE, TALLY, AND ACT LIKE EVERYONE ELSE.
POKE
WE'VE GOT A CHOICE.
WE CAN GROW UP ANY WAY WE WANT.
NOT BE PRETTY? THAT'S CRAZY, SHAY.
ALL THE TIMES YOU TALKED THAT WAY, I THOUGHT YOU WERE JUST BEING STUPID.
MY FRIEND PERIS ALWAYS SAID THE SAME STUFF.
I WAS BEING STUPID.
BUT WHEN YOU SAID THAT I WAS AFRAID OF GROWING UP, YOU REALLY MADE ME THINK.
I MADE YOU THINK?
I REALIZED YOU WERE RIGHT.
I'D CHICKENED OUT ONCE—ABOUT GOING TO THE SMOKE—BUT I DIDN'T HAVE TO AGAIN.

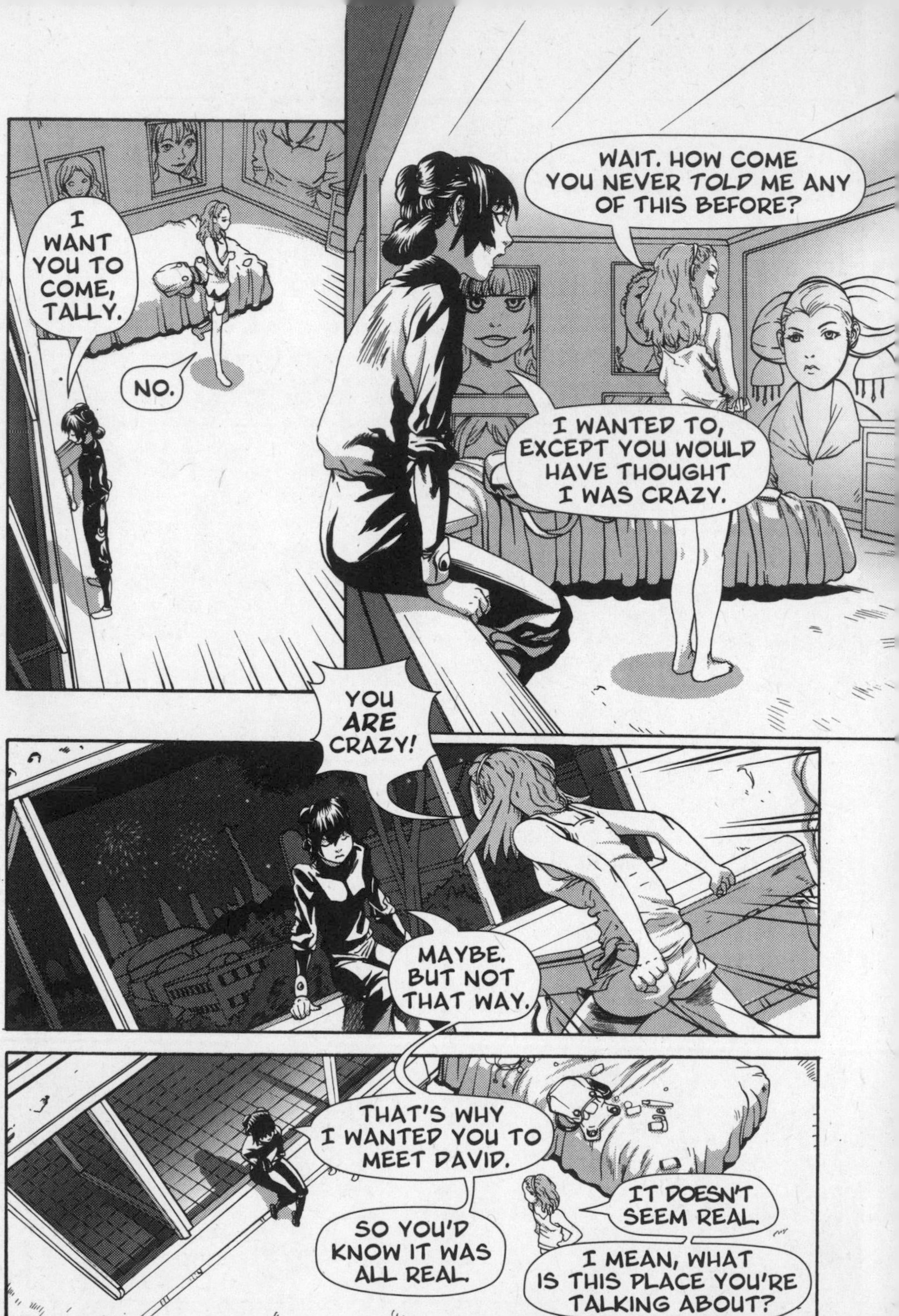
I WANT YOU TO COME, TALLY.
NO.
WAIT. HOW COME YOU NEVER *TOLD* ME ANY OF THIS BEFORE?
I WANTED TO, EXCEPT YOU WOULD HAVE THOUGHT I WAS CRAZY.
YOU **ARE** CRAZY!
MAYBE. BUT NOT THAT WAY.
THAT'S WHY I WANTED YOU TO MEET DAVID.
SO YOU'D KNOW IT WAS ALL REAL.
IT DOESN'T SEEM REAL.
I MEAN, WHAT IS THIS PLACE YOU'RE TALKING ABOUT?

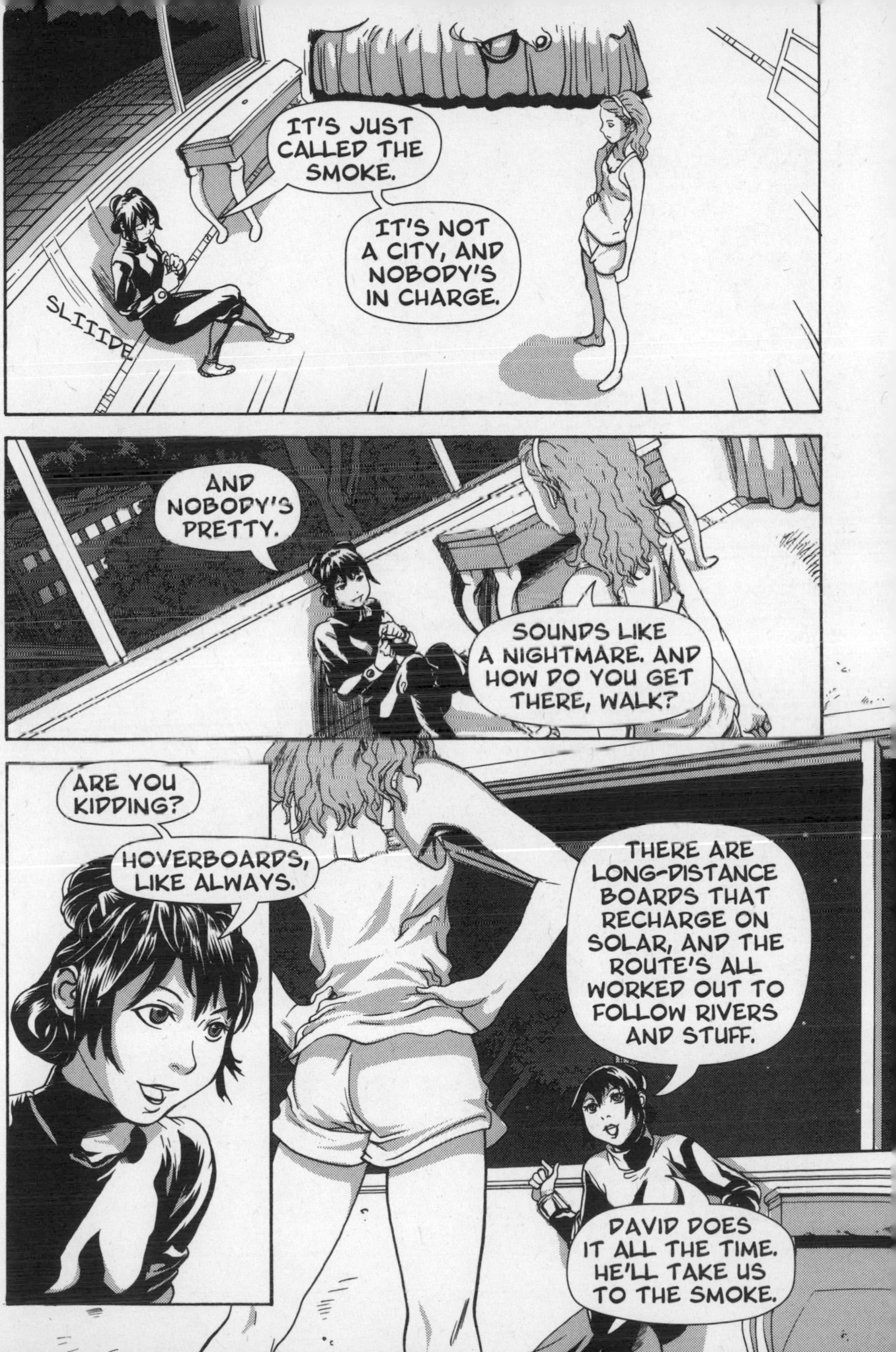
IT'S JUST CALLED THE SMOKE.
IT'S NOT A CITY, AND NOBODY'S IN CHARGE.
SLIIIDE
AND NOBODY'S PRETTY.
SOUNDS LIKE A NIGHTMARE. AND HOW DO YOU GET THERE, WALK?
ARE YOU KIDDING?
HOVERBOARDS, LIKE ALWAYS.
THERE ARE LONG-DISTANCE BOARDS THAT RECHARGE ON SOLAR, AND THE ROUTE'S ALL WORKED OUT TO FOLLOW RIVERS AND STUFF.
DAVID DOES IT ALL THE TIME. HE'LL TAKE US TO THE SMOKE.

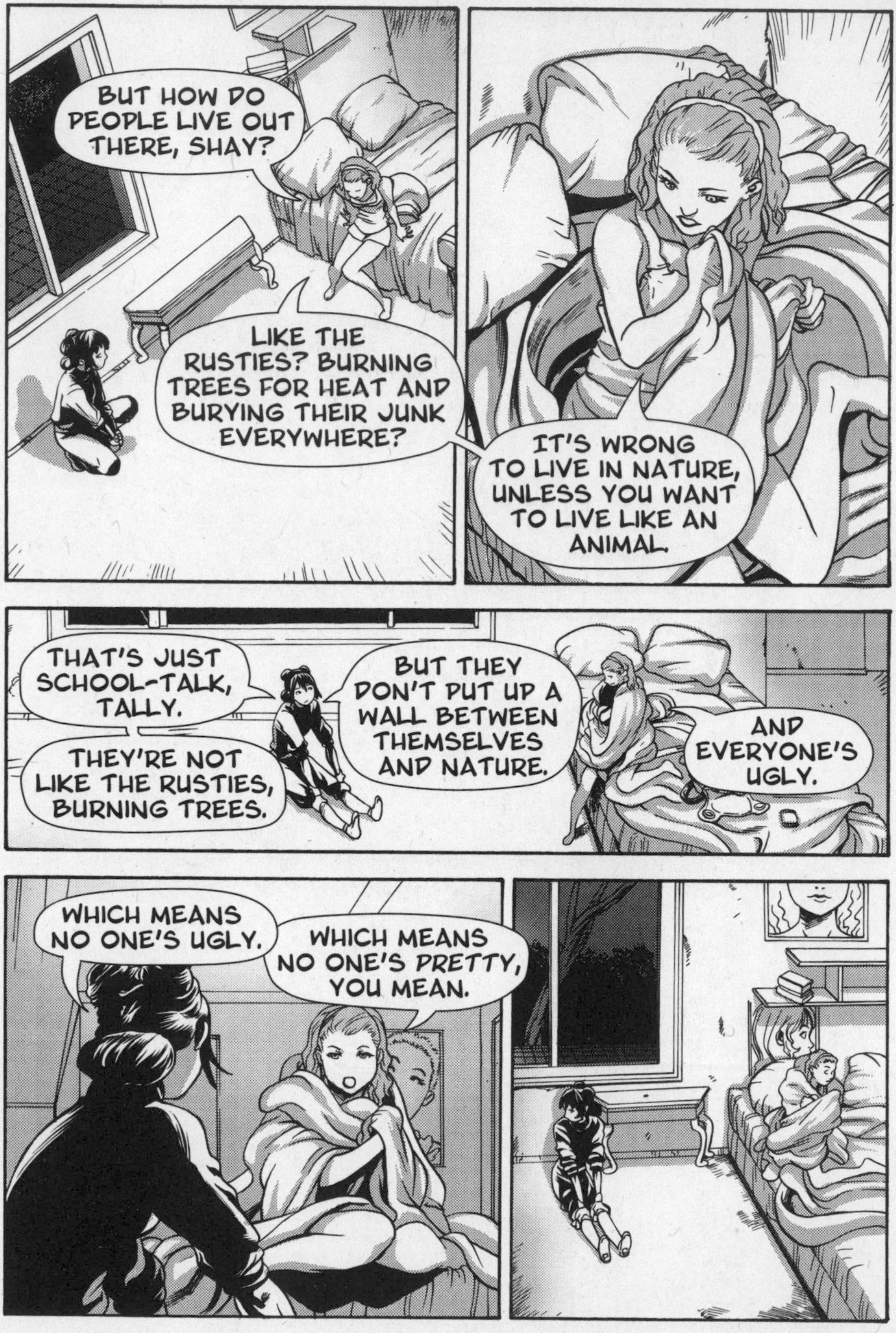
BUT HOW DO PEOPLE LIVE OUT THERE, SHAY?
LIKE THE RUSTIES? BURNING TREES FOR HEAT AND BURYING THEIR JUNK EVERYWHERE?
IT'S WRONG TO LIVE IN NATURE, UNLESS YOU WANT TO LIVE LIKE AN ANIMAL.
THAT'S JUST SCHOOL-TALK, TALLY.
THEY'RE NOT LIKE THE RUSTIES, BURNING TREES.
BUT THEY DON'T PUT UP A WALL BETWEEN THEMSELVES AND NATURE.
AND EVERYONE'S UGLY.
WHICH MEANS NO ONE'S UGLY.
WHICH MEANS NO ONE'S PRETTY, YOU MEAN.

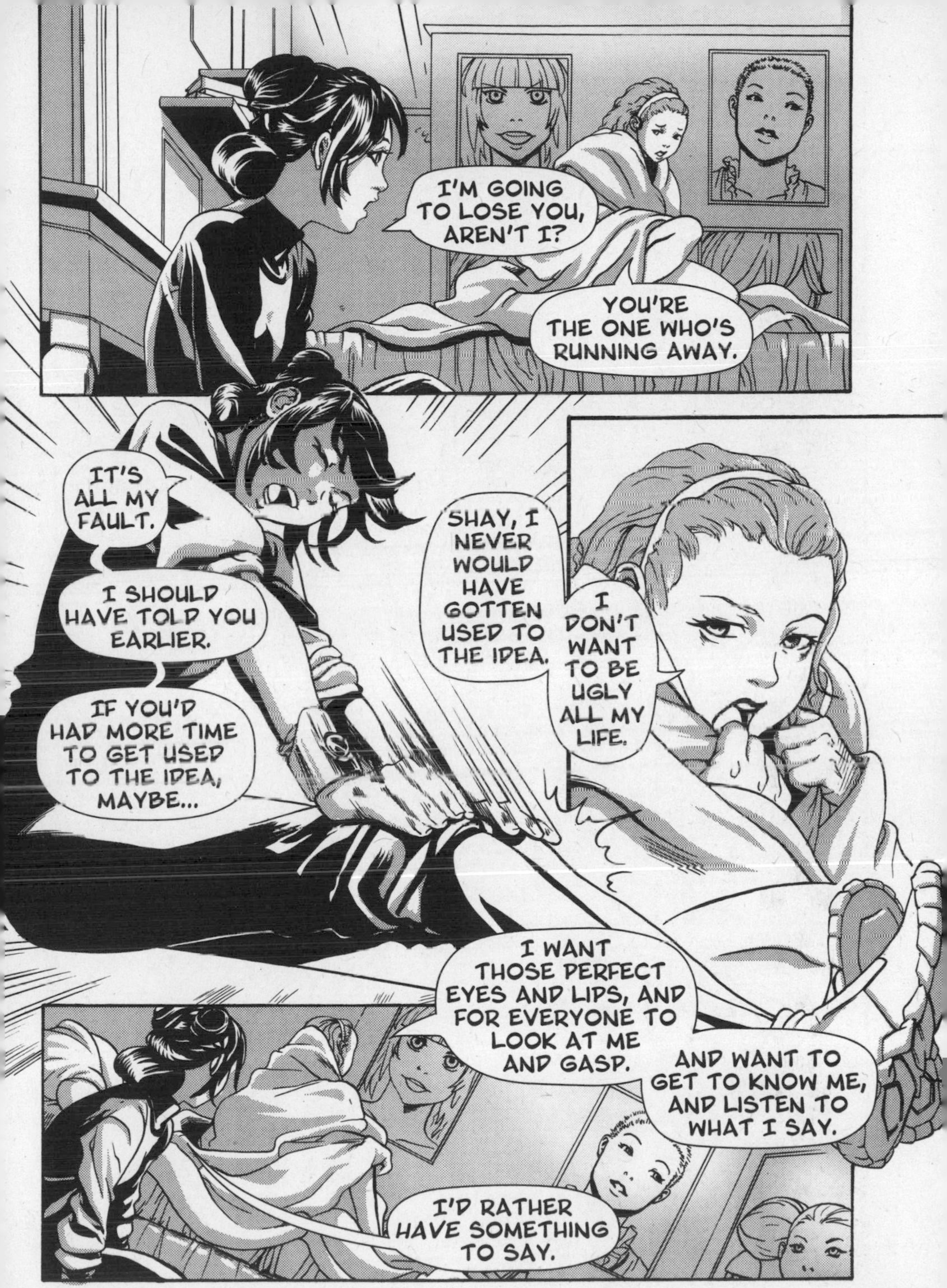
I'M GOING TO LOSE YOU, AREN'T I?
YOU'RE THE ONE WHO'S RUNNING AWAY.
IT'S ALL MY FAULT.
I SHOULD HAVE TOLD YOU EARLIER.
IF YOU'D HAD MORE TIME TO GET USED TO THE IDEA, MAYBE...
SHAY, I NEVER WOULD HAVE GOTTEN USED TO THE IDEA.
I DON'T WANT TO BE UGLY ALL MY LIFE.
I WANT THOSE PERFECT EYES AND LIPS, AND FOR EVERYONE TO LOOK AT ME AND GASP.
AND WANT TO GET TO KNOW ME, AND LISTEN TO WHAT I SAY.
I'D RATHER HAVE SOMETHING TO SAY.

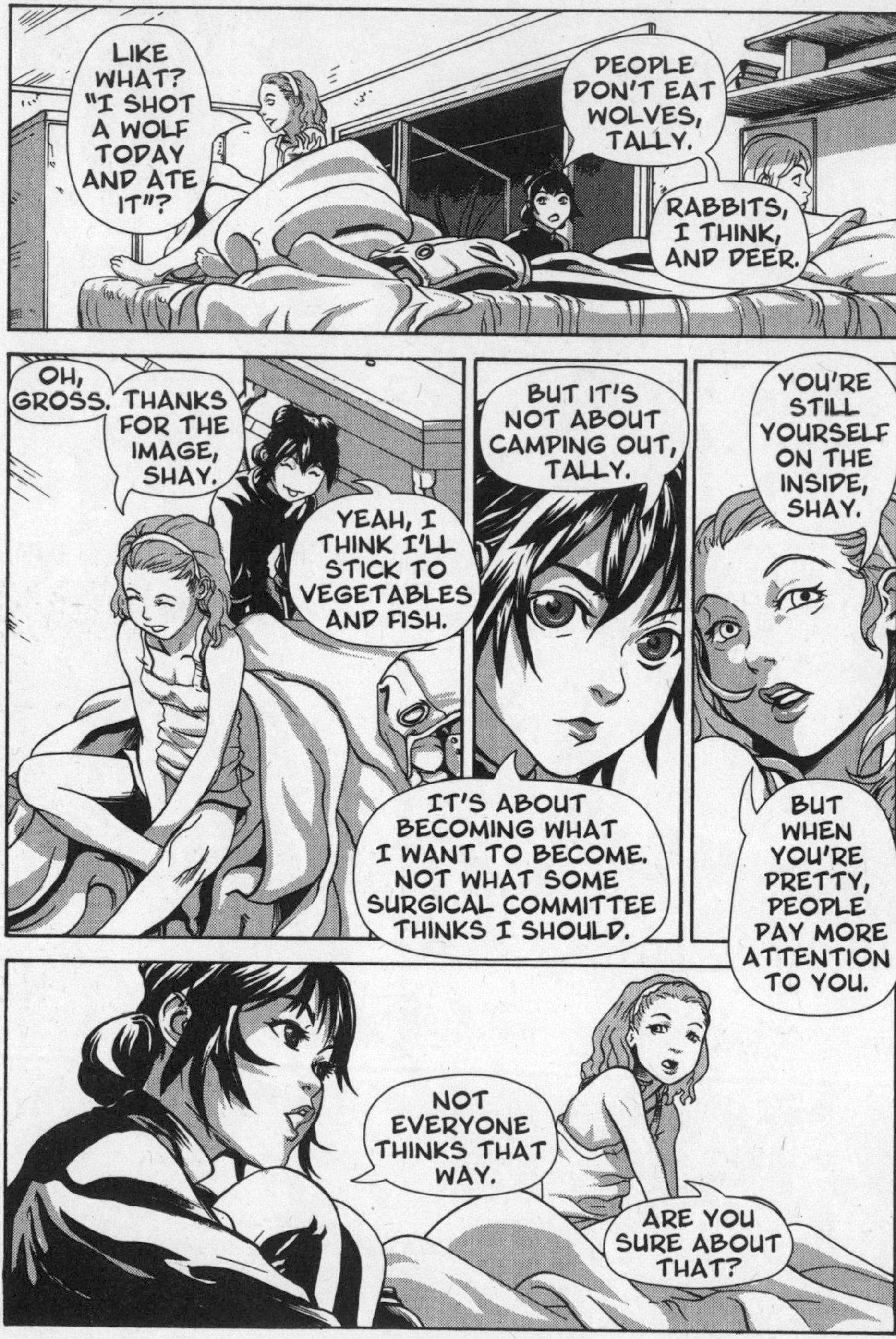
LIKE WHAT? "I SHOT A WOLF TODAY AND ATE IT"?
PEOPLE DON'T EAT WOLVES, TALLY.
RABBITS, I THINK, AND DEER.
OH, GROSS.
THANKS FOR THE IMAGE, SHAY.
YEAH, I THINK I'LL STICK TO VEGETABLES AND FISH.
BUT IT'S NOT ABOUT CAMPING OUT, TALLY.
IT'S ABOUT BECOMING WHAT I WANT TO BECOME. NOT WHAT SOME SURGICAL COMMITTEE THINKS I SHOULD.
YOU'RE STILL YOURSELF ON THE INSIDE, SHAY.
BUT WHEN YOU'RE PRETTY, PEOPLE PAY MORE ATTENTION TO YOU.
NOT EVERYONE THINKS THAT WAY.
ARE YOU SURE ABOUT THAT?

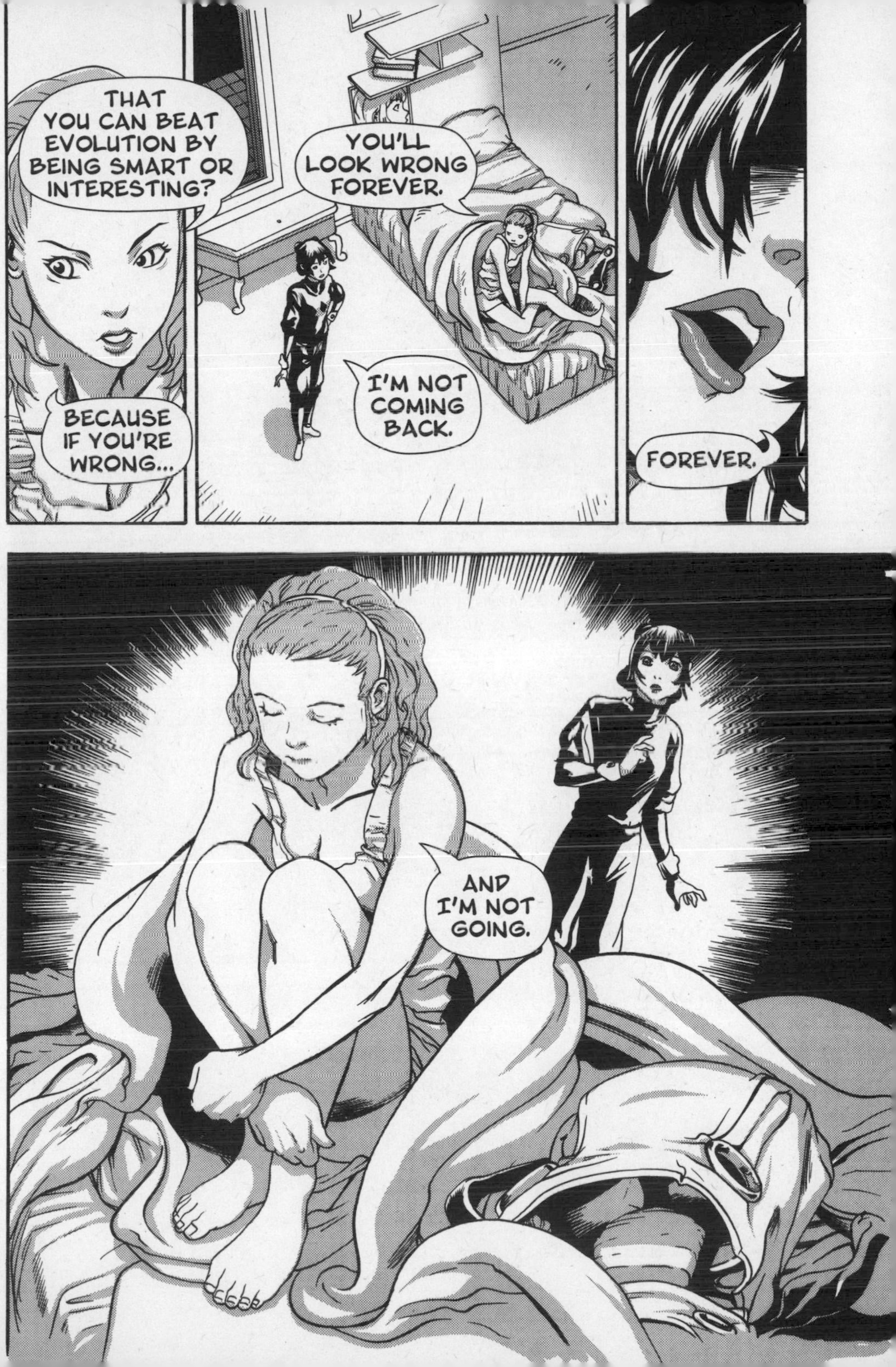
THAT YOU CAN BEAT EVOLUTION BY BEING SMART OR INTERESTING?
BECAUSE IF YOU'RE WRONG...
YOU'LL LOOK WRONG FOREVER.
I'M NOT COMING BACK.
FOREVER.
AND I'M NOT GOING.

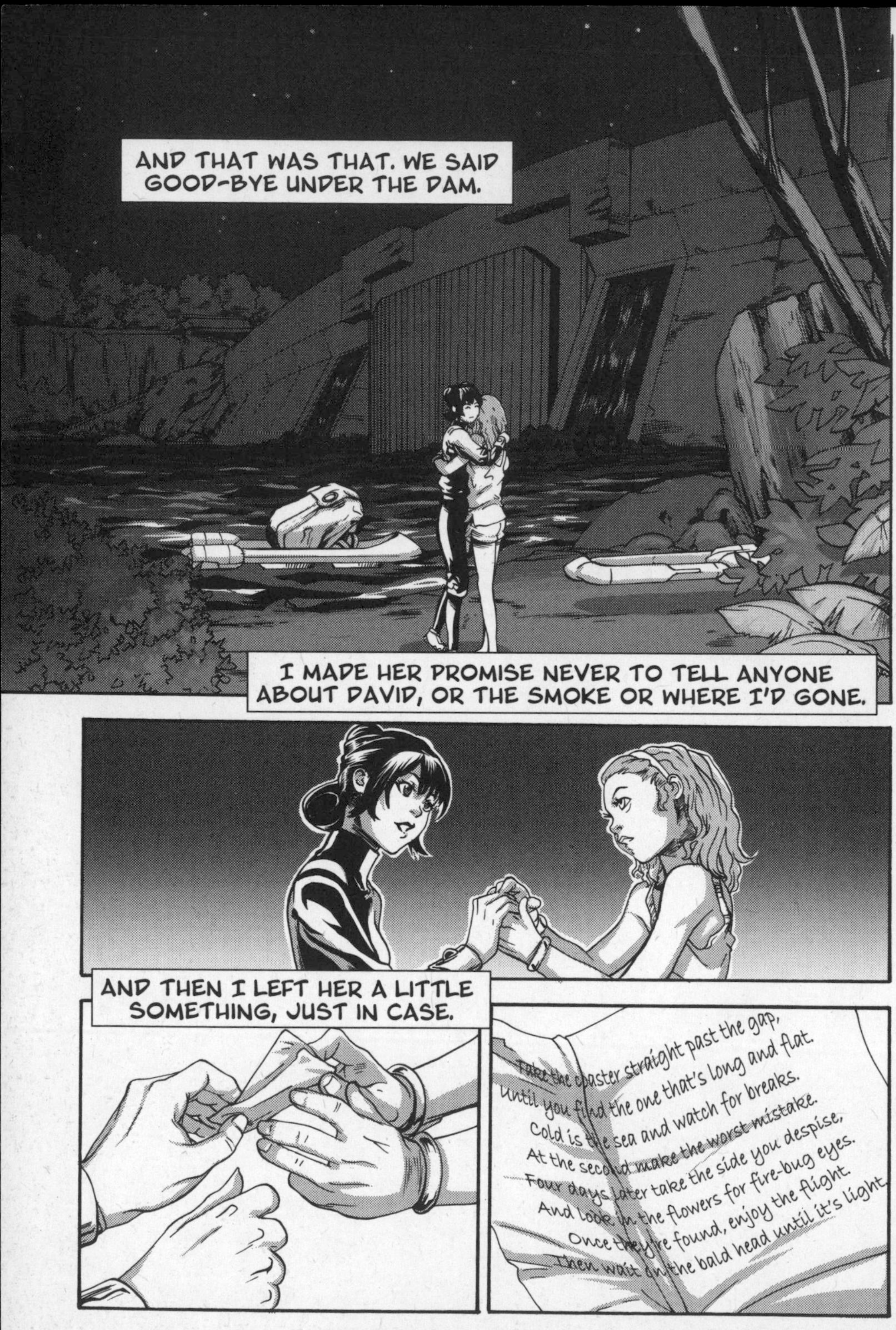
AND THAT WAS THAT. WE SAID GOOD-BYE UNDER THE DAM.
I MADE HER PROMISE NEVER TO TELL ANYONE ABOUT DAVID, OR THE SMOKE OR WHERE I'D GONE.
AND THEN I LEFT HER A LITTLE SOMETHING, JUST IN CASE.
Take the coaster straight past the gap,
Until you find the one that's long and flat.
Cold is the sea and watch for breaks.
At the second make the worst mistake.
Four days later take the side you despise,
And look in the flowers for fire-bug eyes.
Once they're found, enjoy the flight.
Then wait on the bald head until it's light.

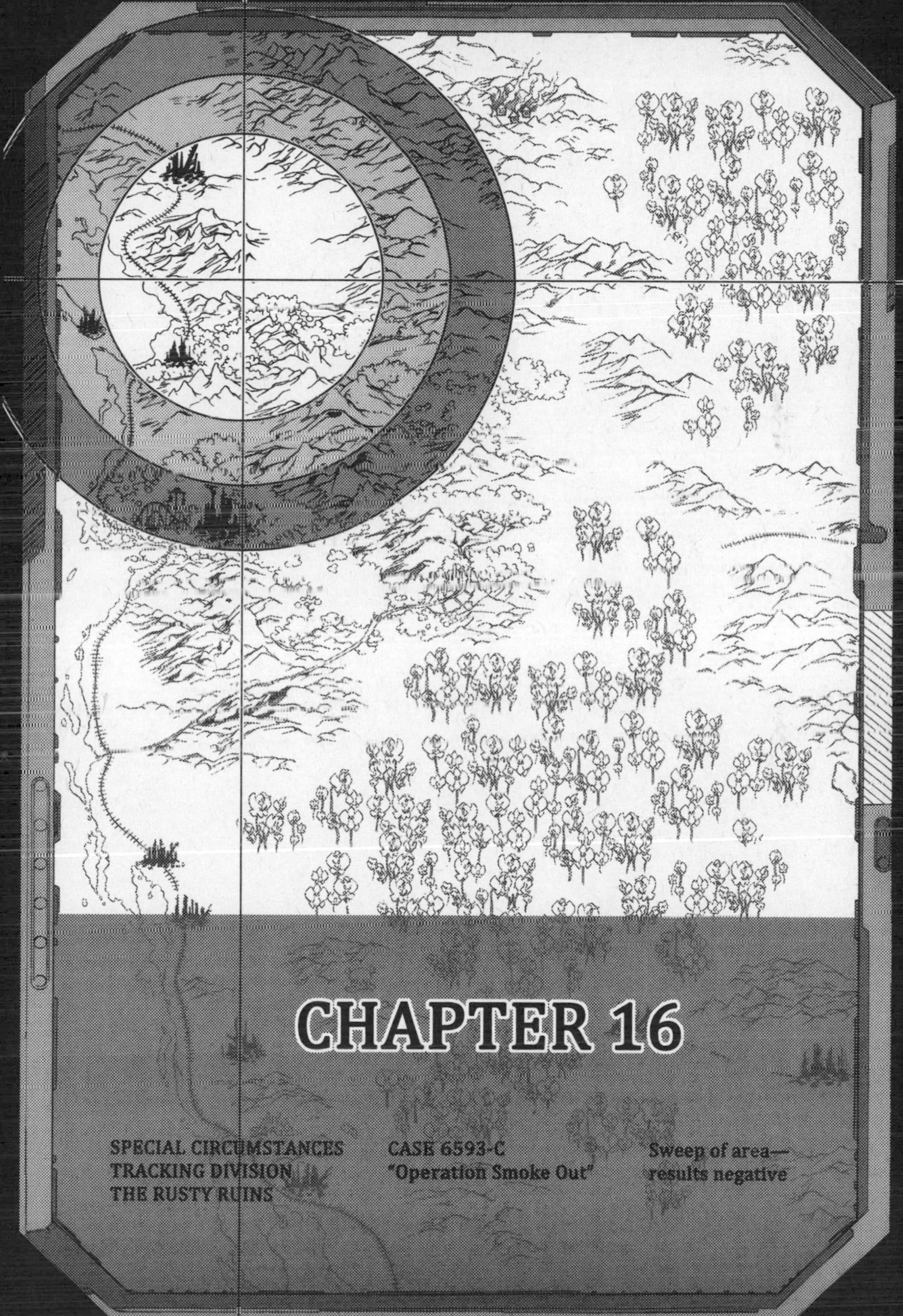
CHAPTER 16
SPECIAL CIRCUMSTANCES
TRACKING DIVISION
THE RUSTY RUINS
CASE 6593-C
"Operation Smoke Out"
Sweep of area—
results negative

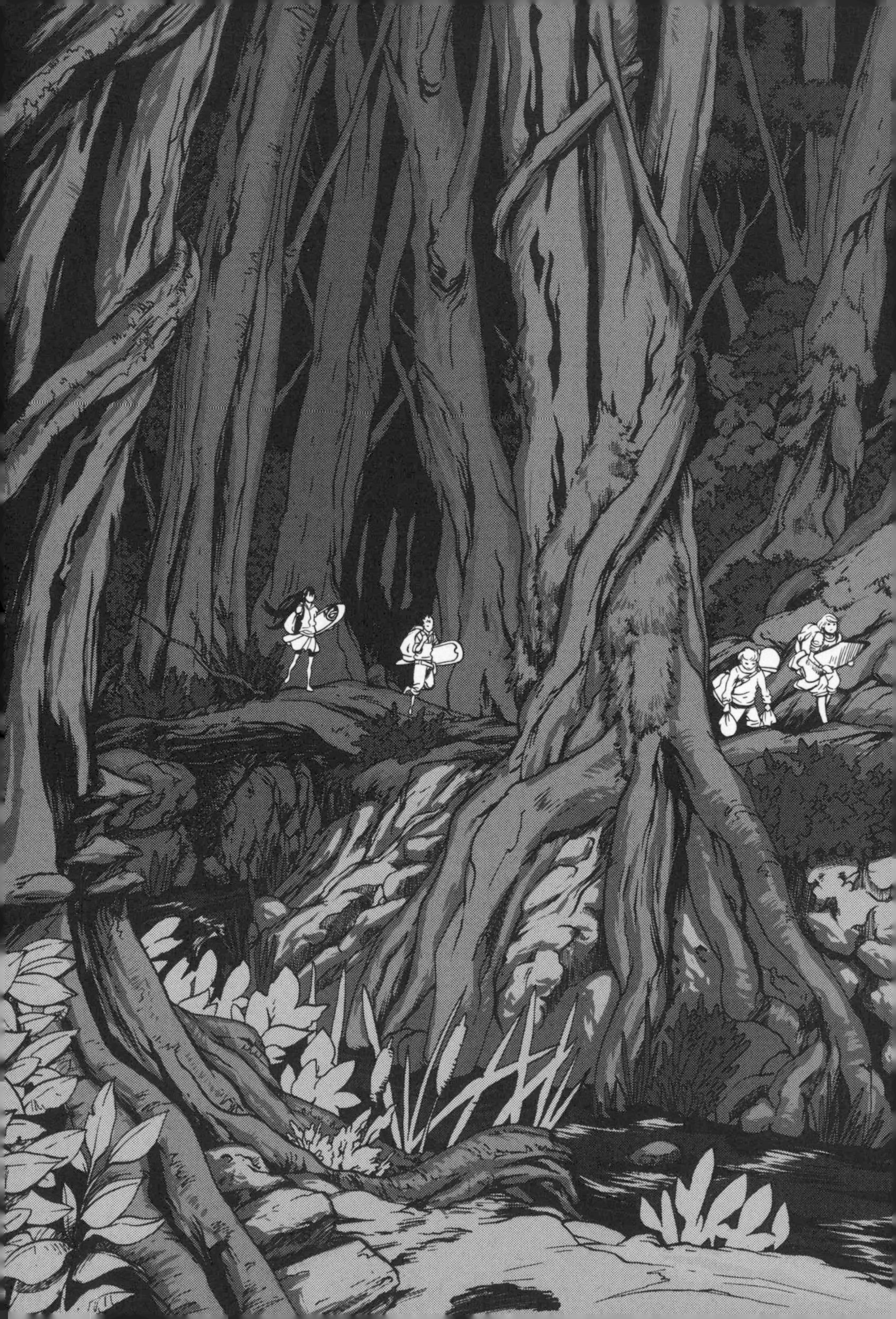

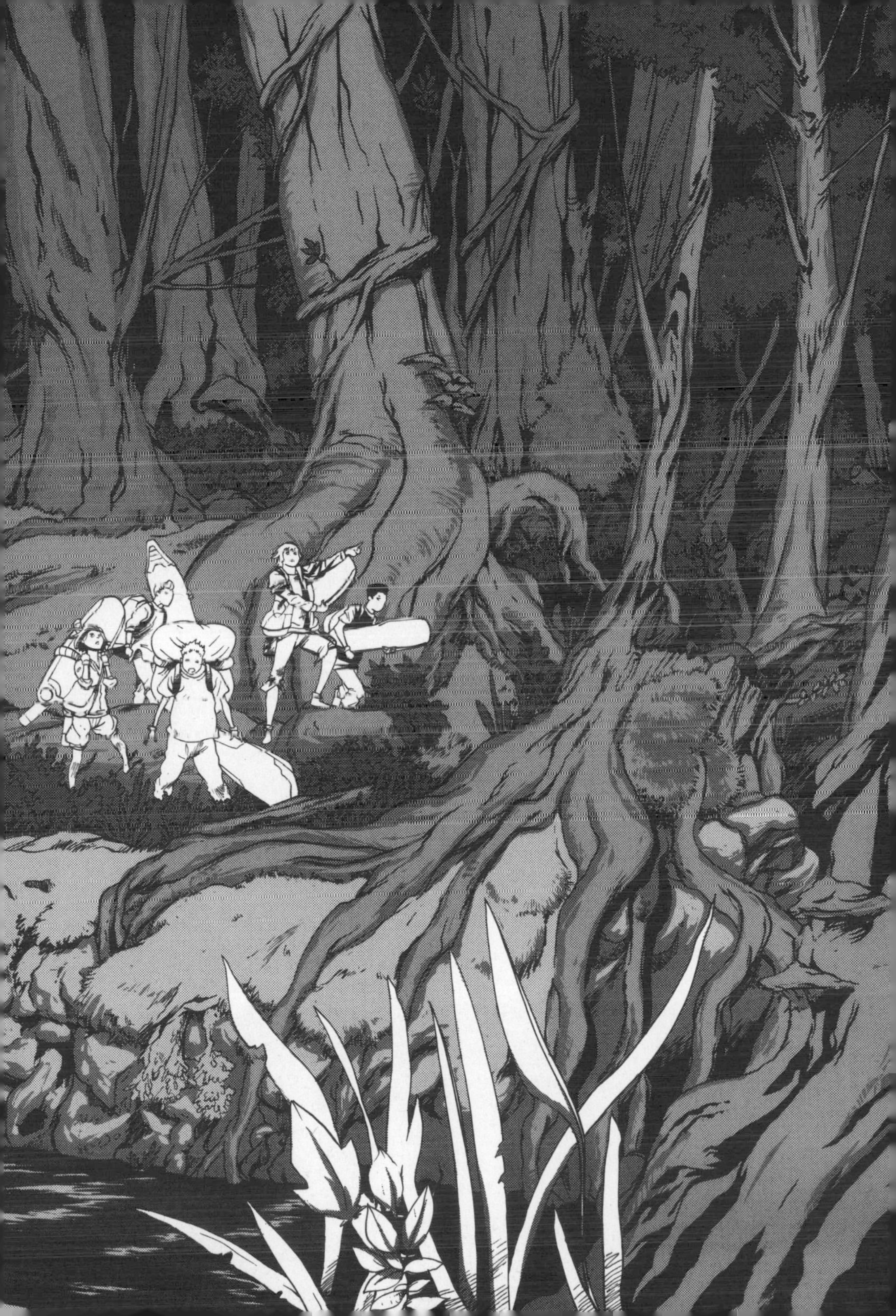

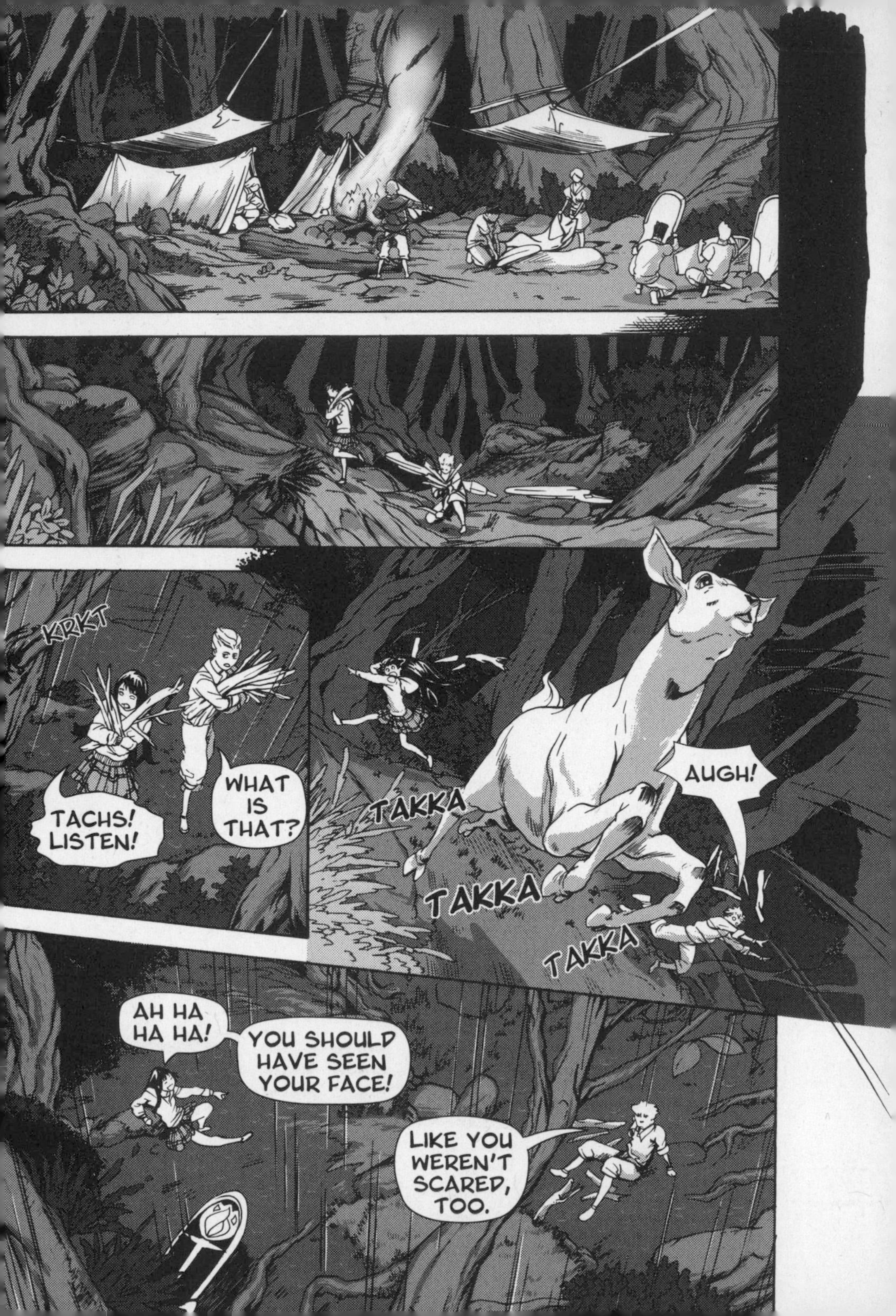
KRKT
TACHS! LISTEN!
WHAT IS THAT?
TAKKA
AUGH!
TAKKA
TAKKA
AH HA HA HA!
YOU SHOULD HAVE SEEN YOUR FACE!
LIKE YOU WEREN'T SCARED, TOO.

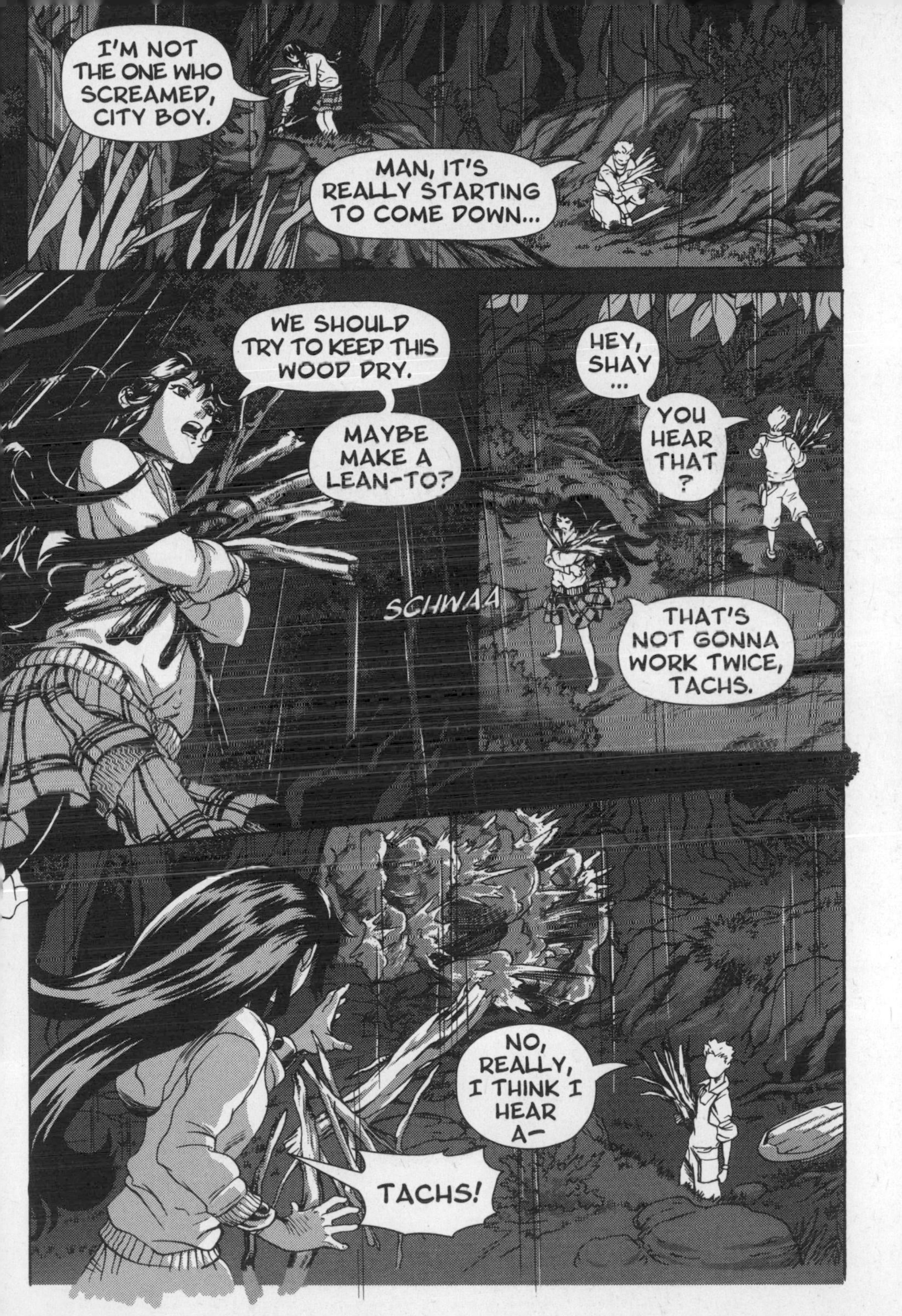
I'M NOT THE ONE WHO SCREAMED, CITY BOY.
MAN, IT'S REALLY STARTING TO COME DOWN...
WE SHOULD TRY TO KEEP THIS WOOD DRY.
MAYBE MAKE A LEAN-TO?
SCHWAA
HEY, SHAY ...
YOU HEAR THAT ?
THAT'S NOT GONNA WORK TWICE, TACHS.
NO, REALLY, I THINK I HEAR A-
TACHS!

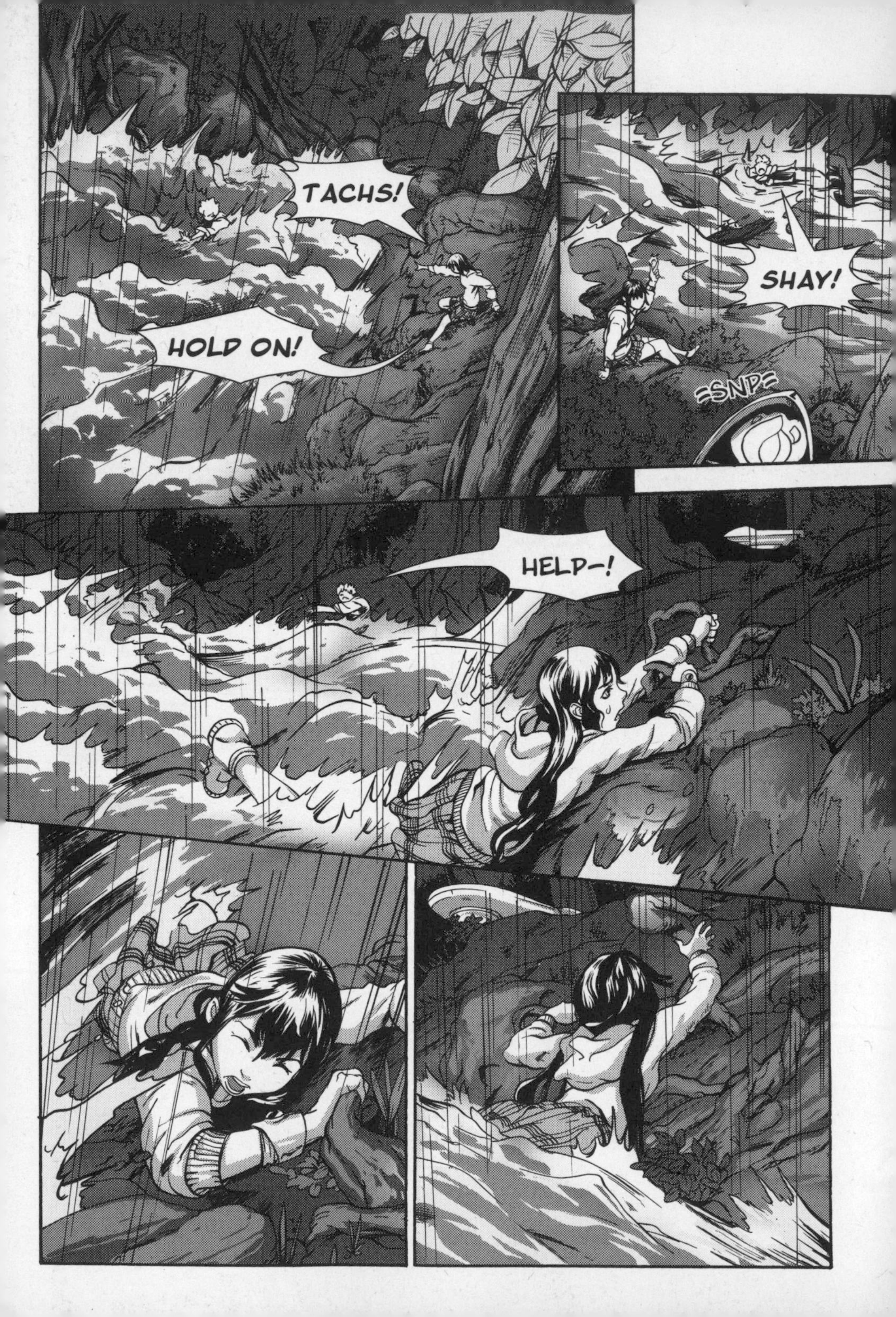
TACHS!
HOLD ON!
SHAY!
SNP
HELP-!

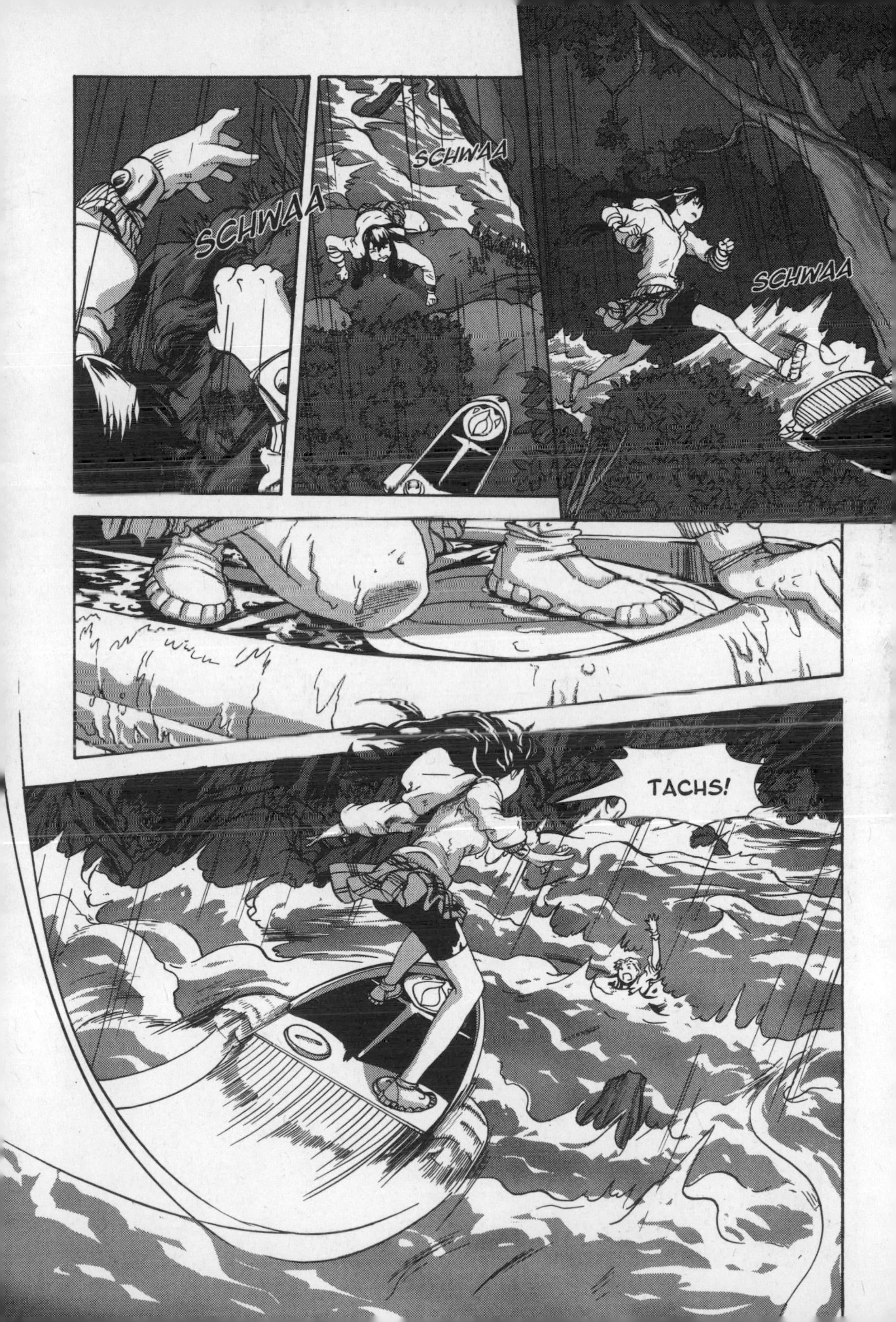
SCHWAA
SCHWAA
SCHWAA
TACHS!

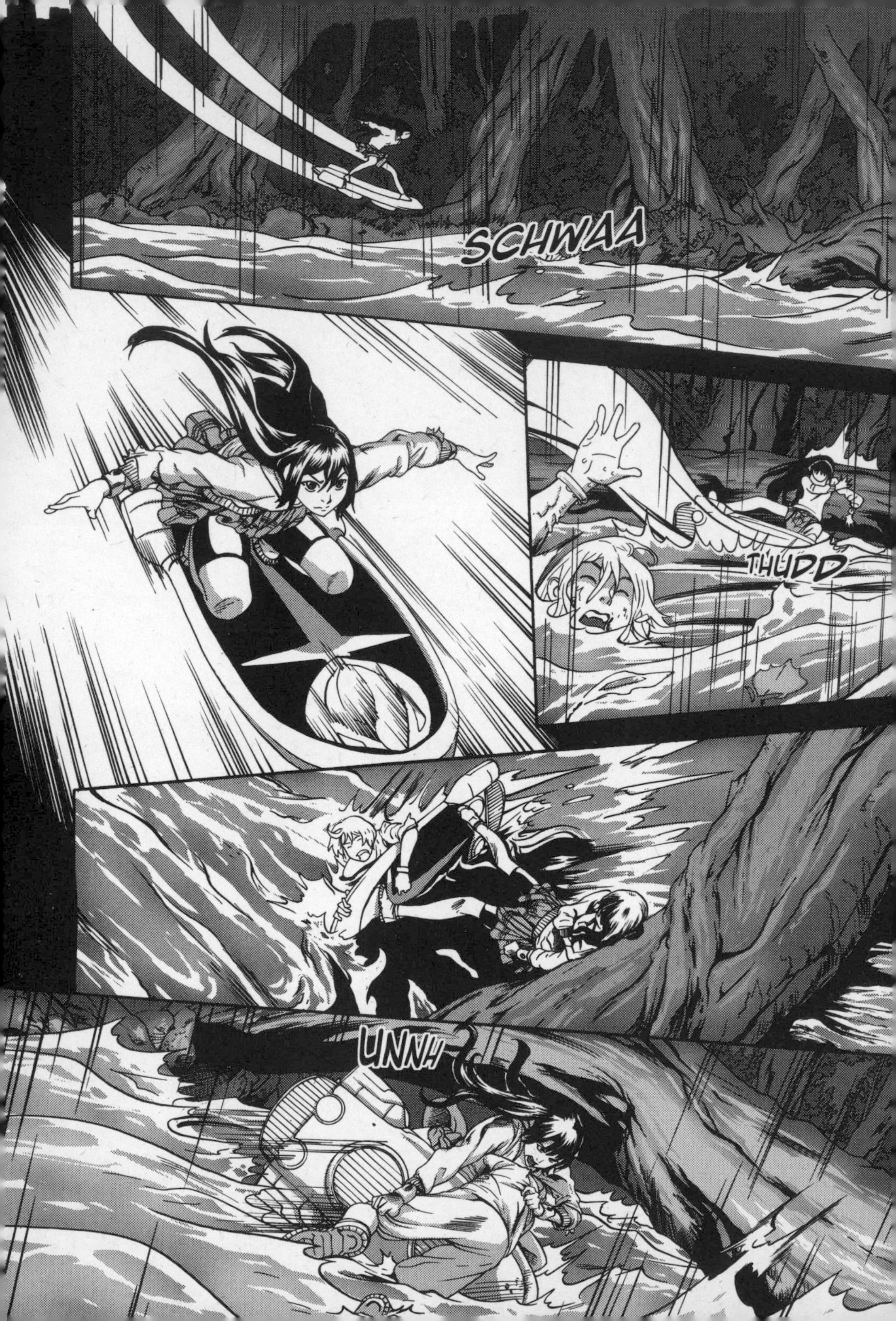
SCHWAA
THUDD
UNNH

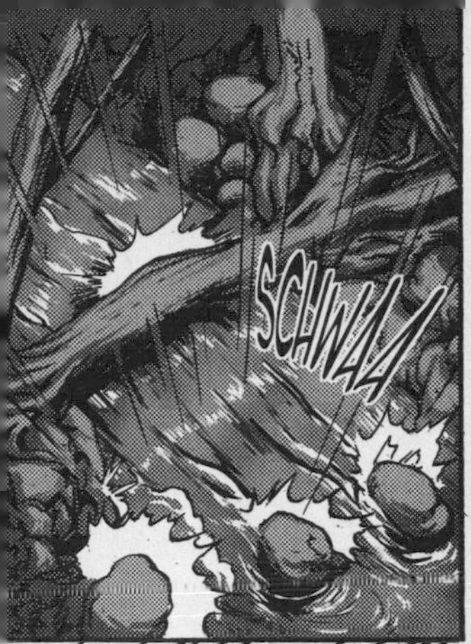
SCHWAAA
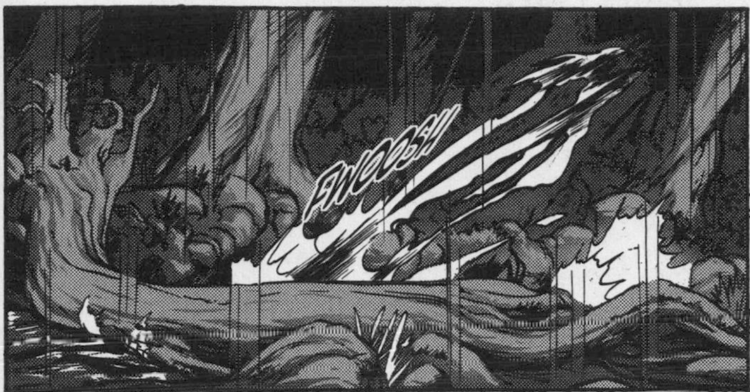
FWOOSH
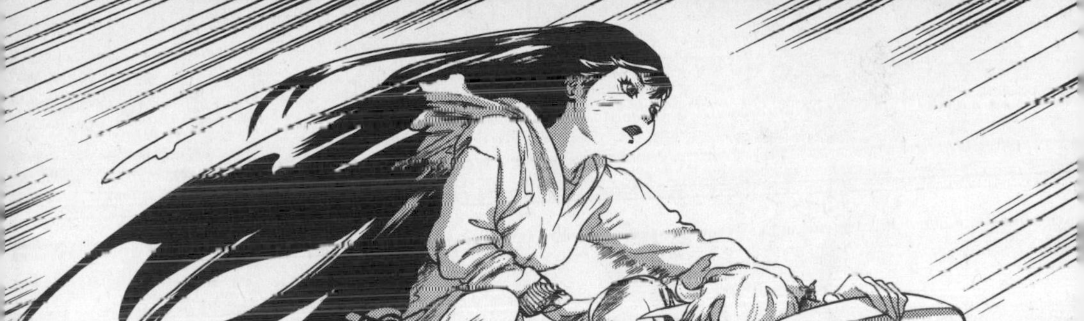
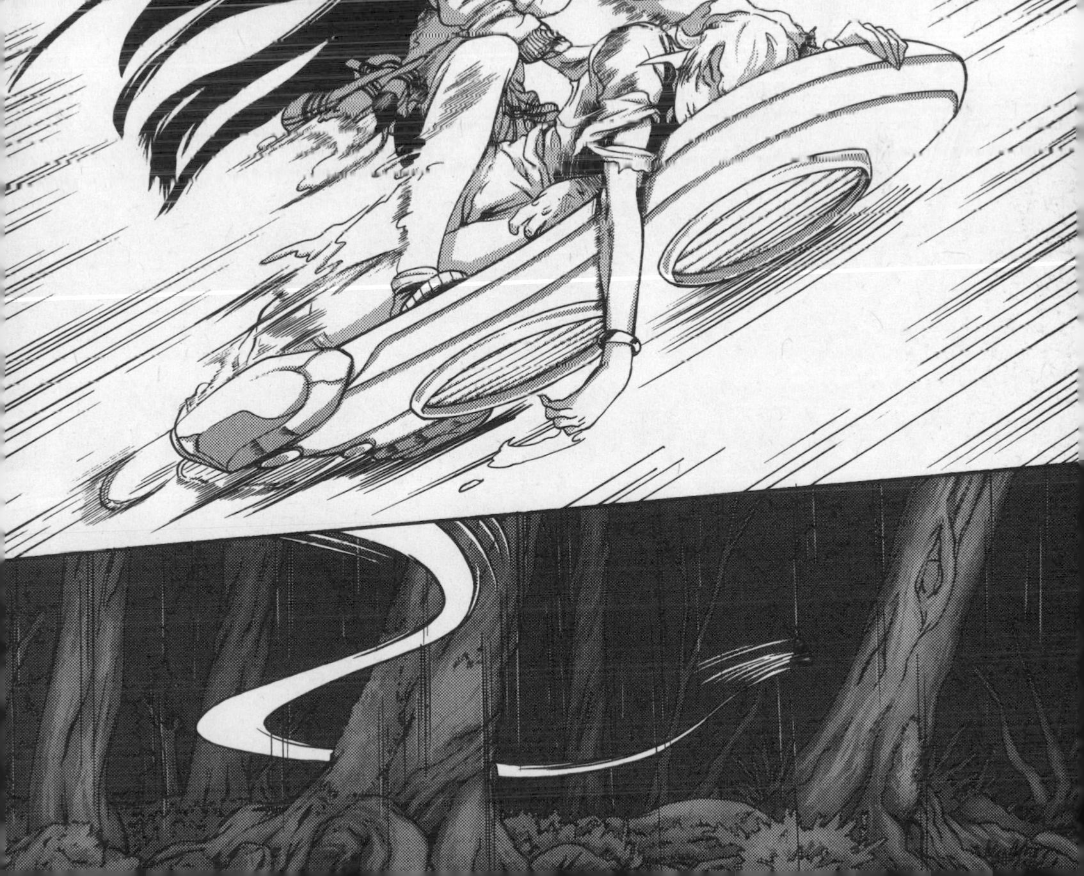

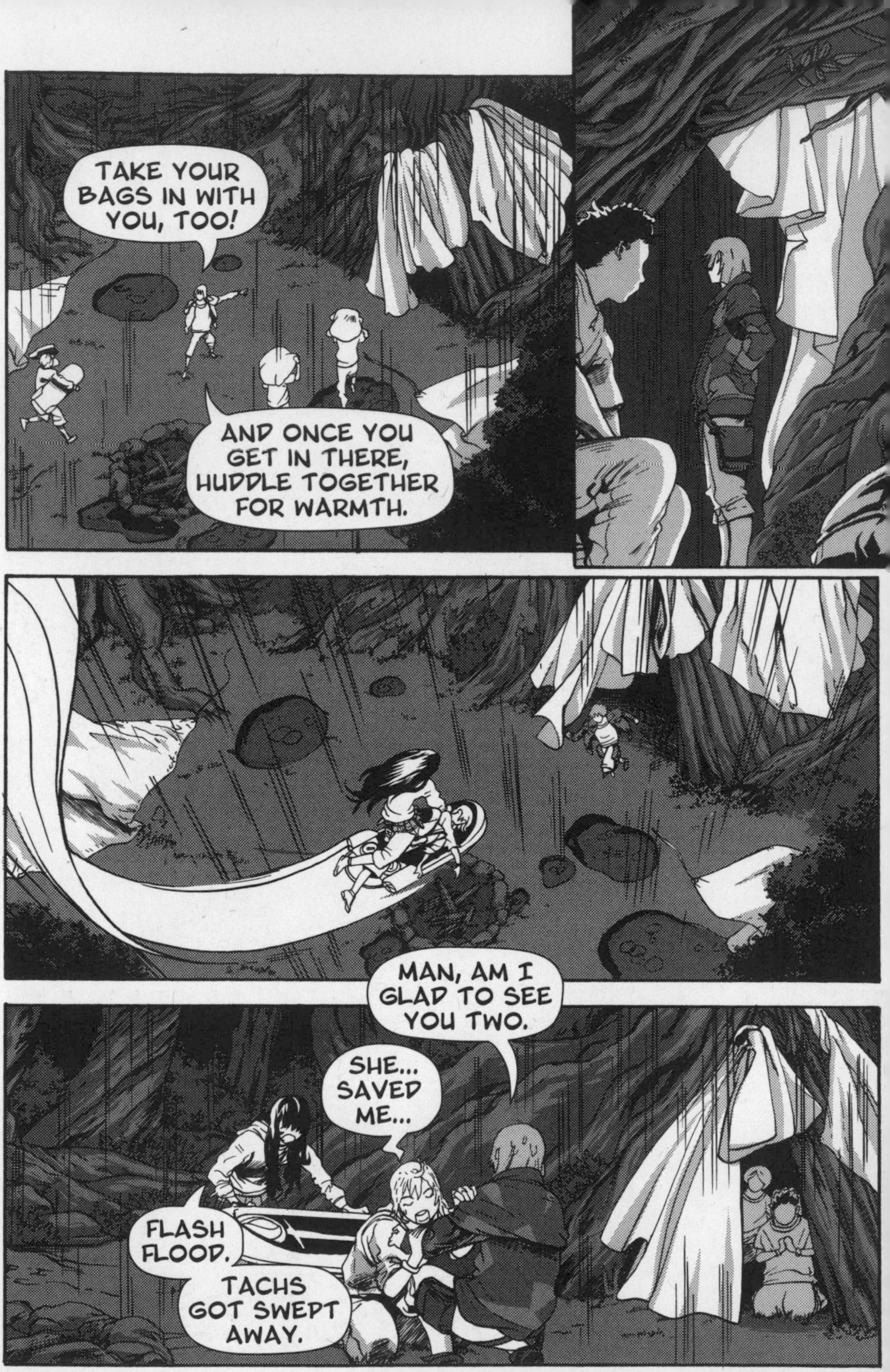
TAKE YOUR BAGS IN WITH YOU, TOO!
AND ONCE YOU GET IN THERE, HUDDLE TOGETHER FOR WARMTH.
MAN, AM I GLAD TO SEE YOU TWO.
SHE... SAVED ME...
FLASH FLOOD.
TACHS GOT SWEPT AWAY.

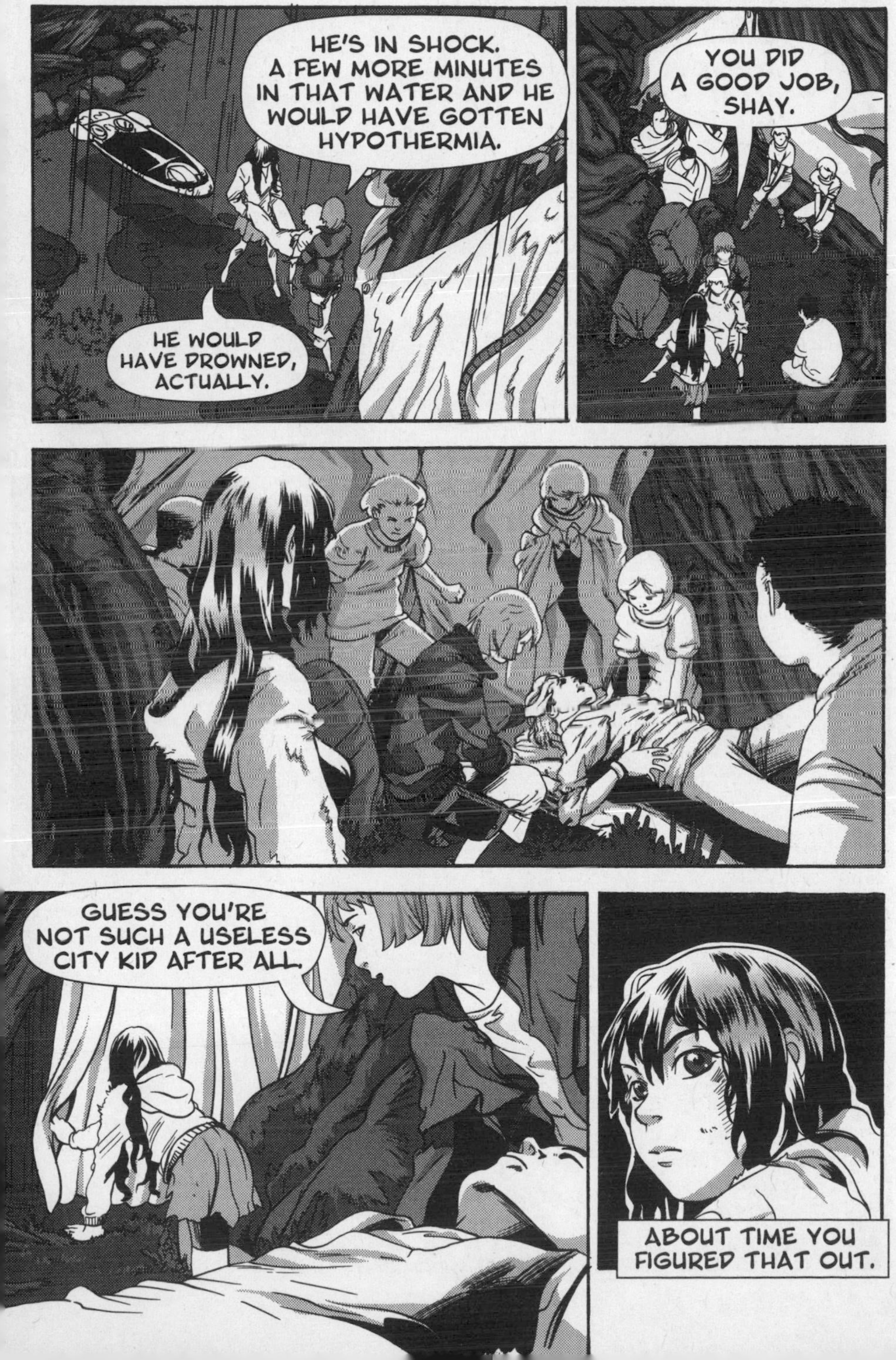
HE'S IN SHOCK. A FEW MORE MINUTES IN THAT WATER AND HE WOULD HAVE GOTTEN HYPOTHERMIA.
HE WOULD HAVE DROWNED, ACTUALLY.
YOU DID A GOOD JOB, SHAY.
GUESS YOU'RE NOT SUCH A USELESS CITY KID AFTER ALL.
ABOUT TIME YOU FIGURED THAT OUT.

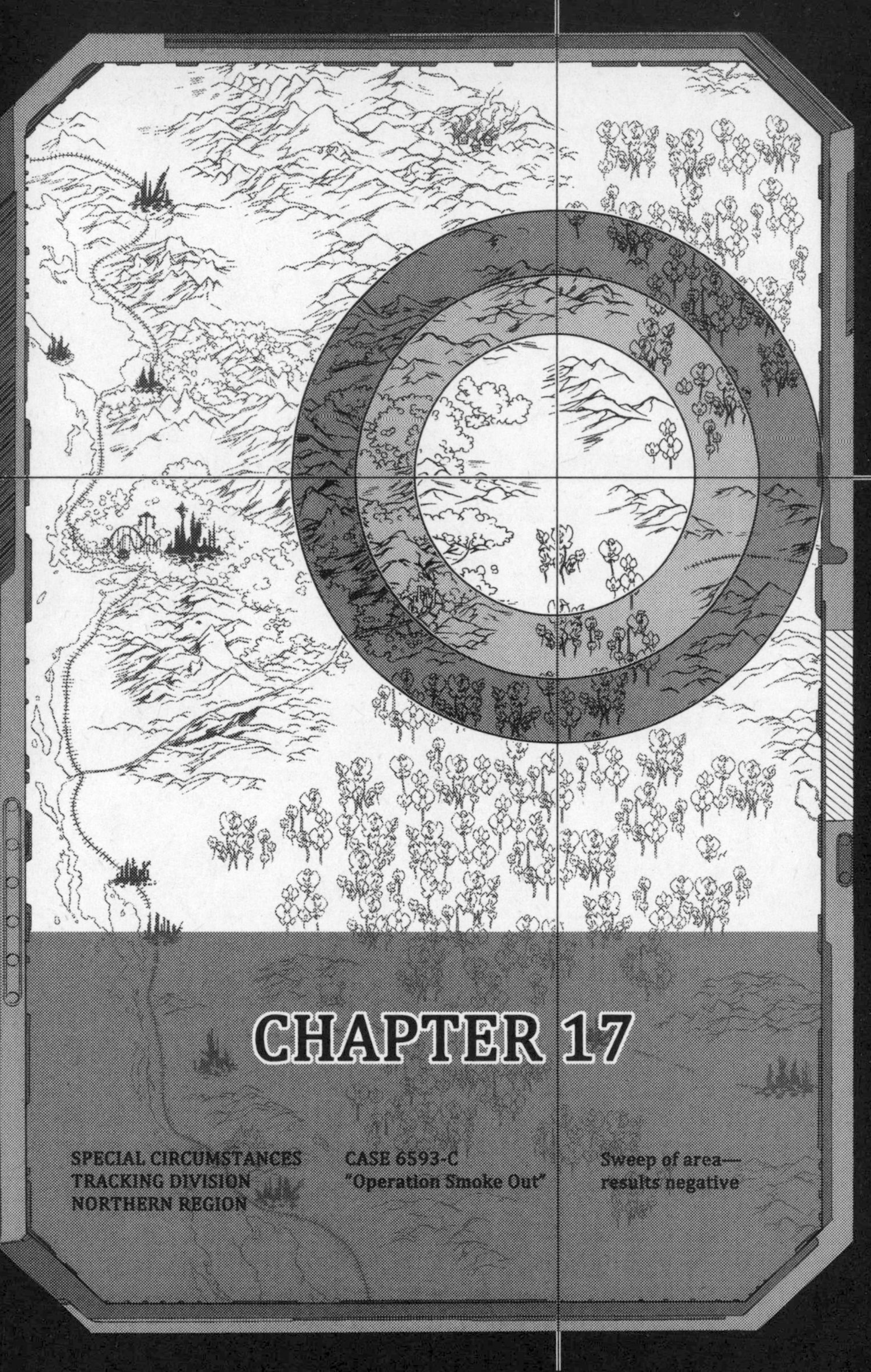
CHAPTER 17
SPECIAL CIRCUMSTANCES
TRACKING DIVISION
NORTHERN REGION
CASE 6593-C
"Operation Smoke Out"
Sweep of area—
results negative

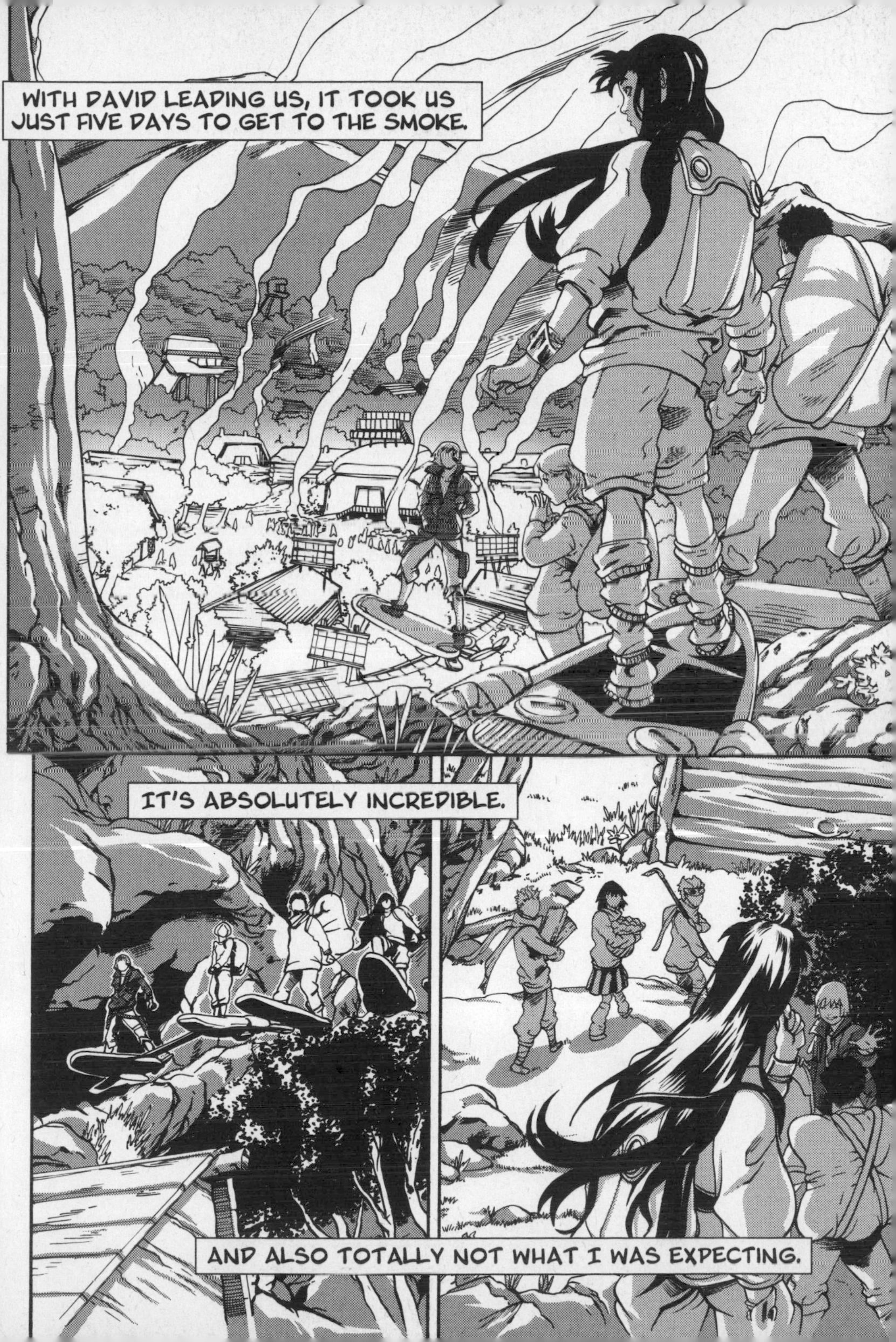
WITH DAVID LEADING US, IT TOOK US JUST FIVE DAYS TO GET TO THE SMOKE.
IT'S ABSOLUTELY INCREDIBLE.
AND ALSO TOTALLY NOT WHAT I WAS EXPECTING.

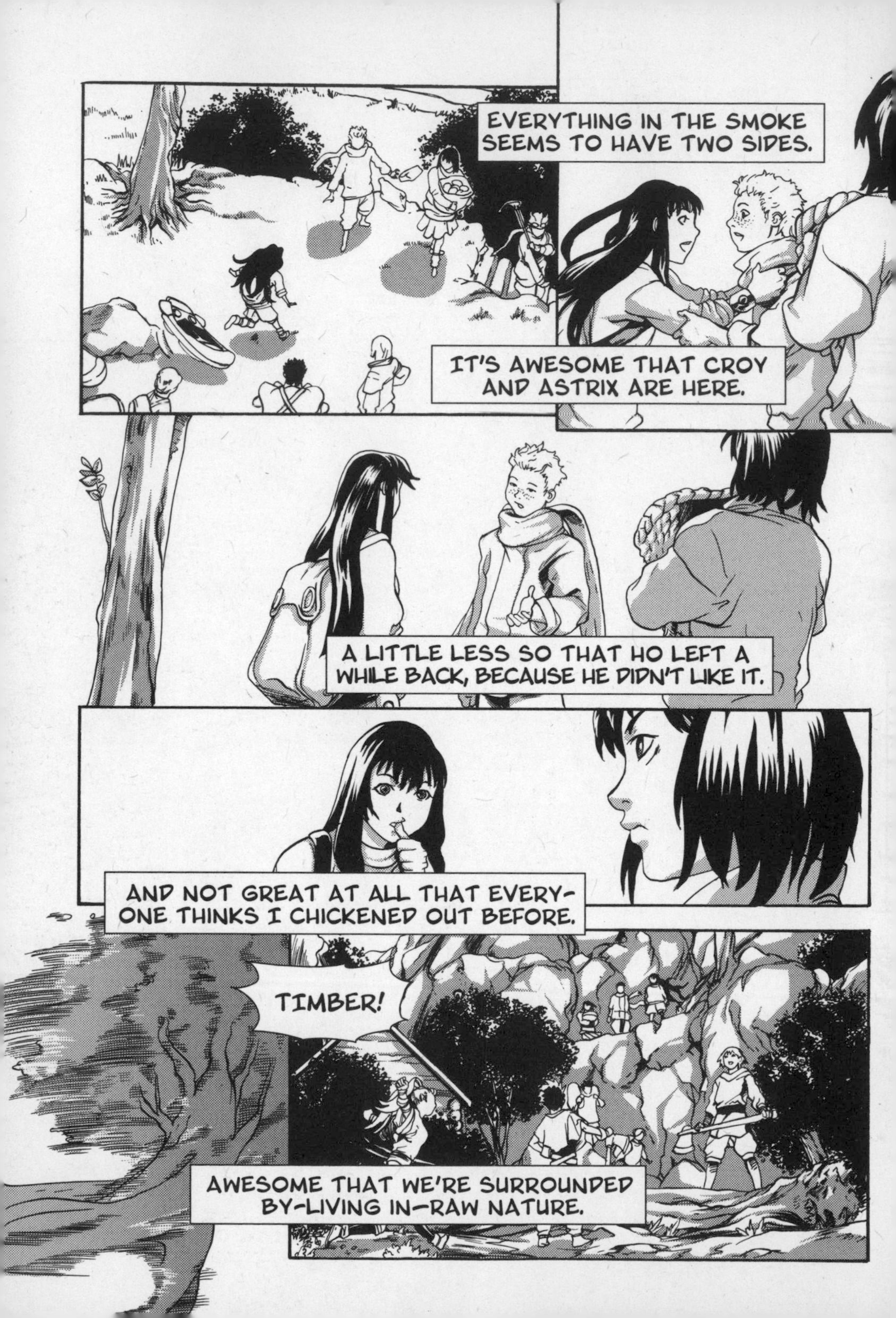
EVERYTHING IN THE SMOKE SEEMS TO HAVE TWO SIDES.
IT'S AWESOME THAT CROY AND ASTRIX ARE HERE.
A LITTLE LESS SO THAT HO LEFT A WHILE BACK, BECAUSE HE DIDN'T LIKE IT.
AND NOT GREAT AT ALL THAT EVERY-ONE THINKS I CHICKENED OUT BEFORE.
TIMBER!
AWESOME THAT WE'RE SURROUNDED BY—LIVING IN—RAW NATURE.

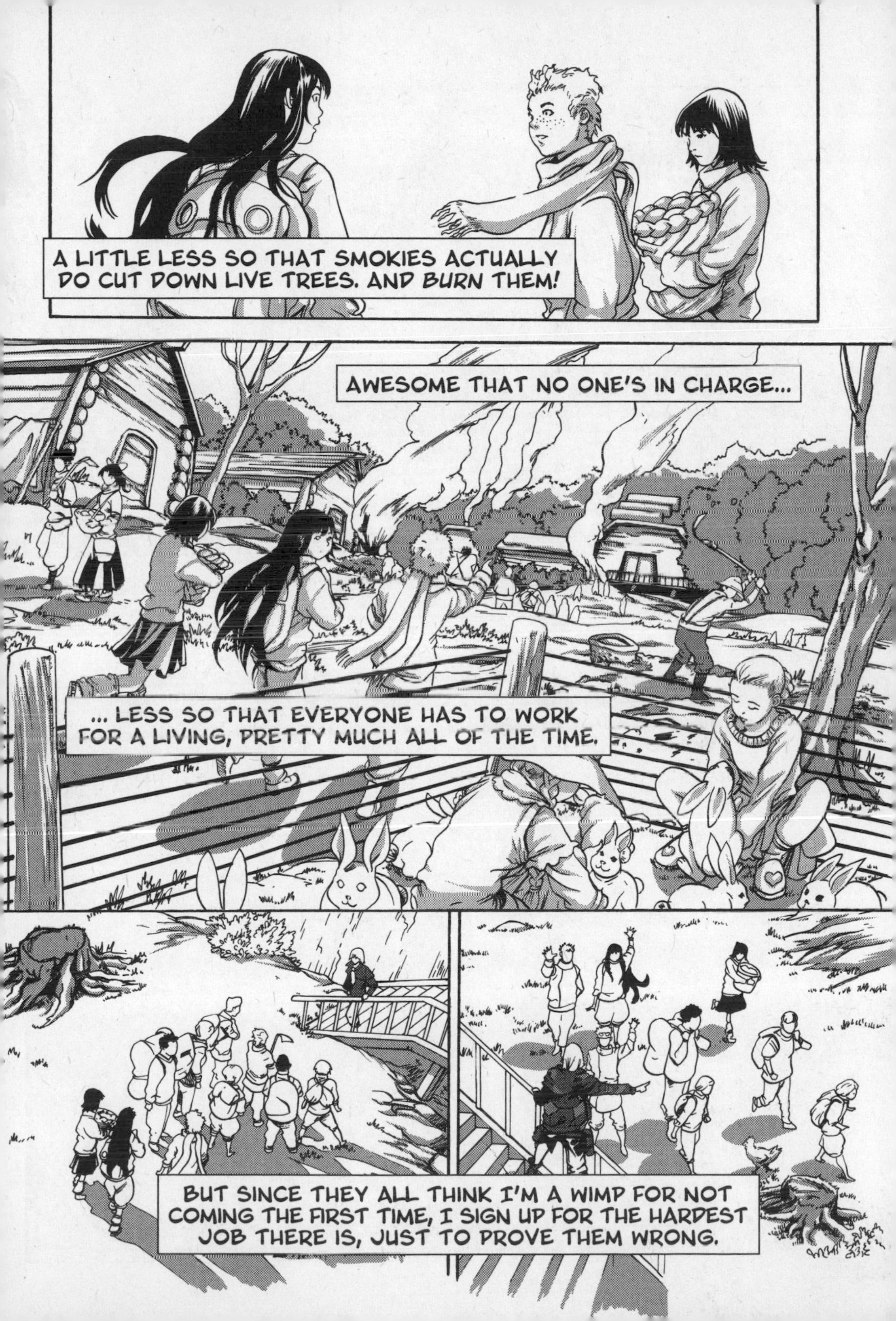
A LITTLE LESS SO THAT SMOKIES ACTUALLY DO CUT DOWN LIVE TREES. AND BURN THEM!
AWESOME THAT NO ONE'S IN CHARGE...
... LESS SO THAT EVERYONE HAS TO WORK FOR A LIVING, PRETTY MUCH ALL OF THE TIME.
BUT SINCE THEY ALL THINK I'M A WIMP FOR NOT COMING THE FIRST TIME, I SIGN UP FOR THE HARDEST JOB THERE IS, JUST TO PROVE THEM WRONG.

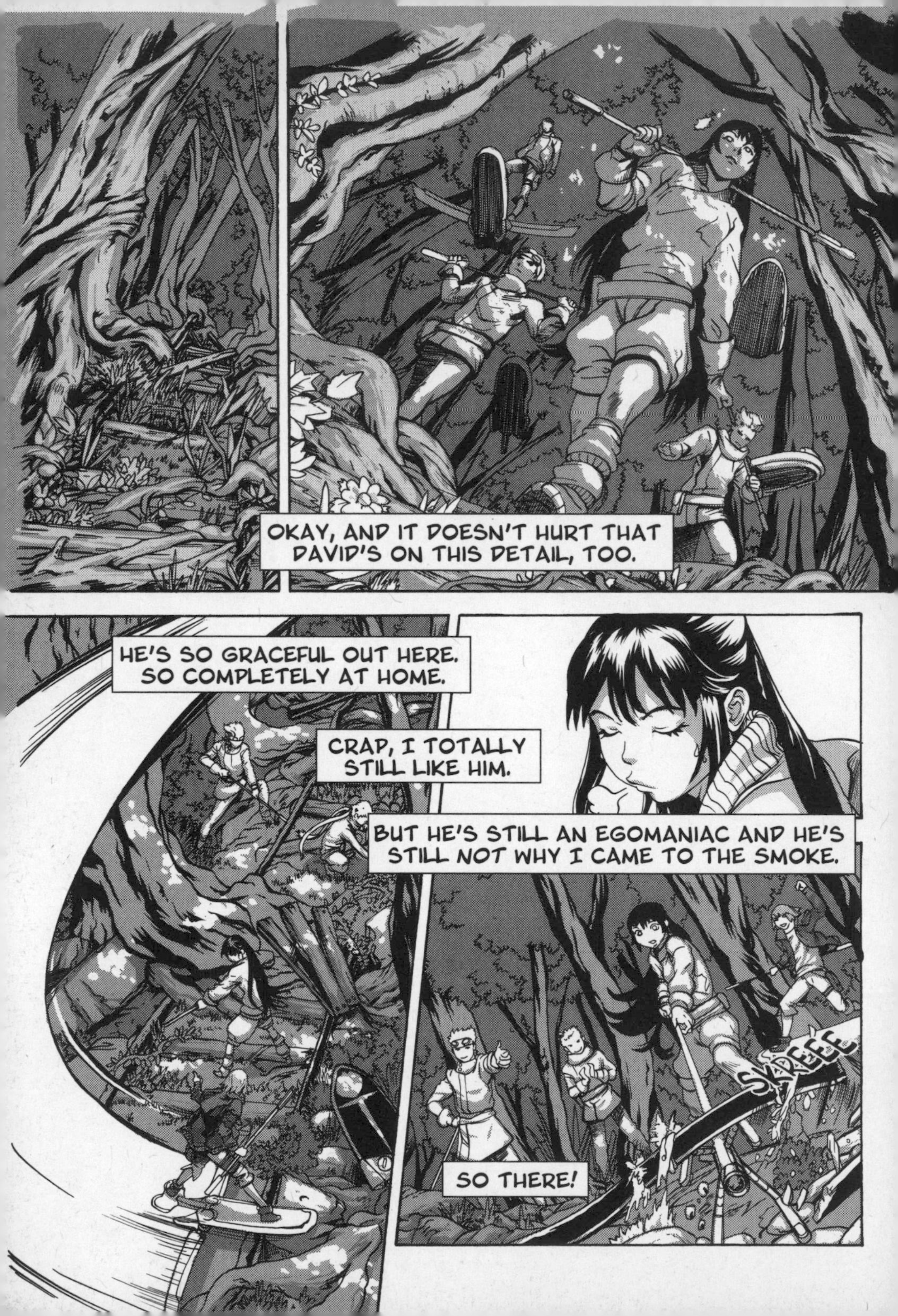
OKAY, AND IT DOESN'T HURT THAT DAVID'S ON THIS DETAIL, TOO.
HE'S SO GRACEFUL OUT HERE. SO COMPLETELY AT HOME.
CRAP, I TOTALLY STILL LIKE HIM.
BUT HE'S STILL AN EGOMANIAC AND HE'S STILL NOT WHY I CAME TO THE SMOKE.
SKREEE
SO THERE!

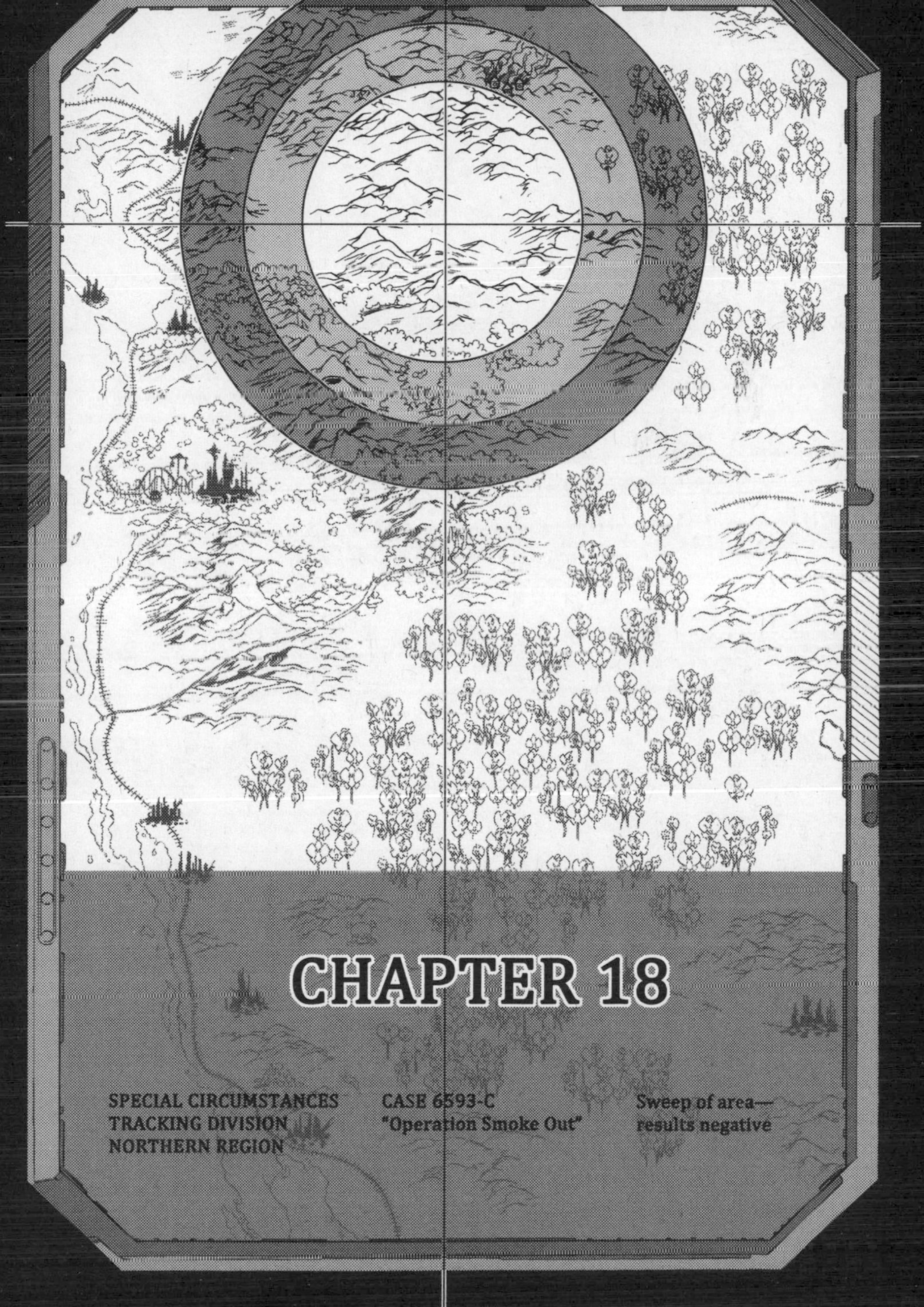

# CHAPTER 18

SPECIAL CIRCUMSTANCES
TRACKING DIVISION
NORTHERN REGION

CASE 6593-C
"Operation Smoke Out"

Sweep of area—
results negative

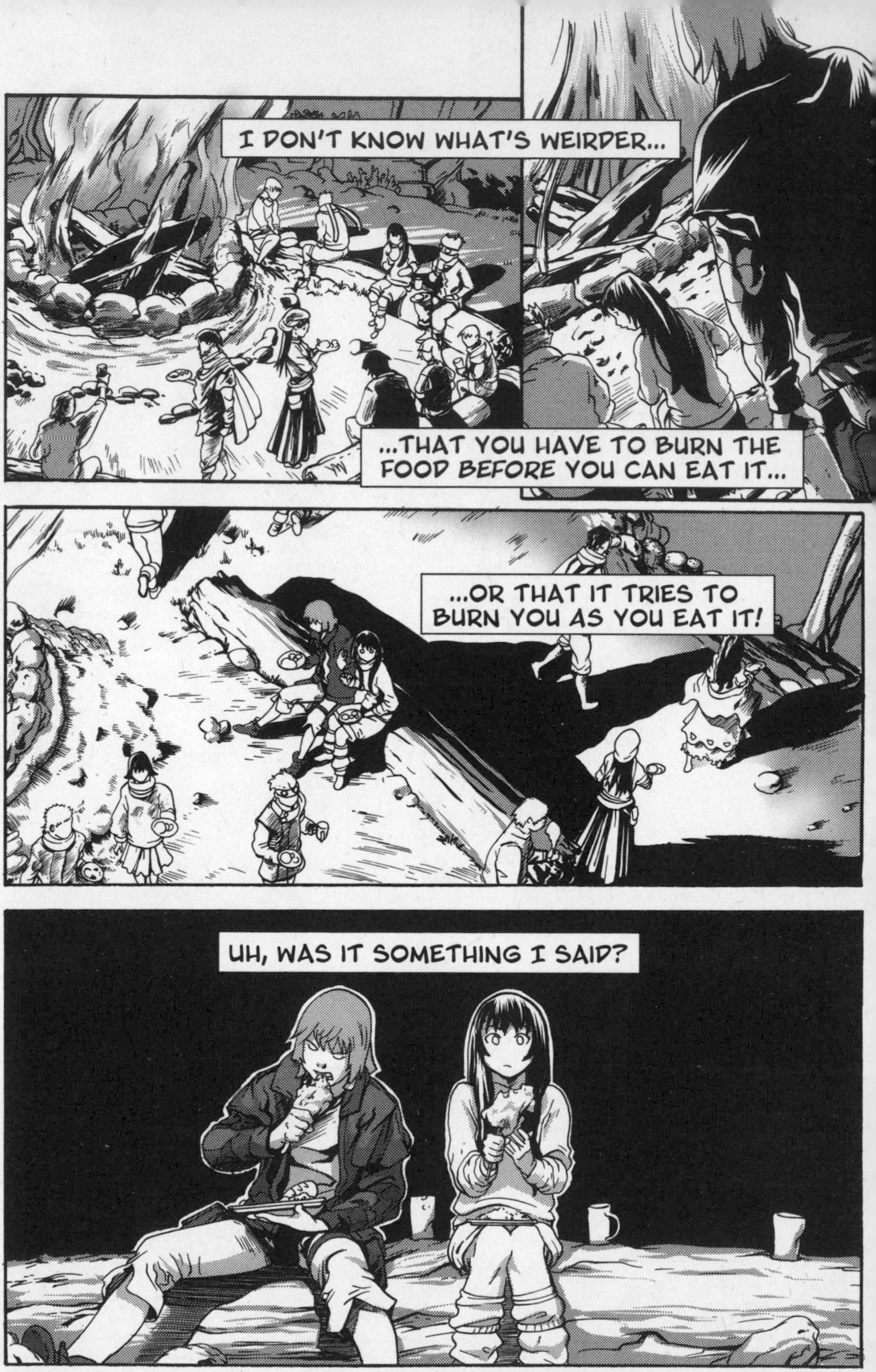
I DON'T KNOW WHAT'S WEIRDER...
...THAT YOU HAVE TO BURN THE FOOD BEFORE YOU CAN EAT IT...
...OR THAT IT TRIES TO BURN YOU AS YOU EAT IT!
UH, WAS IT SOMETHING I SAID?

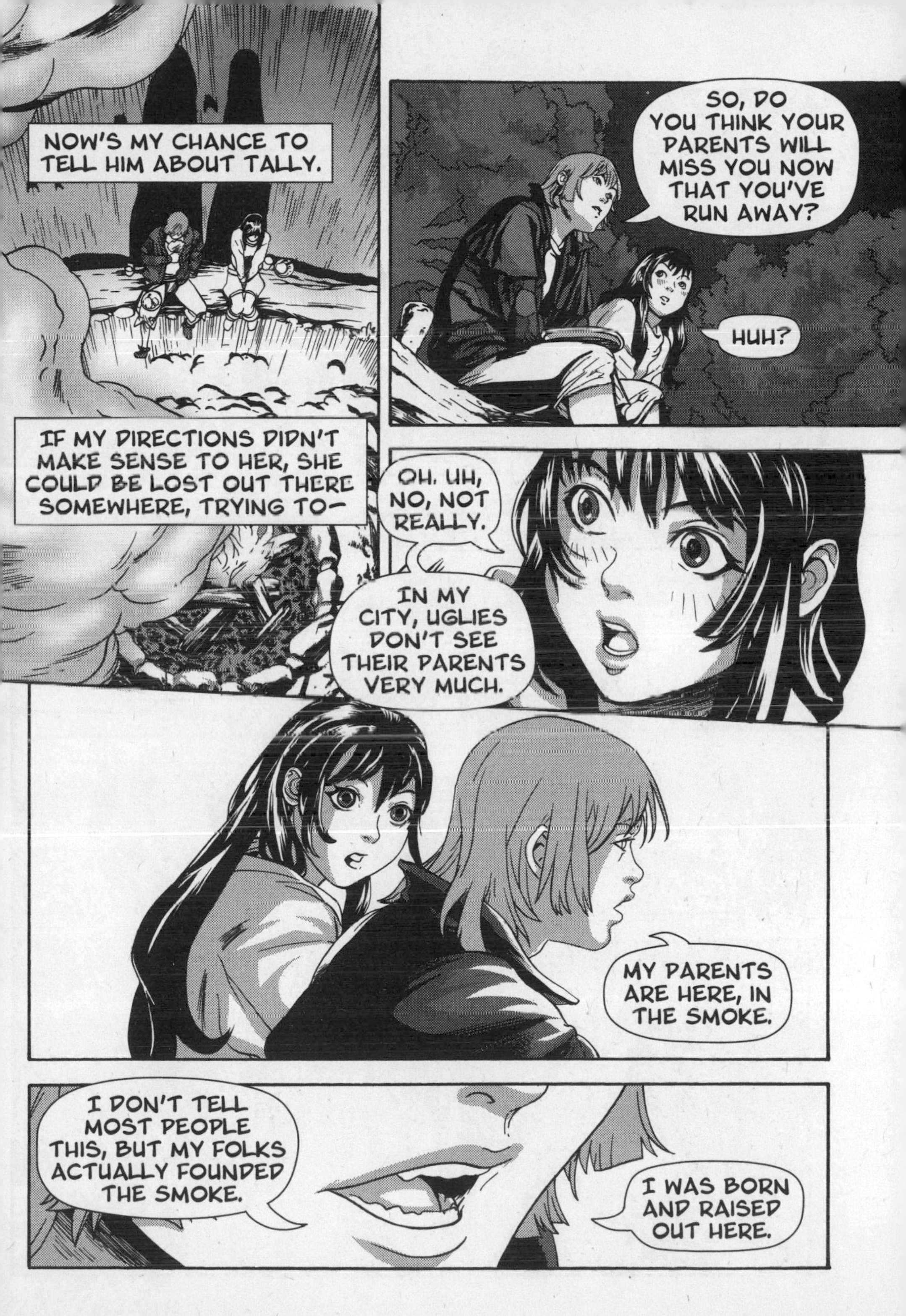
NOW'S MY CHANCE TO TELL HIM ABOUT TALLY.
SO, DO YOU THINK YOUR PARENTS WILL MISS YOU NOW THAT YOU'VE RUN AWAY?
HUH?
IF MY DIRECTIONS DIDN'T MAKE SENSE TO HER, SHE COULD BE LOST OUT THERE SOMEWHERE, TRYING TO—
OH. UH, NO, NOT REALLY.
IN MY CITY, UGLIES DON'T SEE THEIR PARENTS VERY MUCH.
MY PARENTS ARE HERE, IN THE SMOKE.
I DON'T TELL MOST PEOPLE THIS, BUT MY FOLKS ACTUALLY FOUNDED THE SMOKE.
I WAS BORN AND RAISED OUT HERE.

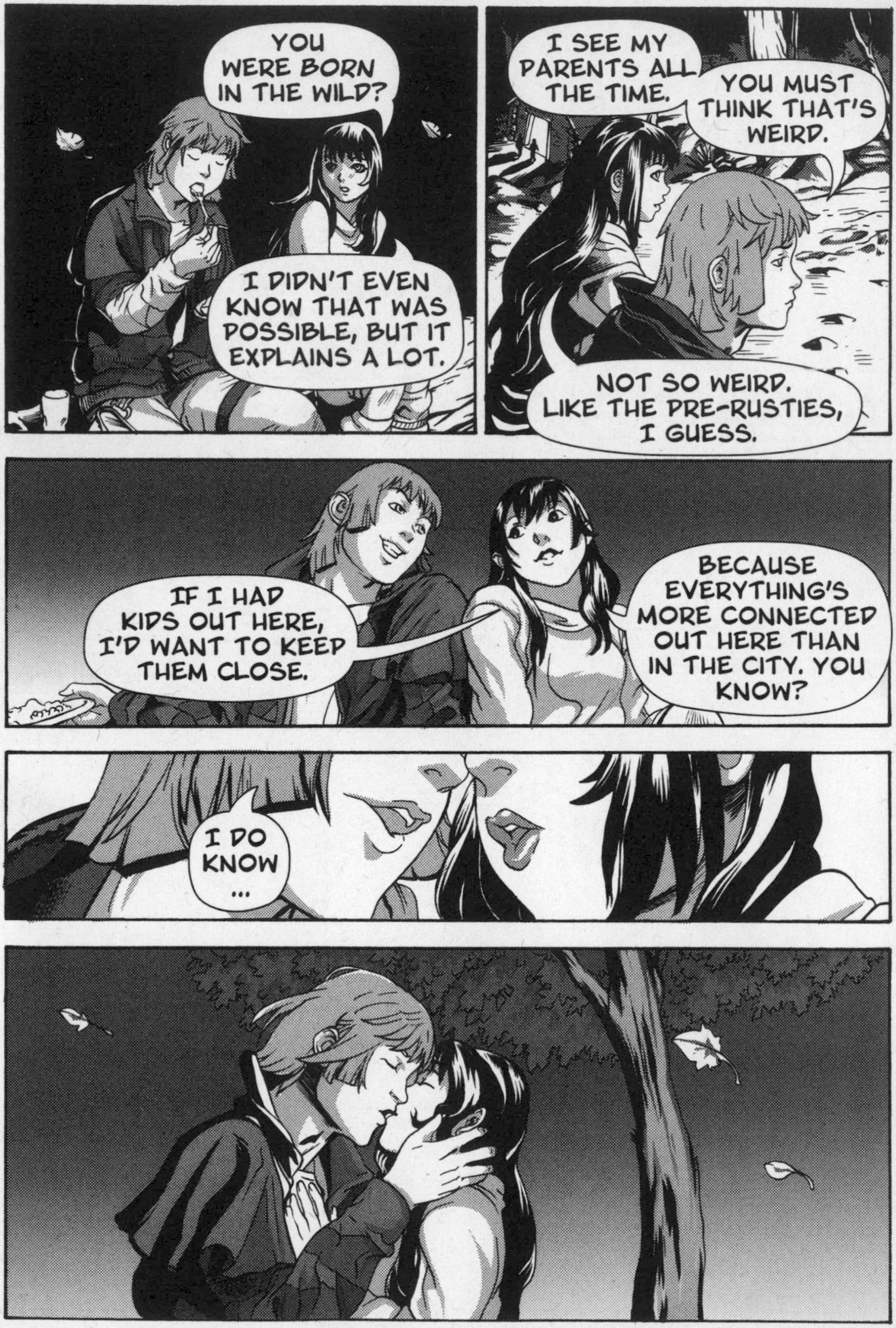
YOU WERE BORN IN THE WILD?
I DIDN'T EVEN KNOW THAT WAS POSSIBLE, BUT IT EXPLAINS A LOT.
I SEE MY PARENTS ALL THE TIME.
YOU MUST THINK THAT'S WEIRD.
NOT SO WEIRD. LIKE THE PRE-RUSTIES, I GUESS.
IF I HAD KIDS OUT HERE, I'D WANT TO KEEP THEM CLOSE.
BECAUSE EVERYTHING'S MORE CONNECTED OUT HERE THAN IN THE CITY. YOU KNOW?
I DO KNOW ...

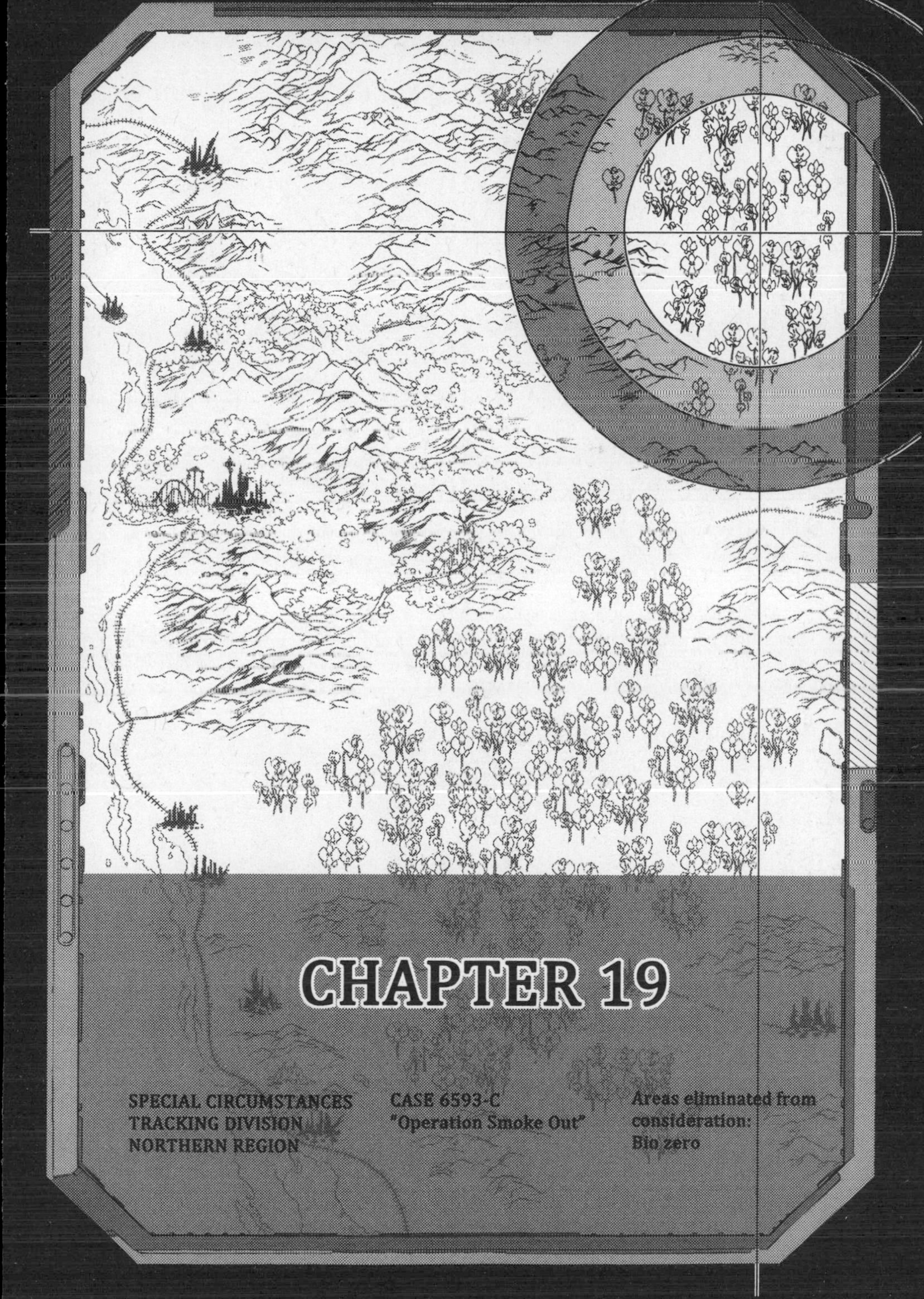

# CHAPTER 19

SPECIAL CIRCUMSTANCES
TRACKING DIVISION
NORTHERN REGION

CASE 6593-C
"Operation Smoke Out"

Areas eliminated from
consideration:
Bio zero

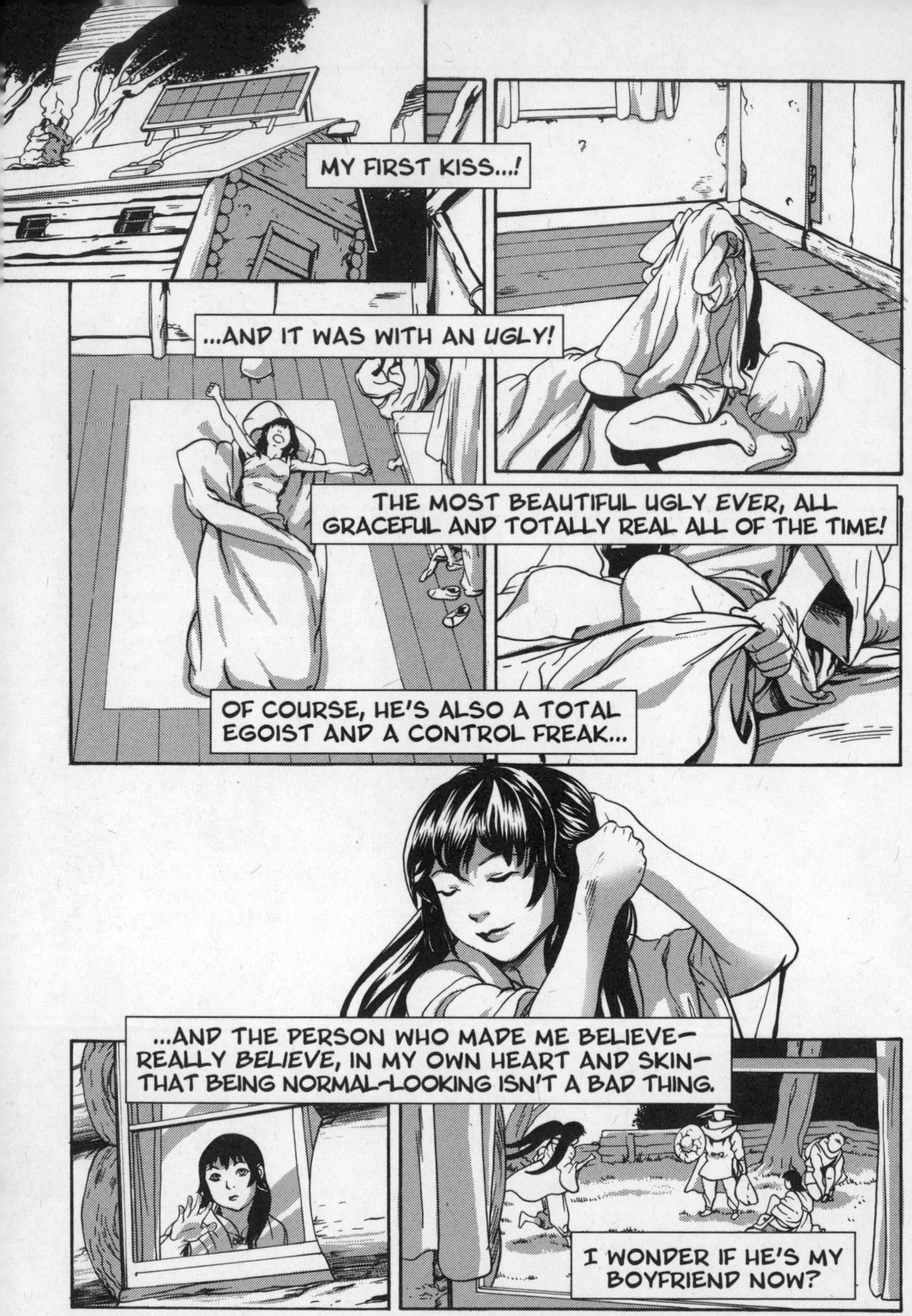
MY FIRST KISS...!
...AND IT WAS WITH AN UGLY!
THE MOST BEAUTIFUL UGLY EVER, ALL GRACEFUL AND TOTALLY REAL ALL OF THE TIME!
OF COURSE, HE'S ALSO A TOTAL EGOIST AND A CONTROL FREAK...
...AND THE PERSON WHO MADE ME BELIEVE— REALLY BELIEVE, IN MY OWN HEART AND SKIN— THAT BEING NORMAL-LOOKING ISN'T A BAD THING.
I WONDER IF HE'S MY BOYFRIEND NOW?

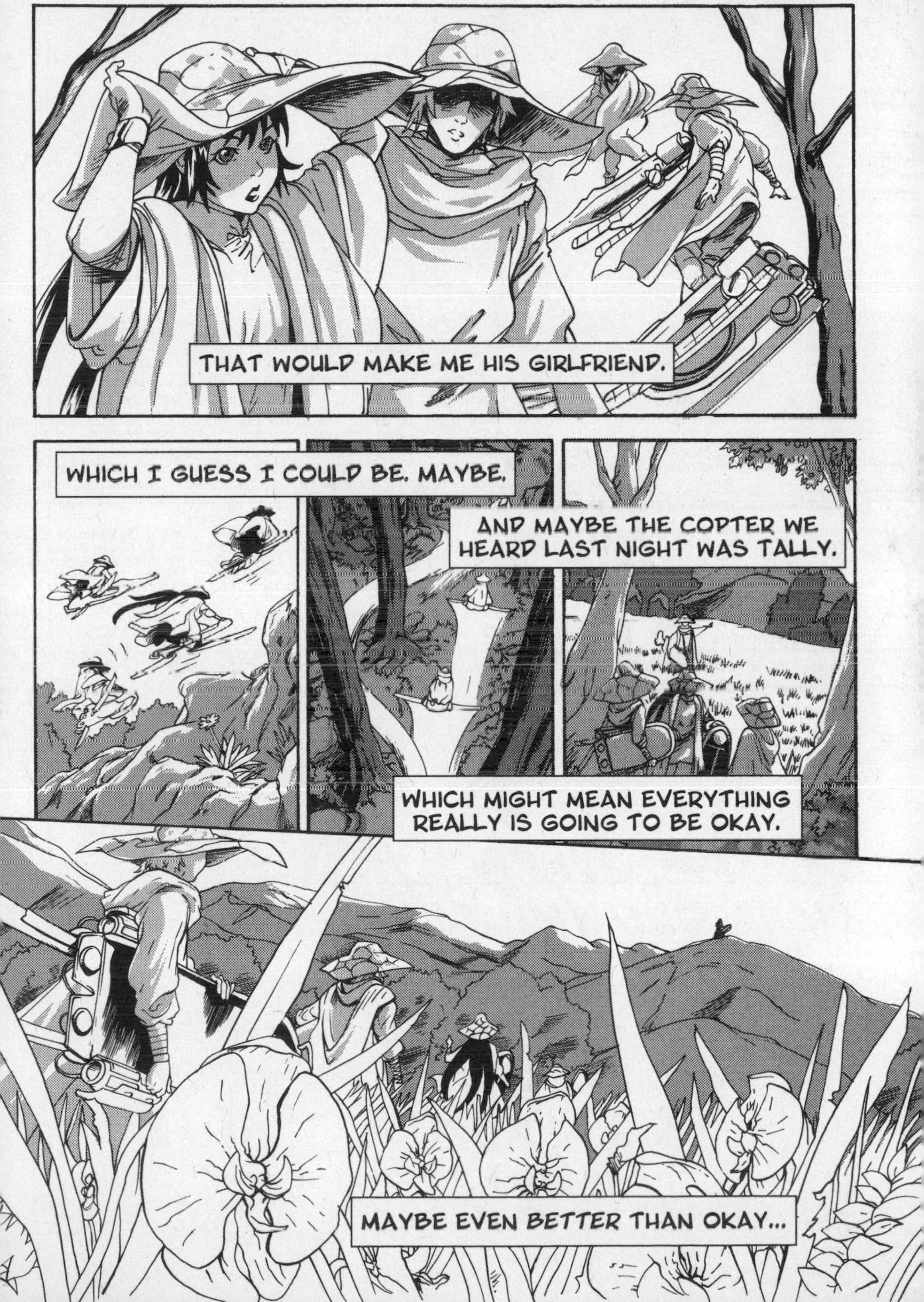
THAT WOULD MAKE ME HIS GIRLFRIEND.
WHICH I GUESS I COULD BE. MAYBE.
AND MAYBE THE COPTER WE HEARD LAST NIGHT WAS TALLY.
WHICH MIGHT MEAN EVERYTHING REALLY IS GOING TO BE OKAY.
MAYBE EVEN *BETTER* THAN OKAY...

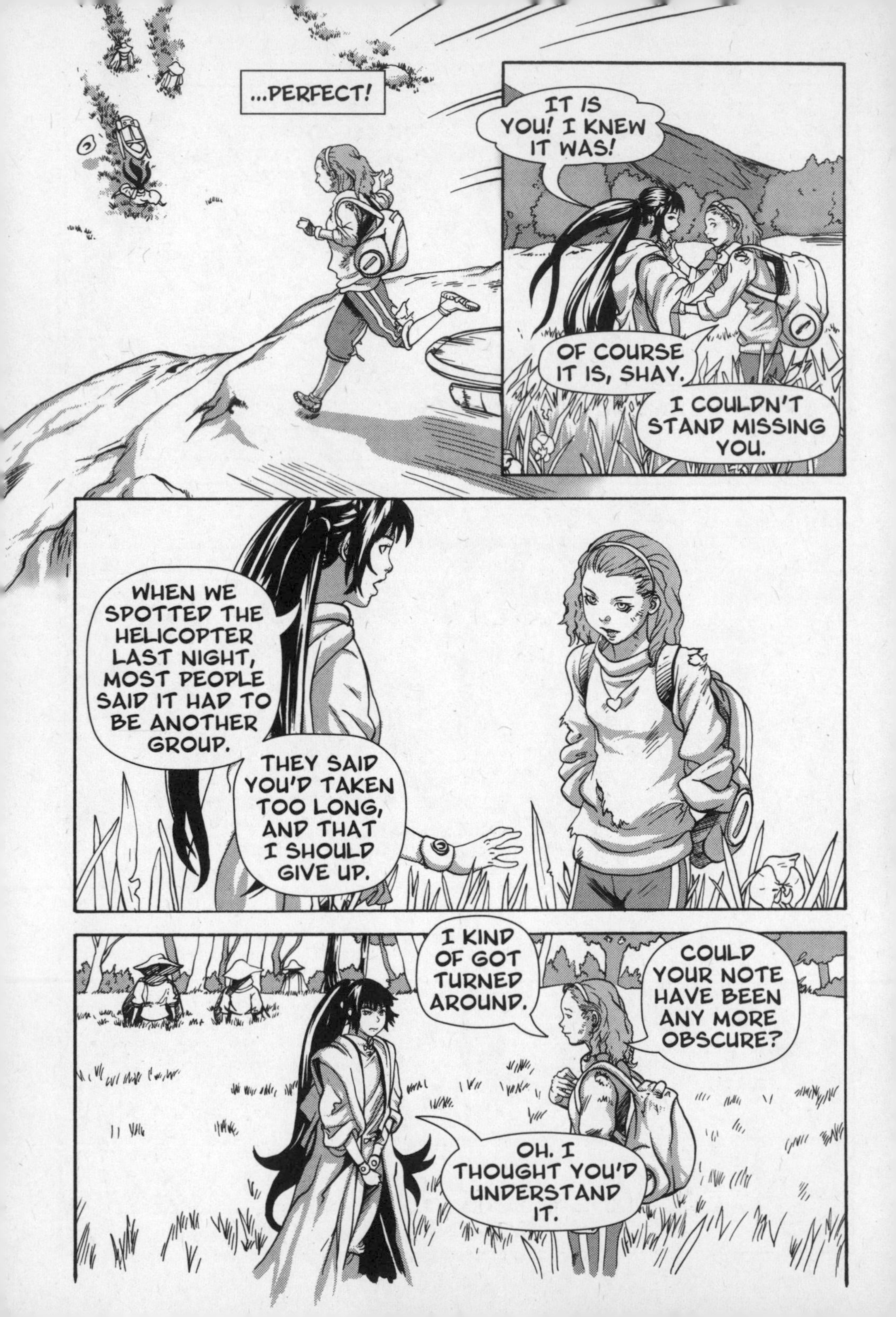
...PERFECT!
IT IS YOU! I KNEW IT WAS!
OF COURSE IT IS, SHAY.
I COULDN'T STAND MISSING YOU.
WHEN WE SPOTTED THE HELICOPTER LAST NIGHT, MOST PEOPLE SAID IT HAD TO BE ANOTHER GROUP.
THEY SAID YOU'D TAKEN TOO LONG, AND THAT I SHOULD GIVE UP.
I KIND OF GOT TURNED AROUND.
COULD YOUR NOTE HAVE BEEN ANY MORE OBSCURE?
OH. I THOUGHT YOU'D UNDERSTAND IT.

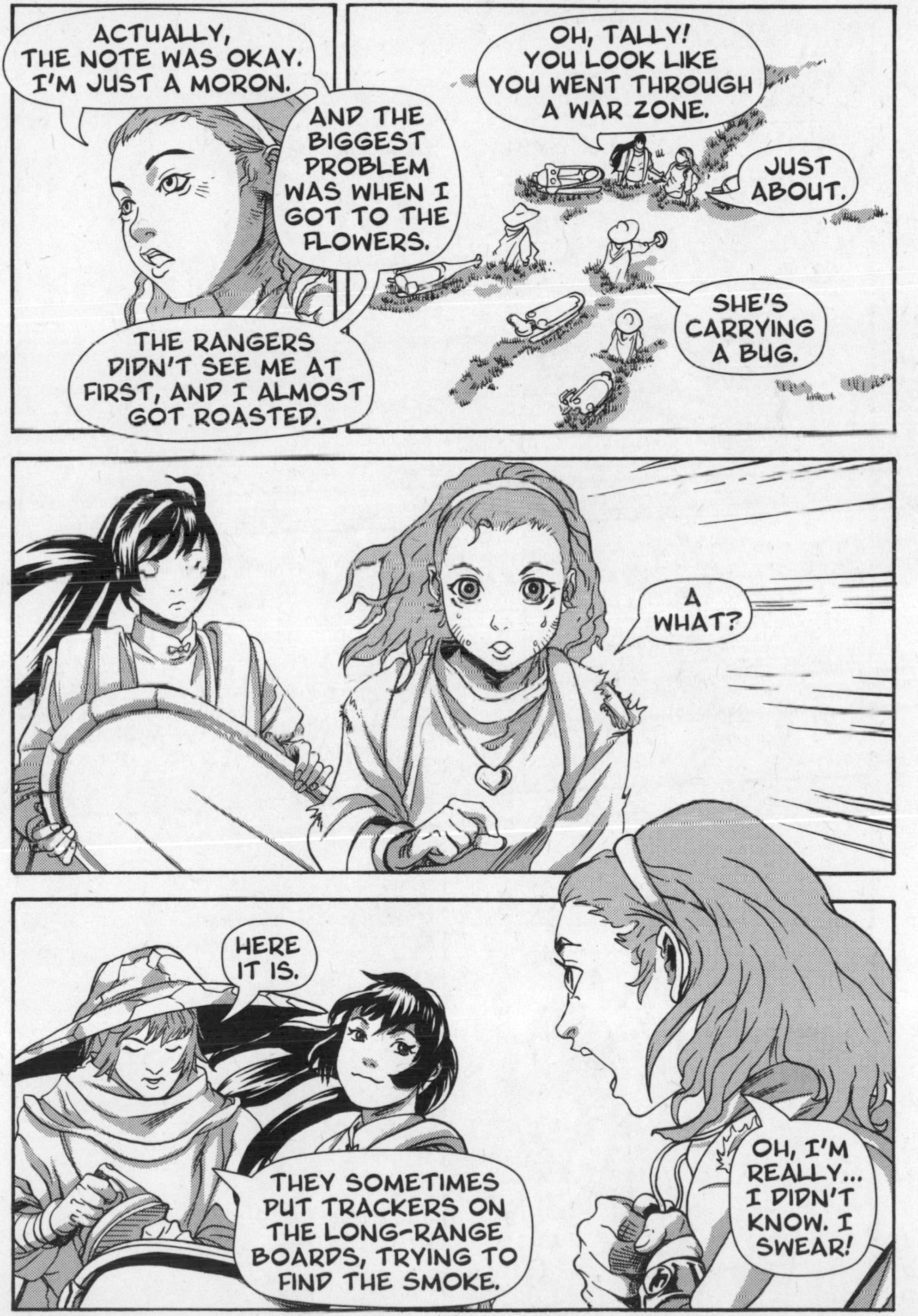
ACTUALLY, THE NOTE WAS OKAY. I'M JUST A MORON.
AND THE BIGGEST PROBLEM WAS WHEN I GOT TO THE FLOWERS.
THE RANGERS DIDN'T SEE ME AT FIRST, AND I ALMOST GOT ROASTED.
OH, TALLY! YOU LOOK LIKE YOU WENT THROUGH A WAR ZONE.
JUST ABOUT.
SHE'S CARRYING A BUG.
A WHAT?
HERE IT IS.
THEY SOMETIMES PUT TRACKERS ON THE LONG-RANGE BOARDS, TRYING TO FIND THE SMOKE.
OH, I'M REALLY... I DIDN'T KNOW. I SWEAR!

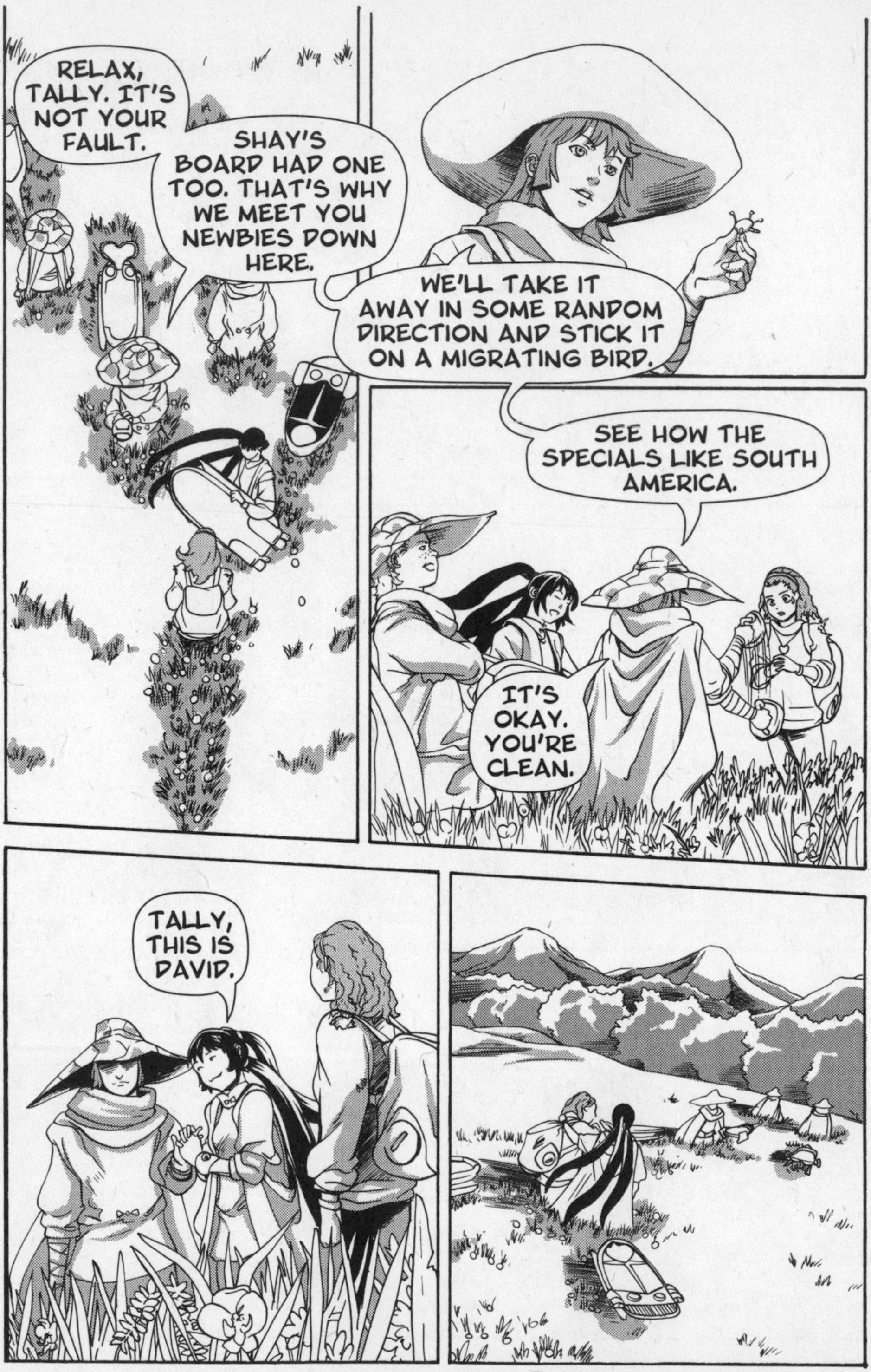
RELAX, TALLY. IT'S NOT YOUR FAULT.
SHAY'S BOARD HAD ONE TOO. THAT'S WHY WE MEET YOU NEWBIES DOWN HERE.
WE'LL TAKE IT AWAY IN SOME RANDOM DIRECTION AND STICK IT ON A MIGRATING BIRD.
SEE HOW THE SPECIALS LIKE SOUTH AMERICA.
IT'S OKAY. YOU'RE CLEAN.
TALLY, THIS IS DAVID.

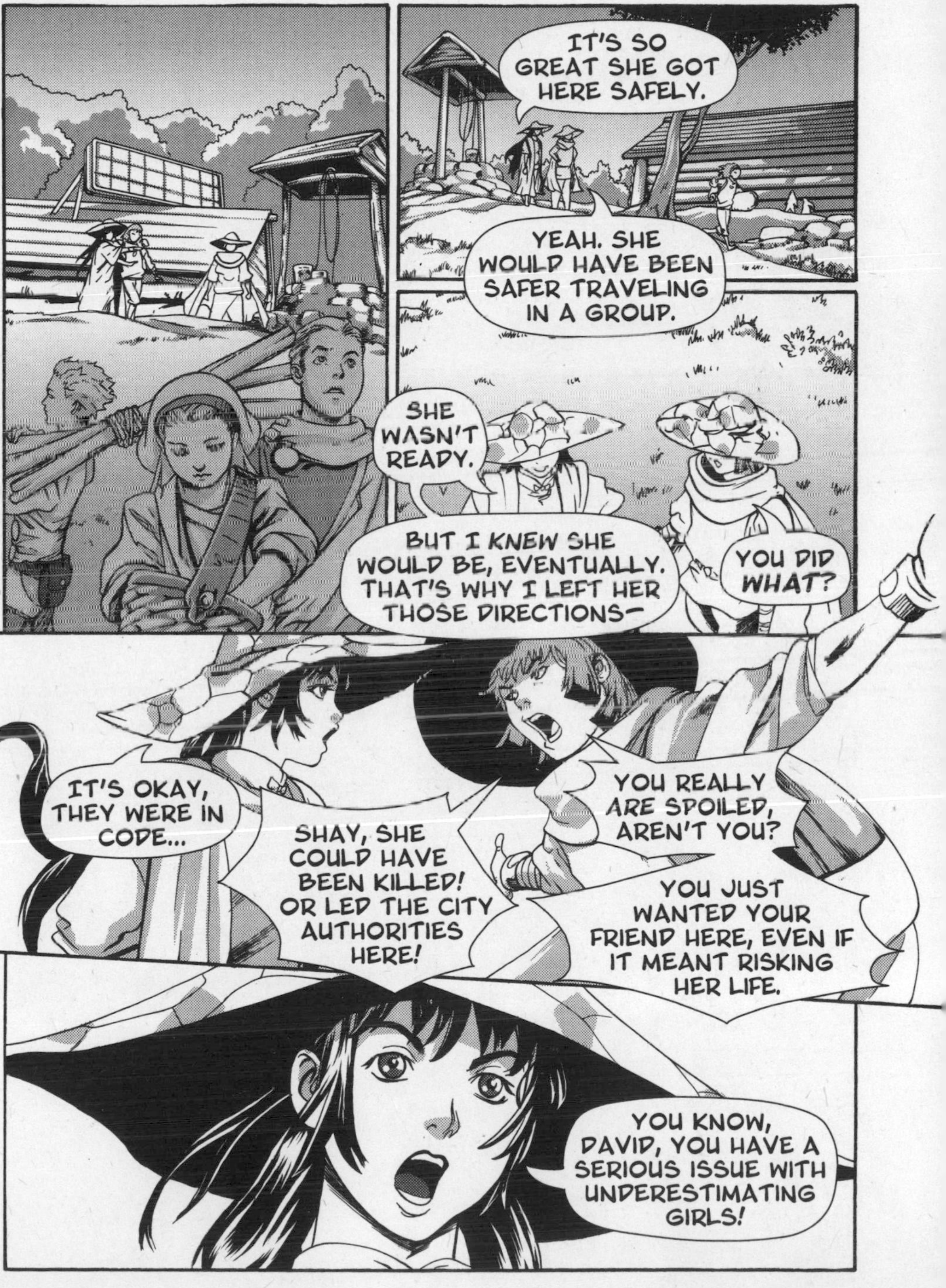
IT'S SO GREAT SHE GOT HERE SAFELY.
YEAH. SHE WOULD HAVE BEEN SAFER TRAVELING IN A GROUP.
SHE WASN'T READY.
BUT I KNEW SHE WOULD BE, EVENTUALLY. THAT'S WHY I LEFT HER THOSE DIRECTIONS—
YOU DID WHAT?
IT'S OKAY, THEY WERE IN CODE...
SHAY, SHE COULD HAVE BEEN KILLED! OR LED THE CITY AUTHORITIES HERE!
YOU REALLY ARE SPOILED, AREN'T YOU?
YOU JUST WANTED YOUR FRIEND HERE, EVEN IF IT MEANT RISKING HER LIFE.
YOU KNOW, DAVID, YOU HAVE A SERIOUS ISSUE WITH UNDERESTIMATING GIRLS!

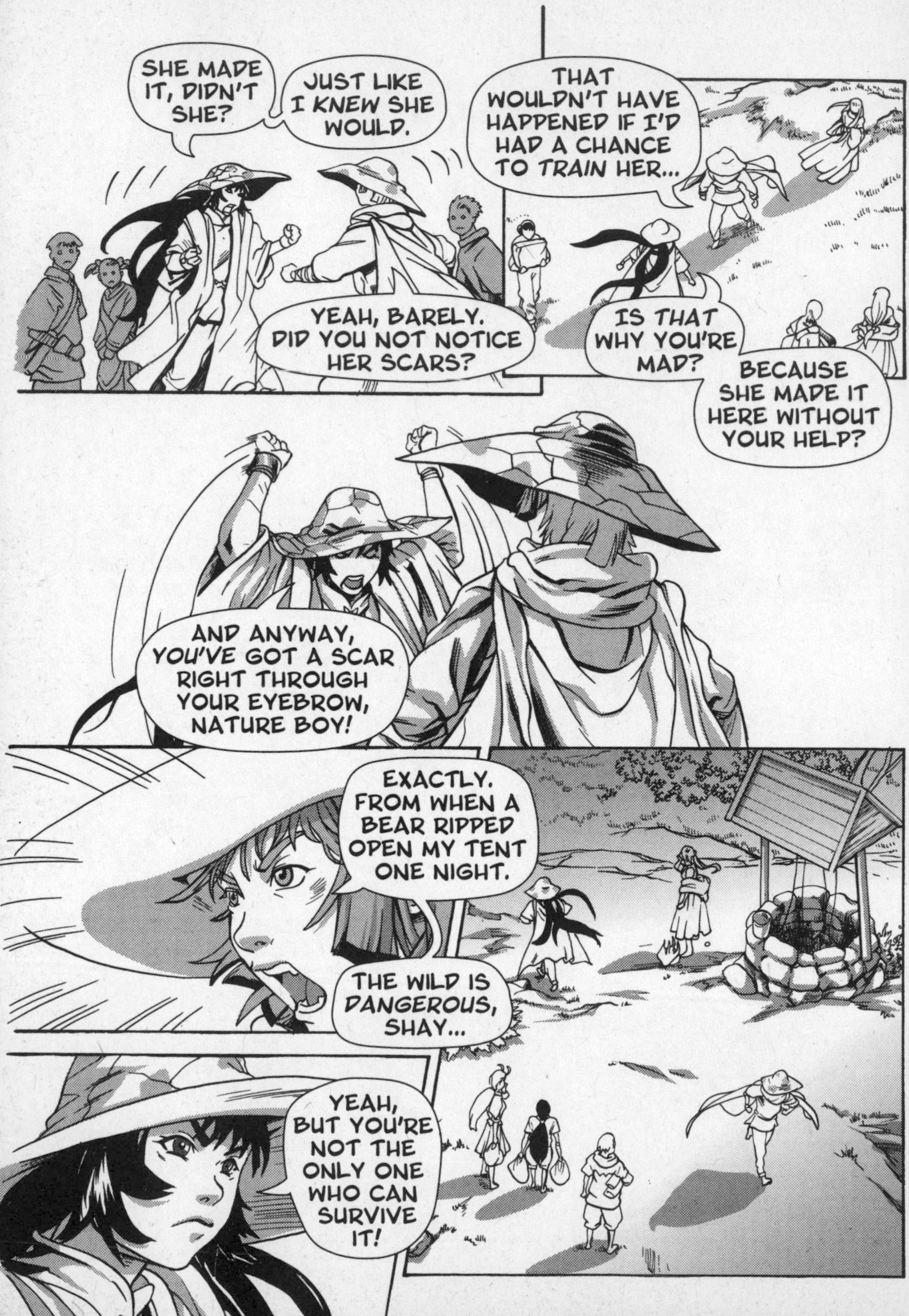

SHE MADE IT, DIDN'T SHE?
JUST LIKE I KNEW SHE WOULD.
YEAH, BARELY. DID YOU NOT NOTICE HER SCARS?
THAT WOULDN'T HAVE HAPPENED IF I'D HAD A CHANCE TO TRAIN HER...
IS THAT WHY YOU'RE MAD?
BECAUSE SHE MADE IT HERE WITHOUT YOUR HELP?
AND ANYWAY, YOU'VE GOT A SCAR RIGHT THROUGH YOUR EYEBROW, NATURE BOY!
EXACTLY. FROM WHEN A BEAR RIPPED OPEN MY TENT ONE NIGHT.
THE WILD IS DANGEROUS, SHAY...
YEAH, BUT YOU'RE NOT THE ONLY ONE WHO CAN SURVIVE IT!

# CHAPTER 20

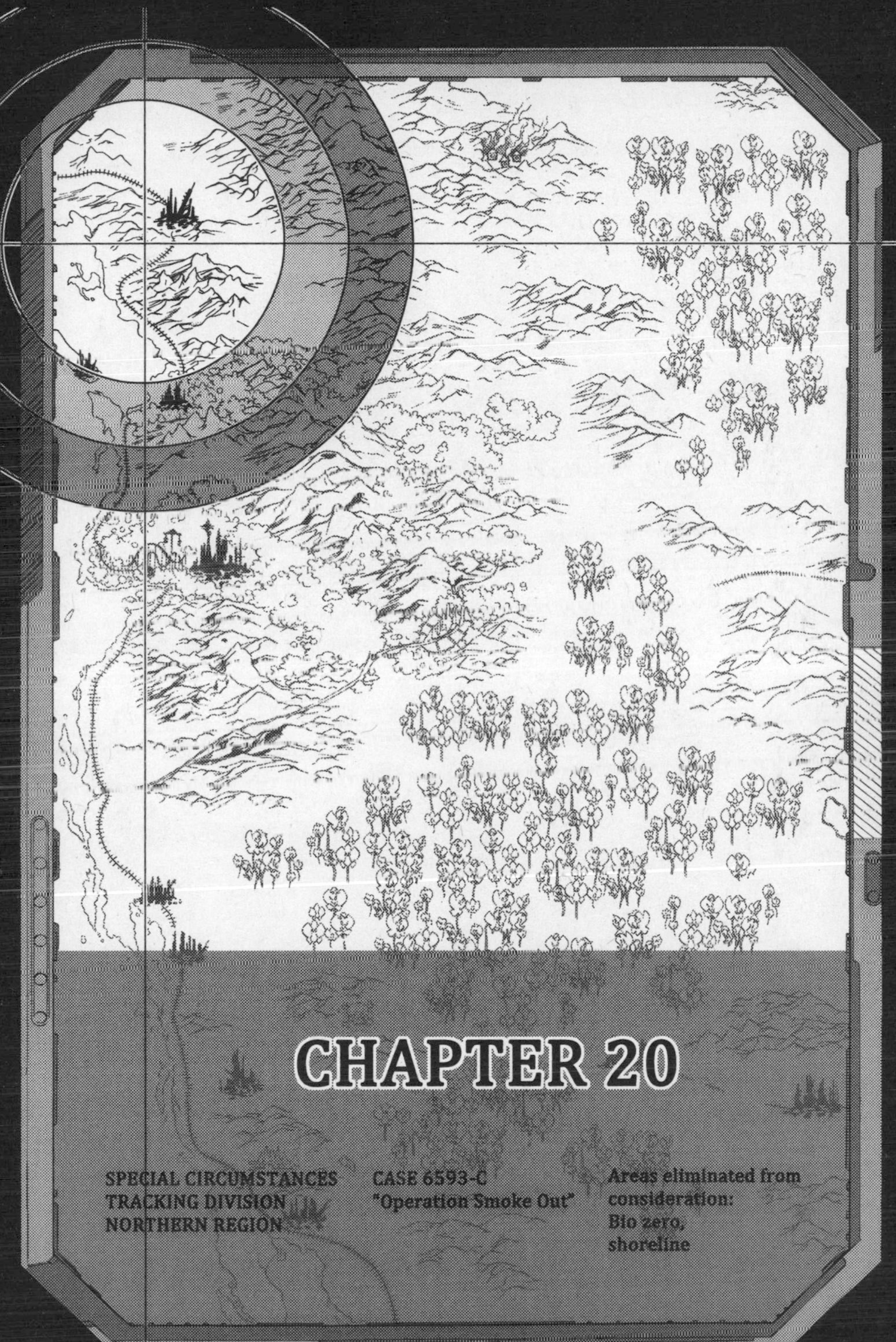
SPECIAL CIRCUMSTANCES
TRACKING DIVISION
NORTHERN REGION
CASE 6593-C
"Operation Smoke Out"
Areas eliminated from
consideration:
Bio zero,
shoreline

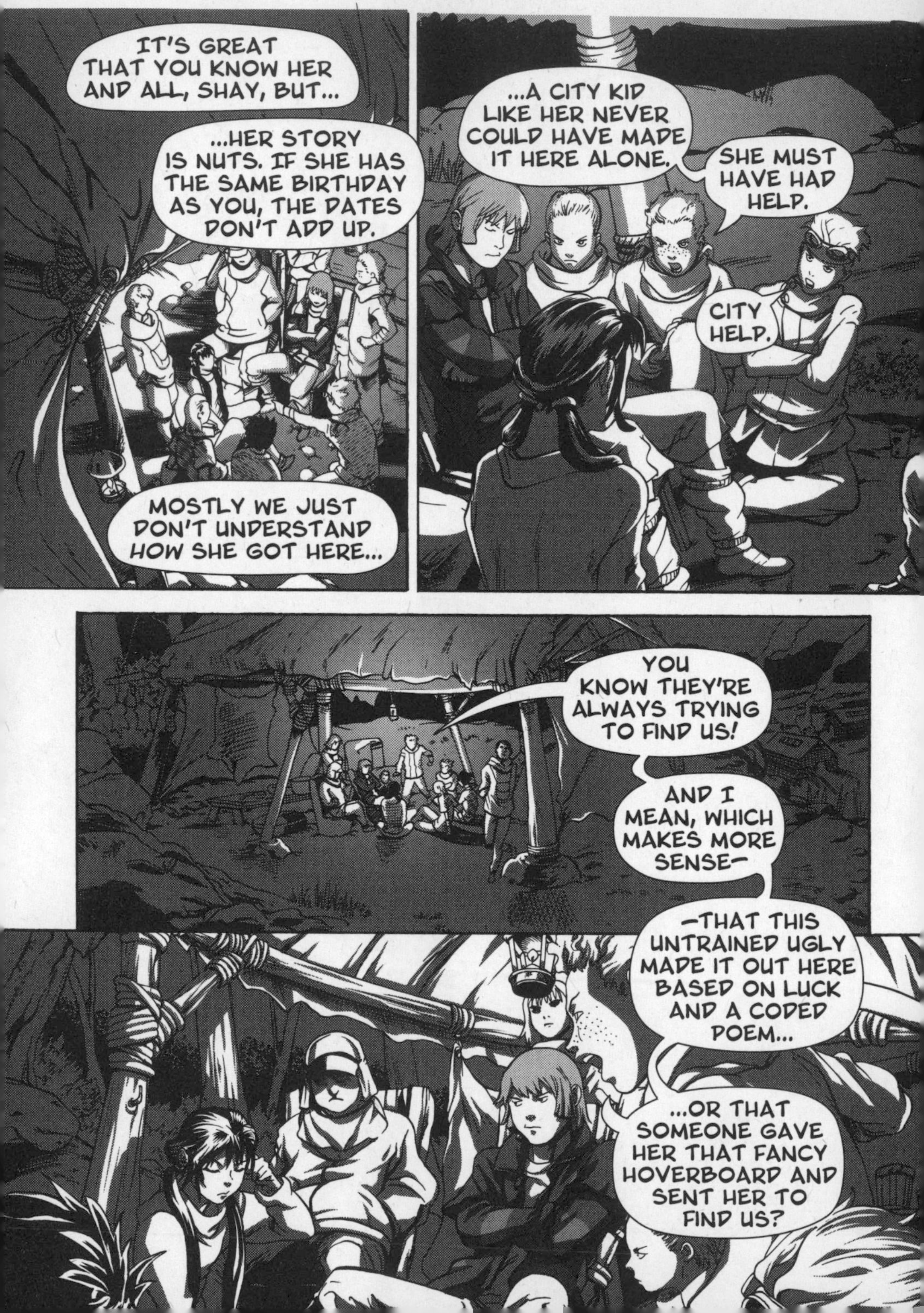
IT'S GREAT THAT YOU KNOW HER AND ALL, SHAY, BUT...
...HER STORY IS NUTS. IF SHE HAS THE SAME BIRTHDAY AS YOU, THE DATES DON'T ADD UP.
MOSTLY WE JUST DON'T UNDERSTAND HOW SHE GOT HERE...
...A CITY KID LIKE HER NEVER COULD HAVE MADE IT HERE ALONE.
SHE MUST HAVE HAD HELP.
CITY HELP.
YOU KNOW THEY'RE ALWAYS TRYING TO FIND US!
AND I MEAN, WHICH MAKES MORE SENSE—
—THAT THIS UNTRAINED UGLY MADE IT OUT HERE BASED ON LUCK AND A CODED POEM...
...OR THAT SOMEONE GAVE HER THAT FANCY HOVERBOARD AND SENT HER TO FIND US?

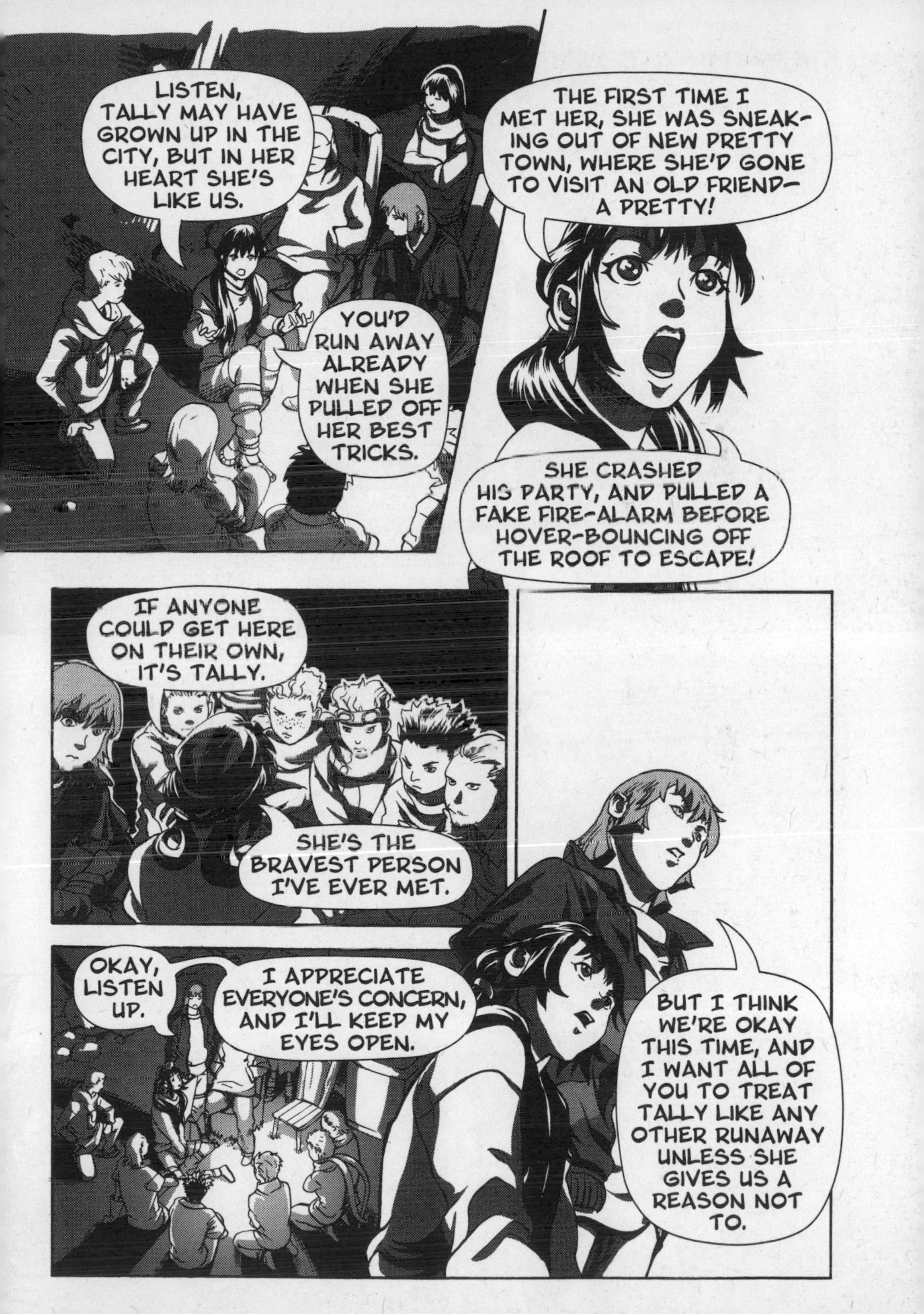
LISTEN, TALLY MAY HAVE GROWN UP IN THE CITY, BUT IN HER HEART SHE'S LIKE US.
YOU'D RUN AWAY ALREADY WHEN SHE PULLED OFF HER BEST TRICKS.
THE FIRST TIME I MET HER, SHE WAS SNEAK-ING OUT OF NEW PRETTY TOWN, WHERE SHE'D GONE TO VISIT AN OLD FRIEND—A PRETTY!
SHE CRASHED HIS PARTY, AND PULLED A FAKE FIRE-ALARM BEFORE HOVER-BOUNCING OFF THE ROOF TO ESCAPE!
IF ANYONE COULD GET HERE ON THEIR OWN, IT'S TALLY.
SHE'S THE BRAVEST PERSON I'VE EVER MET.
OKAY, LISTEN UP.
I APPRECIATE EVERYONE'S CONCERN, AND I'LL KEEP MY EYES OPEN.
BUT I THINK WE'RE OKAY THIS TIME, AND I WANT ALL OF YOU TO TREAT TALLY LIKE ANY OTHER RUNAWAY UNLESS SHE GIVES US A REASON NOT TO.

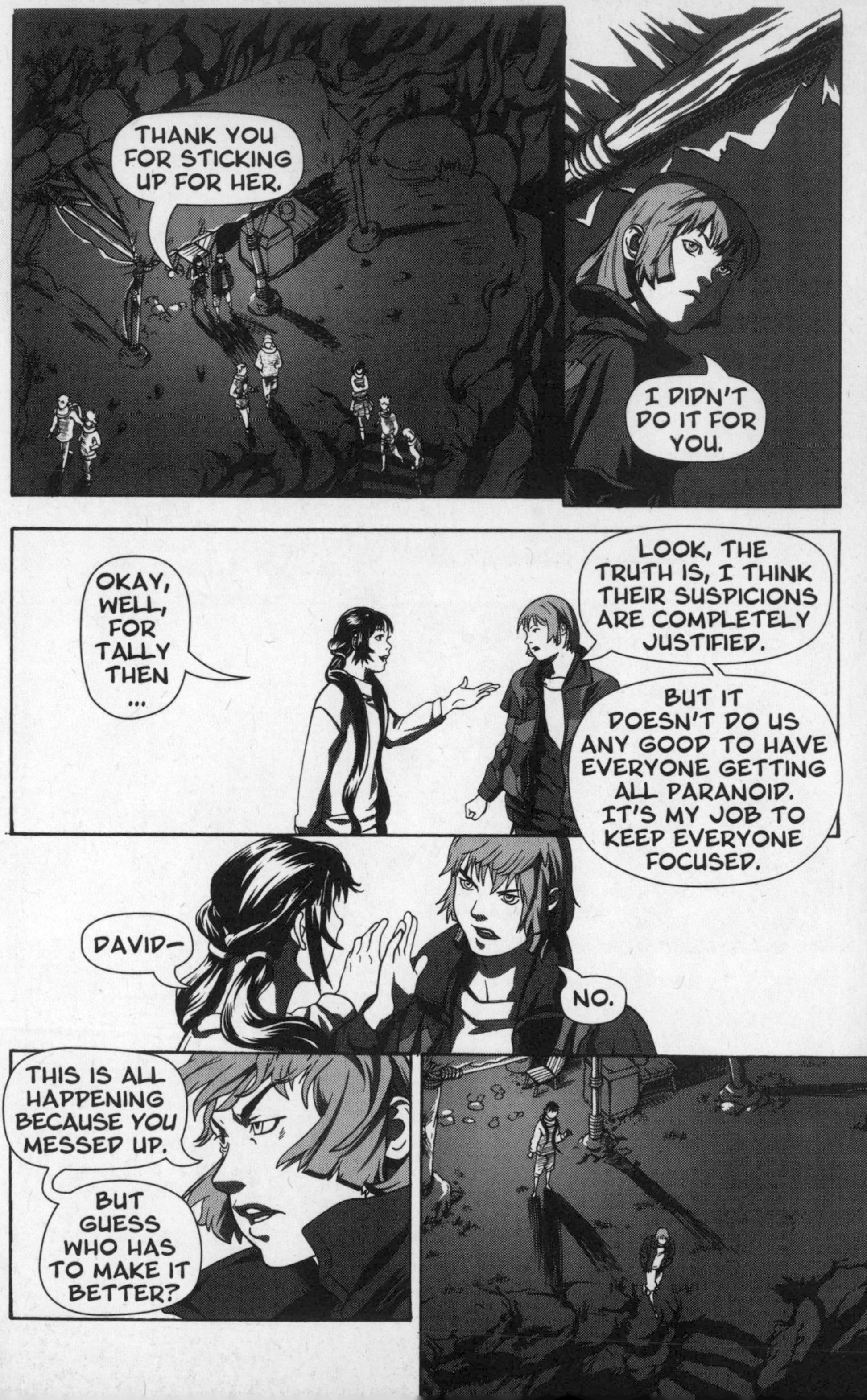
THANK YOU FOR STICKING UP FOR HER.
I DIDN'T DO IT FOR YOU.
OKAY, WELL, FOR TALLY THEN ...
LOOK, THE TRUTH IS, I THINK THEIR SUSPICIONS ARE COMPLETELY JUSTIFIED.
BUT IT DOESN'T DO US ANY GOOD TO HAVE EVERYONE GETTING ALL PARANOID. IT'S MY JOB TO KEEP EVERYONE FOCUSED.
DAVID–
NO.
THIS IS ALL HAPPENING BECAUSE YOU MESSED UP.
BUT GUESS WHO HAS TO MAKE IT BETTER?

# CHAPTER 21

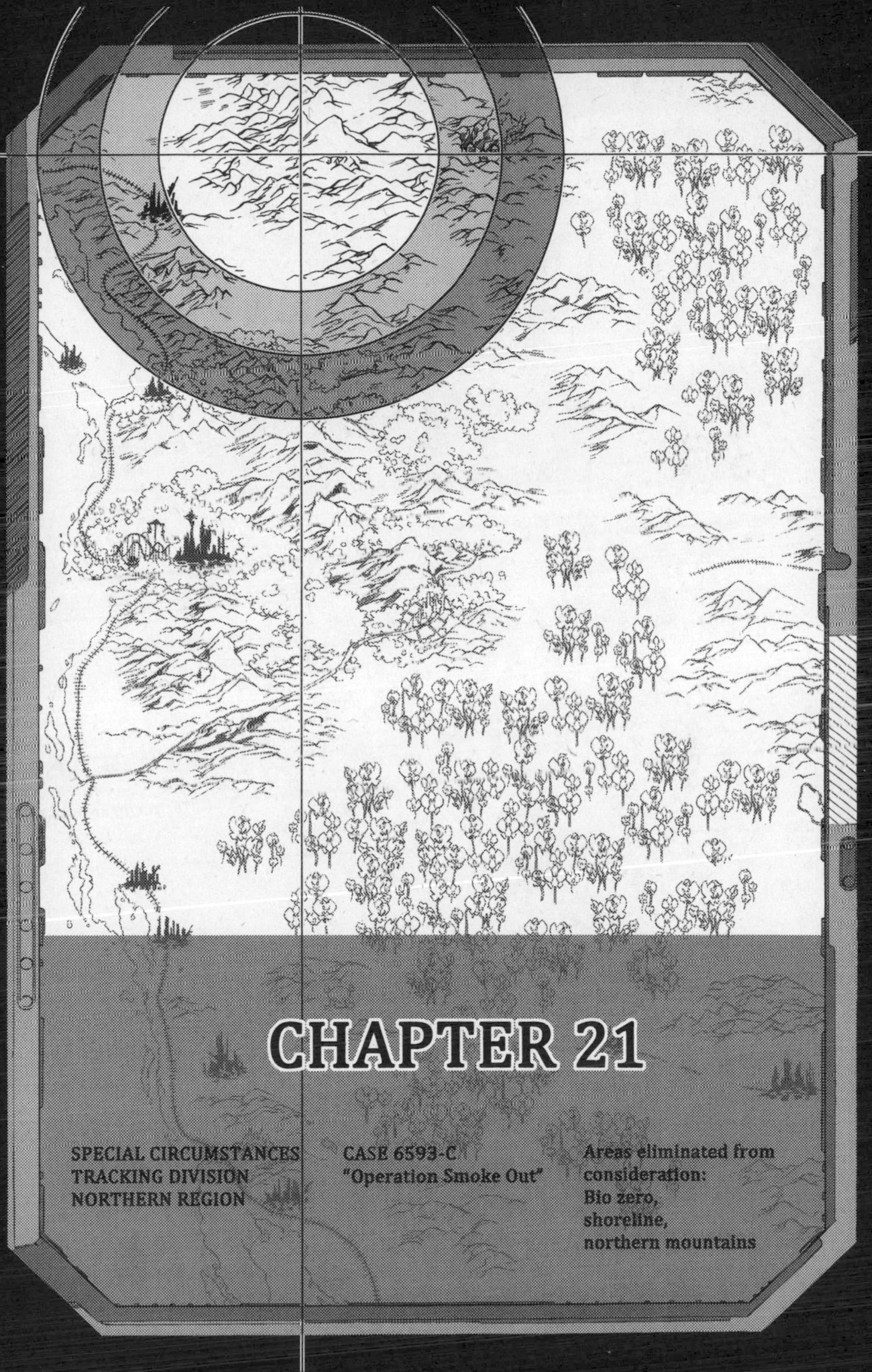
SPECIAL CIRCUMSTANCES
TRACKING DIVISION
NORTHERN REGION
CASE 6593-C
"Operation Smoke Out"
Areas eliminated from
consideration:
Bio zero,
shoreline,
northern mountains

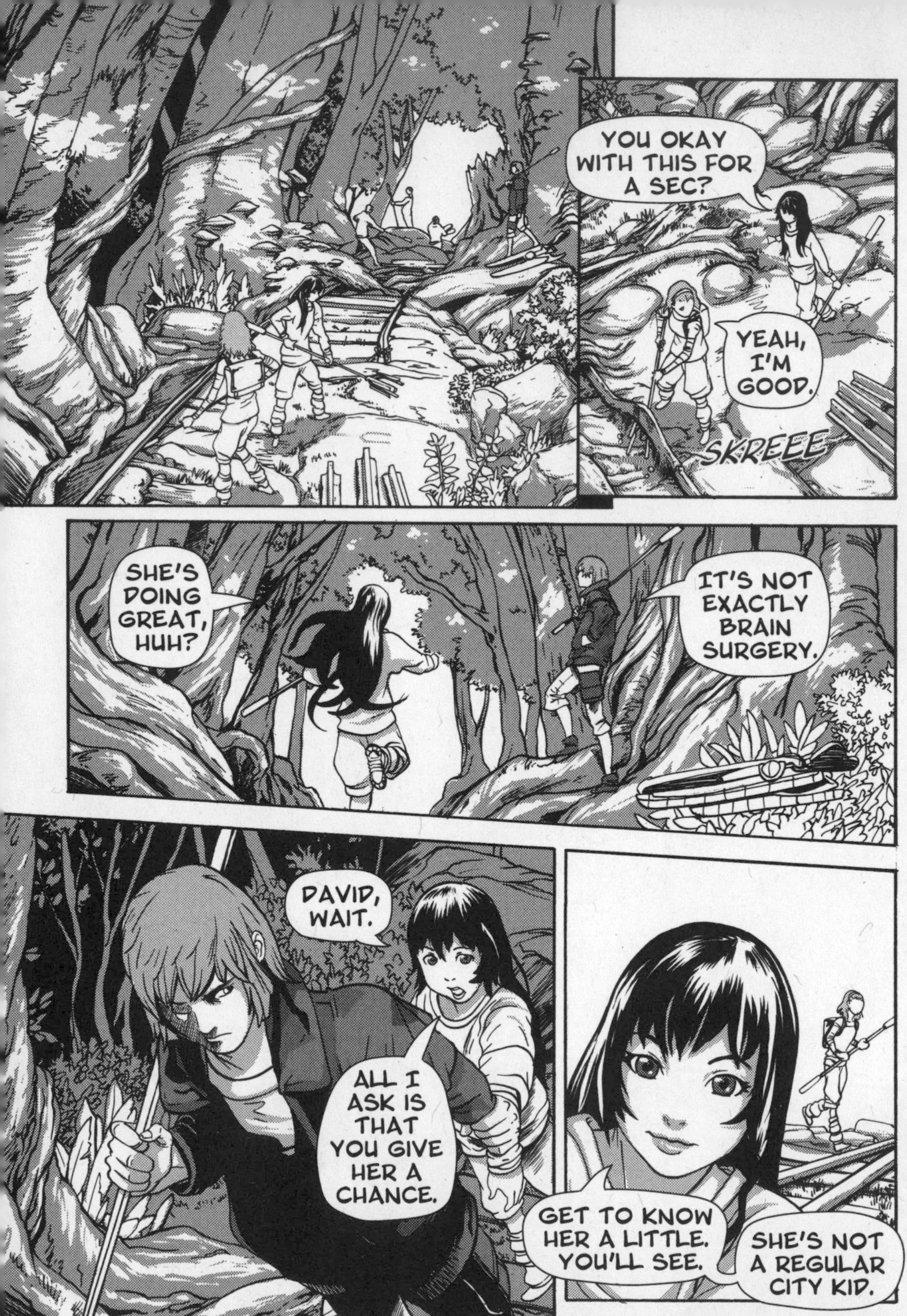
YOU OKAY WITH THIS FOR A SEC?
YEAH, I'M GOOD.
SKREEE
SHE'S DOING GREAT, HUH?
IT'S NOT EXACTLY BRAIN SURGERY.
DAVID, WAIT.
ALL I ASK IS THAT YOU GIVE HER A CHANCE.
GET TO KNOW HER A LITTLE. YOU'LL SEE.
SHE'S NOT A REGULAR CITY KID.

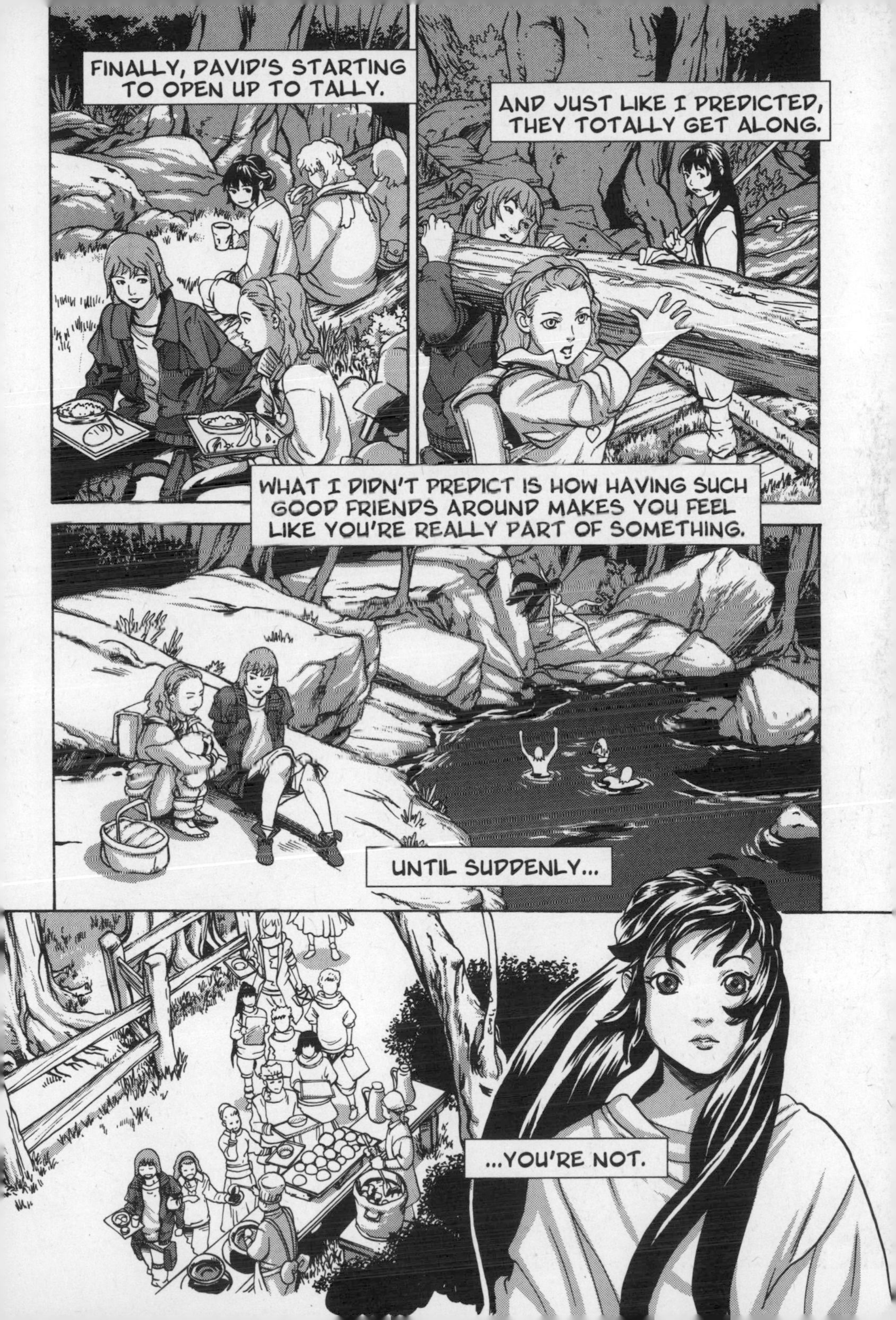
FINALLY, DAVID'S STARTING TO OPEN UP TO TALLY.
AND JUST LIKE I PREDICTED, THEY TOTALLY GET ALONG.
WHAT I DIDN'T PREDICT IS HOW HAVING SUCH GOOD FRIENDS AROUND MAKES YOU FEEL LIKE YOU'RE REALLY PART OF SOMETHING.
UNTIL SUDDENLY...
...YOU'RE NOT.

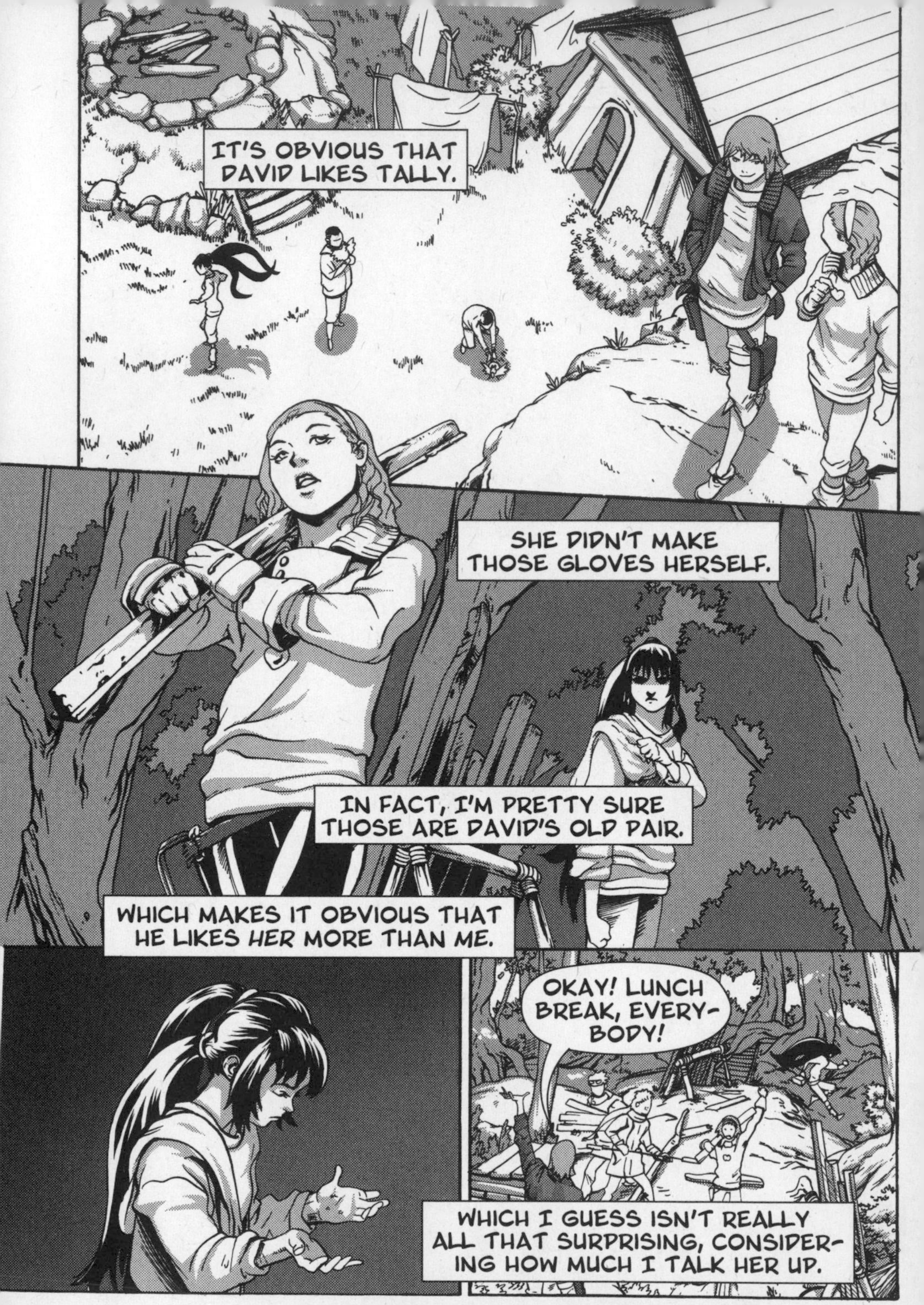
IT'S OBVIOUS THAT DAVID LIKES TALLY.
SHE DIDN'T MAKE THOSE GLOVES HERSELF.
IN FACT, I'M PRETTY SURE THOSE ARE DAVID'S OLD PAIR.
WHICH MAKES IT OBVIOUS THAT HE LIKES HER MORE THAN ME.
OKAY! LUNCH BREAK, EVERY-BODY!
WHICH I GUESS ISN'T REALLY ALL THAT SURPRISING, CONSIDER-ING HOW MUCH I TALK HER UP.

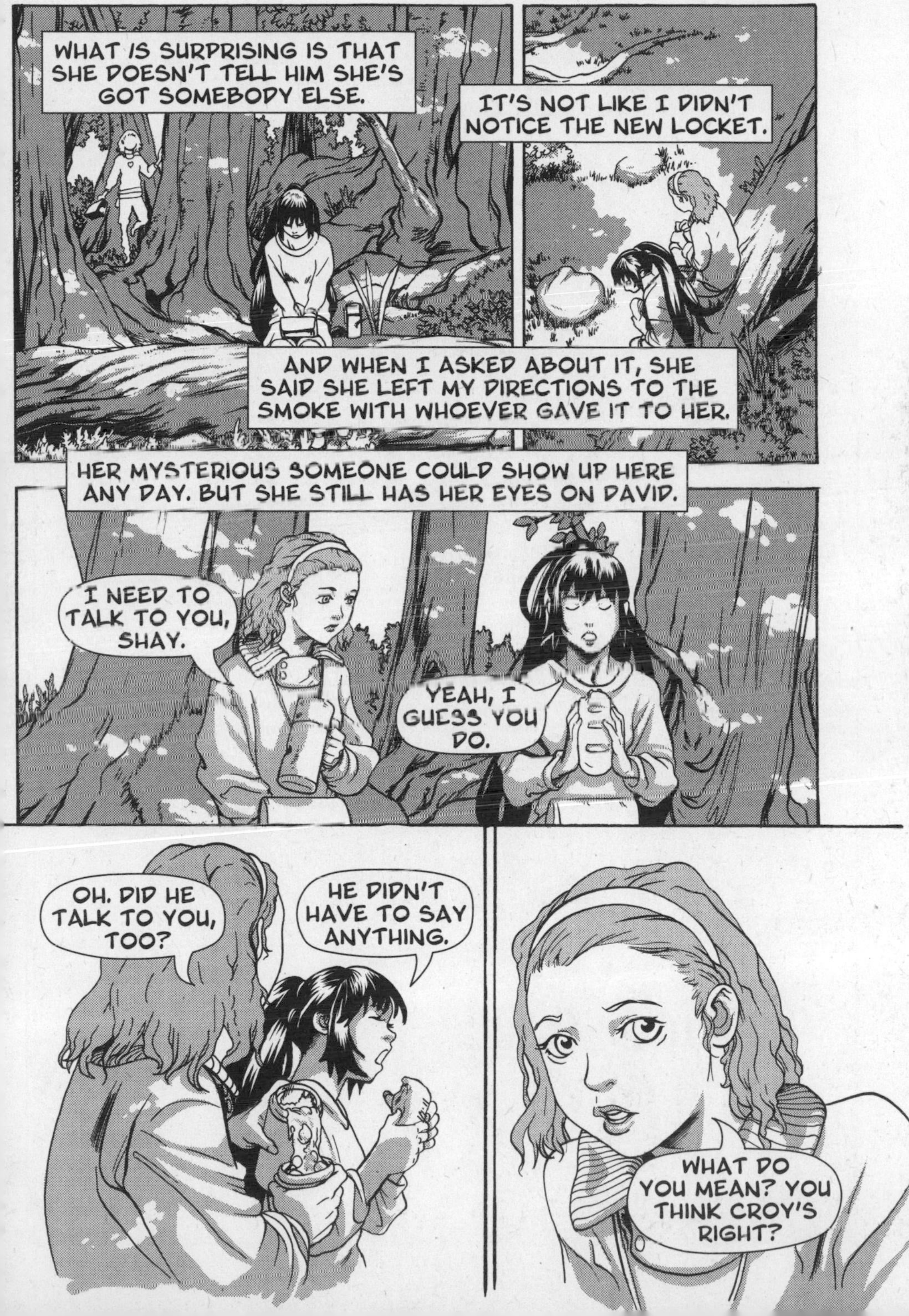
WHAT IS SURPRISING IS THAT SHE DOESN'T TELL HIM SHE'S GOT SOMEBODY ELSE.
IT'S NOT LIKE I DIDN'T NOTICE THE NEW LOCKET.
AND WHEN I ASKED ABOUT IT, SHE SAID SHE LEFT MY DIRECTIONS TO THE SMOKE WITH WHOEVER GAVE IT TO HER.
HER MYSTERIOUS SOMEONE COULD SHOW UP HERE ANY DAY. BUT SHE STILL HAS HER EYES ON DAVID.
I NEED TO TALK TO YOU, SHAY.
YEAH, I GUESS YOU DO.
OH. DID HE TALK TO YOU, TOO?
HE DIDN'T HAVE TO SAY ANYTHING.
WHAT DO YOU MEAN? YOU THINK CROY'S RIGHT?

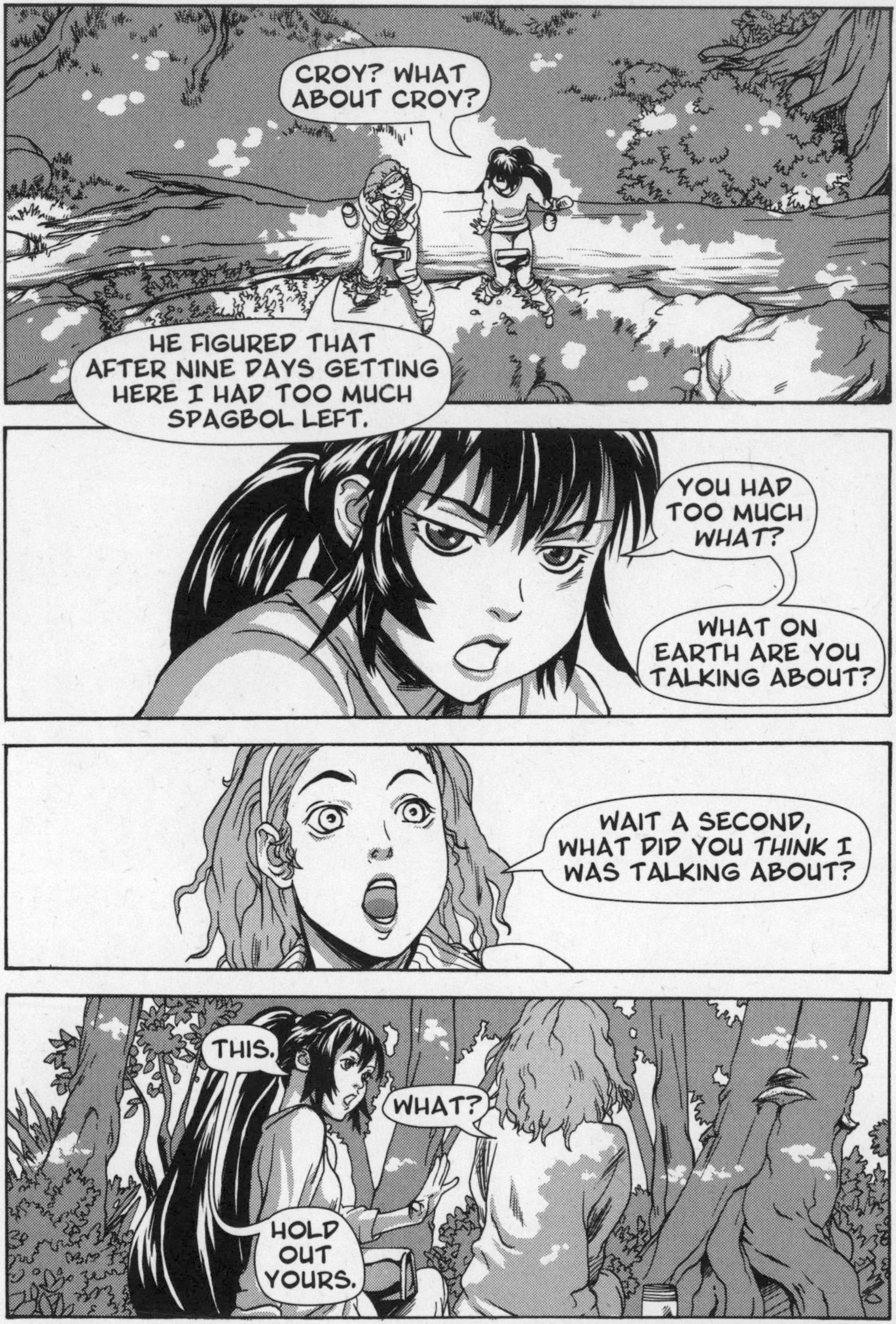
CROY? WHAT ABOUT CROY?
HE FIGURED THAT AFTER NINE DAYS GETTING HERE I HAD TOO MUCH SPAGBOL LEFT.
YOU HAD TOO MUCH WHAT?
WHAT ON EARTH ARE YOU TALKING ABOUT?
WAIT A SECOND, WHAT DID YOU *THINK* I WAS TALKING ABOUT?
THIS.
WHAT?
HOLD OUT YOURS.

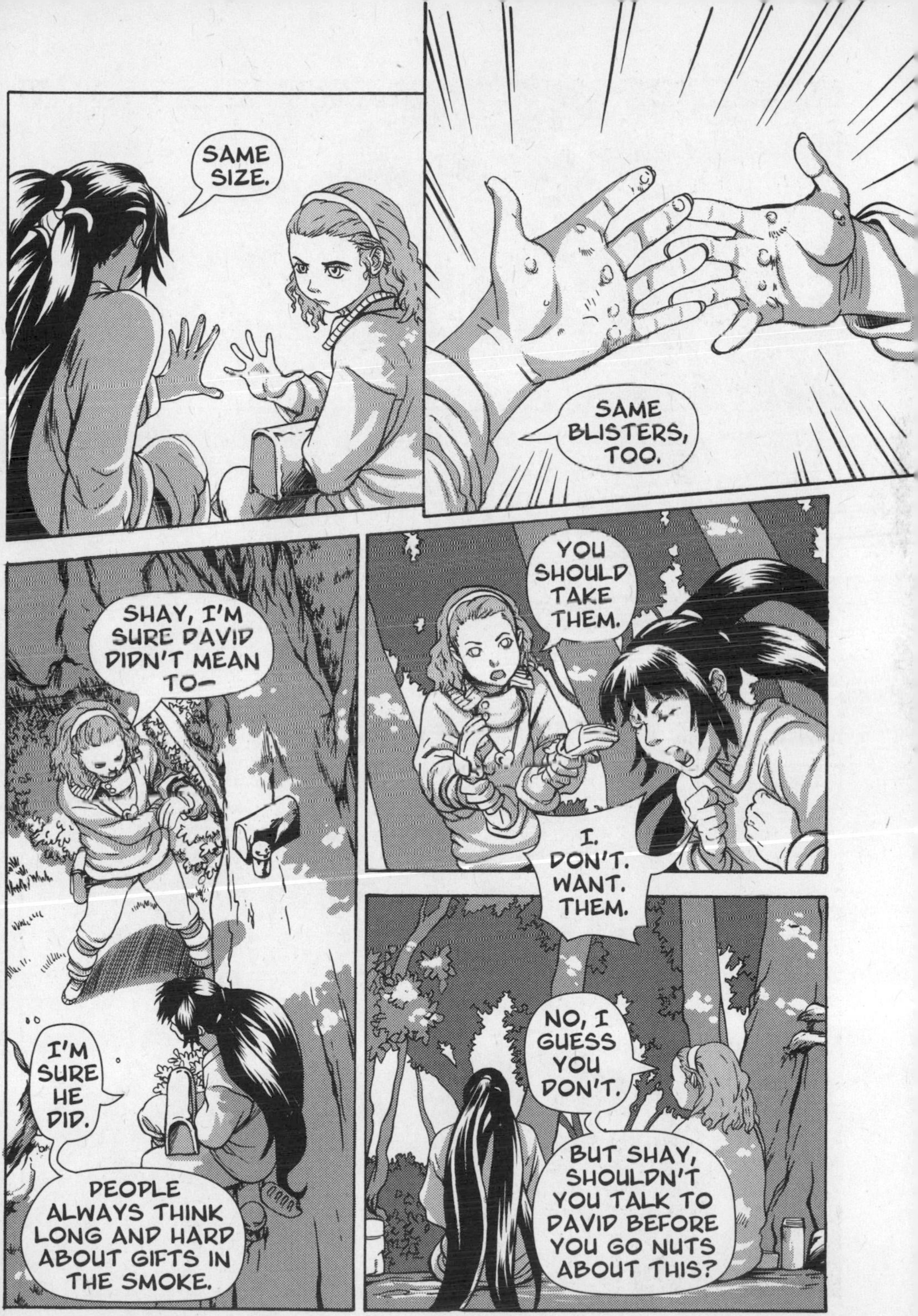
SAME SIZE.
SAME BLISTERS, TOO.
SHAY, I'M SURE DAVID DIDN'T MEAN TO—
I'M SURE HE DID.
PEOPLE ALWAYS THINK LONG AND HARD ABOUT GIFTS IN THE SMOKE.
YOU SHOULD TAKE THEM.
I. DON'T. WANT. THEM.
NO, I GUESS YOU DON'T.
BUT SHAY, SHOULDN'T YOU TALK TO DAVID BEFORE YOU GO NUTS ABOUT THIS?

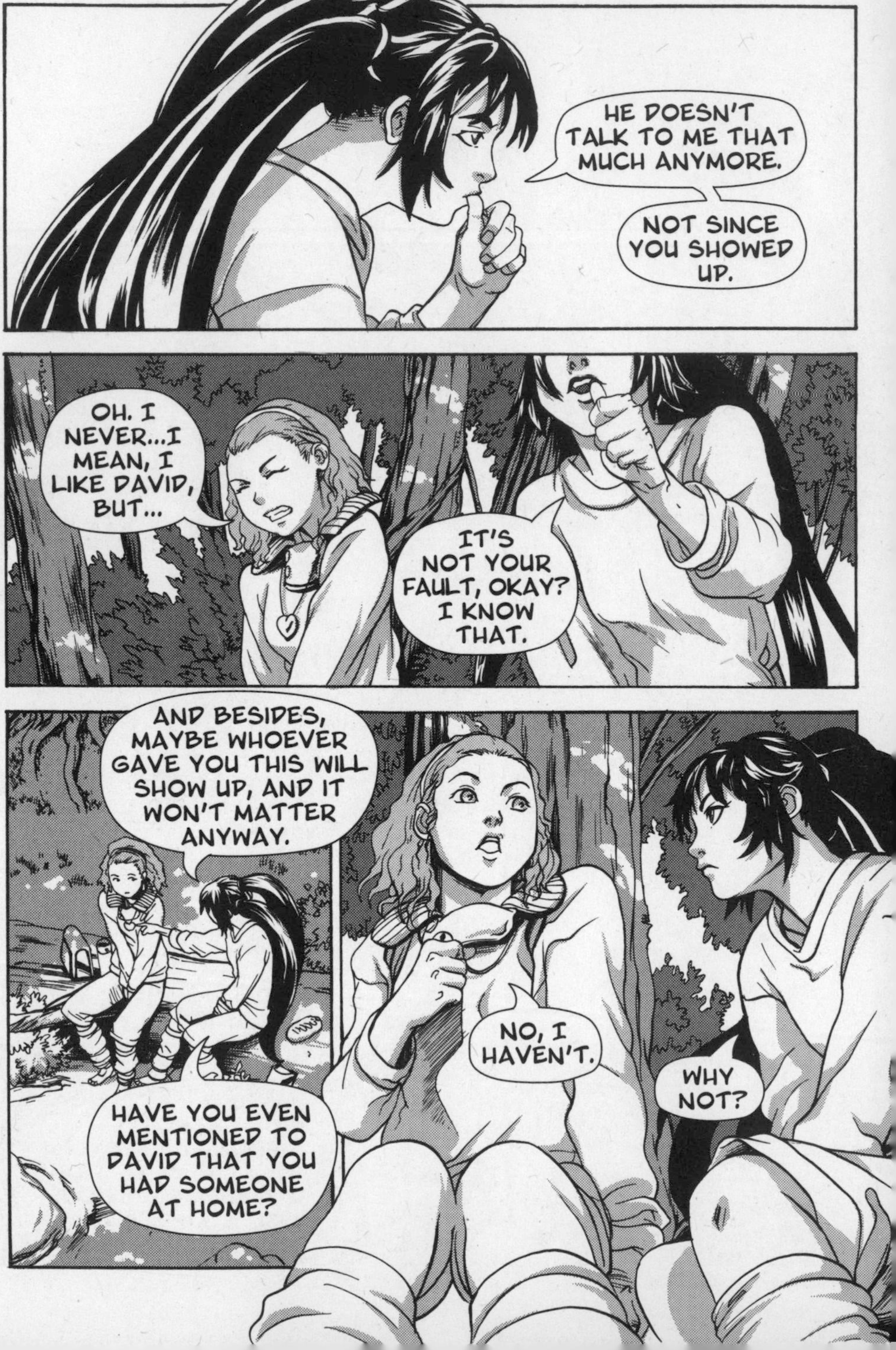
HE DOESN'T TALK TO ME THAT MUCH ANYMORE.
NOT SINCE YOU SHOWED UP.
OH. I NEVER...I MEAN, I LIKE DAVID, BUT...
IT'S NOT YOUR FAULT, OKAY? I KNOW THAT.
AND BESIDES, MAYBE WHOEVER GAVE YOU THIS WILL SHOW UP, AND IT WON'T MATTER ANYWAY.
HAVE YOU EVEN MENTIONED TO DAVID THAT YOU HAD SOMEONE AT HOME?
NO, I HAVEN'T.
WHY NOT?

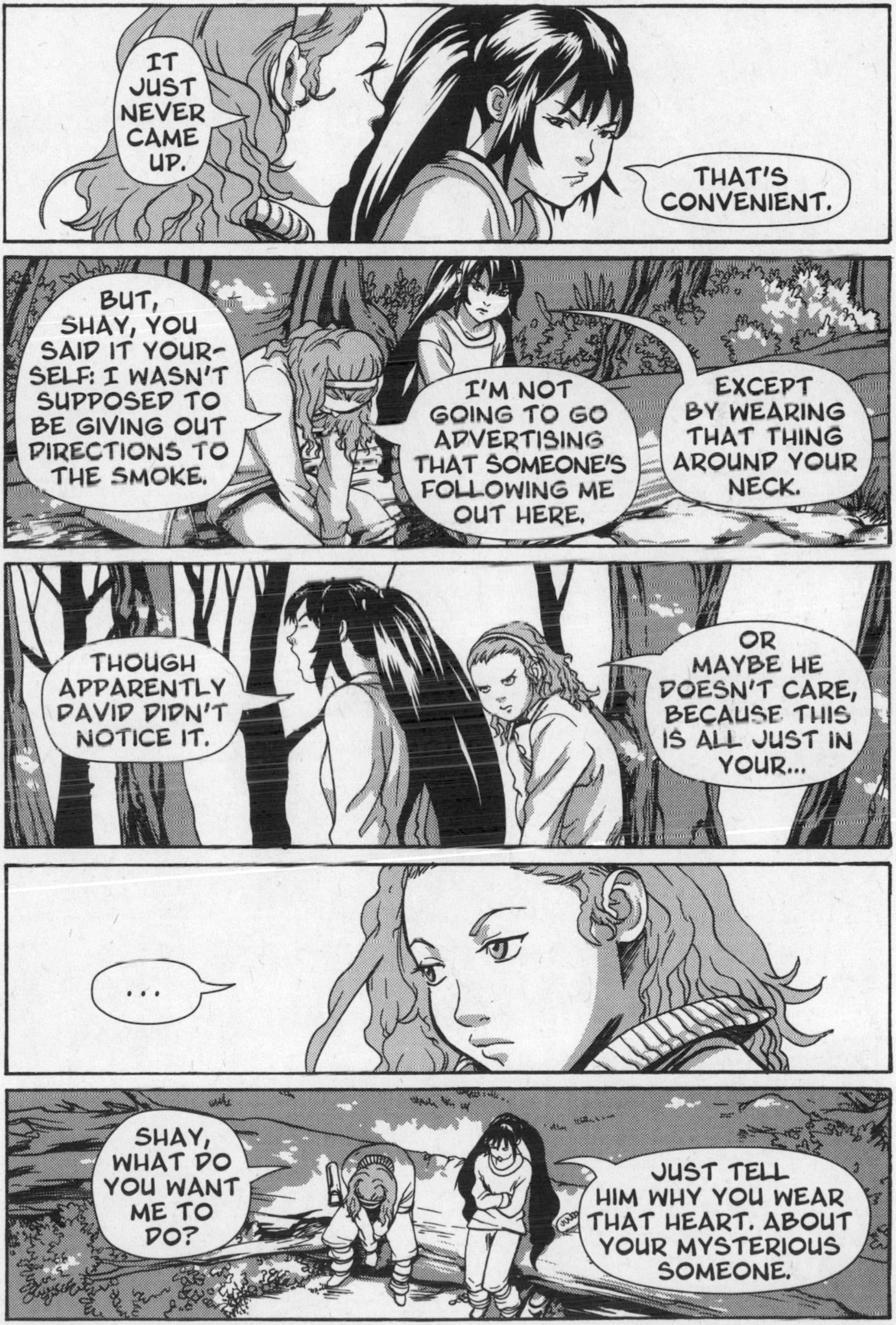
IT JUST NEVER CAME UP.
THAT'S CONVENIENT.
BUT, SHAY, YOU SAID IT YOUR-SELF: I WASN'T SUPPOSED TO BE GIVING OUT DIRECTIONS TO THE SMOKE.
I'M NOT GOING TO GO ADVERTISING THAT SOMEONE'S FOLLOWING ME OUT HERE.
EXCEPT BY WEARING THAT THING AROUND YOUR NECK.
THOUGH APPARENTLY DAVID DIDN'T NOTICE IT.
OR MAYBE HE DOESN'T CARE, BECAUSE THIS IS ALL JUST IN YOUR...
...
SHAY, WHAT DO YOU WANT ME TO DO?
JUST TELL HIM WHY YOU WEAR THAT HEART. ABOUT YOUR MYSTERIOUS SOMEONE.

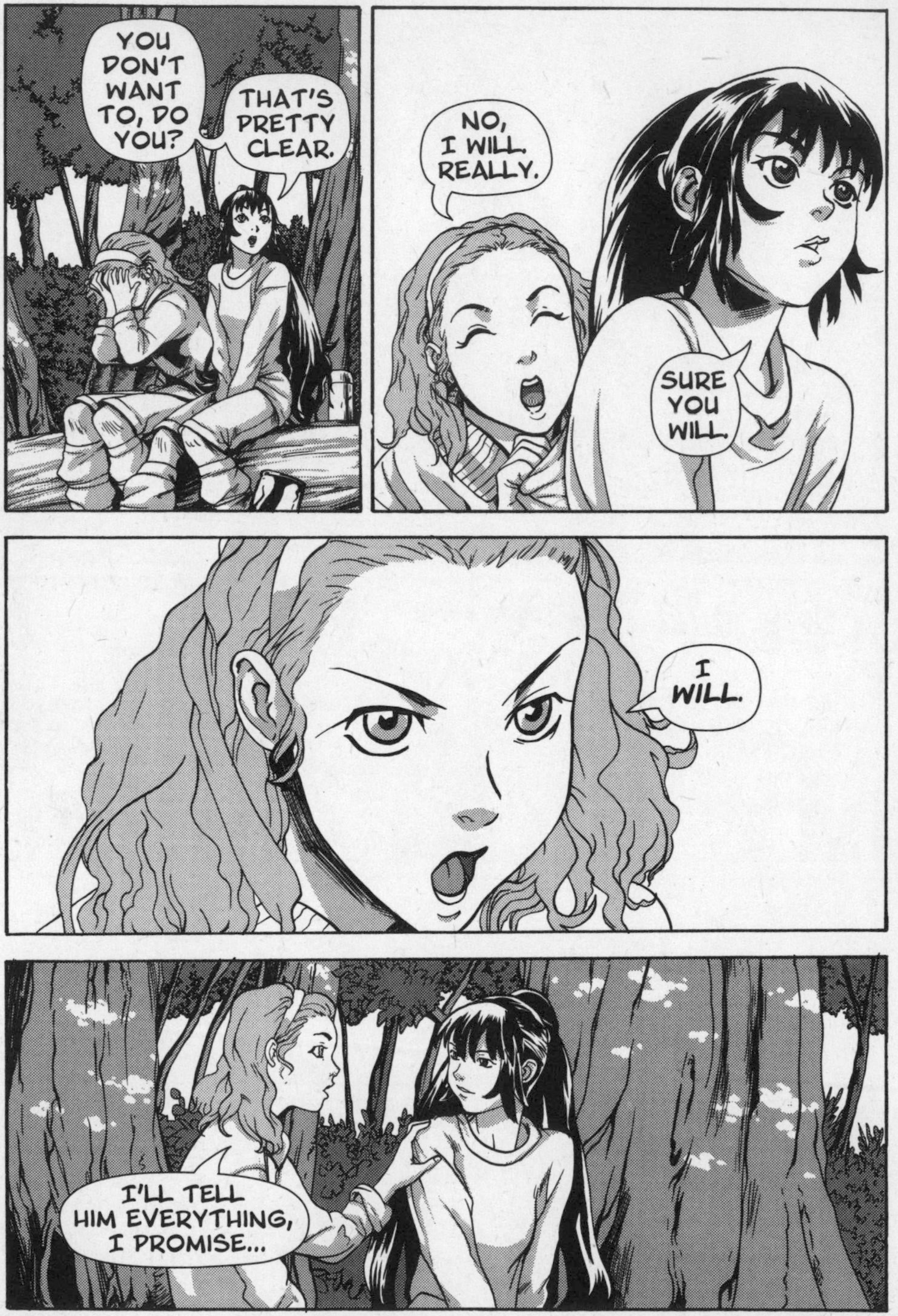
YOU DON'T WANT TO, DO YOU?
THAT'S PRETTY CLEAR.
NO, I WILL. REALLY.
SURE YOU WILL.
I WILL.
I'LL TELL HIM EVERYTHING, I PROMISE...

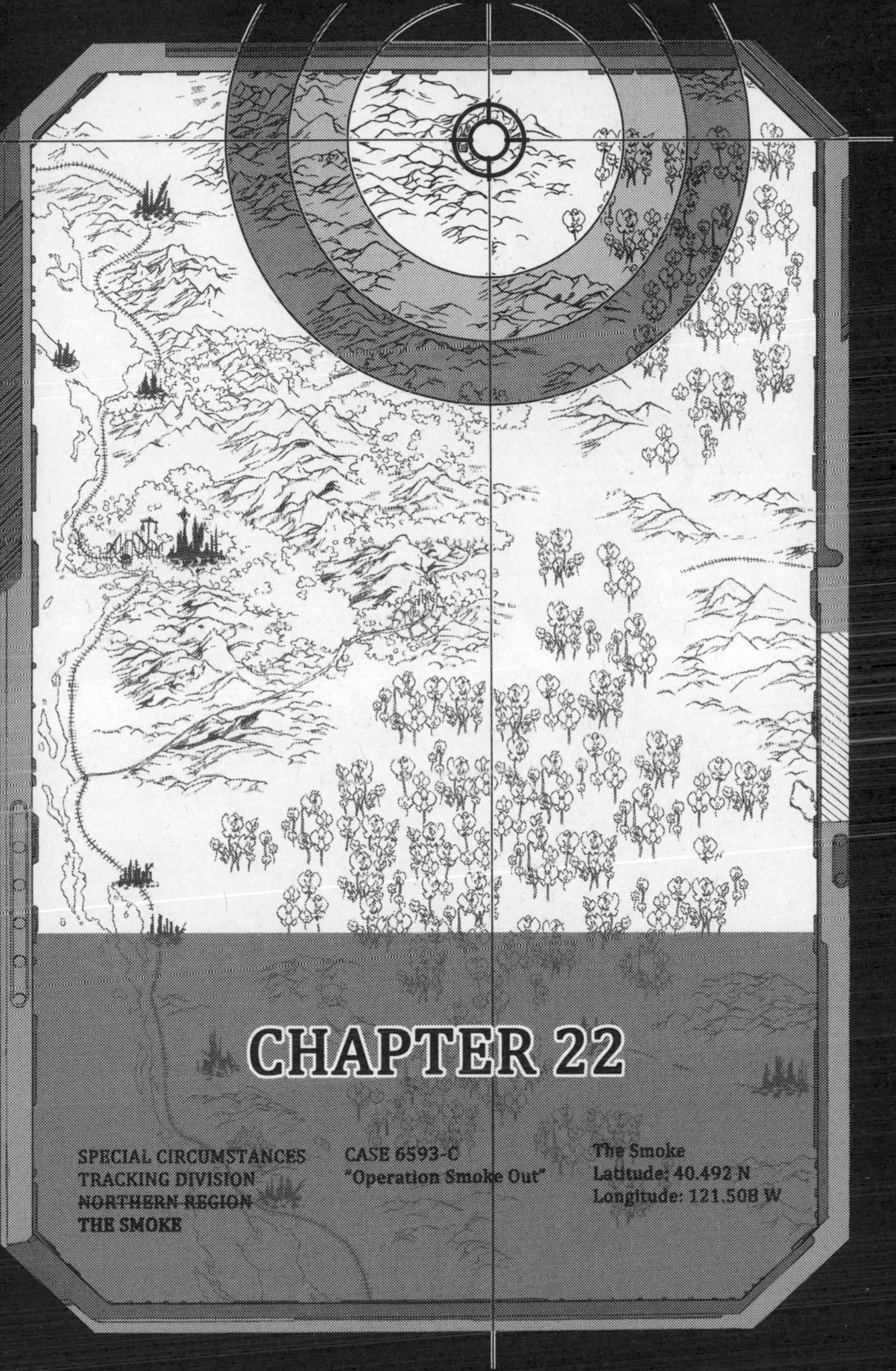

# CHAPTER 22

SPECIAL CIRCUMSTANCES
TRACKING DIVISION
~~NORTHERN REGION~~
THE SMOKE

CASE 6593-C
"Operation Smoke Out"

The Smoke
Latitude: 40.492 N
Longitude: 121.508 W

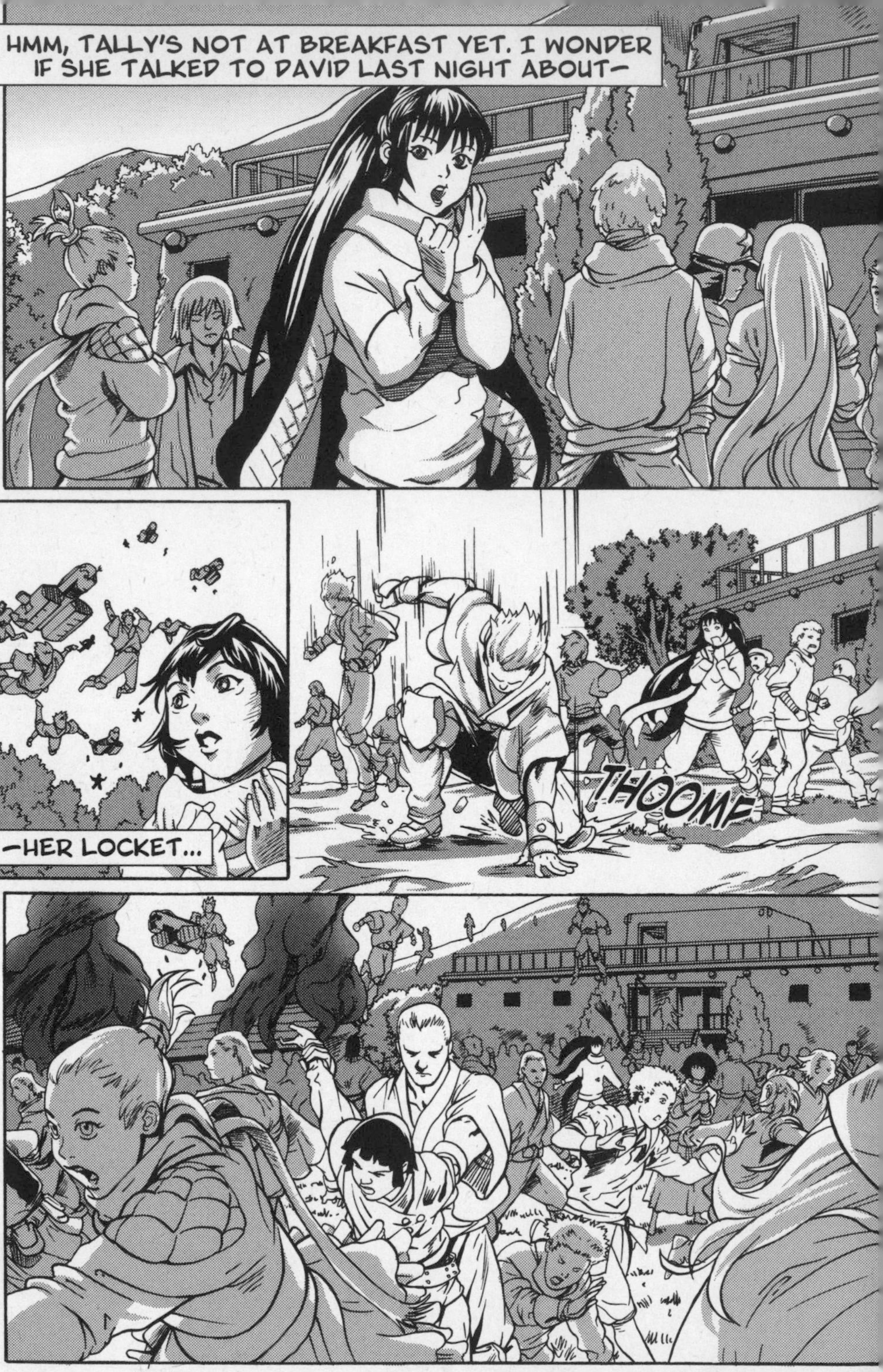
HMM, TALLY'S NOT AT BREAKFAST YET. I WONDER IF SHE TALKED TO DAVID LAST NIGHT ABOUT—
—HER LOCKET...
THOOMF

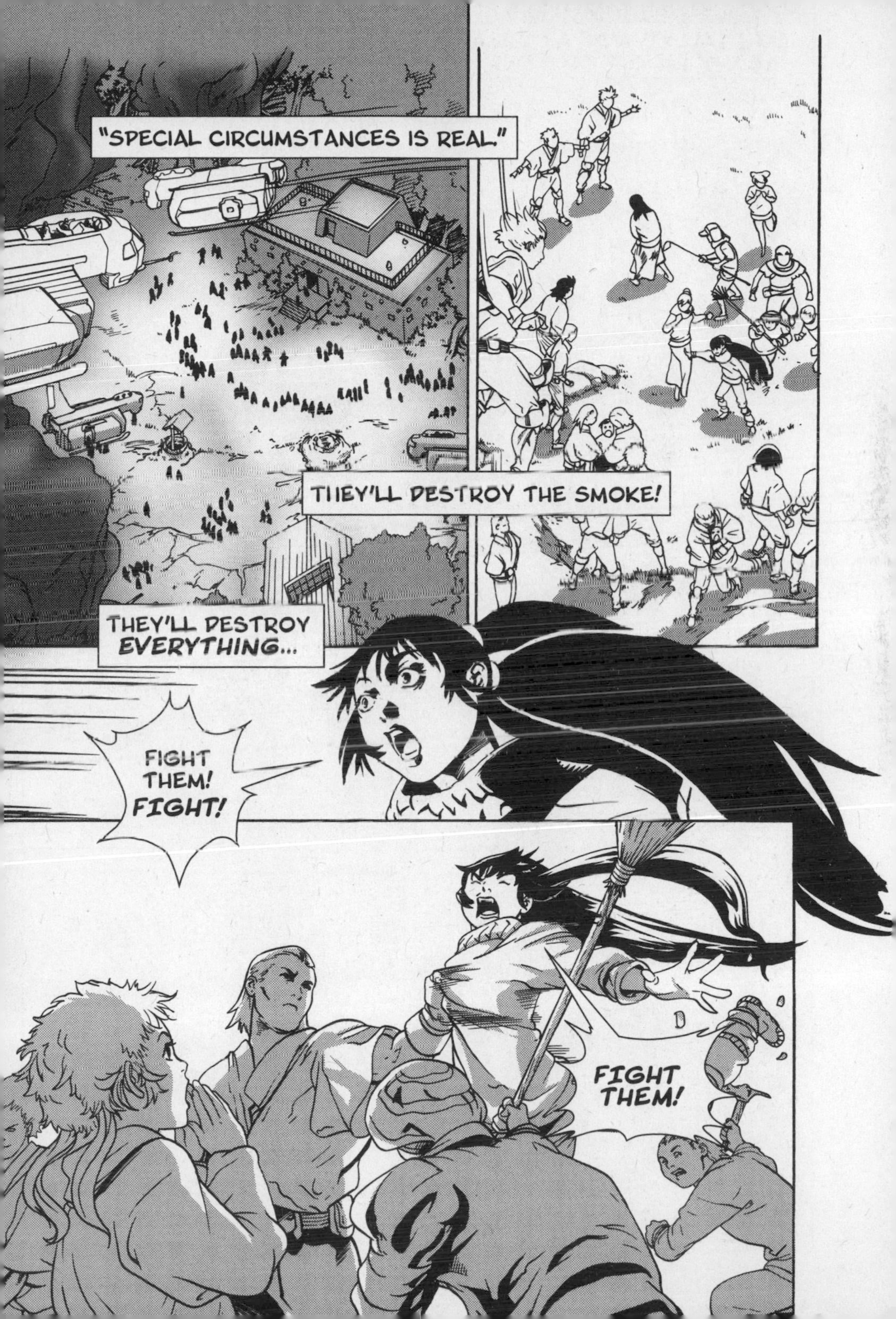
"SPECIAL CIRCUMSTANCES IS REAL."
THEY'LL DESTROY THE SMOKE!
THEY'LL DESTROY EVERYTHING...
FIGHT THEM! FIGHT!
FIGHT THEM!

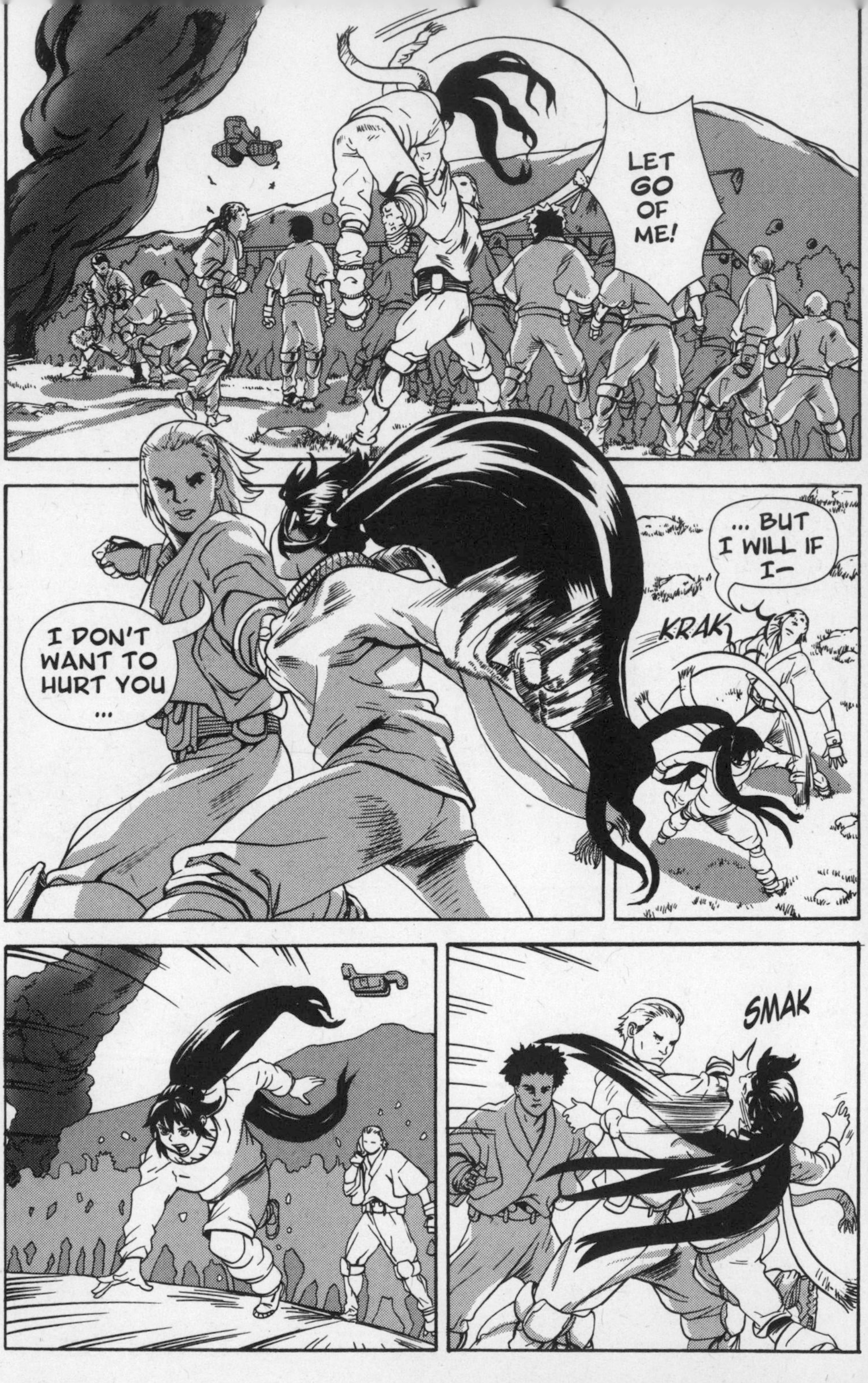
LET GO OF ME!
I DON'T WANT TO HURT YOU ...
... BUT I WILL IF I—
KRAK
SMAK

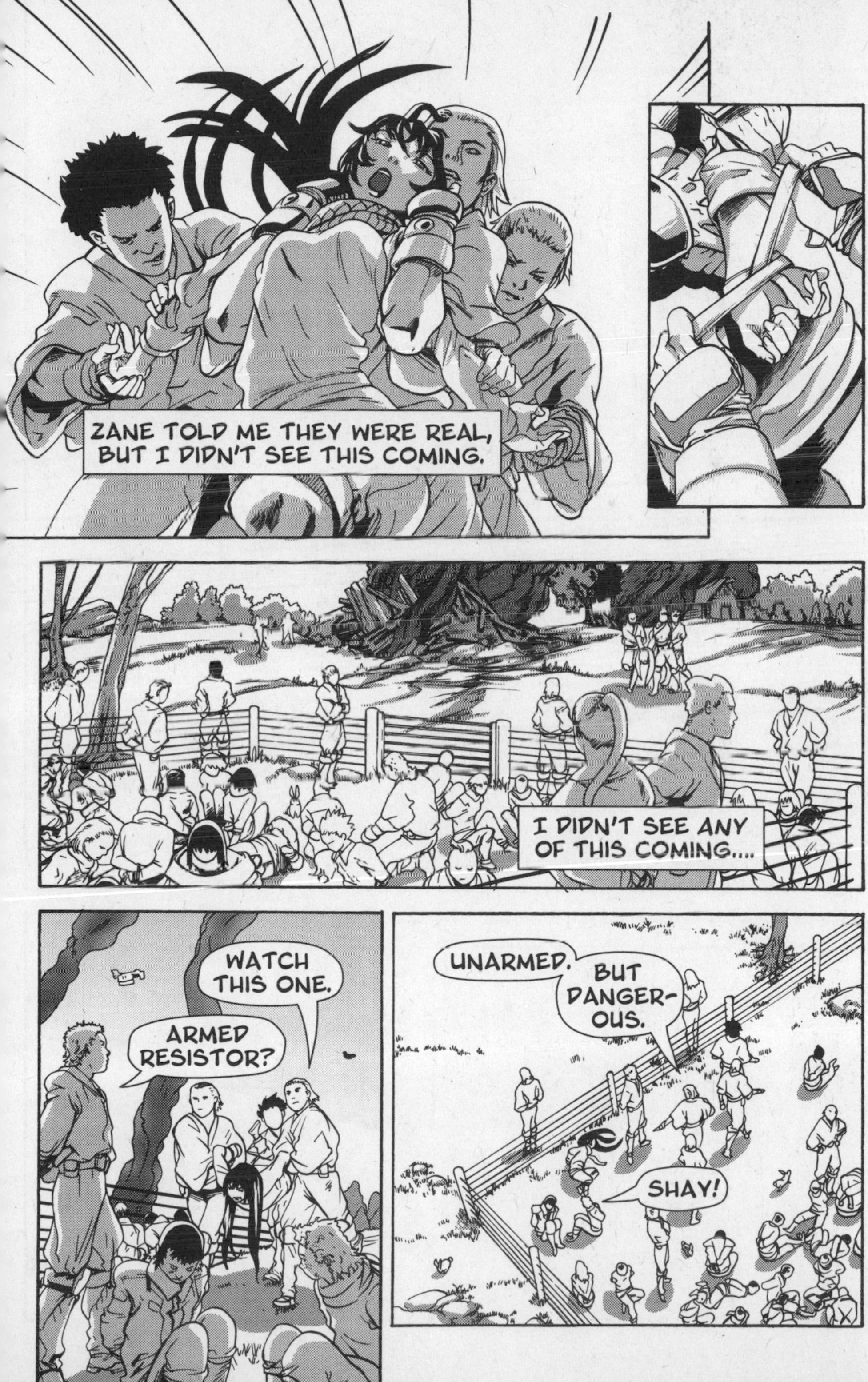
ZANE TOLD ME THEY WERE REAL, BUT I DIDN'T SEE THIS COMING.
I DIDN'T SEE ANY OF THIS COMING....
WATCH THIS ONE.
ARMED RESISTOR?
UNARMED.
BUT DANGER-OUS.
SHAY!

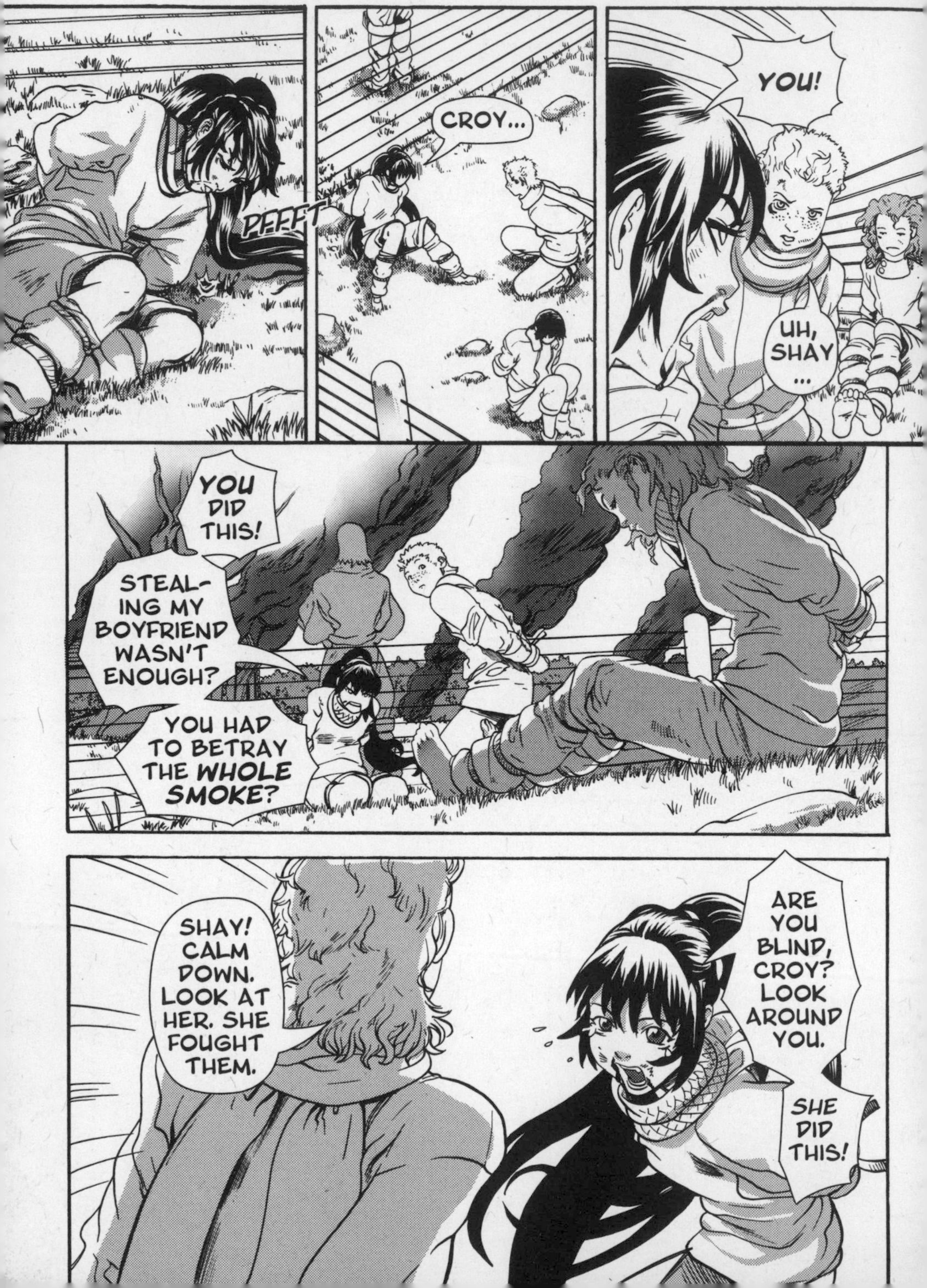
PFFFT
CROY...
YOU!
UH, SHAY ...
YOU DID THIS!
STEALING MY BOYFRIEND WASN'T ENOUGH?
YOU HAD TO BETRAY THE WHOLE SMOKE?
SHAY! CALM DOWN. LOOK AT HER. SHE FOUGHT THEM.
ARE YOU BLIND, CROY? LOOK AROUND YOU.
SHE DID THIS!

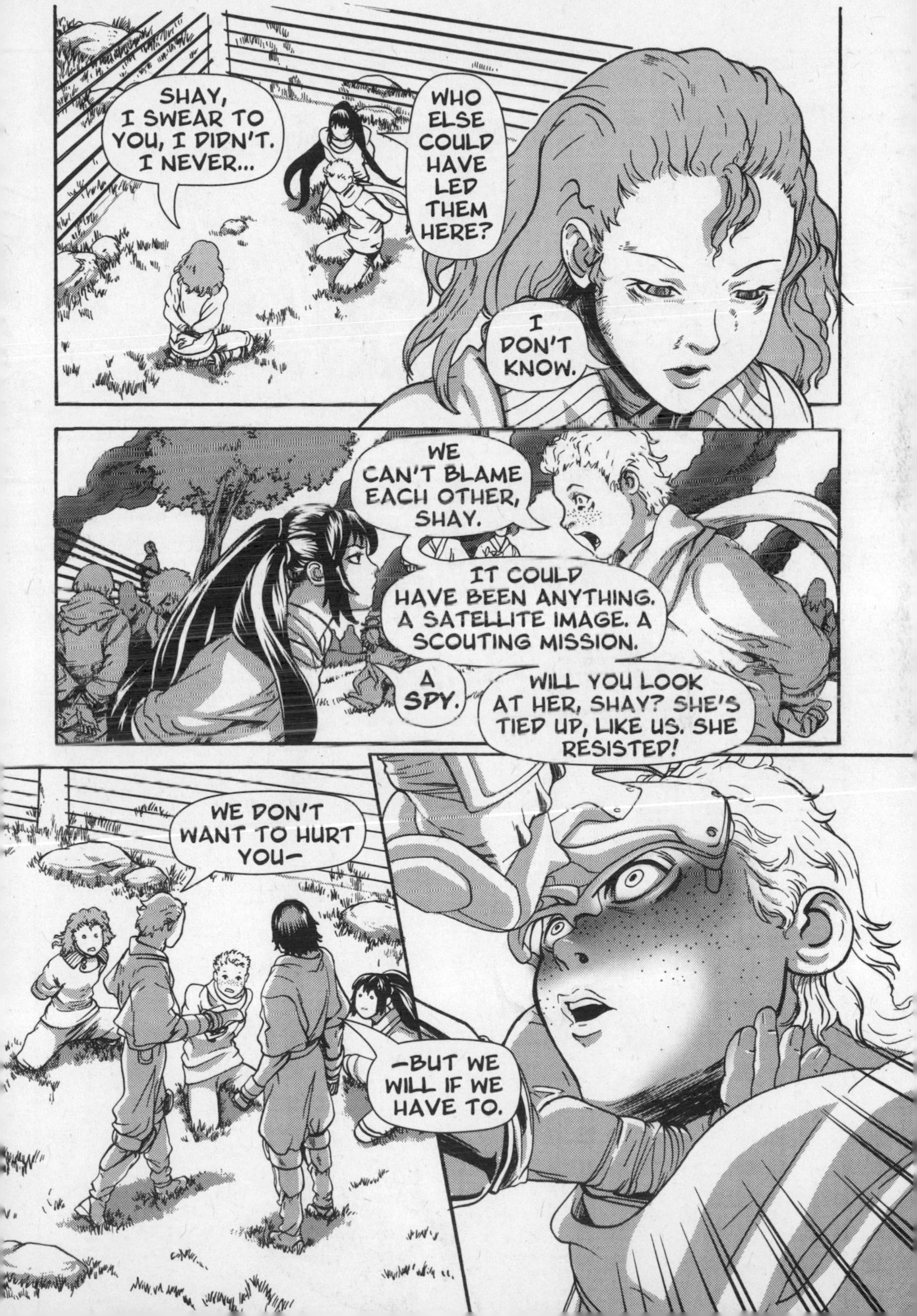
SHAY, I SWEAR TO YOU, I DIDN'T. I NEVER...
WHO ELSE COULD HAVE LED THEM HERE?
I DON'T KNOW.
WE CAN'T BLAME EACH OTHER, SHAY.
IT COULD HAVE BEEN ANYTHING. A SATELLITE IMAGE. A SCOUTING MISSION.
A SPY.
WILL YOU LOOK AT HER, SHAY? SHE'S TIED UP, LIKE US. SHE RESISTED!
WE DON'T WANT TO HURT YOU—
—BUT WE WILL IF WE HAVE TO.

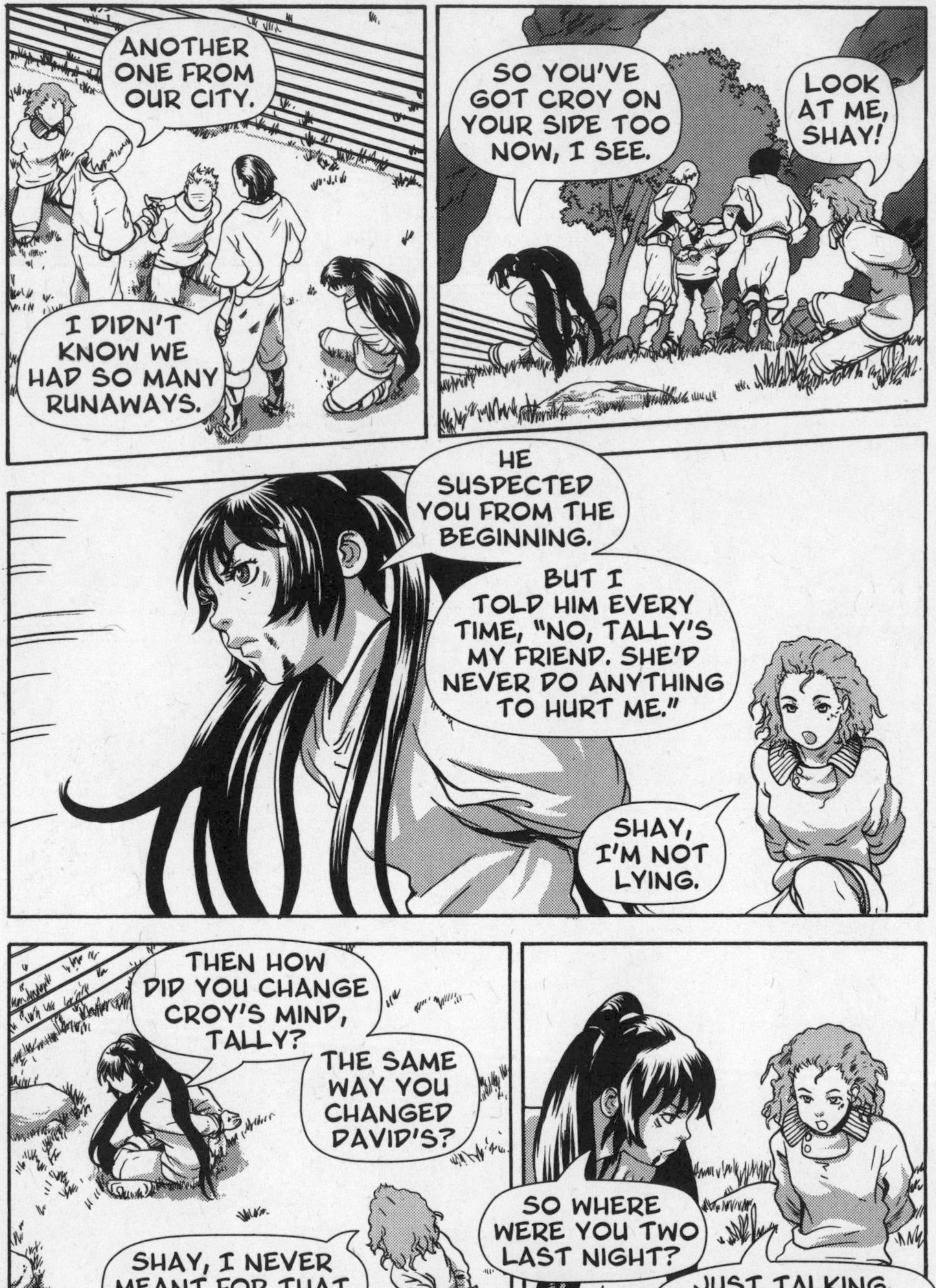
ANOTHER ONE FROM OUR CITY.
I DIDN'T KNOW WE HAD SO MANY RUNAWAYS.
SO YOU'VE GOT CROY ON YOUR SIDE TOO NOW, I SEE.
LOOK AT ME, SHAY!
HE SUSPECTED YOU FROM THE BEGINNING.
BUT I TOLD HIM EVERY TIME, "NO, TALLY'S MY FRIEND. SHE'D NEVER DO ANYTHING TO HURT ME."
SHAY, I'M NOT LYING.
THEN HOW DID YOU CHANGE CROY'S MIND, TALLY?
THE SAME WAY YOU CHANGED DAVID'S?
SHAY, I NEVER MEANT FOR THAT TO HAPPEN.
SO WHERE WERE YOU TWO LAST NIGHT?
JUST TALKING. I TOLD HIM ABOUT MY NECKLACE.

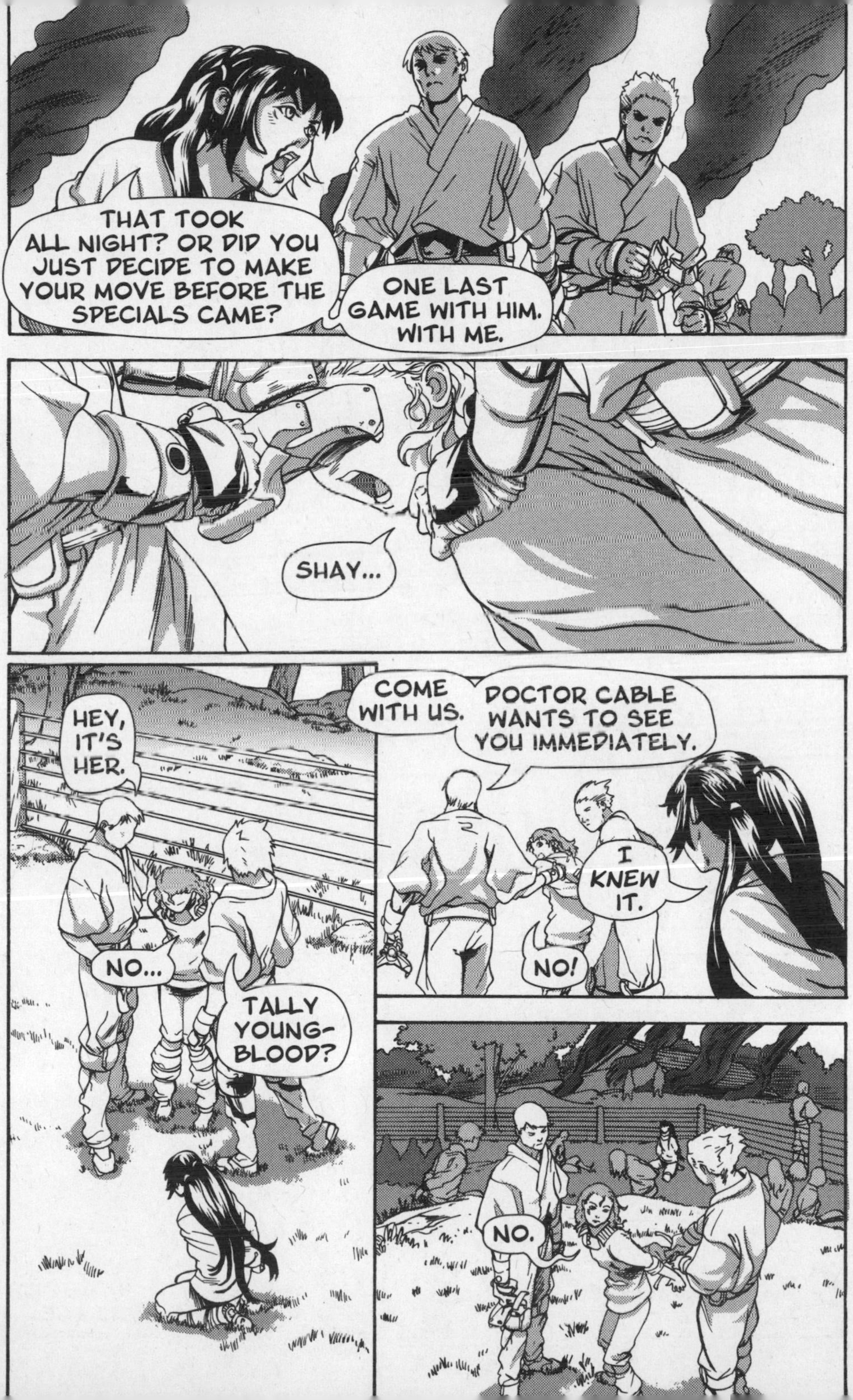
THAT TOOK ALL NIGHT? OR DID YOU JUST DECIDE TO MAKE YOUR MOVE BEFORE THE SPECIALS CAME?
ONE LAST GAME WITH HIM. WITH ME.
SHAY...
HEY, IT'S HER.
NO...
TALLY YOUNG-BLOOD?
COME WITH US.
DOCTOR CABLE WANTS TO SEE YOU IMMEDIATELY.
I KNEW IT.
NO!
NO.

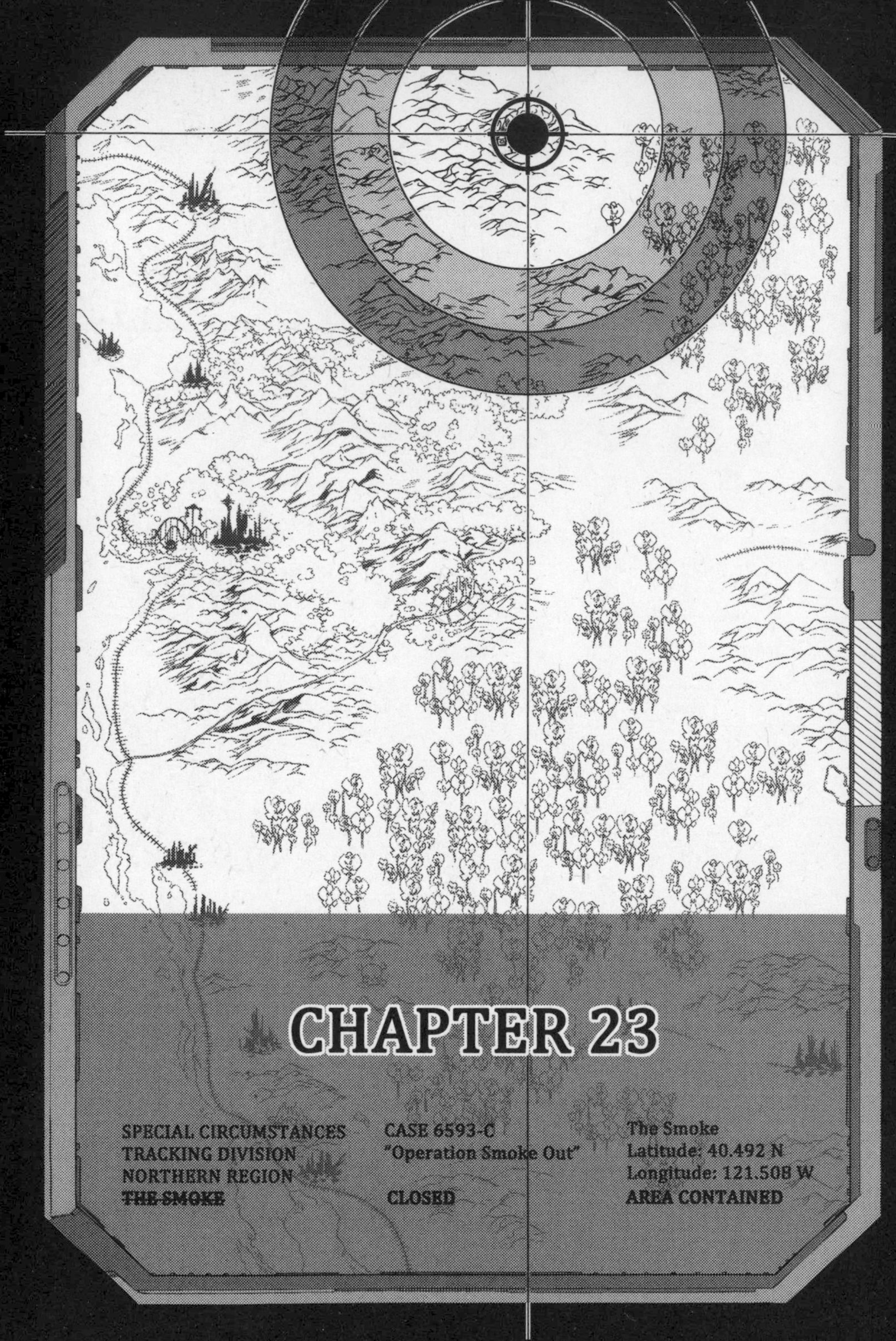
CHAPTER 23
SPECIAL CIRCUMSTANCES
TRACKING DIVISION
NORTHERN REGION
~~THE SMOKE~~
CASE 6593-C
"Operation Smoke Out"
CLOSED
The Smoke
Latitude: 40.492 N
Longitude: 121.508 W
AREA CONTAINED

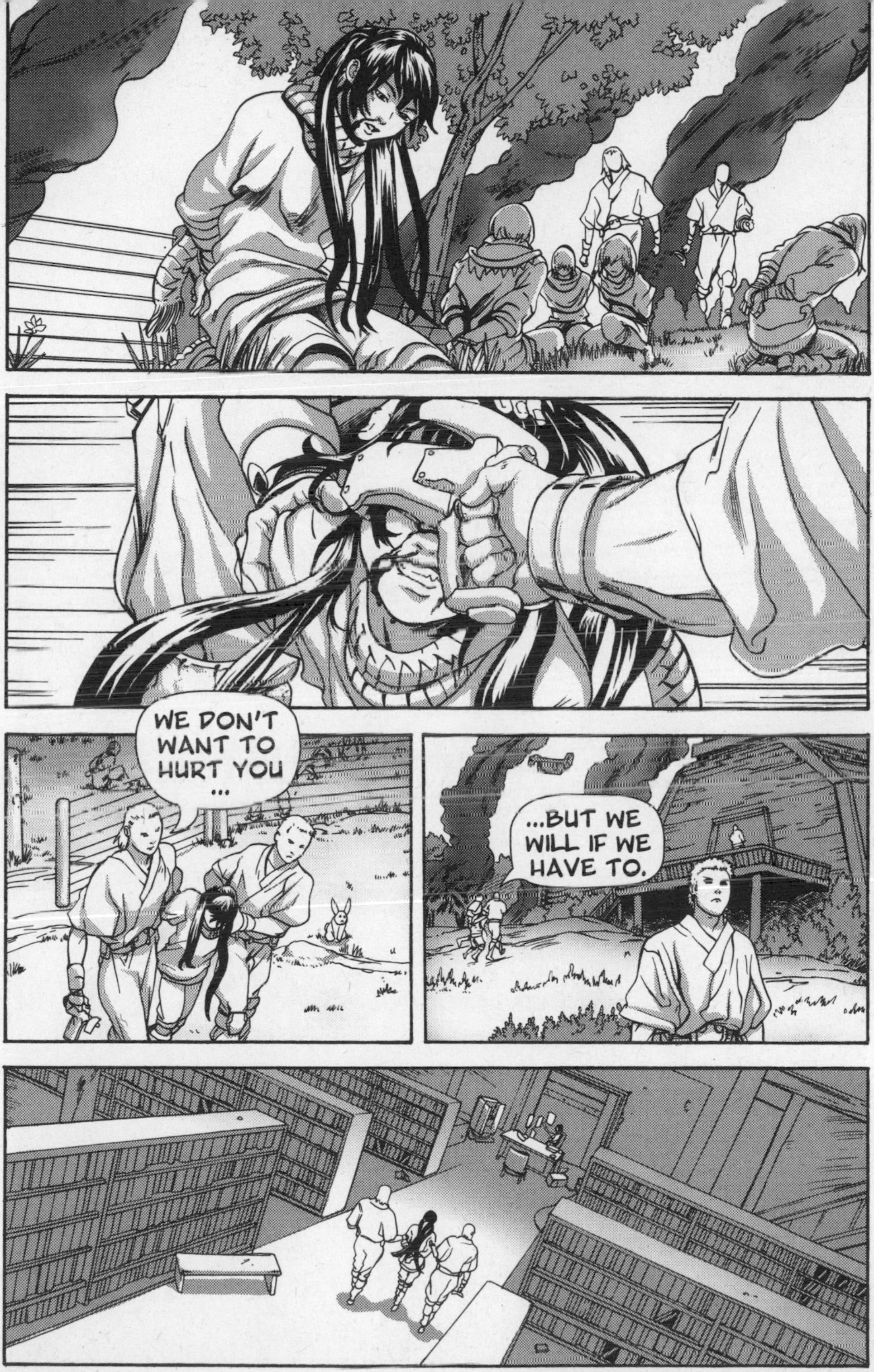
WE DON'T WANT TO HURT YOU ...
...BUT WE WILL IF WE HAVE TO.

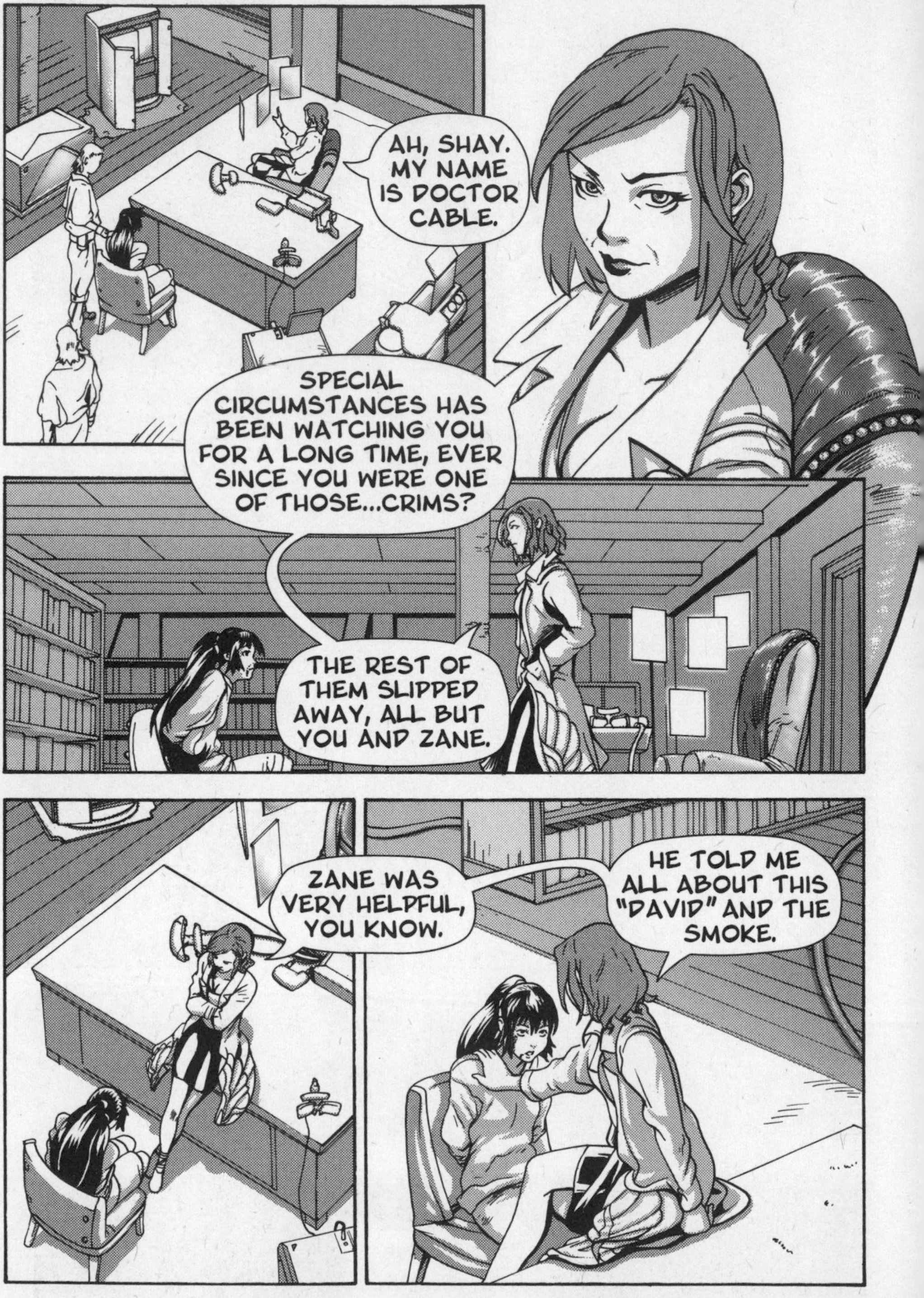
AH, SHAY. MY NAME IS DOCTOR CABLE.
SPECIAL CIRCUMSTANCES HAS BEEN WATCHING YOU FOR A LONG TIME, EVER SINCE YOU WERE ONE OF THOSE...CRIMS?
THE REST OF THEM SLIPPED AWAY, ALL BUT YOU AND ZANE.
ZANE WAS VERY HELPFUL, YOU KNOW.
HE TOLD ME ALL ABOUT THIS "DAVID" AND THE SMOKE.

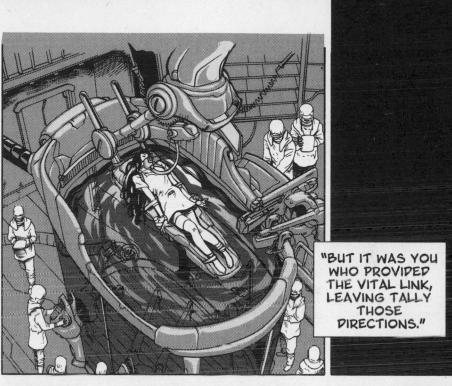

"BUT IT WAS YOU WHO PROVIDED THE VITAL LINK, LEAVING TALLY THOSE DIRECTIONS."

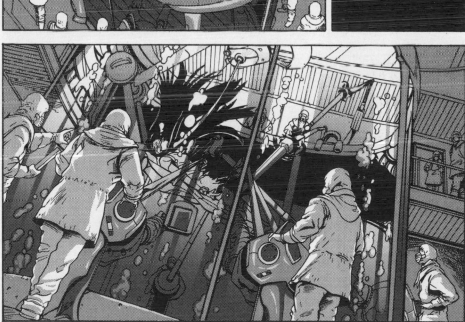

"SO THANK YOU, SHAY..."

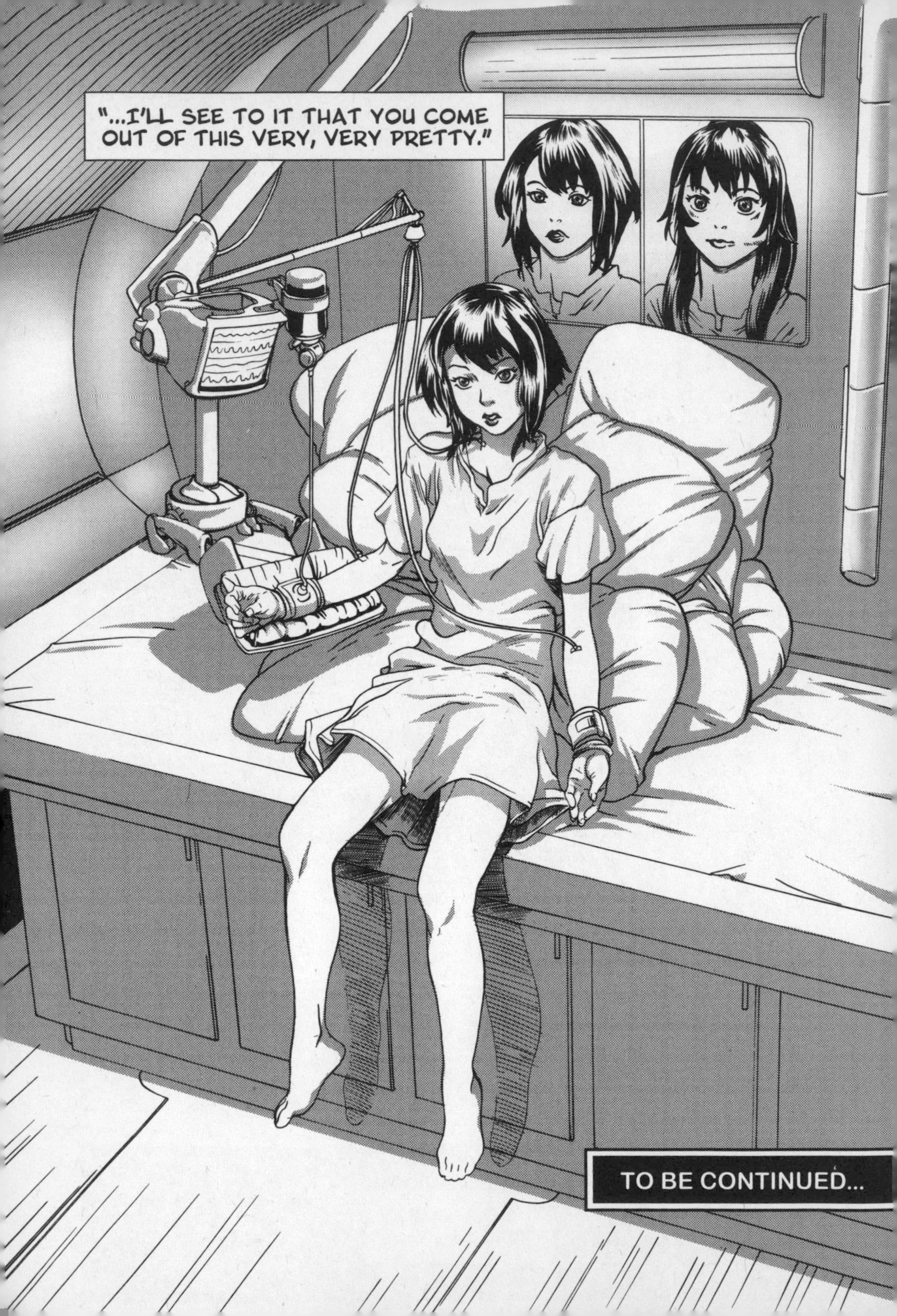
"...I'LL SEE TO IT THAT YOU COME OUT OF THIS VERY, VERY PRETTY."
TO BE CONTINUED...

# ABOUT THE CREATORS

**Scott Westerfeld's** novels include the Uglies series, the Leviathan trilogy, the Midnighters trilogy, *Peeps, The Last Days,* and more. Scott was born in Texas and alternates summers between Sydney, Australia, and New York City.

**Steven Cummings** lives with his family in the magical land known as almost-Tokyo. He has worked for a variety of comic and manga publishers, ranging from Marvel and DC to Tokyopop, on titles including *Wolverine: First Class, Elektra, Batman: Legends of the Dark Knight, Deadshot,* and *Pantheon High.* He is also a member of the Canadian art empire known as Udon.

**Devin Grayson** turned a lifelong obsession with fictional characters into a dynamic writing career. Best known for her work on the Batman titles for DC Comics and the celebrated *X-Men: Evolution* comic for Marvel, she has written in a number of different media and genres, from comic books and novels to videogame scripts and short essays.

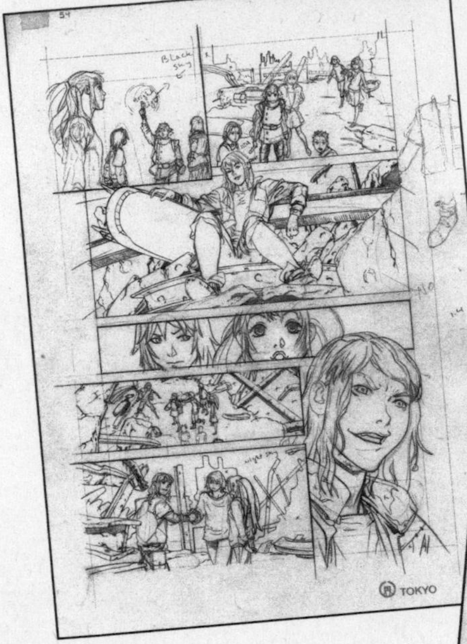
Black Sky
TOKYO
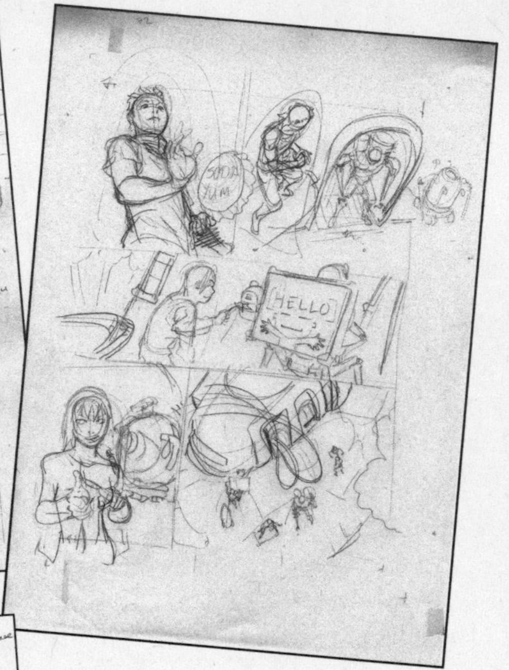
SODA YUM
HELLO
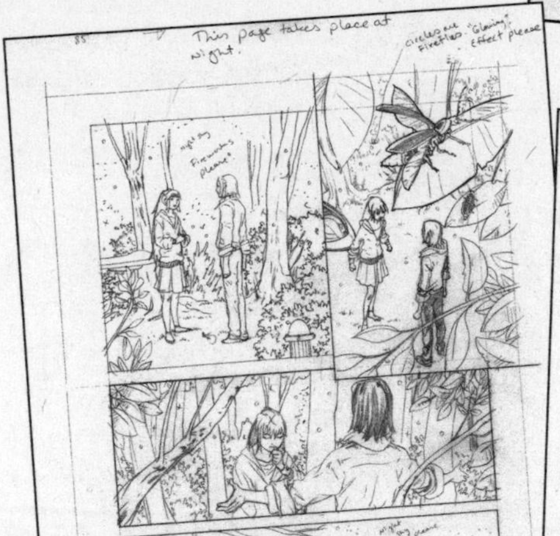
This page takes place at night.
Circles are Fireflies. "Glowing" Effect please
night sky Fireworks please
TOKYO
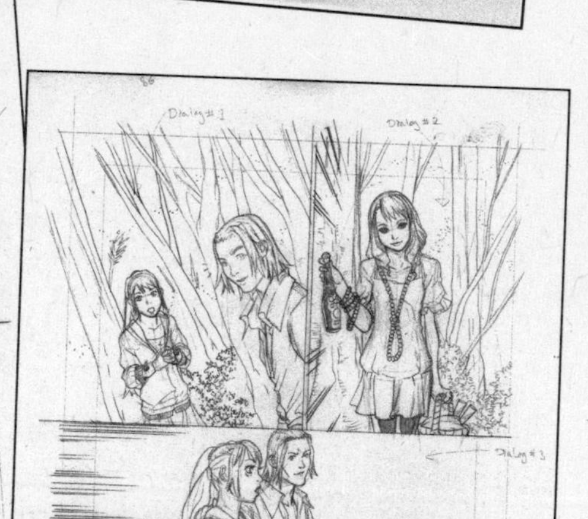
Dialog #1
Dialog #2
Dialog #3
TOKYO

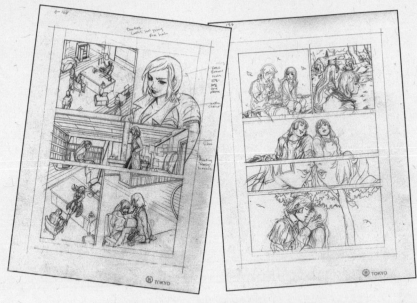

# ARTIST'S SKETCHBOOK

Steven Cummings worked closely with Scott Westerfeld to create the visual look of *Shay's Story*. Steven's first task was to create character sketches based on Scott's descriptions. Shay and Tally came easily. Here is how Scott described each of them:

*Ugly Shay is very slim (her ugly nickname is "Skinny"), with long, dark hair and dark eyes, nice lips, and a slightly angry, defiant look on her face. [Note that "Ugly" just refers to the body in which a person is born, before any surgery is done. It does not mean she is literally ugly. Part of the message of the series is that being normal is just fine—that we don't need cosmetic surgery in order to be happy.]*

*Ugly Tally has light, wavy hair, shoulder length, a little bit frizzy. She has a small nose, light greenish-brown eyes, a typical fifteen-year-old girl's body. Nothing distinctive about her. She's cute, but not beautiful. Her ugly nickname is "Squint," and she is convinced her eyes are too close together.*

# ZANE

Some of the other characters were tougher to come up with—Zane, for example. Ugly Zane doesn't appear in the novels, so Steven had no problem creating a look Scott approved. But his appearance as Pretty Zane had to go through a couple of rounds.

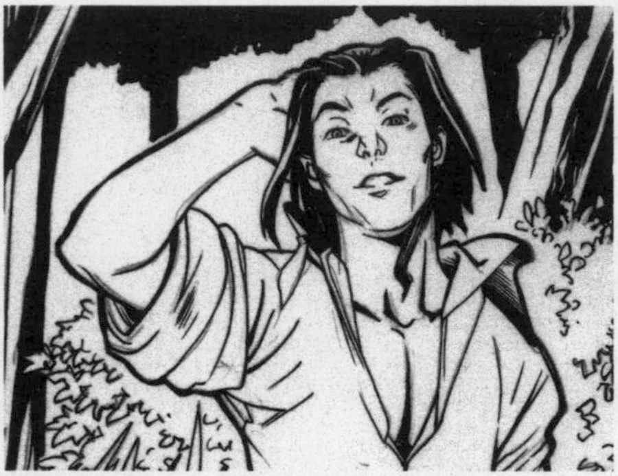

This first attempt just wasn't attractive enough.

Scripter Devin Grayson was a big help in getting to the next level—she went through her manga collection and sent Steven a bunch of "pretty-boy" characters as guidance!

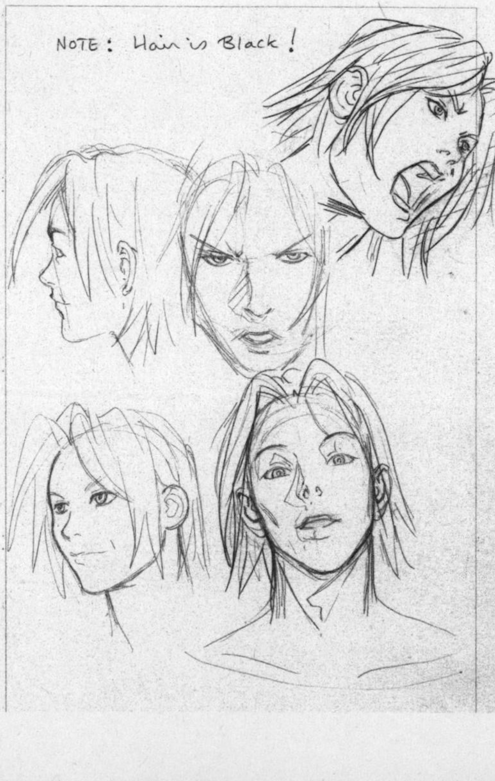
NOTE: Hair is Black!

Scott approved this look with hairstyle A (and minus the wristband).

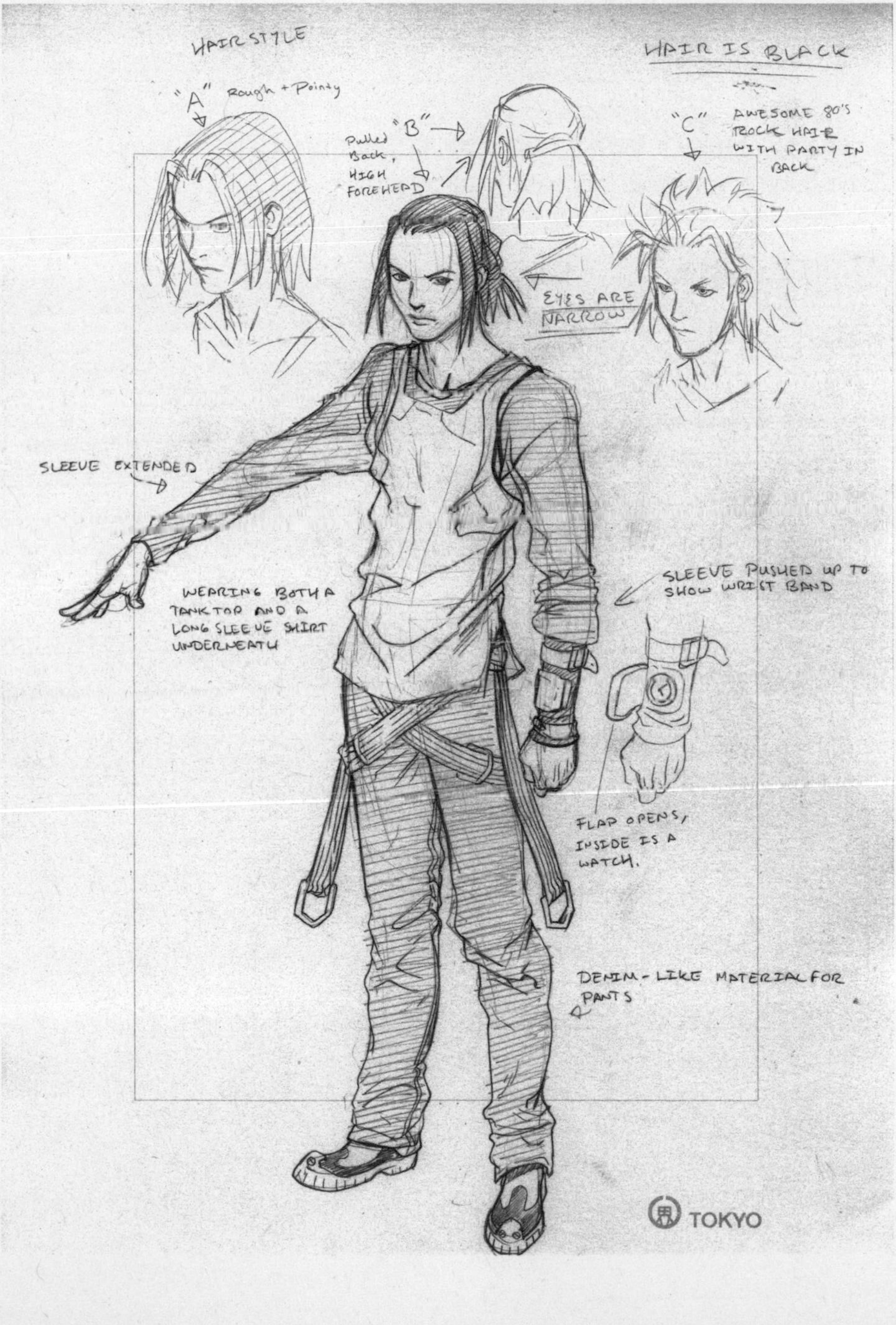
HAIRSTYLE
"A" Rough + Pointy
Pulled Back, HIGH FOREHEAD
"B"
HAIR IS BLACK
"C"
AWESOME 80'S ROCK HAIR WITH PARTY IN BACK
EYES ARE NARROW
SLEEVE EXTENDED
WEARING BOTH A TANKTOP AND A LONG SLEEVE SHIRT UNDERNEATH
SLEEVE PUSHED UP TO SHOW WRIST BAND
FLAP OPENS, INSIDE IS A WATCH.
DENIM-LIKE MATERIAL FOR PANTS
TOKYO

# DAVID

David's look posed a problem as well. Here is Steven's original sketch.

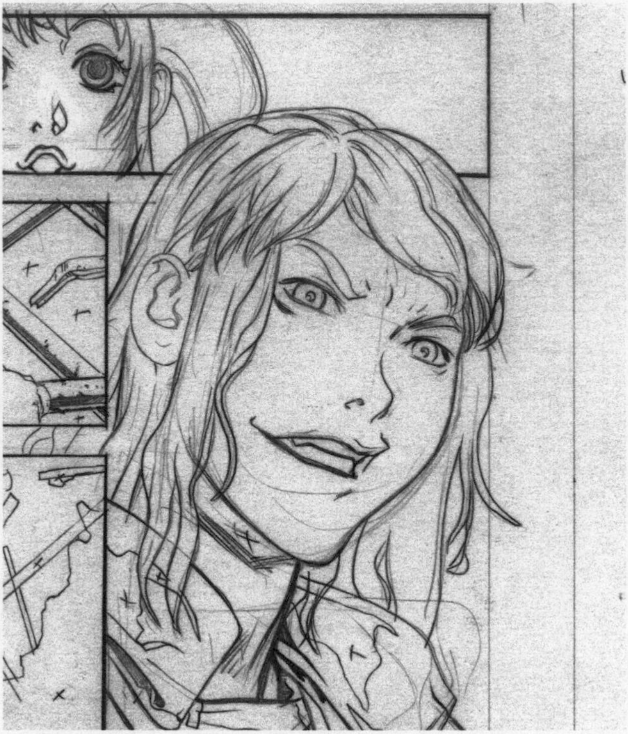

Scott had a lot to say here!

*He's eighteen and should look older. He's a lot more mature than the city kids, having traveled on his own in the wild a lot. He should look a bit stronger than you have him here. He's been chopping wood, etc., his whole life. The cape is wrong. It's not practical enough for hoverboarding through the trees. And the vest is odd. He should look a bit more Daniel Boone and less Victorian. He has a leather jacket in the books and also handmade leather shoes. He's the romantic lead, so he has to be the outdoorsy guy of every young girl's dreams.*

So it was back to the drawing board for Steven!

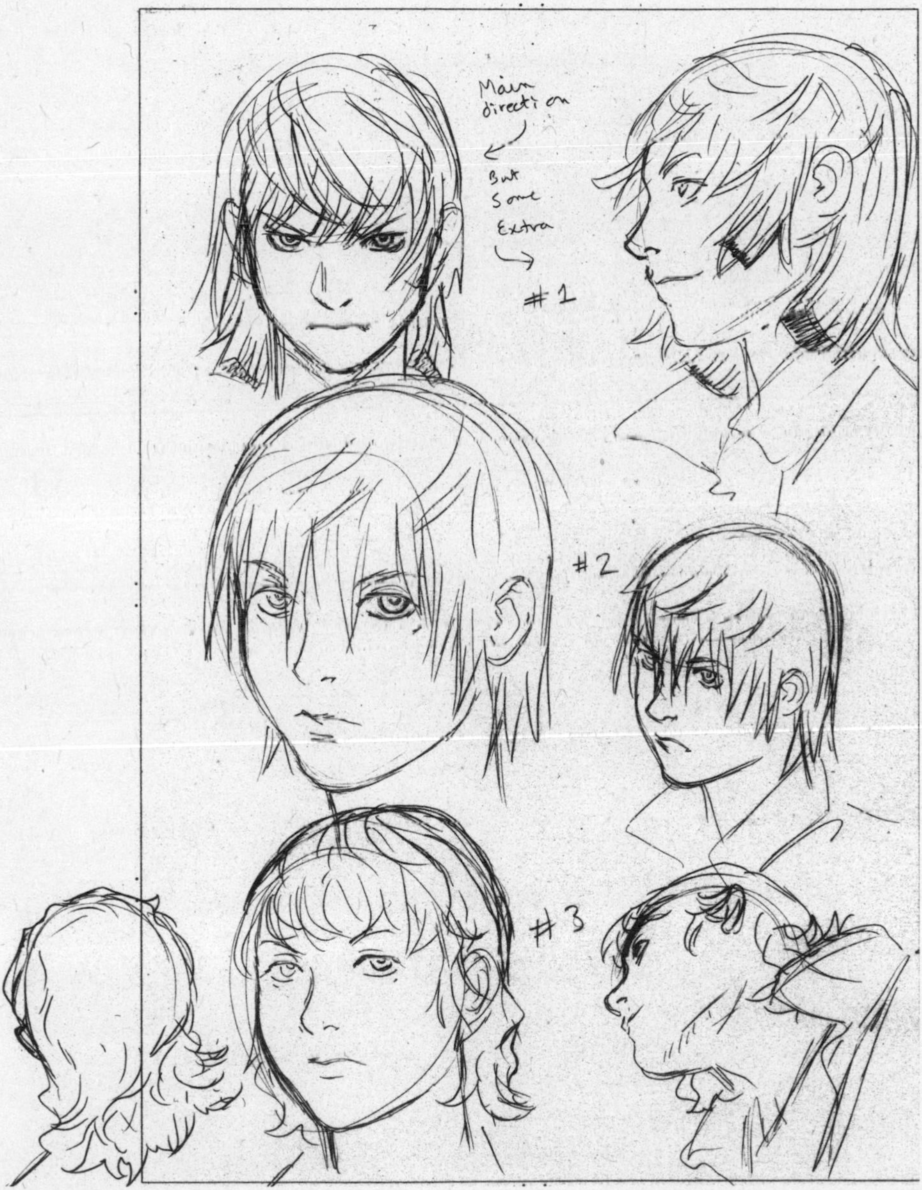
Main direction
But Some Extra
#1
#2
#3

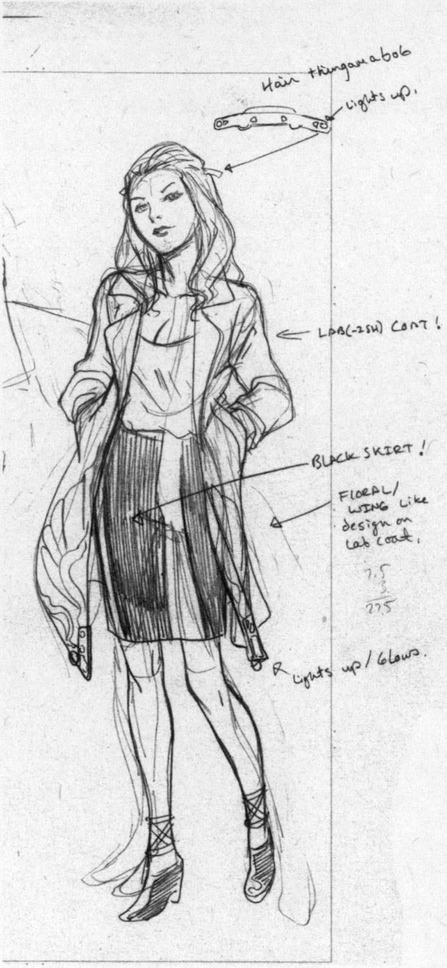
Hair thingamabob
lights up.
LAB(-ISH) COAT!
BLACK SKIRT!
FLORAL/ WING Like design on Lab coat.
7.5
3
22.5
lights up / Glows.

# DOCTOR CABLE

Steven's first sketch of Doctor Cable also needed revision. She's a Middle Pretty, and Scott wanted her to look forty to fifty years old.

Her revised appearance is suitably frightening!

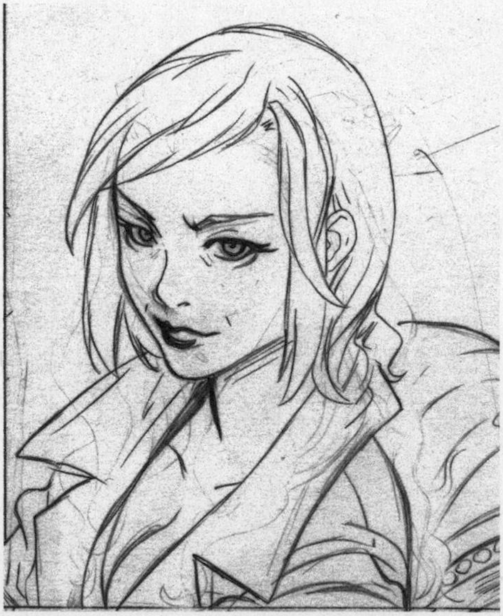

# THE SPECIALS

Doctor Cable sent her Specials to attack the Smoke.
Steven had a great time creating his "Special Storm Troopers"!

SPECIAL STORM TROOPER.

Reinforced sleeves
for fighting.
Good for when
someone swings
a pipe at you!

under the outer clothing is
a body suit

Different
Hair Styles
represent
different
looks & various
Specials.

crash Bracelets (glow!)
Both arms

Boots, stiff
Leather

Silk Top +
Bottom

BELT

crash bracelets
built into the Boots
(also glow).

women's version
similar to the men's

Plastic wrist
Restrainer
container
(x2, left +
right)

TOKYO

Scott liked many elements of the sketches. He told Steven:

*The version on the left looks a bit too superheroic for me. It has lots of flowing capelike elements, which I realize give a lot of motion to the character. But I'm not sure that fits in with the Specials' business-like approach to things. (And as for the mask, Specials never wear anything over their eyes. All their vision enhancements are built in surgically.) The one on the right is much better. It's loose, so it's easy to move in, and it's simple and even a bit formal. It suggests karate without going all the way into ninja.*

*I think Specials do need crash bracelets (and those knee pads could also be lifters), but they don't need reinforced sleeves to block any lead pipes. They would duck rather than block an attack like that. You would never touch them, my friend, with your clumsy lead pipe! Specials are more about speed and stealth (and intimidating beauty) than strength.*

## ABOUT THE NEXT BOOK

The script for the sequel to *Shay's Story* is finished, and Steven is deep
into creating the pages! He and Devin Grayson were joking via email
that it would be a very simple project for him to draw if only Devin
would set all of the action in a snowy whiteout or, alternatively,
deepest darkest intergalactic space. Watch for news of Part 2
on Scott's blog at scottwesterfeld.com.

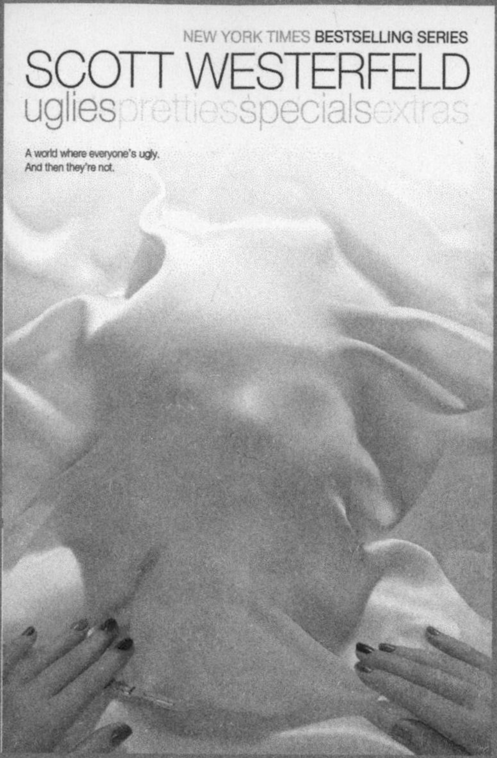
NEW YORK TIMES BESTSELLING SERIES
SCOTT WESTERFELD
uglies prettiesspecialsextras
A world where everyone's ugly.
And then they're not.

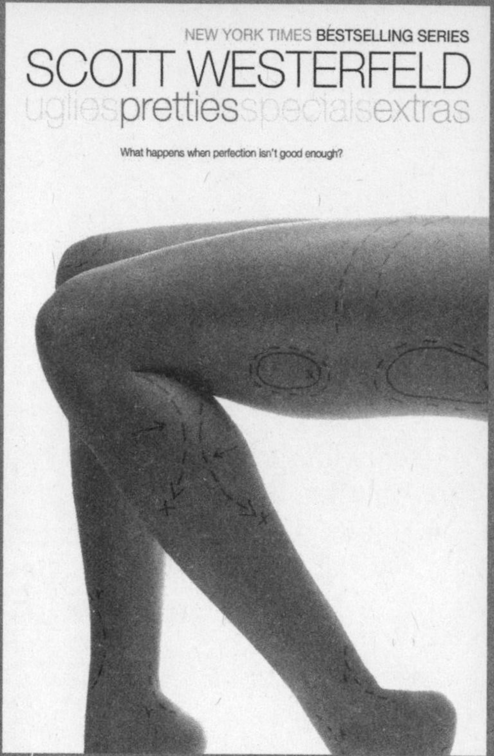
NEW YORK TIMES BESTSELLING SERIES
SCOTT WESTERFELD
ugliesprettiesspecialsextras
What happens when perfection isn't good enough?

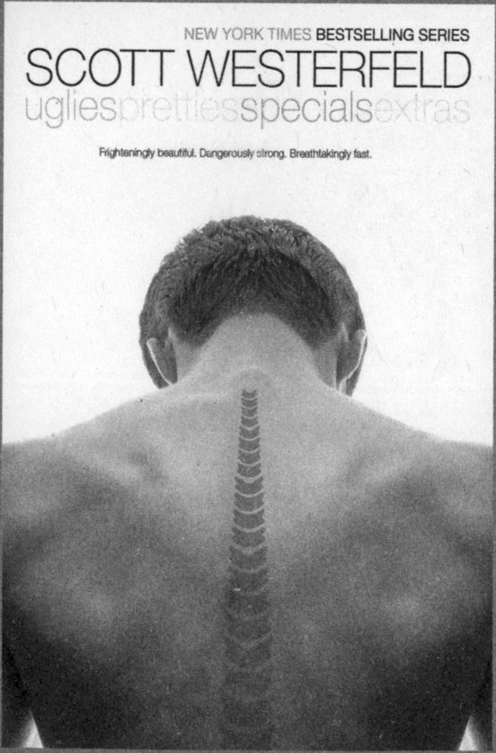
NEW YORK TIMES BESTSELLING SERIES
SCOTT WESTERFELD
ugliesprettiesspecialsextras
Frighteningly beautiful. Dangerously strong. Breathtakingly fast.

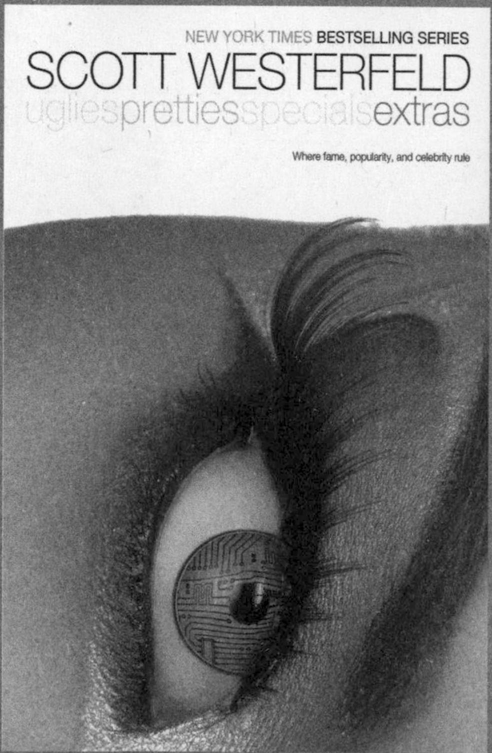
NEW YORK TIMES BESTSELLING SERIES
SCOTT WESTERFELD
ugliesprettiesspecialsextras
Where fame, popularity, and celebrity rule